The Marlen of Prague

The Marlen of Prague:

Christopher Marlowe
and the City of Gold

Angeli Primlani

GUARDBRIDGE BOOKS
ST ANDREWS, SCOTLAND

Published by Guardbridge Books,
St Andrews, Fife, United Kingdom.

http://guardbridgebooks.co.uk

Marlen of Prague, The.

This is a work of fiction. Some events and personages are real, but they have been dramitised for this novel.

Poetry translation from *Elizabeth Jane Weston, Collected Writings*, Ed. And Trans. Cheney, Donald and Hosington, Brenda, University of Toronto Press, 2000.

Cover art © Kate Edmunds.

ISBN: 978-1-911486-75-6

"Well resolve me in this question: why have we not conjunctions, oppositions, aspects, eclipses, all at one time, but in some years we have more, in some less?"

—Christopher Marlowe, *Doctor Faustus*, scene 7.

"The universe is under no obligation to make sense to you."

—Neil deGrasse Tyson, *Astrophysics for People in a Hurry*.

Prologue

Madame.

I do not appeal to you as the representative of any government, crown, religious sect or country. I am technically of the Protestant Christian faith as is my Queen. Such things are decided by the inclination of our rulers in Europe. But not in this country. Here, in Bharat, the land at the meeting of the two oceans...but of course you smile when I say that. The real ocean is far away. This is a city, and there is only a river. But the real meeting of two oceans takes place in the heart. Your son, his blood, his very existence he owes to this fragile state of tolerance. But I need not explain that to you, Madame.

Your son told me to come to you for help. He said I could tell you the entire truth and nothing I said could shock you. He thinks that much of you.

You judge me already although I have scarce begun. You sit wrapped in sea-coloured silk and gold like the queen of my own country. But you, Madame, are a humble scholar, and perhaps a poet as I am. I cannot read your language well enough to judge, but I'm working on it. At any rate, your son said you could help me read the works in the library here, and that my story would be your price. He said you like stories.

Oh right, I should begin with the passwords.

The fire is warm

The fire is old

The torch still burns

The torch burning downward

That which keeps me alight, extinguishes me

That which nourishes me, destroys me

Madame, my name is Christopher Marlowe, poet, scholar, one time agent of Queen Elizabeth of England. I am a magician of no small ability, a decent swordsman, one of the Gifted, who walks in the spirit world, whether he will or no. I have come to your garden of peacocks and hibiscus flowers, a refugee from the wars of Christendom, to beg for help at the court of Emperor Akbar of Delhi. I am, like you, a Merchant of Light, and with these passwords and tokens you are sworn to give me aid.

Oh, and in my own country I am reckoned to have died five years ago.

Shall we begin?

Chapter 1

There is an early morning that is a crystal in my mind, because it was just before the world changed. I contemplate every sweet, affectionate, and ordinary facet now. It was the last time I was certain of the substance of the world.

At dawn, a few days after we'd heard that the Spanish Armada entered the English Channel, I opened my eyes when the bells began to ring. I sat up blinking in the darkness. It was warm and humid, like a damp cloth squeezed on us both. My bedmate, Thomas, reached his soft sweaty arms around me and pulled me back against his chest. "You beautiful man," he said. "Do not leave me."

"Shan't," I said, giving myself over to his kiss. Thomas was generous in darkness, his hands rough and his lips smooth, the salt in his skin ambrosial and warm. As soon as the sun peeked through the window, he would grow distant, puritanical, and thin lipped and pretend that we merely shared room and bed as other struggling young men do. But in the hours before sunrise, he still belonged to me.

"Have the Spanish come?" he murmured into my hair.

"Hush."

"But the bells..."

"Mean nothing," I said, cupping his member. "The London city fathers run drills all the time. Stay."

He pushed my hand away and sat up, the dreamy sensuality of half sleep was gone, alas, gone. "If we could only cast a spell to stop them."

"You'd never endanger your immortal soul so, Thomas," I said, resting my chin against his shoulder blade.

"You take every word I say so literally." The affection bubbled under the tremble in his voice. "But on this morning, had I your Gift, Kit..."

"You are not afraid?" I sat up and touched his arm. I could not see his face.

"Of the Inquisition?" He laughed without humour. "But it is different for you. You have no trouble bending the knee to any orthodoxy, since you hold all doctrine in contempt."

I kissed him. He tasted like apples. They were all we had to eat the night before. All the taverns were shut, foodstuffs hidden from the invaders. But it was August and apples were plentiful, if a bit green.

"Not all doctrine," I whispered.

"Do not repeat your blasphemy about Christ and John the Evangelist now," he said, hoarsely. "We have so little left of freedom."

"You should go to the river."

"Five minutes more," he said. "What is five minutes on our last day as free English men?"

"All right," I said. And for a time, we said no more. But the black sky turned grey; the grey turned pale blue. The bells went on.

As the sun's first rays came in through the high open window overhead, there was a sharp rap on the door.

"The Watch," said Thomas. "Put your britches on."

I did, quick as I could. Thomas started to rise, tripped, and fell sprawling. The knocking grew more insistent. I picked up the bedclothes and threw them over him and went to open the door.

It was not the Watch. Or to be precise, it was, but not as I expected.

"Hello Kit," said my sister Anne. She was dressed as a boy, wearing the badge of the city Watch, and carrying a package of sausages.

We were almost the same height but looked nothing alike. She was ruddy and freckled while I am fair enough to see veins spider web under my skin. Her hair was golden and thick, unlike my loose, brown mop. Her eyes were green, and mine brown. She had no breasts to speak of and was considered a plain woman, while most judged me a handsome man. But we were alike in temperament. She accepted my perversions and heresies. I accepted her black tempers and her generous relationship with honesty. We were bad characters, but as a man this qualified me for employment with Her Majesty's Secret Service, while poor Anne was trapped at home. Or she should have been. She made a convincing boy in the poor light, and on this day the Watch might not notice her sex, or care.

"What on Earth are you doing in London?" I asked.

"I've come to fight the Spanish. The sausages are from Mother." She sailed past me into the room. "She's certain the whole city is eating rats already. Tell Thomas not to get up."

Thomas emerged from the floor bringing most of the bedclothes with him, his fair hair all askew and his eyes still half closed. "Why does she know who I am?"

"I've come to make you breakfast before the fight, Master Kyd." Anne took a small skillet from her bundle and set it atop the papers on the table. "I read your Spanish Tragedy. Oh, and Kit tells me everything, we have no secrets."

Thomas squinted. "I don't know who you are. That's a secret."

I bowed. "Thomas Kyd, may I present my sister Anne Marlowe."

"Put on clothes. There are sausages."

"Enchanting," he said, yawning.

"Do you have anything to add to this?"

"I've some apples," I said.

3

"Be useful and cut them up together."

She set about starting a fire. I found my knife in a jumble of papers on the table and sliced the sausages and apples. Anne swept the pieces into a pan she found propped behind my atlas.

"So, you are a loyal Englishwoman this morning? All tricked out to fight the Inquisition?"

"English priests are bad enough but at least they belong here."

"And if the Spanish catch you?"

She made a gesture that I didn't know she knew.

"If Her Majesty can take the field, why not your sister?" said Thomas, grinning.

"Thank you, Master Kyd," said Anne, spearing a bit of sausage on her knife for him. He popped it into his mouth, still spitting grease. He moaned in pain, but chewed manfully.

"Eat quickly," she said. "The Duke of Parma could be crossing the Channel right now. Half the city is at the river already."

I shrugged and speared a bit of sausage. Thomas looked peevish.

"What is it?" asked Anne.

"Kit's bound for Greenwich," Thomas said.

Anne made a sour face. Thomas nodded at her, sighed, and went back to his breakfast.

I tasted the bit of sausage. "This is good."

Thud went the pan on the table, apples and sausages bouncing. "He's doing magic for the Queen," she said to Kyd.

Kyd nodded.

I did not hear what Anne said then because she boxed my ears. I slapped my hand over her mouth. She bit me. I yelped but did not let her go. She struggled until her cap went flying and her hair started tumbling down.

Kyd shrugged on his doublet. "See if you can't make him see sense," he said. "Thank you for the food."

He hesitated at the door. He gave me a look heavy and wet with desire, but whatever my lover would say to me before going to war, he would never say in front of my sister. He slapped on his cap and stalked out of the room.

"Why?"

"You should not be here at all."

"I can fight."

"And I've the scars to show for it." I put my hand to my left arm, where I would bear the marks of her teeth to my grave.

She hit me just in case I'd forgotten what it felt like. It felt quite unpleasant.

"Will you be still?" I asked. "Let me explain."

She nodded. I let her go. Anne retrieved her hat, collected her injured dignity about her, and re-braided her hair.

"What do you know about the Merchants of Light?"

"The Queen's Witch Masters?"

"They're not witches, Anne. They are the Queen's most trusted scholars."

"Well enough for the Great and Near Great. Folk like me are just called witches." Her eyes narrowed. "They will use your Gifts and spit you out."

"At least my life will be of use," I said, more sourly than I meant to.

"What?" she said. "Oh, poor me, poor Kit Marlowe. I see spirits. I indulge in perversions and tarry at the doorway of Hell. What piteous lot is mine."

"You see spirits, too. And here you are, ready to die in battle. Same as me. Do I criticize?"

She collapsed into a chair. I sat too, my arms across my chest, leaning back in my chair. My long bare legs had a tiny trail of bedbug bites. They looked like I had the pox, if pox could be confined to a man's legs. The bells were going again. London's churches calling London's citizens to lay down their lives in her defence.

"Your masters," she asked, slowly. "Are they like us?"

I sighed. "They understand our Gifts well, for they study such things. They are not themselves Gifted."

"Never trust anyone who cannot perform his own magic. That was your rule. And some of these men are not even Englishmen. Some are Catholics themselves."

"Better to trust our fate to Merchants of Light than to the Inquisition, who burn folk like us as witches and heretics. Is that what you want?"

"Do the Spanish attack us with magic?"

"His most Catholic majesty does not truck with magicians."

"Then why must we?"

"We are Protestants and that makes us practical."

"It is wrong, and you know it."

"Worse than killing with sword or fire?" I scoffed. "What do you think war is about, Anne? The size of the Spanish fleet is one of the worst kept secrets in Christendom. One hundred and thirty ships, including two full squadrons of galleons."

I tried to speak as if I were sure I was right, and Anne was wrong, and perhaps I fooled her a bit. Anne frowned. She detested displaying her ignorance of military matters. "A squadron is?"

"Ten ships. So twenty galleons, ten of them the heavy Portuguese make, and several odd warships from Naples."

"Is that an unusually large fleet for an invasion?"

"Yes," I said. "The Duke of Parma has ground troops massed across the Channel, ready to hit London as you know. But the real force will come from the Atlantic, and we don't have enough ships."

"But Francis Drake?"

"A few pirates make a pathetic navy. We have nothing to

match the Armada, Anne. So, I will let the Merchants of Light use me any way my Queen requires..."

"And if you fail?"

"We will not fail," I said.

"If you do?"

I shrugged. "They will kill the Queen, certainly. Close the Protestant churches, establish the Inquisition. Bloody Mary's reign will be a pleasure party by comparison."

"Still..." Anne said, "it feels...dishonest."

I grinned. "Afraid for my soul? How sweet."

Anne took my hands in hers and squeezed them hard. "Even without Perdition, there is such a thing as a fair fight. You knew that when you fought schoolboys in the Canterbury mud. What changed you, brother?"

I wouldn't have tolerated this lecture from anyone else. I was not happy to hear it from Anne. It was a little too much like the days when I still believed God saw my every wicked impulse. But though I squirmed under my sister's judgment, I said nothing. Fighting Spain was paramount in my mind.

"I think I will go to the river," said Anne, patting my head. "In case you come to your senses and the invasion comes after all."

"Let me walk with you."

I dived into my bed for my stockings. I pulled them over my itchy legs, the little pattern of bug bites looking like lace under the thin white cloth. Anne laced up my doublet. She threw her arms around me. Then she clouted me on the side of the head, so I would not think her gone soft. She wiped her belt knife on her sleeve with as much dignity as a cardinal. And then there was a rap at the door.

I opened it and found Matthew Roydon, splendid as Adonis and delicious as cake. He wore his best shabby blue doublet and a cheap paste drop in his ear. He was dressed for court, not a hard

ANGELI PRIMLANI

ride to the coast. I might have wanted to rip his clothes off on the spot, were it not for Thomas.

"I have come to fetch you."

"Now?"

"Doctor Dee cast a horoscope or somesuch and says we must be ready by noon precisely. But I see you are entertaining." Matthew eyed my sister with mixed curiosity and pique. "Does Thomas know?"

"Allow me to introduce my—"

"Brother," she said. "Anthony."

"Anthony Marlowe, this is Matthew Roydon."

Anne curtseyed. Then she bowed. Then curtseyed again. She inched past Roydon and shimmied down the stairs.

"Wait for me."

"Let her go," said Matthew.

I reached for my one really good suit, copper red and gold thread that glinted in the bright morning sun. Matthew devoured the last of the sausages, mopping the drippings in the pan with his finger.

"Matthew?"

"Aye?"

"Are you afraid of what we do?"

He grinned. "Thomas has been filling your head with nonsense?"

"Not Thomas."

"Then fetch your ritual knife."

It was on the table. I pushed some papers out of the way to locate it. Some were mine, others belonged to Thomas. I swept them up together and shoved them into a box to make room.

I did not think about the contents of those pages. I thought myself safe in the hands of Thomas Harriot, John Dee, Walter Ralegh, each high in the Queen's esteem. More fool me, I believed

8

Matthew and I would save the country with magic and be back in time for supper.

We did save the country. We were even home in time for supper. Anne was there with a bottle of something strong. She matched me drink for drink. She always could. I did not speak of what happened and she didn't ask. Kyd stayed away until dawn. He looked troubled, but we did not speak of it, not then and not in the years that came, when our bed grew cold, our friendship thinned. Not even when they arrested him, and it was all my fault.

Anne went home, and I stayed. I adopted new habits: smoking and cruelty, poetry and worse, anything that would shut out the memory of the Armada Spell. In time, I wore out Thomas' patience. He sent me packing.

The papers remained in his box. I did not think of them until five years later, the day he was arrested, before my official death in Mistress Bull's tavern. Put this on my tombstone, should I ever get a proper one. Here lies Christopher Marlowe, who would have done less harm to those he loved except he did not think.

Chapter 2

Let's be clear. I knew exactly who Richard Baines was when he sat down next to me. We had worked together abroad on the Queen's business. He was a provocateur. On this day, I was the man he meant to provoke.

He offered to fill my pipe with tobacco. I had no illusions when he leaned over his ale in the dark corner of the tavern, the firelight casting ribbons of orange light across his pockmarked face as he whispered his infernal question. But it had been near upon five years since the Armada spell, and I no longer cared what happened. It was winter of 1593, the plague year. I'd mastered the art of the sneer, in the face of quarantine marks chalked on the doors of friends.

"I did meet the Algonquin chiefs at Master Harriot's house."

He smiled, that rat's smile, that has no feeling, only the bones under the skin holding the pink of his lips in position. "You are quite brave to converse with such savages."

"Not especially." I placed my hand on the round pommel of my dagger, but it would do me no good. Baines would give me no excuse to fight him. Violence did not suit his purposes.

"I meant morally," he said, his eyebrow raised.

"You must be joking, given what we've both done."

He whispered. "I do not speak of venial sins of the bedchamber."

I regarded the fine stitching on his doublet, his warm cloak. I was not fooled for a second by his conspiratorial wink. "Nor do I."

Will Shakespeare and some few diverse players came in at that moment. The small piece of my soul that still had a care for my safety thought to get up out of this infernal corner and join them at the fire. Will and I were not close friends. I do not think he was really close to anyone. Not a bad actor. Good voice, passable leg. But he was the sort who everyone met, and no one knew. He could have been a Government Man himself, were he not so stupid and Christlike.

But panic grew inside me like a wart on my heart. I tilted my head, brushed Baines' leg ever so gently with mine, and gave him a smile as false and skeletal as his own. "Did you offer to fill my pipe?"

"I did," said Baines.

I offered my pipe to him. "All those who love not tobacco and boys are fools."

"Say you so?"

"I swear it."

Baines lowered his lashes to his cup. He meant to look flirtatious, but I knew that glance well. He was trying to hide the triumph in his eyes. He could not know that this fish was swimming toward the hook, not away.

His hands did not tremble as he unlaced the top of his pouch. The sweet strong smell of the leaves made me glance away toward the fire. Will was looking at me. He raised his eyebrows but did not move. I wondered if he knew who Baines was. Will always saw more than you thought he did. He turned back to his friends, and I turned back to my self-destruction.

I lit my pipe. It was heavenly. "The Algonquin do not conceive the world as Christian men do. It would be imprecise to call their views heresy. Their imagination resembles that of the noble pagans who lived before Christ. They have stories older than Adam's creation, assuming that date can be reckoned by counting the years that Scripture says the patriarchs lived."

"You share their views on the age of the Earth?"

There we were, dangling together on the precipice. "I see no compelling evidence to contradict them."

"The truth must be in Scripture," said Baines. "Come, man, we are friends. Speak plain."

We were not friends. I tasted my drink. "What did Old Sir Francis Walsingham say about speaking plain?"

Baines leaned forward, as if he would kiss me like Judas Iscariot. "I have heard whispered some of your thoughts about the nature of Christ."

"Which thoughts?" I said, the honey taste of the ale filling my throat. "That Mary was a bawd, and that Christ and John the Evangelist might have been lovers? And now that lax attendance at services won't be tolerated, neither will dangerous speculation about the age of the planets nor a defence of Greek love?"

Baines' eyes narrowed. He moved away on the bench, dropping all pretence. "Atheists are as trustworthy as Papists."

"Which precise blasphemy would you repeat to your masters?" I snarled at him. "Shall I say religion itself is a sickness?"

A gloved hand rested on my shoulder. "Kit, come join us," said Will Shakespeare.

"Stay out of this, Will."

"Yes, Master Shakespeare," said Baines. "By all means let him speak."

"Miracles finer than those of the saints are performed by the men who visit with Master Harriot..."

"You've had a lot to drink," Will said, urgent, with a subtle hint of command. I gaped at him in shock, but I spoke no more. Who guessed Will Shakespeare was Gifted?

"No matter," said Baines, rising. "Your friend has said more than enough for my purposes tonight."

Baines gave a little bow. I lurched to my feet, knife in my hand, but Will was somehow in the way. Then Baines scurried off to report my words to whatever Thought Master he served now. Indeed, what was the point of fighting it? Come death, and welcome. Were there a just God, or any God, I would be extinguished from this Earth before I could do more harm.

"I'll take you home," Will said, but I staggered out of the tavern into the dark empty street.

Will found me some hours later lying drunk in a carriage rut in the road that ran through Shoreditch into London. He lay down beside me, though the ground was cold with frost. He was always companionable in drink. "I should have let you stab him."

"It would not shut him up."

"It would if he were dead."

I opened one eye to look at him. "When did you go all bloodthirsty?"

"I understand the danger you are in," said Will. "Better than you know."

"You couldn't possibly." Then I remembered the one reason he could. "Are you a Catholic? Is that why you stayed clear of university?"

Will folded his hands over his heart. "I obey the law and love my Queen."

"Will Shakespeare a secret Papist."

Will sighed. "You can be so literal sometimes."

It was something Thomas would say. I put my thumb up to the brilliant star where no star should be in Cassiopeia. That star had existed before we did the spell. Astrologers all over Christendom wrote of the brilliant new light, the Fiery Trigon, the harbinger of a new and better age of Mankind. I remembered showing it to Anne, lying in the grass on a warm night. I remembered my schoolmasters arguing that it could not be there, Aristotle had said the realm of the stars was fixed and unchanging, and yet there it was, brighter than Venus, visible by day for weeks.

I remembered when it faded in 1574.

But there it was again, the *Stella Nova*, brand new, blazing in Cassiopeia as if it had never left us. The night was deadly clear. There wasn't even any moonlight. It was not just the stella nova. The constellations were no longer the shapes I knew. Will was Gifted. Perhaps he could see what I saw. "Do the stars look wrong to you?"

"You look wrong to me."

"Be serious."

He regarded the sky and shook his head. "What do you see that looks wrong?"

"Everything."

"You are drunk," Will said.

"I know all the stars. I am a mage."

"Well, aren't we grand."

"Do you remember the new star that appeared when we were young?"

He patted my bare hand with his gloved one and got up. "I am cold. And the constable will be here soon, all the noise you made."

He gave me a nudge with his foot. I rose, feeling the world around me giving way. "Does Henslowe keep your plays?"

"Pardon?"

"Old scrolls the actors use. The texts you give the Registry."

"The ones we use the most, sure. Why?"

"Because I've been looking for reference to the Fiery Trigon in astrological texts and checking navigational maps and I can't see any reference to that star appearing suddenly, and slowly vanishing."

"And you think one of your poet friends put one in a play?"

"Possibly," I said. "It is one of many possibilities."

Will looked up. "Church doctrine says Aristotle is correct and the heavens are immutable."

"You can speak freely to me."

Will gave me a significant glance. "I just did."

"With the evidence before you, a star that appeared and disappeared and reappeared, you shrug?"

"I'm not Thomas Kyd," he said, softly. "I don't love you enough to risk prison for you."

The hairs prickled on my forearms. It was cold. "Take me to the Rose."

He put a hand on my shoulder and looked me in the eye. "What will the plays tell you?"

I stumbled and fell. The icy ground jarred my knees, and the pain sobered me. The glint of the frost on the ground mirrored the glint of the altered stars. I, a mere juggler, no god, or prophet like Moses, had made and unmade stars. What else must have changed?

"Will?" I asked. "Who wrote the *Spanish Tragedy*?"

"I don't know that play."

I leaned over and vomited. Well, perhaps I was a little drunk. Will pulled my hair out of my face and made vague noises.

"Thomas wrote a play," I said, numbly.

"I didn't know that."

"Burbage did it three times. It was popular."

Will offered me his hand. I stared at it, but did not move, nor look him in the face.

"God's teeth! You were *in* it, Will. You played Balthazar."

Now he looked truly unnerved. I shook him hard. Anne would have kicked me. But Shakespeare was an even-tempered man. "All right, I'll take you to the Rose. Just...stop doing that."

It was easy to break into the theatre at night, although it was dark and full of odd items to stumble over. Will found a box of old scrolls and a candle. We sat down on the stage, in the starlight of the roofless pit, and went through the scripts together. He kept the light trimmed and the smoke out of my eyes as I read every line. Most were actor's sides, which only contained the lines from a single character. None of them were from Thomas' play, but that meant nothing.

I couldn't be sure the stars were changed either, without talking to someone else from the night of the Armada spell. But they were scattered. Ralegh was in and out of prison, Harriot hunted his missing colony in America, and Matthew was on the Continent. Providence alone knew where Dee was. I was the only one in London.

Will found a bottle of old wine hidden among some prop swords. He poured some in a gilt-painted wooden cup. It was not bad, for the stuff players drink. "Might I speak plain?"

I put the heel of my hands to my sore eyes. "Is it possible to stop you?"

"This is School of Night business, isn't it?"

"That's not what they're called."

"I made the name up." He grinned. "What do you call them?"

"It is not safe to know about them."

"You've been babbling about spells gone wrong and witch masters for a long time, Kit." He glanced down at his hands. "You'd be better off seeking wisdom from men of the theatre than that of the great and grand. We value what you are, not what you do for us."

"Thank you, Master Shakespeare. Your wisdom is beyond price."

"You did some sort of spell. And you think it changed the plays and the stars and maybe other things."

"Maybe not," I said. "I don't understand exactly what it did. Lord Manteo taught it to Thomas Harriot who taught it to me. It seemed to work. At least we weren't invaded. But now those who ordered it done have turned to the likes of Richard Baines to solicit my confession of heresy."

"They fear English Catholics more than ever," said Will, grimly.

"I was unkind to you about that."

"Oh, they fear atheists too. You shouldn't drink in public if you cannot keep your mouth shut."

I rose and staggered to the middle of the stage. "Stand still, you ever moving spheres of Heaven. That time may cease, and midnight never come!" I shouted. I spun around, and the theatre spun with me.

"You're not Faustus."

"Oh, so you remember my *Faustus*, but not Kyd's *Spanish Tragedy?*"

Will shifted uncomfortably. "It might not mean anything. We perform five plays a week. I've acted or managed nearly all of them. If you didn't keep aloof from your creations, you'd understand."

"I'm a scholar, not a player."

"You're about to be a prisoner so I wouldn't put on airs."

I sank heavily to my knees on the stage. I had drunk enough that the walls kept spinning after I stopped. "Men like us need patronage, Will."

"I am not a magician."

"You could be a Merchant of Light," I said. "You are Gifted, and not merely with words. I knew men at Cambridge who were reckoned brilliant men, who had not half your mind or your talent."

"I pay my own way," he said.

"You scratch out rubbish for pennies."

"Better that than be at the mercy of powerful men."

"You could be more."

Will sighed. He leaned back on his hands and looked up at the stars. "We make our own rough magic here, I think. Change minds. Change hearts. There's power here too, Kit. I thought you understood that after *Tamburlaine*..."

"You mean after the thugs took my words and used them to harass Dutch Protestant refugees."

"Well, I didn't mean that particular incident." Will's breath was visible in the air between us. He rubbed his hands over the candle. "I hate your...colleagues. They are poison."

The venom in his voice stung my eyelashes. It couldn't be tears. I was too tired for that. "What do you want of me, Will?"

"Walk away. There's no one on the Bankside who would not fight for you, no matter what trouble you're in."

I put my head down and closed my eyes. "You're not a fool, Will. Stop pretending you are."

"I am a fool," Will said, stroking my head. "Poor, lonely fool. Ignorant of the grand designs of the realm. What does it matter if the stars changed or are as Aristotle said, forever fixed?"

"Isn't it enough I erased Thomas' life?"

"That wasn't you, Kit. That was the authorities."

But it was worse than that. I had erased his fame. Somehow *The Spanish Tragedy* ceased to be, and with it something in Thomas had died. He'd become ever more tormented by the conflict between what he was and who he thought he should be, so when the Queen's men came to break him, he didn't fight. Baines arrested him because of the papers they found in Thomas' rooms, papers I left the morning of the Armada spell. While the spell unmade all the moments wherein Thomas put pen to paper, it left that moment alone, forever trapped like the stars were supposed to be.

It would not be the first night I'd slept in the theatre. Some nights it was the only place that felt safe. That was an illusion. Baines or someone of his ilk would find me soon. And Will's doughty players, for all their valour, could not possibly protect me.

Chapter 3

"Whoreson," Ingram Frizer said.

I opened my eyes and wished I had not. His next blow made my eyes water. My neck was sore from jerking about every time he hit me. Strange to tell, but I could not feel my head anymore. I could not see Ingram Frizer either. My vision was shrouded in reddish sweat, occluding all but the lank hair outlining his pudgy, beardless face. It grew redder, his face. Or mayhap t'were just my eyes, red from a burst blood vessel. I have seen that, in prison. Cannot remember which prison. A man hit a prisoner 'til he cried blood. Messy that.

My neck jerked. Frizer must have hit me again. "I'm going to kill you."

"Right," I said. "Get on with it, then."

"You'd like that, wouldn't you?" said Frizer.

I struggled a bit in his friend's arms. Skeres clasped me against his thick, cork-barrel chest, sweating against my twisted arms. I could not feel my arms either anymore.

"I can wipe that smirk off your face," said Frizer, reaching for the laces on his breeches. "You, Master Marlowe, are going to suck my cock."

I might have done it if it would save my life. Even if he did smell like dung and beer and something sweet like chicken, I'd have jammed his thick, disgusting maggoty member in my mouth and hung upon him until he spent. But he had his orders, see. I did not want to vomit before I died. A corpse has so little dignity.

"Terrible sin, that," I said.

I spat blood, perhaps a bit of tooth. They both hooted like deranged waterfowl.

"Yeah," said Frizer. "Much you care."

Skeres pushed me to my knees, but I saw Frizer's poxy cock, and I thought...it felt like hearing a soft voice from very far away except it was all my own...hell with this. I rammed him in the nuts with the top of my head.

If he hadn't been drunk, he never would have fallen for it, but his balance was not its best. Did he ever howl! Skeres was laughing too, so I yanked forward and used his own weight against him. He went down, plop! My shoulder rang loud, banging peals of pain. I yanked free, jumped to my feet, and snatched Skeres' belt knife out of the cheese he'd left it in.

I waved the square dagger at Frizer. He staggered to his feet now, howling in time with the throbbing in my shoulder. He lurched toward me. I ducked and went under his arm. I grabbed my short cloak and flung it into Skeres' eyes. This distracted Frizer enough that I got past him and flung open the door.

There stood Matthew Roydon, elegant in soft velvet, perfumed, with new a pearl drop earring, only a bit smaller than the one Lord Ralegh wears. I had not seen him in five years, but he still looked delicious. Just this moment I was not in a position to appreciate it.

"Hello Kit," he said.

I saw a strange red...cheesecloth...over everything. I dared not faint

"Hello Matthew," I said. "New suit?"

Skeres grabbed me from behind. I didn't resist. If Matthew Roydon were here, I might as well take the knife and plunge it into my own eye.

"That is not necessary," said Roydon. "Leave us."

Skeres dropped my arms. He and Frizer scuttled out of the private tavern room where I'd been their most reluctant guest. I stood shaking and filthy, stupidly holding the knife. Roydon gently took it out of my hand, put it on the table, and placed a heavy velvet purse next to it.

"Sit," he said.

I slid to the floor.

He blinked and offered me his hand. "At the table, if you please."

He wore new embroidered gloves. I was ashamed to sully them with my filthy paw, but my limbs ached so. I would never rise on my own. I let him help me into the chair like an old man.

"Which cup is yours?"

"My hosts..." I spat. "Did not grant me my own cup."

He held the bottle out to me. I took it but did not drink. I held it against my chest, like a lover's token. Roydon closed the door, found a chair, and sat down across from me.

"How did you find me?" I managed to ask.

He barked a little laugh. "I am here officially. But not *officially* officially, if you take my meaning."

"I surely don't," I said, through my dry tongue and the pounding in my head.

"*Officially*," said Matthew Roydon, "Christopher Marlowe died this day, 30th May anno domini 1593, in this tavern in Deptford, fighting with a few old friends over...the bill, let's say."

This did not make an overabundance of sense. I took a drink from the bottle, but it only made my head spin. "Say again?"

He crossed his legs and leaned forward, the snowy lace on his collar seemed blinding. His expression wasn't entirely inhuman. "Officially you are dead, Kit."

"Go to hell."

He smiled. "One day. But first let me give the mistress orders to clean up this mess. And then we'll have your funeral."

"Funeral?"

"You've become a poet of some renown on the Bankside. All the players in London are in mourning, and the wags at court.

21

Even the Queen noticed. There will have to be an inquiry and a funeral. You cannot simply disappear."

"Only to reappear one day like the Stella Nova in Cassiopeia. What do you know about that, Sweet Matthew?"

He hesitated, but he nodded, looked away, fiddling with the fringe on his sleeves. "I am in touch with a few Merchants. None of us know why that star returned."

"But you've guessed?"

"I don't need to *guess*," he whispered, leaning forward. "Other things are...different."

"What other things?"

He leaned back again. "Like I'd tell you, sure."

I wished I did not sound so weak. "So am I off to prison?"

Matthew patted my arm. "Think of it more like school."

Now I was truly afraid. Death I could accept but not what I suspected. "School?"

"The Armada experiment proved such a success—"

"Success?" I choked.

Matthew rolled his eyes. "It kept the Inquisition from our shores, so yes, Master Marlowe, in my view that is a success."

"We don't know that," I said, sitting up, fury being a powerful counterbalance to my headache. "Lord Wanchese told us it was possible they might have been blown off course anyway—"

"And it was possible they might not," said Matthew. "Infinite possibilities, we selected one thread on the loom of time and pulled ourselves closer to it."

"So, we know this thread is different but not what is different about it."

"Was our Queen executed? Are there auto-da-fé peppering the landscape? What do I care if not everything is exactly the same? What is now is better than the days of Bloody Mary and quite acceptable..."

"...to the English crown," I said. "And that is your lodestar."

Matthew sat up quite straight. "I am a Merchant still."

"The hell you are."

"The hell *you* are," he replied. "All you do any more is drink and brawl and talk and write rubbish and talk and talk and did I mention the talking?"

"The Merchants." I scratched my head and licked my lips. I kicked the leg of the table, trying to find the words. "It's a higher calling, Matthew. The Merchants of Light are a living thread from pagan times to our own, collecting, preserving, and protecting knowledge."

"Until conditions exist where such can flourish again," said Matthew. "You've been approached by the Order of Merlin before this."

"Invited to join your spy network, English wizards, devoted to the Crown." I laughed right in his well-powdered face. "I'd prefer prison."

He laughed back in mine. "You? In prison?"

"Wouldn't be the first time."

"Real prison, though, with no helpful word in some magistrate's ear? Real torture? Real hunger? Real disease?" Matthew shook his head. "The Order of Merlin is not a terrible fate, Kit."

"Obviously not to you. So, I'm to use the magical arts to bend the world to Her Majesty's will? That's just lovely."

"You and I engaged in manipulation, coining, fraud, and various diverse mundane betrayals. Why does adding magick to the mix change things for you?"

"Bugger off," I said.

The smile vanished. "Kit, please. You must have known we could not let you continue as you were."

I could see myself sweeping those heretical papers off the table the morning of the Armada, tossing them in with Thomas' things. No matter what we did, that still happened. Unchangeable, inviolate, trapped in time in the hours before we changed things. I had erased his fame, but not that.

"Why did you keep those pages?" Matthew asked. "That was foolish."

The truth was I could not bear to burn them. I had only just met the American chieftains at the wizard Thomas Harriot's house. The received wisdom of the Bible was that we could reckon the age of the Earth by counting the ages of the patriarchs and by adding in recorded history, we could have been here no longer than 6,000 years. But Lord Manteo the Algonquin chief explained that the world existed many millions of years before Man walked the earth, far into the depths of time.

I should have taken more care. I should have thought at least of the Spanish, who might land on our shores and burn me for them. I never dreamed that five years later my own government would come calling and the one who would answer the door was Thomas.

But all I said was, "Because I'm still a Merchant, Matthew. Some oaths can't be undone."

"You've taken oaths to the Crown as well. The Armada..."

"Was an emergency. And it went wrong, you know it did."

"That's an affectation. This has nothing to do with the Armada spell. You've gone mad since Thomas was arrested. Writing secrets into your plays, reading atheist lectures to Richard Baines, of all people. The guilt is destroying you."

"Well, that which nourishes me, destroys me, as the Merchants would say."

"That is not what the Merchants say." Matthew leaned back in his chair, crossing his arms, disgust in every angle of elbow and knee.

"It's in the Merchant's charter, written by one of the last of the pagan writers at the very cliff of the Dark Age. He knew—"

"She. Hypatia," said Matthew.

"If it was Hypatia."

"Tradition says it was Hypatia of Alexandra."

"Tradition also says we do not compromise the ideals of the Merchants to do the will of princes, Matthew."

"Well, you're about to," said Matthew. "You're one of us. Or you were. Before Thomas."

"Shut up."

"You lost one love to death, so you've been courting death in his stead. You think you're the first?"

"This isn't about Thomas," I said. "I'm done with the English Secret Service, Magickal or Otherwise and you can tell her own Right and Christian Majesty in those words. If the other choice is the death I crave, you can jolly well give it to me."

Matthew couldn't, though and I knew it. I was Gifted. He was Gifted too, though not in my league, and I'm not sure he ever grasped the difference between us. Lord Manteo the Algonquin chief did. He told me to listen to what I knew, even if lesser men told me I was wrong. Manteo was the only man I'd ever met more Gifted than I, except possibly Will Shakespeare.

Matthew did not flinch. "Even if we scoured the countryside for university students and country apprentices with Gifts, we might not find enough Englishmen who could be trusted. So unfortunately for you, I was able to arrange for you to be inducted into the Order, sent abroad where you'll stay out of trouble."

"I thought I was here because I could not be trusted."

"If that were so, you would be dead years back. But you've kept the most important secret, and that has not gone unnoticed. So, once you are trained, we will set you loose on the Continent. Our Marlen." The bastard smiled when he said this, as if making a pun from a common spelling of my surname was somehow clever.

"So you, Sweet Matthew," I said, trying to sound as if I did not care. "You're mighty comfortable perverting the mission of the Merchants of Light into the narrow interests of the English Crown."

His chin lifted. "We did that spell so England can be free."

"Is England free?" I asked. "Denunciations, secret trials, lice like Baines reporting on every unguarded word. And this Order of Merlin? The greater magicks of the Merchants of Light turned to weapons. And now all Christendom falls into armed camps of Catholics and Protestants, and if a real freethinker like Giordano Bruno appears, which side will kill him faster? The Merchants don't serve Catholic or Protestant or the crowned heads of Europe. We're here to keep men like Bruno from being crushed between them."

"That will do," said Matthew. He placed his hands on his velvet covered knees and drummed his gloved fingers on his thighs, his thoughts turned inward. "This was the best your friends could do for you. Accept it as a barely tolerable alternative to your execution."

I felt a barely tolerable urge to spit blood in his direction. But poor Roydon's face was so sorrowful, I managed to smile.

"Right," I said. "Thank you. Friend."

I vomited blood and wine all over the floor.

Chapter 4

The Order of Merlin induction was a quiet affair in the crypt of the church at Deptford. Only Lord Cecil and Matthew were there, as befit a secret ceremony. I was asked to renounce my allegiance to all other societies that would interfere with my work, and I spoke the words. Matthew was not fooled, but like the Queen he did not require more than outward obedience. Lord Cecil, though, was quite convinced. He placed his hand on my head and spoke nonsense about the sacred nature of my service to Queen and Country. I simpered like a virgin meeting the betrothed her family chose for her.

Then I was bundled into a closed wagon and driven across country until I lost all sense of where I was. The Order of Merlin's training facility was in a former monastery. I could see gaps in the walls where the local saints had been violently ripped from their thousand-year resting places. My room was in small tower inside the old-fashioned closed keep. It looked out over the sea, so we were somewhere in the West. I seldom left that chamber. I could not see much beyond the square of the blue beyond my window. The sun rose behind me and set over the ocean, and that was all I knew of my whereabouts. It was not bad as prisons went. I had a warm, comfortable room, plenty of food, books, and wine, the freedom of the courtyard on Sundays. I liked listening to the wind and the crash of the waves. I even came to like the cold air and darkness, when I was lucky enough to have time to sleep.

I expected to be instructed by real scholars, if not the calibre of the Merchants of Light, at least men with Gifts. Instead, my teachers were two Un-Gifted old men named Wood and Reeve, with identical beards and scholars' robes, full of rips and food stains. Wood was lean and fair; Reeve was plump and dark.

Neither were attractive and neither were inclined to sociability. They had no practical skill in the magical arts but had apparently read every metaphysical and theological book in Christendom. They lectured about Hermes Trismegistus until I wanted to scream with boredom.

The Order of Merlin's program did not include practical experimentation. Both my tutors looked scandalized when I suggested it. Wood said I could not be trusted with a ritual sword, which is as deadly a weapon as the ordinary kind after all. But in truth I think they did not know how to do formal ritual at all.

By Michaelmas we had exhausted theory, and my keepers decided they could not train a magical spy without letting me practice any magic. After some deliberation they decided that remote viewing was safe enough. I sat through endless, cold days with charcoal and scraps of butcher paper, trying to visualize the number and configuration of troops on the French coastline.

My sketches were not much use. I was always terrible at remote viewing on command. Matthew could do it, and Harriot's sketches could be extraordinary. When they asked me to show them where the French priests were hiding, I sketched Notre Dame Cathedral in Paris. I caught Reeve smiling over that one.

They gave up that project a week before Advent. After a bit of an argument, they decided to allow me to learn astral projection, which was unintentionally hilarious because I've been Walking since I was a boy. Reeve gravely explained that all of the Order of Merlin needed to be proficient at leaving our bodies, the better to report back to our masters while serving at foreign courts. It was a very serious endeavour. They required preparation through prayer, lack of sleep, and a bread and water fast, which I didn't enjoy very much. I didn't need any of this. I have no idea if Un-Gifted folk could walk the spirit world at all or if any of these things would help. I could do it feasting, drunk, and in the midst of revelry or on one occasion battle.

Still, this presented an opportunity for me, so I did as they bid me. As instructed, I lay down on the wooden bed, smelled incense that Wood burned, and listened to Reeve chant. I easily drifted into a familiar state between dreaming and waking.

I tried for London. London was familiar, and there were several among the Bankside players who had Gifts, including Will. I immediately realized I was nowhere near there. I heard screams. The ships were on fire. A storm. Men escaping ghost ships, swimming to the Irish coast, to have their heads crushed by tribesmen who found them exhausted on their shores...and me safe in the circle, holding a candle and chanting the words...I started to scream with them, but a thin, bony hand placed itself on my head.

"Open your eyes," said a woman's voice, gentle as a bell. "We are in the Library."

It was silent after she spoke. I looked up, and sure enough, I saw books, walls full of books. I was sitting on a stone floor, but it was not real stone, it gave slightly when I pressed on it. The owner of the hand was a spirit, that was clear enough. She had translucent skin, sweet black eyes, and thin arms. She stood over me and took my hand.

"My name is Madimi," she said. "I am a member of John Dee's household."

"Doctor Dee keeps a spirit in his household?"

"He doesn't keep me." She seemed confused, not offended.

I looked past her down an endless hall, with tall shelves on either side that went up into darkness, oblivion. I could not see how high the walls were, or how vast the hall.

"What is this place?" I asked.

Madimi frowned and thought a while. When she answered she spoke slowly, as if translating from another language. "The Library is a place outside of time and space where all the books ever written are kept."

"All of them?"

"Yes," she said. "Your lover's quarto too. The Spanish Tragedy. We could find it if we looked hard enough. There is a version of the world where it is still read 500 years later."

"Read?"

"Studied. By scholars. Not performed. Not much anyway. And not in the world you live in now. In that world you are..." She glanced away and wrung her thin fingers.

"Dead? In fact, not in reputation."

"I don't mean to be rude. That man, Baines, killed you in that other world."

Madimi seemed quite anxious. I bowed as respectfully as I could. "Honesty gives no offense, my lady. You can see in all the worlds?"

She beamed. "If I tried, but there are so very many and some make no sense at all; there aren't even people, or worlds, or stars. Come and sit."

She led me into the endless corridor, but at last it was not endless. We came to an alcove where a massive fire roared in a fireplace. There were two richly upholstered chairs by the fireplace, and a delicately carved table between them. When I glanced back the way we came, I discerned only dark emptiness, shadows, cold and thin.

"How long have I been in prison?"

"Seven months," she said. "Longer perhaps? Time is different here. You must have left your body before. You are an adept."

"Of a sort. I learned magick under Lord Manteo's guidance," I said.

She nodded. "The Algonquin."

"So, there are many worlds?"

"Worlds uncountable, and this place in between them all."

"I've Walked many times before, but I've never come here."

"Doctor Dee sought a place where a man in one city could speak with a man in another city, so agents of the Queen might share knowledge across great distances."

John Dee. Company man. Of course, why did I think otherwise. *"Lovely. So, Magister Dee created all this?"*

"No. It was always here." Madimi smiled. *"This is a place where friends far away in space and time have always met."*

"Are we friends, spirit?"

She tilted her head. *"If you will have me."*

I shuddered under her trusting gaze. *"I don't think I am a safe man to befriend."*

She shook her head, her thin hair falling around her shoulders. *"I need a friend badly. You will serve."*

My head began to throb. *"Because the stars are wrong? The nova appeared in the sky 20 years late."*

The spirit frowned. *"The star did not appear. It was always there, beyond human sight, but it...I guess I should say it exploded. It became bright and faded. The world where you live now, it exploded a little later than the world you were born in. That's all."*

"Stars explode?" My mind was spinning. *"Like gunpowder?"*

"No." She rubbed her arms as if she were cold. *"And yes. The process is not important."*

"So, we did not change the world at all," I said. *"We just shifted ourselves, world to world, like steppingstones across a pond. We didn't hurt anything at all."*

Madimi looked up into the dim mists of the Library shelves and said nothing. She seemed to be thinking of someone far away from her. John Dee perhaps. Her hair hung long and straight on her shoulders, much like Lord Manteo's and nearly as black.

"Or help anything either, I suppose," I said. *"The other world,*

those poor bastards still exist under Spanish rule no doubt."

She turned to me and smiled. "Do not fear, Master Marlowe. The effects of the Armada spell are confusing, but I can help you—"

My shoulder suddenly jerked in pain. Candle wax dropped on my skin. Reeve in his enthusiasm had let the beeswax taper tip in his hand.

"Where did you go?" asked Wood.

"Nowhere."

"What did you see?" asked Reeve.

"I saw nothing."

They believed me. Un-Gifted men, why wouldn't they. But it was their job to teach me their methods. "We'll try again," they said, in concert. And in a few days, they did.

"I know I trouble you," Madimi said. "I am sorry for it. It is difficult to speak with most people. You have a natural gift for Walking through worlds. It is why they needed you for the Armada spell, though you were still young and untrained."

"Is this the only place we can go?"

"I can take you anywhere," she said, her chin lifting proudly. "Look up."

We sat together on the crest of a vine-grown ziggurat, while the angel of death overran the city below. Oh, yes, it was very much a city, however primitive. It stretched in three directions around a monstrous and slow-moving river. A city of dark, black-haired people. Most of them were dying. The plague-ridden bodies fell into the wide, lazy river, a river so vast it seemed like the sea itself, as if the world were indeed flat and China just visible across the horizon.

I tried to keep my trembling hands still. "I do not know this place."

"This city is called Cahokia," said the thin-armed girl. I noted

then that she sat atop a gravestone. As did I.

"But where is that?"

"America," she said. "In the places beyond your maps."

The Spanish discovered ancient cities in the jungles of the South America, or so it was said. I had heard they were made of gold, not mud and sticks and plague. "The Spanish brought the plague here?"

"The Spanish have never been here. But that is not necessary for disease to spread."

"Will they die?"

She wrung her hands together and, at first, she did not speak."Nearly all. The Mexica brought grain, and the grain brought pestilence. Your pestilence."

"My pestilence?"

"Your people's, I mean. All of Christendom, not the English specifically."

The moans of the dying grew louder. There were bodies strewn all over the ground. There were more of the dead than there were of the living. The living had not the strength to do more than lie in their own filth. The stench was immeasurable.

"So can you take me anywhere?"

"I cannot leave the Earth. The Library is the only place outside your dimension—"

"Dimension?"

"Your world, Marlen, your...reality. The one you're in now, not the one you were born in." *Madimi frowned.* "I'm not good at explaining—"

I was back in my cell with Wood and Reeve peering down at me.

"Where did you go?" asked Reeve.

"Nowhere."

"What did you see?" asked Wood.

"I saw nothing."

"Try again."

Quite seriously, this nonsense went on for months. It was endlessly preferable to reading theory. I just wished I could have meat and wine once in a while.

We were back in the Library. Madimi sat, her hands folded primly, her back straight like a well-trained young woman, although who could say if one such as her could be called young or a woman. I walked down the long corridor into darkness for a long time. I saw no other fireplaces, no other comfortable nooks. I saw no ceiling either. Maybe a foot above my head you began to see scrolls, and up, just at the point where I could barely see, there were a few stone tablets.

I came back to the fireplace and sat down next to Madimi. "If this is all the books ever written, can they tell me what the Armada spell did?"

"The magicians who crafted that spell did not write books," said Madimi. "So their wisdom cannot be recorded in the Library."

"That makes no sense."

"Magick has rules. It uses symbols. Writing is a symbol, just as you are a symbol, my Marlen."

"Do stop calling me that," I said. "I detest magick."

"A wizard who hates magick is like a fish who hates water."

"I also despise spirits," I said. "No offense, to you, lady. You seem a worthy representative of your kind."

"No offense taken," she said.

"Doctor Dee has no love for me. He used my Gift, but it did not endear me to him. Much like you I suppose."

"Doctor Dee did not send me," Madimi said. "I need your help."

"I have no power to help you."

"Not yet," she said. *"But I will help you, and in time, you will help me."*

"With what? I'm a prisoner. Even when they let me out, they won't leave me unfettered. How can I possibly help you?"

Something in her smile chilled me. "I am working on the problem."

Two days after the holy feast of Easter, I cautiously approached Reeve, who had a barely perceptible touch of wit and independence. "Would it be possible for me to leave my chamber at night to observe the motions of the stars?"

He blinked his watery and glassy eyes. "Master Marlowe, you know that is not possible."

"Are you afraid I'll throw you off the walls of this place? Or slide down the tower and make my escape?"

Reeve folded his veined hands over his open copy of Hermes Trismegistus. "Master Marlowe, for myself, I trust you. A man who has served the Queen as you have...well I had a brother who died fighting the Armada. You should be honoured among men, not closeted up here with two old fools. You've forgotten more about astrology than Wood and I ever learned. But we've been particularly ordered to prevent you from a serious study of the stellae novae."

"*Stellae novae?*" I asked. "There's more than one?"

He spread his hands. "I am forbidden to discuss it. Take heart. In time they will assign you abroad, and you will leave our tiresome company and go on adventures. Won't that be nice?" He patted my hand like a schoolboy then and turned back to his book.

Sometime around the Feast of the Assumption, the door opened during supper. Matthew Roydon strode into my cell, dressed in fine green silk to visit me at the end of the world. Wood and Reeve put their cups down and left without a word. I said nothing. I licked my lips. It was summer but they were as dry as if I'd stood three hours in a North wind in January.

He took off his plumed hat and placed it on the table next to the candle. "Well, you look exactly like those two old crows."

"Do you come to spare my life or end it, Sweet Matthew?"

He took a crystal out of his pocket. It was polished quartz, amber and smoky, but if you let the light hit it just right, you could see things in that crystal. It was a proper seeing stone, perfectly round and polished. It barely fit into the circle of his index finger and thumb. It was neither clear white nor black obsidian as was Doctor Dee's stone, but amber coloured, like sunlight and tobacco smoke haze. I'd seen it at Thomas Harriot's house, on the wretched day of the Armada spell. It belonged to Lord Manteo.

"How did you get that?"

He did not answer. I wiped the sweat from my eyes. I reached for the stone despite myself. It felt cool in my bare fingers as Matthew placed them there. He pulled his own gloved hands back as if he were releasing a hot fork. It had no real power, not in itself, and yet it was a focus for those like myself who did.

"Quite a risk, giving me this."

"Please. You never needed crystals. We're giving you an assignment."

He took off his gloves and sat down in the seat Reeve had vacated. "Master Dee is missing. He is rumoured to be at the court of the Holy Roman Emperor, Rudolf II. We would have you bring him home. This is your token. He will recognize it and assume you represent the Merchants of Light."

Dee? I wondered if Madimi had anything to do with this. Matthew was Gifted. Perhaps he too had been to the Library?

"Why send me? Dee and I have no special love for each other.

Why not go yourself?"

"He will listen to you," said Matthew.

"Oh, I see," I said. "I am not the only one of the old gang who has gone a bit out of bounds, am I?"

"No," said Matthew. "Not six months ago, Dee was in Prague. He met with many scholars, was heard talking about a mad and all-encompassing spell. Something that could rewrite the world."

"Dee told other scholars about the spell?" My fingers gripped the cool, hard crystal. Good lord, I could have killed him myself.

"The agent who reported to me didn't understand the details. It's hard to say what Dee said. But several alchemists clearly know the Armada wasn't blown off course by the will of God."

"And that alone is dangerous," I said. "If Philip of Spain realizes supernatural means were used—"

"He'd take his American gold and start a witch hunt that will rip Europe to shreds. Lucky for us, Philip's view of his nephew Rudolf is not good."

"All Christendom knows Rudolf is mad."

Matthew leaned in close. He smelled like powder and horse and the outside world. He put his hand on my shoulder. He'd never been my bed partner, it wasn't the way he inclined, but we were once closer than lovers. I felt that old feeling stir within me as he whispered in my ear. "We think it plausible that Doctor Dee has given the emperor the spell already."

"That's treason." I could imagine Dee being a little indiscreet, he could be effusive when an idea had hold of him. But this...

Matthew shifted his head from side to side, thoughtfully. I leaned forward. Matthew's lips were shiny and red, his skin paler than usual. Cosmetics? Probably. He looked cold, as if the wind off the sea bit at him. "Rudolf is Gifted?"

Matthew shrugged. "He's surrounded by magicians. He doesn't need to be."

"Wouldn't he have used it by now?"

"Would we know if he had?"

This was true, and yet I knew – I didn't know how I knew, but I knew – the spell hadn't been repeated. I could feel it in my heart. "You don't just want me to find John Dee. You want me to kill him."

Mathew shook his head, his thick curls danced against his shoulders. "I would not ask you to kill a Brother. Just find him. We'll assess the situation and deal with him." He sat back, folding his hands in a pyramid. "Prague is not a burdensome post. It's full of heretics. You'll probably love the place. I thought you'd be delighted."

"Ecstatic." I was only a little ironic. "But are there conditions to my parole? You would not just let me loose on the Continent."

"To the world, Christopher Marlowe is dead and dead he must remain." He poured me a glass of wine. "Your family, your friends, most of all your audience must never know."

"I accept," I said, quickly.

"And..." he hesitated. "Above all, you must not write. Not for the stage or publication, under your name or any other. Not on any topic whatsoever."

"I would not write about the *stellae novae*, they have to believe—" My head began to pound.

"The Council insisted," said Matthew.

I pulled an indignant face, but my stomach turned over because I already knew exactly why. This had nothing whatsoever to do with the *stellae novae* or the Armada spell. Matthew had the decency to look uncomfortable.

"The trouble your play *Tamburlaine* caused—" he began.

"I had naught to do with the anti-immigrant riots. What do I have against Dutch Protestants? Is it my fault the thugs liked my play?"

"It's called inspiration, you nit. You incited rebellion," He crossed his arms across his chest. "And in *Faustus* you conjured a demon on stage using a complete Hermetic ritual."

"I had to stage the entire ritual, or a demon would be left unbound after every performance."

"And we will not speak of your *Massacre at Paris*."

"'Tisn't even my *Massacre at Paris*. The censors rewrote most of it."

Matthew's cheek twitched, real anger bleeding through his mockery now. "I saw your version of the script. You made Sir Francis a monster."

"Walsingham was a monster."

Matthew raised his fist, but he did not strike me. He hovered for a second and then sat down. "We in her Majesty's Service do not speak ill of our honoured dead."

"They tortured Thomas Kyd," I said. "They knew those papers were mine. Why torture Thomas?"

Matthew looked at his hands. Whatever they'd done to Thomas was not Roydon's fault, but I wanted him to feel shame.

"I can write in Latin if I wish. Who would know?"

"I am sure the Catholic authorities will be even less accommodating than we are, but I have conceived a simpler remedy," said Matthew. "If you speak of what you should not speak, or if you write at all, an anonymous man will step out of the shadows and stab your sister in the heart."

I blinked.

"Anne, wasn't it?"

I had a sudden painful vision of Anne slipping past Roydon on the stairs.

He leaned in close. "And by no means am I leaving you on your own."

Then he kissed me. At that moment I knew what my next play

might have been. I should write about Judas Iscariot. It was a role I knew to the bone, betrayal with a kiss.

Matthew smiled and straightened my collar. "Let me introduce you to your new companion."

"Another wizard?" I managed to sound indifferent, though my stomach turned.

"No," said Matthew. "He's not Order of Merlin. Indeed, he isn't overfond of wizards, so watch your tongue around him. But he knows the country and the language. You may find him useful."

Matthew opened the door. The new man carried a large candle. I heard the heavy tread of his boots as the door whispered shut. My eyes adjusted. Behind all that light stood a young, pale fellow, with blonde lashes that gave his grey-green eyes a peculiar lidless look.

He bowed. "Master Marlowe."

"Who asks for him?" I said, through a tongue wrapped in leather.

"I am Edwin Mooney," he said.

"My keeper?"

Mooney flushed. His eyes were like a pair of polished mirrors.

Matthew stood and bowed. He put his hat on his head, its ridiculous feather dancing in the firelight. "I'll leave you both to it. Do your duty, Marlowe."

I rose unsteadily and lifted my cup. "Not for Queen and country, and certainly not for you," I said. "For Anne."

I did not need crystals to leave my body or wander the spirit world, but controlling where I landed was another matter. It wasn't the easiest thing to do after a full meal and several cups of wine. As little as half a cup of wine can interfere with the astral body's navigation. But it had to be now. Wood and Reeve were older men and had grown lazy about watching me, but once I was on the road with the lidless Edwin Mooney, I'd have no privacy.

And I had Lord Manteo's crystal to aid me.

I lay in my narrow bed listening to the crash of the waves below and prepared to leave my body. When Reeve began to snore, I crept out of bed and sat on the floor as the Algonquin chiefs did, my back straight, my legs crossed, and lit a candle. I held the crystal so that the flame reflected against its shiny surface. It was mottled and flawed, warm and rose-brown. It felt like Lord Manteo, the particular smell of his sweat, so like and unlike that of Englishmen who lived their lives within walls. I breathed in and...left.

The chair I sat on was soft and warm. I could sink into it and sleep for a hundred years, so I forced myself to stand. I looked about me. The bookshelves reached upward into darkness on all sides, the fire was banked, still burning but low, giving off heat but very little light. I tried not to worry about the symbolism of that.

"Madimi?"

Madimi appeared from the shadows. She sat down on the heavy leather-covered chair opposite me. Her eyes seemed blacker than before. "You've returned."

"You said you can take me anywhere."

She blinked, tilted her head sideways. "I did."

"Take me to my sister," I said.

"I don't know your sister," she said. "You will be as a ghost to her."

"She is Gifted as I am," I said. "If I can see spirits, she can."

"Possibly."

"Please try. I must warn her."

Madimi frowned. She seemed to be weighing a much heavier question than the one I posed for her. At length she nodded. "Show her to me."

"How?"

"Picture her in your mind. I will see."

She placed my hands on either side of her head. Her skin was soft but dry, like parchment. I imagined Anne as she'd been the Armada morning, wisps of blonde hair escaping her boy's cap, scepticism in her blue eyes, the slight sheen of sweat around her eyebrows, the pockmarks and freckles on her hands.

"I found her," Madimi said. *"She is drunk."*

I smiled, the joy in my chest filled me unexpectedly. *"Usually."*

"Drink is hard on the Gifted," she said. *"Even if she sees you, she may not remember what you say."*

"It's all right, I'll give it a try."

"If it's a warning, it's important that she remembers, Marlen." Madimi put her hand on my wrist. It was cool, like the wind off the sea. *"Is there someone else? Someone Gifted, but in the world, whom you trust to take her a message?"*

My other sisters had no talent at all. The other poets in my set were as sensitive as bricks, and Thomas...well if he was out of prison...if he was still alive. But there was Will.

I put my hands on Madimi's temples and pictured Will, his wispy little beard, lumpish figure, the ditch water brown hair, tacky clothes.

She beamed. *"Oh! I know him!"*

"Of course, you do."

"Look up Marlen."

Will did not recognize me at first. When he did, he threw his inkstand at me, just like Martin Luther and the Devil. It went through me and splashed blue black ink all over the dingy whitewash walls of his shabby rooms. The ink stain was not visible in the sputtering light of Will's candle, and it probably was not the only one to grace the wall. There were ink stains on his table, his hands, and the threadbare lace on the cuffs of his shirts.

He slapped his hands to his eyes and left a smear of ink on his *face.* "*Avaunt ye spirit!*" *he cried.*

"*Not a spirit,*" *I said.*

He made the sign of the cross.

"*Will, don't go all Catholic, I need your help.*"

"*Where are you?*"

"*Cornwall, I think.*"

Will grinned. "*I thought you would say Purgatory. What the angel said is true, then?*"

"*The angel?*"

"*Madimi.*"

"*She's not an angel.*"

"*Not as such, no.*"

"*You do not question her intent?*" *I asked.* "*That's lazy.*"

He poured himself a bit of wine. There was not much. He should be doing better than this. That wretch Henslowe was cheating him. "*Not everything must be dissected and catalogued, Kit. I accept her as the miracle she is.*"

"*You'd be a terrible mage. You shouldn't trust me.*"

"*I did just try to exorcise you.*"

"*Badly.*"

I told him as much as I thought prudent about the fix I was in. For a long time, he said nothing, just rolled his wine cup between his hands.

"*May I tell the others?*" *he asked.* "*Nashe and Greene and all?*"

"*You can't.*"

Will touched his hand to his throat and swallowed. "*They wouldn't talk.*"

"*Are we speaking of the same Nashe and Greene?*"

"*They grieve your most unnatural murder. Without talking. Do your friends not have the right to any knowledge that could save their lives?*"

I might not have been so angry if I didn't know he was right.

43

"Shut your pustulant mouth."

"Are you going to hit me?" Will was crying. *"But you cannot touch me, can you? You're a mere shade, if in truth this is not a dream."*

"Find Anne and protect her."

"I swear I will do so."

"You would swear though you think this is a dream?"

"Dreams can be true. You really never understood that, did you?" He raised his hand as a pledge, and the world around us dissolved as I felt myself slip back into my own body.

Stupid Will. Gifted, Christlike Will. How strange that as the noose grew tighter around me, it was Will I turned to.

Chapter 5

I might have given Mooney the slip while we crossed the French countryside. I knew the land better than he did. But the thought of Anne kept me still. Matthew could be pork-fisted, but he was efficient. And I did not esteem Dee's skin so highly that I'd risk Anne to protect him.

I was content to pass the long hours on horseback in silence, enjoying the fresh air and meditating upon the scanty details I knew about my silent companion. Mooney probably was not his real surname. His accent was from the north. His Flemish was indifferent, his French worse. He claimed to be fluent in German and Czech. I supposed he lived in Prague as Sweet Matthew had and studied at the English Catholic college there. Certainly, he would have the advantage over me in Bohemia, so I should be on my guard.

I'd never been to the Golden City. Prague was the very heart of Christendom, the golden capitol of the Holy Roman Empire. The court of Rudolf II was a refuge for alchemists and magicians. Most of them were charlatans, but as exile went, a city could suit me worse. I might have quaked with anticipation, were I travelling as a free man.

Of course, I used the scrying stone to find Doctor Dee. It never worked. Sometimes I ended up in the Library, but it was empty, no fireplace, just books and dust and darkness.

Other times, I would see strange sights.

Once I found myself in a jungle. The trees were full of squirrels. Madimi lay in the grass like a child, watching them, fascinated. She was splendidly attired in a red gown trimmed in a deep, unnatural green. Her hair fell to her shoulders, and she wore soft red leather gloves.

She pulled herself up on her elbows and beckoned. "Join me. But be careful"

I lay down beside her to see what she saw. A squirrel leapt over our heads through the trees. No, this was no squirrel at all. His eyes were azure blue, round like robin's eggs, and its hands were shaped almost like a man's. He gazed down on us with bald curiosity, his long, ringed tail wrapped around the branches to steady him.

The girl said, "What goodly creatures are there here. What brave new world that has such creatures in it."

"Beg pardon?" I asked.

"Shakespeare."

"Will never wrote anything like that."

She frowned and shook her head. "Perhaps not yet."

"Goodly creatures, these, and strange," I said. "And quiet. So very quiet."

"They are called lemurs. They make no sound when they are slaughtered for meat. Soon the biggest ones will disappear. Very soon."

Ah yes, I knew there had to be a slaughter someplace. "Where are we?"

"The underside of the world."

"The Underworld? You mean Hades?"

"The island Madagascar," she said. "Past the horn of Africa, at the bottom of the world. Consult your atlas."

"I haven't got one, Madame. I am travelling."

She wrinkled her freckled nose, and her brown eyes twinkled. "Are you?"

"Seeking your master in fact."

"Good," she said. "Very good."

The goodly creature leapt into the trees, the better to regard us from a distance. All the trees were adorned with the silent monsters, thoughtful and unblinking, hanging from their tiny, man-like hands. We heard shouts, and slight, sharp popping sounds, and the creatures in the trees began to die.

Another time, I found myself in a large, outdoor palace, with a chessboard on the floor and men and women wrapped in billowing silks, all dressed up as pieces. There was no ceiling but a crimson and gold tent. The sky that showed as it flapped in the wind was an intense, bright blue I'd never seen in this world. A man with a large moustache and turban sat on a dais surrounded by more women. He barked orders and the pieces would move. I could not tell if there was another player or if he was playing himself.

"Fatehpur Sikri," Madimi said, behind me.

"What's that?" I asked.

One of the players lifted his white bishop's cap and looked in my direction. He was darker than the man barking orders but had a similar moustache. He frowned as if he was trying to place where he'd seen me before. The man on the dais shouted another order, and he slapped his hat back on his head. The move took him to the other side of the board. Check.

"Did he see me?" I asked Madimi.

"Emperor Akbar?" she asked. "Surely not."

"Why can't I find Doctor Dee?"

"You aren't looking correctly."

"These far off shades you show me, spirit. Are they real?"

"Yes."

"Why show them to me."

"T'is what I do."

"Yes, but why?"

She sat silent, her hands wrapped about her knees. When she spoke, it was with effort. "I need help."

"Madame Spirit. I am little better than a prisoner." I shrugged. "I cannot even help myself."

Madimi touched my face. "You are not yet dead, Marlen."

I often found myself with Anne. She was always in the pub. Merry Anne, singing and dancing. Surly Anne, pulling the hair of some hapless constable. Senseless Anne, slumped unconscious over a table. Exhausted Anne, ale at her elbow, baby at her breast. She could not hear me even when I shouted.

One night I found her lying in the grass outside of town, hair askew, her skirts torn and stained with wine. She watched the moon arcing across the sky, and cried for a long time, those lovely, heartfelt, honest sobs that were cleansing because one could pretend not to remember them. They were the healing madness that drink alone could give. I cried like that the night they took Thomas Kyd.

I lay down next to her and touched her hand. She turned and looked straight at me. "Why did you have to die?"

I stroked her hair. "I am not dead."

"Oh Kit. No one else...likes me."

"What of your husband?"

She sniffed. "He says I'm no fit mother. He took the baby to his Mum and won't come back unless I mind him."

I snorted. "Must I sort him out?"

"He's not a bad man," she said. "I do drink."

I put my spirit hand over her warm one. She turned back to the stars. They were in fine form tonight, a great stretch of jewels peppering a vast ocean of darkness. We always watched the stars together when we were little.

"Anne," I said. "Please listen. You are in danger."

"Danger?" she mumbled.

"Men are coming to kill you."

"I don't care."

"I care, Anne."

She sat up on her elbows and stared right at me. "If you are not dead, come back right now."

"If I do, they'll kill you for sure."
She lay back down. "You went away long before you died."

I felt a hand on my shoulder. "Master Marlowe?" said Mooney.

Mooney was a blur in the guttering light of the candle. I was lying in the corner of a common room. Men snored all around me. The sounds and smells of humans and sausages and dogs came back one at a time.

"Are you well, Master Marlowe?"

"Quite well, Master Mooney."

He frowned. I put my hand to my face. Oh. Tears.

Mooney sat back on his haunches. He regarded me through those pale lashes. I could not tell if I saw pity or scorn or some other feeling there. It occurred to me, like a shout from across the sea, that I was afraid. Was this small weakness enough to trigger Anne's death?

He put his hand on my shoulder. It was soft and heavy, not a workman's hand or a soldier's. A scholar's hand. I looked up at his lashless eyes again. They weren't really. In the firelight the light colour caught a hint of gold. His eyes were hazel and looked like amber. For the first time Edwin Mooney had what I reckoned to be a human response. His skin flushed red, to the tip of his pale, thin hair. He took his hand away.

"Go back to sleep." His voice was very low, in a very familiar timbre. He rolled over and turned his back to me.

I closed my eyes and listened to Master Mooney's uneven breathing. Well, that was interesting. That was very, very interesting.

After some weeks on the road, Mooney and I met a troupe of actors. Players were not always well received so instead of risking any unpleasantness with the burghers, the troupe made camp outside the gates. They circled their covered wagons around a large bonfire, long ribbons and pennants playing about in the breeze. I could hear thin strains of lute music over the wind.

Mooney told me to wait while he talked to the master of the troupe. When he returned he announced, "We've joined the company."

"Why?"

"They're headed home to Bohemia. They've agreed to take us along."

"They're awful trusting, taking in strangers."

"I've worked for Jahoda before. The fat man. The Master of the Company."

"So, you are an actor?"

"I was with Burbage's company at the Rose with Master Shakespeare," he said. "Do you not remember me?"

"No."

He turned red and walked away. Proof piled upon proof. All manner of men seek refuge in the playhouses and one sort of man in particular. I wondered if I dared put that notion to the test. Although if he worked on the Bankside, it was probable he knew all facets of my reputation. He would be on his guard.

I did not contemplate bedding Master Mooney for my own pleasure. An experienced agent would not confuse lust with affection. He would not lower his guard just because I slaked his thirst. The mere hint that he inclined toward men gave me a sliver of hold over him. If he were to prove that in unmistakable terms, that sliver might become leverage. If that could turn into power which could be used to protect Anne, it had to be tried. If I could make him love me...or merely make love to me...he might become an ally. If there was any man for this job, it was probably me.

Mooney handed me over to the women, who placed me by the

fire with a tin plate heaped with stew and a hunk of brown bread the size of my hand. There were ten players, six men, four women. The women acted too, as was the custom on the continent. They spoke with Mooney in German, but amongst themselves they conversed in Czech. It was unfamiliar to me. I couldn't make out any words. Two spoke French. None spoke English or Flemish, and Latin made them laugh.

They set to the serious business of eating, drinking, and having a laugh and left me alone. Mooney sat with the bottle in his hands, not drinking from it. I picked up my cup and joined him. "I am sorry I did not remember you played at the Rose."

He shook his head. "No reason you should. I played servants, watchmen, girls, that sort of thing."

"But you know who I am? As a poet I mean."

The blush returned. "Everyone knows who you are."

His voice shook a little, and he did not look at me. Well. Well, well, well. I sat down very close to him, not touching but just close enough that he could feel the heat of my skin. He poured some sweet-smelling drink into my cup.

"I hope to play your Doctor Faustus, one day, if the chance should come."

"They still play *Faustus*?" I despised myself for caring.

He glanced up, his long lashes playing Helen rather than Faustus. "The author is better remembered on the Bankside than can be spoken openly."

Will had alluded to the silence enforced upon my friends. They were all being watched, probably by men not unlike Mooney, actors who played in the secret theatre as well as the stage. Mooney was not remotely pretty enough for Helen. Even in youth he wouldn't have served, with that weak chin and lip. But those eyes. In the firelight they were almost green.

"I tried translating it," he said, abruptly.

I came out of the reverie over the jade flecks in his eyes. "Translating what?"

"*Faustus*. Into Czech. It's an important legend where we're going."

"There must be plenty of Faust plays."

"Just Mystery plays, Virtue and Vice. Nothing to touch yours. I've tobacco." He shook his head and took his pipe from his pack.

"Thank you, sir." I lit the pipe, gratefully, inhaling the woody smell of the tobacco. I fought the suddenly vivid memory of Lord Manteo sitting across the fire, chanting softly over the smoke. "So, you admire *Faustus*?"

Mooney turned his eyes back to me. "The devil's words about damnation, a state that follows you, Hell as a place you carry within." He put a tentative hand on my shin.

Well. Well, well, well. I handed him back the pipe and poured a little more drink into his cup, leaned against him just a little closer. "While you were playing bit parts, they closed all the houses because the Plague was in London."

"Bit of an obstacle to my career, that was."

"So, you joined the secret theatre instead."

Mooney smiled. It made his rabbit face almost attractive. "That's a mighty pretty name for it."

"What do younger men call it?"

He shrugged. "I'm just a messenger."

"Matthew's messenger?"

"Master Royden, you mean? I am, you might say, on loan. I was at Rudolf's court, his personal retreat at Brandýs nad Labem, among English Catholics plotting against our Queen, when I heard some rumours about Doctor Dee. I was ordered to report to him."

So Mooney was the man who told Royden that the emperor knew about the spell. "And now you are my handler."

He looked at me without answering for a long time, as I looked at him. Master Mooney was not entirely without merit as a physical specimen. He had an actor's leg and a slender arm that was hard muscle. He was a swordsman, and not just on the stage. It would be no great burden to bed this man.

"I suppose you may as well know," said Mooney.

"Know?" I smiled my best lazy smile, like a predator lying still.

"About our mission."

I blinked with disappointment. "Finding Dee."

"Yes, but Master Roydon did not tell you everything," he said. "This is why we need to find him."

He removed a paper from a pocket in his sleeve. A block of numbers filled the page, laid out in 16 lines like a sonnet. I stared at it in the firelight.

"It's a cipher."

"I can see that."

"Can you read it?" Mooney asked.

"No," I said. "I assume you think Doctor Dee can?"

"He will try if you ask him."

I laughed. "Matthew overestimates my powers of persuasion."

He stretched out his hand for the paper. "I assume you have already attempted to seek him using your...particular skills."

He would not meet my eye. It goaded me. "Using magick, you mean."

Mooney frowned. He shrugged. "Did it work?"

"No," I said. "We'll have to seek him using mundane means."

He sighed, even smiled a little. "Good. You can stop doing whatever you're doing when you think I'm asleep."

He looked up again. He was almost beautiful in the firelight. I hated that I noticed. "You prefer honest spycraft then?"

"I suppose so."

I gave him back the letter and watched carefully while he

tucked it in his sleeve. He could hide it someplace else on his person, but maybe he would not, and I could pluck it while he slept. "No interest in learning our methods then?"

"I know all about the Order of Merlin, sir, and all the gold in Christendom could not compel me to join you."

"You are wise beyond your years, my boy."

"I leave you with my pipe, sir," said Mooney, suddenly cool. "We leave early in the morning."

He walked away. Of course. Mooney was no fool. No easy provocation would achieve my lascivious purpose. I would need more time. Still progress had been made. I was no longer travelling with a silent guard, but an ordinary companion, possibly even a friend.

Jahoda's troupe performed a bastardized mix of commedia del'arte, music, juggling, and fairy stories in low German. Mooney's fluent German allowed him to join the company as a player, but my accent marked me as an Englishman. I kept backstage. I sewed, hammered platforms, scrubbed pots, combed horses, and even milked goats.

One evening, Mooney sat next to me, chewing on a bit of chicken while I knelt in the mud scrubbing pots. "Sweet Jesu. You've really begun to smell like a drudge."

He licked his fingers and looked across the river. He hardly seemed to see me. I was losing my charms, fast becoming the most pathetic drudge in the poorest wandering theatre company in all Christendom. That would not serve my purpose with him.

"Your friends do not trust us," I remarked.

"Should they?" he said, twisting a single lock of hair behind his ear.

"You said they were Protestant."

Mooney turned back to sucking on a chicken bone. "They are

whatever is convenient. Their patron is a Protestant nobleman, Petr Vok z Rožmberk, or in German Rosenberg."

"Lord Rožmberk who holds South Bohemia?"

"That's his cousin. In any case, we're not going there."

"We should. He was Doctor Dee's patron."

Mooney flung the chicken bone into the river. "Look across the river, very slowly."

I looked up. There was an encampment on the other side of the river. I ducked my head back into the pot I was scrubbing. "Just some Travellers."

"Haven't you seen that group of Gypsies before?"

I thought about it. "Hard to say. They are all through these parts."

He shuddered. "I hate Gypsies."

"These in particular?"

"Perhaps."

"Have you seen them before, Master Mooney?"

Mooney looked peevish, his skin waxy under the freckles. "Everywhere. Prague. Dresden. Munich. Krakow. That band is always around. Following me. They're rotten with spies."

Generally speaking, the Romany ignored the entire Protestant-Catholic business, preferring to make money fleecing winners and losers alike. This was evidence of their good sense in my opinion. But Mooney was clearly troubled.

"It would be easy for a dark Italian to hide amongst them, or a Turk. A Spaniard, even. But I don't know many Travellers as'd take on the risk."

"They will do near anything for money. And the man who tried to kill me in Brandýs nad Labem is with them."

"Which one?"

Mooney leaned his head slightly in the direction of the camp. "The big fellow, with the moustache and the red sash."

All the men had moustaches. Most of them were big. Half wore sashes that might be called red. But I knew which man Mooney meant. He was just as dishevelled as the others, but there was something apart about him. None of other Travellers touched him. And there was something familiar about him.

I bent back over my work and reminded myself to breathe. I let silence hang in the air. If I waited, he would speak.

He leaned over and hissed over the wet dishrags. "Some feel that the Right Catholic Holy Roman Emperor just isn't Right or Catholic enough. They believe he tolerates Protestants in his lands because he is impious, or perhaps mad. There have been attempts on his life."

He trailed off, so I prompted him. "What monarch in Christendom has been spared assassination attempts?"

"Some are agents of the Spanish King. Some are from his brother Matthias."

"The spy works for someone in Rudolf's family?"

"He did try to kill me."

I raised my eyebrows. "Perhaps he did not like the look of you."

He scrambled to his feet and kicked over my pile of cooking pots. "Mock me then," he said and stalked away.

I laughed. I shouldn't have teased him. It tore his conspiratorial mood like a boy's stick through a spider web, though it was fun to watch the blood fill his ears.

But when I turned back to my chores, I noticed the Gypsy who wasn't a Gypsy looking at me. I wondered where I had seen him before.

He smiled. And then he turned away.

Chapter 6

The feast day of All Saints was the last day of full sunlight. On All Souls morning, the mists came down and met us as we climbed the white, limestone hills, lovely veils of thin spun lace caressing the pine topped hills as we crossed into Bohemia.

Once we entered their own country, Master Jahoda brought Mooney and me to his own fire for some stomach-burning liquor and sausages. He urged on me more drink than I ought to have accepted. "You will forgive us for your cold reception. While we were in Catholic lands, it was best we speak as little as possible."

"Are we not still in Catholic lands?" I asked. "This is the Holy Roman Empire."

"This land here, sir, is held by Vilem z Rožmberk," Jahoda said, puffing up his round body. "The right Protestant lord of these parts."

"You are Protestant, sir?"

"All Czech people are Protestant."

I looked at Mooney.

"Many Czechs are Catholics," said Mooney, a bit sourly.

Jahoda gave him a droll look. "Even Czechs who are Catholic are Protestant. The real Catholics are Germans. You want more sausage?"

He took another sausage out of the pan and looked stern and sorrowful until I consumed the entire thing. He did the same with Mooney, who looked like he was becoming a mite ill.

"When the emperor moved the capitol to Prague, he made a pact with the Czech people that there would always be religious toleration in the land. This is because we have a long tradition here of the Czech Brotherhood."

"You're not Lutheran then?"

"Oh! Jan Hus reformed the Czech Christians many years before Luther," said Jahoda. "Most people attend whichever church is handy. We never really answered to Rome. The Holy Roman Emperors have the good sense not to make a point of it. They answer to Rome for us, and everybody is happy."

"Even Lutherans and Jews are tolerated," said Mooney. "And atheists."

"Mohammedans, them, he might question because of the war with the Turk. Though I've heard it rumoured some Gypsies are Mohammedans. They came north from the plains of Hungary, driven by the Ottoman janissaries."

"And magicians?" I asked. "They are tolerated too?"

Jahoda looked amused. I imagine I was not the first foreigner to ask. "Encouraged, rather. We have many mages at Lord Rožmberk's seat at Krumlov. He seeks an heir. The alchemists are at it night and day, to keep my lord's...interests...upright."

I laughed so hard I breathed liquor into my nose. Even Mooney cracked a smile at the thought of grave alchemists plying their skill so one high-born man could get it up. I knew the importance of dynastic conundrums – I was English after all – but it was still funny.

"Will you go with us all the way to Prague?" I asked.

"We turn south to Krumlov. You can take this road west a bit and follow the river north to Prague."

"I know the way," Mooney said, stiffly.

Jahoda raised his eyebrows significantly. "You will seek Tadeáš Hájek, I suppose."

Mooney glared. "What do you know of our business, Master Jahoda?"

"I know you are Englishmen," Jahoda said. "I know the emperor has imprisoned a certain important Englishman. I know that if his family does not reside with Magister Hájek, he will know where they are. This information must be useful to you."

Mooney's scowl did not trouble Jahoda in the slightest. He rose, smiled warmly and kissed me on both cheeks. He did the same for Mooney, who suffered the embrace like a block of wood. Then the playmaster wobbled to his wagon, to his mistress and more of her fiery liquor.

Mooney grabbed my collar. His temper was a storm on a dark sea. "Everything they said of you is true. You have no discretion."

"How is this my fault?" I protested. "I don't even know who Master Hájek is!"

He raised his hand as if to cuff me. But he thought better of it and flung himself down by the fire. I stood, shaking. I had no idea what I might have done if he'd struck me. I could not fight him without killing him, and either way might risk Anne. I would have to surrender to a beating, and I could not bear it. No, I could have. I've taken beatings plenty of times. Like a battered wife, I offered him my pipe to sweeten his mood. He accepted with ill grace.

For a time, he smoked in silence, and I was quiet until I felt it was safe to speak again. "I humbly apologize. I do not know this country. I will be more careful."

Mooney nodded. "I beg your pardon. That was...wrong."

I blinked, surprised at his sudden capitulation. "Thank you."

He indicated I should sit next to him and share the pipe. "Jahoda is trustworthy enough. But please be careful. Not everyone here will wish you well."

"Who is Master Hájek?"

"Court physician."

"An alchemist?"

Mooney shrugged. "They're all some sort of mage in the city. I don't know a philosopher from an astrologer. But he's one of them."

"Dee knows him."

"Oh yes," said Mooney.

"Wait," I said. "Jahoda said a certain Englishman was in prison? Did he mean Dee?"

Mooney grimaced. "He meant the court magician, Magister Kelley. He and Dee made quite a name for themselves, running around the country, casting horoscopes, turning wine into water or stone into bread."

"Lead into gold."

"Whatever it was, they performed miracles in all the finest houses in the Empire. Apparently, Kelley could speak to angels."

I gaped. "Dear God, you do not mean *Edward* Kelley?"

He stared at me with his large, golden fringed eyes. "Yes."

I laughed. It took time to get hold of myself. Mooney waited, his brow furled.

"You are acquainted?"

"A bit," I said, wiping my eyes. "Are you?"

"Kelley was one of Rudolf's favourite magicians until Kelley killed one of his officers." Mooney smiled a little, though it did not reach his eyes. "Not the sort to consort with angels, then?"

"Walsingham had him watching every occult circle in the British Isles. He was called Edward Talbot, then. He knew precisely how to get into Doctor Dee's confidence, but he was completely headblind. Wouldn't know a spirit if he kissed one."

"Well," said Mooney. "That makes me think better of him. I'd heard he'd sold his soul to the Devil."

For a moment I imagined that he trembled.

"You really despise magicians."

"I like some magicians a bit better than others."

I thought the moment as good as any to make my move. I put my arm around his shoulder. He smelled of greasepaint, a sour poultry-fat scent. For a moment he reached around my waist and, with tentative pressure, returned my embrace.

"Kelley and Dee were famously close," he said. "If anyone in the Empire can find him, it might be Kelley."

"He is in prison."

"So, he's easy to find, and inclined to be grateful for any kindness. A word from his family, perhaps the possibility that we can get him back to England, and he'll be cooperative."

"He has a family," I said, my throat growing tight. "I suppose they would be leverage."

Mooney pulled away. The firelight made his light hair shine like a halo. I risked touching it. It was soft and cold though the skin under it was warm. "We won't hurt them," he said. "We are not monsters."

"Yes, we are."

I tried to smile and pass it off as a bit of flirtation, but Mooney looked steady at me until I turned away. "Is this reckless behaviour how you survived Walsingham's service?" he whispered.

"Ahh, Master Mooney, I did not precisely survive."

"Stop calling me Master Mooney," he said, taking my hand. "Edwin."

I swallowed. His lips glistened in the firelight. "Would you call me Kit?"

He smiled, lowering those golden lashes. "I would be honoured."

"Is Edwin your real name?"

"No."

He looked up, and for a moment I thought he would kiss me. But then he moved away. He put down the pipe and dusted off his knees, looking around into the trees. I forced myself to breathe. Not yet. Not yet, but soon. I felt his resolve failing.

"Good night, Edwin."

He stood and looked down at me for a long time. "Good night...Kit."

We left the company together the following morning. That evening, we stopped a village with an unpronounceable name where no one spoke German. I asked Edwin if we were lost, and he said not at all. He knew this place and he wanted me to meet the priest.

The village church was little more than a daub hut, but it had a proud little onion-shaped dome, glinting with new brass. It was Catholic, or at least the Latin Mass they chanted in the tiny, close room was identical to the one said in any Catholic village. Edwin dropped to his knees, the very image of a wandering pilgrim, falling at the feet of Our Saviour as if His grace was the water he thirsted for. I was hard put not to laugh. That's generally the hardest part of spy-work, not laughing.

I crossed myself, knelt beside him, and endeavoured not to fall asleep. The Latin Mass is tedious, but I've always been lulled by the poetry. In translation its power is much diminished. How could the Church of England hold a man's heart in its hand without the lyrics forged by the poet-priests of the late Roman Empire? The Puritans were smart enough not to try.

The crucifix offends me and not because of hatred of Popery or any of the usual reasons. I've seen men tortured to death. I can bear watching such things rendered in flesh, not stone. But I cannot bear the worship of it. Old Sir Francis never received the obvious lesson of the Passion: Don't break a man's bones, 'tisn't nice.

Officially there is no torture in England, but Old Sir Francis Walsingham, heartfelt Puritan, had a passion for the rack and hot pokers. He conducted interrogations in person. Walsingham felt that a thing done for God and Queen should not be left to lesser men.

As I told Matthew: a monster.

Our monster, though of course the Inquisition was worse.

Without our monsters, the Spanish would have put the whole island to the stake. That should have been enough justification for me. Perhaps if I were a believer, it would be. But like the Arian heretics of old, I can scarce believe the man in the New Testament was a god. And what might that man have said over the obscene picture of his emaciated self, hung tortured on the cross, I had no idea.

Edwin did not take communion, so I did not either. I wondered why he refrained. It would have been prudent to do so merely not to call attention to ourselves. Still, when it was over, he got to his feet, looking cheerful.

"Come, sir," he said. "I will introduce you to my friend."

The priest was sharp faced, and his body was gnarled and small. He stooped like an old man, and his hands were almost as spotted. When he came up close, I realized he was younger than I'd reckoned. He greeted us in Latin.

"Greetings, my dear Eduard," he said, leaning up on tiptoe to kiss both of Mooney's cheeks.

"Peace be with thee, Father Tomáš," Edwin replied in Latin, returning the kiss and the handshake both.

"You are in need of food."

"And information. My brother seeks news of Magister Dee."

The priest patted Edwin's face with genuine affection. "Ionnas Dee left this country some years ago, my boy."

"We heard that he has returned, Father."

"That is unlikely. He and Magister Kelley had a serious quarrel."

To my credit I did not stare at Edwin as if he had grown a new head. This was not grammar school Latin. These two men spoke it as naturally as if they stood together in the Coliseum.

The priest patted my arm as if I were a horse he did not know. "Eduard?"

"My apologies," said Mooney. "This is Christo—"

"Christopher Talbot. I studied with Magister Dee in London," I said in Latin, thankful we had a language in common.

The priest took both my hands in his and kissed my cheeks. "Welcome, Master Talbot. Yes, you are most welcome. I am Father Tomáš. I knew Master Dee well. A gentle man for a heretic." He frowned. "Are you a heretic too, my son?"

I stiffened. Edwin laughed. "Father, you are cruel to tease him."

"Ah, yes, after all, what is heresy," said the old man. "There is only you, me and," he pointed upward, "God. Come, we eat."

His house was little more than a cell, but it was warm inside. He laid a rich barley soup and bread for us. It was as flavourful as if there were meat, with large rich-tasting mushrooms and plenty of broth.

"I also studied with Doctor Dee," said Father Tomáš. "Oh, but I was a young man then. Ready to battle the lions of authority."

"You are an alchemist?"

"Astrology was my true interest," he said. "But I lacked the mathematics. I must admit that I felt closer to God in my prayers as the elements mixed in the laboratory below than I ever have before or since."

"I too am only a novice. My real course of study was Divinity." This was true. Always best to tell the truth as far as you can. You make fewer mistakes.

"Ahh, this is why your Latin is so fine." He gave Edwin an inscrutable glance. "You are a priest?"

"No," I said. "Many of my fellow students took orders, but I—"

"Master Talbot is a poet," Edwin offered.

I tried not to look at Mooney although there was no chance my poetry was known here. "A humble translator of lyrics," I mumbled.

"Of course," said Father Tomáš. "Ovid. Virgil. I too was a young man once. The *Amores*... ahh! Such sensuous riches as a godly man should not set eyes upon but what poetry! Did you attempt the translation of such works?"

"Into English, yes." Again, still true.

He clapped his hands together with the bread still in one hand. "But Eduard, surely—"

"Father, what of Magister Kelley?" Edwin said. "Is he still in Prague?"

"You have heard this, yes?" said the priest. "Magister Kelley killed one of the emperor's men in a fight. The emperor grew angry and locked him away. You know, Magister Kelley and your Master were very great friends."

I blinked. He couldn't know Kelley once worked for Old Sir Francis, could he? No, he meant Dee, my alleged teacher.

"Kelley was a great seer," Father Tomáš said. "Once he looked into the black glass and saw the Archangel Michael himself looking back at him. He spoke in the tongues of angels. Remarkable."

Edward Kelley was notorious for looking into shiny objects and claiming to see all manner of things. I wondered how he fooled the good Father Tomáš. He seemed to have a measure of common sense, unlike Doctor Dee who was, for all his brilliance, the most gullible man in Christendom.

"Think you that Doctor Dee has returned to aid the emperor in his illness?"

"The emperor is ill?" I asked.

Edwin and Father Tomáš exchanged a droll look.

"The emperor is always ill," said Edwin.

"Now Brother Eduard," said the priest. "Be kind."

"That is kind."

Father Tomáš put a wrinkled hand on mine. "Rudolf grew up

in the court of his uncle, Philip of Spain. He saw terrible things there that broke his mind."

"Broken minds run in that family."

"Brother Eduard!"

"Forgive our rudeness," I said. "Philip of Spain..."

"He did terrible things to your country too, Eduard." Tomáš nodded.

"That was the work of Queen Mary," said Edwin.

"Under his influence," said Tomáš. He patted my hand again. "Never fear. Philip is not well loved here."

"I cannot imagine Doctor Hájek requires Dee's help," said Edwin.

"Doctor Hájek is a great man," said Father Tomáš, "but his arts have proved insufficient."

I did not think Doctor Dee was much of a healer. His best work had been in astrology and navigation. In the charting of the seas by mathematics he had no peer. Although he was a government man, a Merchant of Light. I could not know everything about him.

"Who is administering the realm?" I asked.

"Sorry?" They both looked amused.

"You said the emperor was ill."

Tomáš put his hand on my cheek. He looked into my eyes. "The emperor is still King of Bohemia."

"What does that mean?"

"We should be on the road, Father," Edwin said, standing suddenly.

"No, Brother Eduard," the older man said, plaintively. "Rest here tonight. We'll make merry until the saints weep with envy. The last of the burčák is buried next to the well."

"New wine," Edwin translated for me. "And we cannot stay."

I reluctantly stood with him. Walking into the cold evening

landscape was not an inviting prospect. I liked the thought of sitting with the old scholar, discussing Ovid over a drink.

It was dark in earnest before we finally left the priest's house, burdened with four cheeses, his entire store of dried pork, and a flask of new wine. We could walk for scarcely two hours before we were forced to stop and build a fire. By that time the wind had picked up, blowing the clouds across the moon and biting into my face and hands. It took a long while to get a fire going, and even so it was dim, sputtering and gave no warmth.

"It will be cold sleeping here," I said, irritably, rolling my blanket out by the small, imperilled fire.

"Are we too grand to do without a roof overhead, good sir?"

I shivered, despite myself. "I don't like to in November for pity's sake. Not when we could have stayed—"

"I would not imperil the old man by staying in his house," he said, sharply. "I am a bastard, but not that sort of bastard."

He dropped down next to the fire, huddling over it to shield it from the wind. I uncorked the flask the good Father gave us and took an experimental sip. It was rich and sweet and tickled my nose. I handed it to Edwin. He did not refuse although he must know I wanted to loosen his tongue. He took a deep gulp of the wine and wiped his lips on his sleeve with a sigh.

"You have had me at a disadvantage these many months, Edwin," I said. "You know all about me while I know nothing about you."

He grinned. The warming liquor made his lips deep red. "A gentleman such as yourself wouldn't have shared two words with a poor player like me before you tumbled so far down in the world."

I took the bottle from his hands. I wished for some tobacco, but it was almost gone. "I'm no more high-born than you, I dare say. How did you come to know Will?"

"Master Shakespeare was my schoolmaster."

"In Stratford?"

"York," he said.

Lord. When was Will Shakespeare ever in York?

"So, dear Brother Eduard," I said cutting a hunk of cheese for him. "What university did you attend?"

"I? Attend a university?" he said, his northern accent growing stronger as he chewed.

"That was not grammar school Latin."

"Master Shakespeare is fluent in Latin. He never went to university."

"Few men are Master Shakespeare."

"Oxford." He looked away and blushed hard.

"I thought Old Sir Francis preferred Cambridge men."

"I put myself in debt to some important people. They sent me to Balliol College on the Queen's business, to sort of work it off."

"To infiltrate the Catholics there," I said. "So, you were a government man before you were an undergraduate?"

"We had a bit of trouble in the North, you remember."

I did. The North barely tolerated the Church of England even now. He took the bottle back from me and took a long sip that made him sputter. "Well, you made good use of your time."

"Had to," he said, his Northern accent growing broader. "As far as the masters knew, I was just another scholarship student. I had to keep up or I'd have been packed off."

"Did you receive your degree?"

"It became known what I was about. The other students did not take kindly to my presence."

"So, you went to London and Master Henslowe took you on as a player?" I wondered if Shakespeare knew what Mooney was. Then I realized he must have. A boy from the North, embroiled in intrigue. Will hinted he knew more than he was saying that night in the Rose. Will probably sought to save Edwin from my sorry fate.

"No," he said. "I went to Prague. I lived among the Catholic exiles, studied, did my bit for the Queen, you know. Same as you. But a man gets a hankering for his own country, and back I went."

"So, whom do you work for?" I asked.

"Sorry?" he blinked at me.

"Well, you said it wasn't Royden. Thomas Walsingham? Or Lord Cecil?"

Edwin took another swallow of the brandy. A grin broke across his homely face. "I work for the Queen. Don't we all?"

He kissed me. I am not often without words. I'd been angling for weeks and here I was the one caught. His mouth tasted sweetly of the juicy new wine, stilled all thoughts. It was so sudden, so seemingly unguarded that I laughed.

He blinked at me, dejected. "I...I did not mean to cause offense...I..."

I clasped him in my arms. It felt good to have a man's soft skin against my hands, his body hard against my own hardness. I could feel him shift his balance so that his weight rested on my own. I held him up and kissed him and kissed him and kissed him.

He rested his head against my shoulder. "How long have you wanted to do this?" I whispered.

"Long," he said, his voice hoarse.

"I would not take from you anything you did not wish to give me."

"I would give you my life," Edwin said.

He spoke so sincerely that it could not possibly be true. I disentangled myself and set him gently on his own feet.

"Nay do not leave me," he said. "Devil."

"I will come back, Sweet," I said. "But first, I must piss like the Devil."

I stepped back and slipped into the woods. I did have to piss, but I needed to think. The story Edwin told me was probably true, or at least not entirely false. By his own admission, he had been an agent provocateur since his youth. He was immensely good at getting close to a man, gaining his confidence, even his sympathy.

And Edwin had my sympathy. Spying on fellow students, friends, leaves a poison in one's mouth. I've spit that one out myself.

But would he know that? All of London knew Kit Marlowe, the Brat Prince of the Bankside. How well did Edwin Mooney, whatever his real name was, know Christopher Marlowe, government man? Would he know exactly the story to tell me that would open my heart to him? While I thought I was seducing him, was he seducing me? And to what purpose? Much as I thought of his ugly face and fine figure, I must keep my head.

I'd walked all the way to the river. I undid my breeches, relieved myself, and knelt at the riverbank to splash water on my face. Was continuing the seduction the best course? It would serve to keep us both warm at any rate. Or I should ply him with more *burčak* and keep traveling down the dangerous road of unguarded conversation.

I had just about decided on nice, safe fornication, when I saw the Man Who Was Not a Gypsy pissing against a tree on the other side of the river. He seemed as surprised to see me as I was to see him. The moonlight flashed on his teeth as he grinned in embarrassment.

I did not know what to do, so I bowed.

He bowed in return, although his had a few more flourishes. Then he tied up his breeches and walked away.

I crept back to our fire and touched Edwin on the shoulder. "We must go."

Chapter 7

Edwin asked no questions, just gathered his pack and calmly smothered the fire. We headed off the road into the woods, heading west, instead of continuing north. The ground was rough beneath our feet. I stumbled more than once but the trees grew so thick they broke my fall. We walked in silence for perhaps an hour before I paused. I felt Edwin's hand on my arm.

"Father Tomáš."

I felt a pang. "He let him be to follow us."

"Please, Kit. He's no longer young. If he goes back for him—"

"Why would he?"

I felt his breath, warm on my face, as he hesitated, making some sort of calculation. The moon made pale streaks of his ice coloured lashes.

"Stay here if you like," he said, and ploughed off to the south.

Had I been the cold, heartless fellow a government man ought to be, I should have knocked Edwin to the forest floor and sat on him. Instead, I swallowed a delicious piece of blasphemy and followed him. At least it would throw our pursuer off our path. He would not expect us to crawl back into the lion's mouth.

I wished I had a decent sword. We both needed weapons. I kept myself warm and reasonably calm planning a persona that would make it credible that we carried weapons openly. Rapiers are the privilege of gentleman in London, but I didn't know the rules here. I would ask Father Tomáš if we found him still alive.

We saw a light at the priest's cottage, and Edwin gasped with relief. I gave him a slight kiss, but I pushed him down into the ruts by the road. He nodded. He would wait and I would investigate, and if there were trouble, he would rescue me. Although again, how we would fare with only belt knives, I had no idea.

I put my hand on the pommel of my dagger and walked slowly forward. The moon turned the surrounding marrows into a sea of silvery light. If there were archers anywhere, they would make me easily. I did not think there were. There were no trees nearby. I would have seen anyone as easily as he saw me.

The priest appeared in the doorway. I took a breath and did not speed my pace. It was best to seem ordinary, unafraid, just a footsore traveller who might beg a bit of bread from a stranger's house. He sat down heavily, waiting for me. He must be tired, I thought. After all, he was very old.

He vomited.

I stopped walking.

The priest slowly sank to the ground, his head pillowed in his own spittle. He mouthed something, but it was not my name or any words that made sense.

Turn around, I said to myself. Walk. Take Edwin away. But my limbs did not obey. I walked slowly, pace by pace, to the shivering, dying priest. I lifted his vomit-soaked head into my lap.

"Book," he said.

He wanted the last rites, of course. No man should die without his rites. It was a hideous, lonely crime that he was unshriven. Death was frightening enough.

I lifted him onto the bed. The sacraments had to be here someplace. Damn you, you stupid God, all this blood on your hands, where are your bloody instruments! I must have blasphemed aloud. His eyes fluttered open. He touched my collar.

There was no time.

He deserved better in death than I could give him now. All right, Kit you idiot. You studied to be a priest. How does the bloody prayer start?"

"In the name of the father..." I whispered, the words coming to me in English.

"Book," he said, again.

He wants it in Latin. I started over in Latin. "In the name of the father, the son and..."

Father Tomáš shook his head. He patted me on the chest. His bowels let go and the stink was incredible. "I...sleep."

He died.

I pulled up his jerkin. No wounds. I felt for welts. It might still be plague but I didn't think so. Plague doesn't come on so sudden. I put him down as gently as I could. Someone had poisoned the poor decent man.

I looked up and saw the spirit Madimi. She shivered in the chill; her arms bare but for the golden snakes that wound around her shoulders. In the hovel's dim firelight, I thought they were moving. I closed my eyes and opened them again. She was still there.

"Am I dreaming?"

"*Of course not,*" she said impatiently. "*Take the book, my Marlen.*"

Book. He had said, book. "Which book?"

She pointed to the table. A small volume lay open by a sputtering candle which gave poor light. I picked it up, wrapping my hand in a bit of my sleeve. I had seen poisoned books before.

Madimi shook her head. "*There is no time, Marlen.*"

I thrust the book into my doublet, where it rested near my skin. If it were poisoned, I'd be dead soon. But figment of my scattered mind or no, the spirit was right. We had to get out of this place.

"Kit?" said Edwin. He stood, clutching the doorjamb, his dagger in his hand. "Someone is coming."

I tried to push him out the door, but he saw Father Tomáš. For a moment I thought he would do something rash: throw himself on the body, stab himself, refuse to leave. But when I dragged him to the door he came. Then again, he had already seen what awaited us in the moonlit road. A dozen men were walking toward us.

"Gypsies," Edwin said.

I squinted. "Those are no Gypsies."

They were monks. At least they were men dressed like monks and they carried a large cross before them. Monks were fat, sedentary men, with stooped shoulders and bowed heads. These were strong looking men. Their heads stood high. One of them saw us and shouted.

Without thinking we both turned and ran across the moonlit fields to the woods. Oh, we outran them, sure. They would have caught us if they tried, but they stopped at Father Tomáš' house first. And then they came after us in earnest.

We heard the outcry. Edwin paused. I grabbed his arm and forced him forward. We had moments only. We were no match for a dozen men, and if they reached the village church and rang the bell, we'd have the entire town to contend with. I found cover, a cut that plunged down to a tiny creek below. I dived into it and pulled Edwin with me. The brush here was tall enough that I could pull it over us.

A man looking down would not see us, even in moonlight. But he might hear us, because one of us was sobbing.

"Stop crying," I whispered.

"Sorry," he said. He wiped his eyes on his hand. "At least they will give the old man a decent...they will care for him, won't they?"

"Come," I said. "Now."

The cut went on for some way, following the creek through the ground. It was headed north and west. If we crept along the bank on hands and knees, we could go far without being seen from above. We crawled on our belly in some places. I did not mind. I could swim like a water snake at need. I only wished there were no moon. We dared not wait for moonset. It would be too close to dawn.

The bell began to toll, but by then we had covered some distance. It took an hour to reach the woods. No, truly it must have been less time than that. It only felt so long. We followed the creek a long way into the woods until I was satisfied that no one was pursuing us. Then we crawled out of the ditch and collapsed on the forest floor. I lay breathing the soft mulching leaves.

I wanted to sleep for a thousand years. I turned over on my back, to say something to Edwin, only to discover that he was now crying in earnest. I went to him and awkwardly put my arm around his shoulder. He scrubbed the tears away with the heels of his palm.

"He was a friend," he said, when he found his voice.

"I am sorry," I said. "I liked him."

"Didn't give a rat about Protestant or Catholic. He just wanted to *know* things. Worth more than kings and scholars and us lot. He was *decent*."

He pushed himself away from me and flopped on the ground. I could not see his face, but I knew it was twisting with anger. I lay down next to him and took his hand.

"They will think we killed him," he said, in time.

"Yes," I said. "They might."

"But we didn't," he said.

"No. So, who did?"

"The Gypsy," said Edwin.

I had no reason to know that, but it wasn't impossible. "Perhaps."

"Oh," Edwin growled. "I am going to take him apart!"

I patted his shoulder, gently. "I will help you."

He shuddered, a last, tiny sob. "Thank you," he said, sniffing. "That's...it's unbelievably decent of you. Considering your... considering I'm your..."

"Rest now, my gaoler," I said. "Just rest."

He fell asleep. I dozed beside him, waiting for the sun to come up. When the sun rose, we would see where we were. My sleep was very busy that night, which didn't surprise me, but was disappointing. I imagined I'd earned dreamlessness.

It was a cold winter night in London, sharing ale with Will Shakespeare. He and I were both writing by the light of a single taper. Will's nose was nearly pressed to the page. A bit of ink had found itself on his right ear where he'd been pushing his hair from his eyes.

This was memory, not Walking. I looked down at the draft before me and knew not only where we were but when. It was the winter of 1593, the year of Plague. The ink beneath my fingers read:

At every stroke, betwixt them he would slide
And steal a kiss, and then run out and dance,
And as he turned, cast many a lustful glance,
And threw....

The lines from Hero and Leander *trailed off in a long blot, rendered by my own hand. I stared at the paper, the ink bleeding everywhere, the blood everywhere, so many friends dead in this winter pestilence. Out in the night Thomas Kyd was still alive and whole and did not yet hate me! I stood quickly, almost knocking over the ink.*

"Where are you going?" Will asked

"I have to find Thomas."

"This is a dream," Will said, without glancing up.

"What if I wrote plays and sent them to you?" I said. "You could put your name on them, say they were yours."

"No, thank you," said Will. He pushed his paper over to me. I could read only the top line in the firelight: Venus and Adonis.

"The sincerest flattery," I said. "You've parodied Hero and

Leander."

"*I would flatter you with all joy,*" he said. "*But it is no parody.*"

"*So, you are my rival now?*"

He raised his cup with a grin. "*It will stand on its own.*"

Will dug a bit of tobacco out of his pocket and lit his pipe. He held it against his heart before passing it to me, as Lord Manteo the Algonquin prince had done, before the Armada ritual, all those years ago. I smoked, pressed the pipe to my heart, and reverently passed the pipe to him.

"*You know Edwin?*"

"*I know nearly everyone.*"

"*He worked with you. Did you like him?*"

"*I like nearly everyone.*"

"*What am I to do with him?*"

He smiled. "*You need him.*"

"*I've been nearly killed twice today. Can't say I need him much.*"

"*You are already dead, brother.*"

"*That joke is tired.*"

"*You are tired of being dead. That's what ails you.*" *Will cut a slice of apple and used his knife to leverage it into his mouth. He winked at my angry face.*

"*Should I trust him?*"

"*Maybe the question is: should he trust you?*"

"*Stop riddling and help me.*"

He put down the pipe. "*You like him.*"

I crossed my arms. I crossed my feet at the ankle. I crossed my eyes. "*As if my taste is worth a fart.*"

"*Truer words were never spoken. Or you would not have wasted time with Thomas Kyd.*"

"*Thomas was a friend, and I lost him the worst way a man could lose a friend.*"

Will touched my hand gently. Why, among all my friends, did I never share a bed with him? "You did not intend to leave those pages in Kyd's rooms."

"Intentions." I snorted. "If the world were just, I would throw myself off a cliff and be done with it."

"You are not the devil, Kit Marlowe" Will said. "You only wrote him."

"That's full of good sense."

"Sometimes good sense is what you need."

I stared out the frosted windows at the darkness.

"Right," I said. "What would you have me do?"

"Take love when it's offered on a plate."

I opened my eyes and saw Edwin looking down at me. His deep green eyes were round with fear. This close I saw they were flecked with brown. I shifted a little. He took a ragged sharp breath.

"What is it?" I murmured.

"You slept so deeply," Edwin said. "I thought—"

"You thought I was dead?"

"No."

He lied, of course. He had only just this night found one friend dead. In the gloomy morning mist, strange thoughts would plague any man.

"I'm not dead," I said, touching his hand as Will had touched mine.

Edwin swallowed. "You were so still."

I sat up. The stench of mud, vomit, and unwashed skin assailed me. "I might die yet."

"Do not joke."

I pulled his mouth down to mine. I meant it kindly, as sort of an apology, but he shuddered softly, like a man who letting go of all restraint. His mouth opened to mine like a devouring spirit. He pulled me up into his arms and we knelt there together, our bodies entwined. An unbidden thought crossed my mind. I was lighter and slenderer than he was. If we were ever to fight, he would get the better of me quickly.

I rested my weight against his wiry arms and looked up at him. "Have you done this before, Sweet Edwin?"

He did not speak at first. I could hear the sound of the brook beneath his soft breath. His green eyes were grey in this light. His lashes were long, longer than any man I'd known save Thomas Kyd. I tormented Kyd about his thick, girlish lashes. I tormented Kyd about so many things.

But this wouldn't do. The poor boy was trembling, in terror of his immortal soul. This was no time for me to meditate on the past.

"Edwin," I said gently, "Do want me?"

"Yes," he said, barely a whisper.

"Do you understand what to do?" I put myself, none too gently, against him.

"I've read Catullus," he said, with a flash of temper.

I laughed gently, running my hands up his back. He breathed heavily. He could still be playing me. But when I met his eyes, I knew one thing was true. He had wanted men all his life and never had he let himself kiss one. "There is more to this than book learning."

He did not speak at once. And then he whispered, "Show me?"

"Lay down with me," I said, my lips just sweet against his hair. "There is a little time before sunrise."

I kissed him again. I pulled him down to the cold ground, the uneven slope of the bank making all my efforts precarious, but my knees would no longer hold me up, and Edwin was weaker than I. I unlaced his doublet and shirt. I pressed my lips over his heart.

His skin tasted of cloves. He shuddered, wrapping both hands behind my head, grasping me to him with firm, gentle pressure as if I were a baby lamb. I kissed his torso, his belly, flicking my tongue into his navel.

He was straining up to meet me. My hand went to his belt. "No," said Edwin.

I leaned up on my elbows. His eyes were the size of moons. I reached up to touch his freckled face. It was wet with tears. "Too much?"

"What are you doing to me?"

"Giving you pleasure."

"But I thought..." He frowned.

The freckles went all the way down his chest. I found a particularly large one on his clavicle and kissed it. "Did you think I would just throw you to the ground and take you like a horse?"

"No?" he said, clearly meaning yes.

I bit his left nipple. "Is that what you'd prefer?"

"No!" He sat up quickly, dislodging me. I slid away, my knees shrieking in pain as they hit the roots of a tree. Edwin bound up his shirt quickly, looking away into the woods like a haunted creature.

"I am very sorry," I said.

"It isn't what you think," he said. "I am not frightened, or disgusted. I am...it is just..." He turned his round, elemental eyes upon me. "Not like this."

I took a ragged breath. My own body was screaming in protest. But I simply reached up and picked a bit of leaf out of his hair. "A tryst on the cold ground may be fine for a line of poetry," I said lightly. "But it loses something in life."

"No, it just...seems wrong to be so happy," he said. "I mean...Father Tomáš..." He bit his lip and stabbed me right in the heart. Oh Will. Take love when it is handed on a plate indeed.

"You loved him?"

He sighed. "He loved me as son. Just as I was."

"So, he knew?"

"There was little to know." Tears stood like fishponds in his eyes; he stared through them as if he could hold them back at will. "What a confession I would make to him if I could this morning."

He smiled, but tears fell. I took a bit of my sleeve and wiped them away. It was nearly black with dirt, but he did not seem to mind. He took my hand and kissed it. At last, we lay entwined, all elbows and knees with our lusts unspent. Edwin eventually slept, smiling like a child. My head hurt, and no matter which way I turned, I felt as if something was digging into my chest.

I must have dozed because it seemed a moment later when the clouds parted suddenly and cleared away the dark morning fog. The sun beamed down upon us. It was warm and bright, like awaking from a dream.

Edwin sat up agitated. "We should go."

He was right. We couldn't be sure we'd lost our pursuers. I dragged myself, stench and all, down the hill to the creek and splashed water on my face. I looked down at my doublet. It was caked with mud and probably ruined. I daubed it best I could before I gave it up.

I suddenly realized what sharp thing had been digging into my chest. The small book I'd taken from Father Tomáš' house was still tucked between my linen and my doublet. I inspected it in the morning light. It was a slim leather-bound copy of Ovid's *Metamorphosis*.

I don't know what I expected, but it was not this. If Edwin was to be believed, Father Tomáš was that rarest of all creatures: a truly innocent man, a country scholar, murdered for our sakes.

Still, it was no bad thing to have a copy of *Metamorphosis*. It would pass the time when we camped. I put it back between my shirt and my doublet and climbed back up the bank to Edwin. He looked worse than I did, all tears and sweat, his doublet torn, and his linen streaked with mud.

He smiled at me, and he was beautiful.

"What is it?" he asked.

"We need clothes."

Chapter 8

I did not give in easily to this feeling of tenderness for Edwin Mooney. I wasn't that big a fool. He was an intelligencer, an actor, every word of his story could be a lie. He told me himself Edwin wasn't even his name. Take love when it's handed on a plate? Only Will Shakespeare would be that naïve. Love handed on a plate was like any other bribe. You may think you've gained in the transaction, but the corruption owns you.

By the time Captain Christopher Talbot and his servant Ned Cooper rode within sight of the gates of Prague, the corruption owned me completely. Every glance from him was a knife, every sigh felt drawn from my own heart. I fancied he felt the same. I knew it was a fancy. I schooled myself silently as I rode. The sun on his hair was only sun, not some purer substance that drew the evil of his former life away. There was no alchemical process that made his sweet lies true and yet I knew one thing. He came to me as a virgin. If he was a player, oh what sweet craft was this?

I had two wishes as we approached the gate. I wished my bum would stop aching, and I wished the hat I'd bought from Jahoda had a bigger feather. Our dark brown horses were neither the youngest nor the best-tempered creatures. Edwin's mount was merely stupid. Mine had spirit, but also the distressing habit of eating everything in sight, including shoes, plants, and the hair of passing young ladies. Still, I cut a reasonably impressive figure. My suit was deep red velvet with a snowy lace ruff. Edwin, as my valet, wore a simple green doublet and a dun-coloured cloak, but he draped the cloak well.

We did not spend our nights together. Captain Talbot needed a spotless reputation. Edwin could wave at folk and joke with children on the road, but as the gentleman it was beneath my dignity. If I were arrested, I did not want to do without a gentleman's privileges in prison, so we needed to make an entrance, and if I looked slightly ridiculous, so much the better.

We came into the city riding along a stream through the tall limestone cliffs to the north and west. The mist since the early morning had been devilish and it felt as if clouds decorated the trees and leaves all around us. I did not know them. That is the nature of travel. You grow up knowing every tree and leaf, what their uses are, which are edible, and which will kill a healthy sized man. And then you find yourself in unfamiliar forests, where it is all still green and yet ever so slightly wrong.

When the mist lifted, we were on the bluff above the city. Caught in the late afternoon light, Prague looked like gold and rubies, sewn across a rolling green carpet like the gems on one of Queen Elizabeth's gowns. The city lay along on both sides of the river Moldau, which twisted around the limestone bluffs like the virgin Diana's girdle. The castle was several hundred years old, but its current occupant had been making improvements. The new summer palace perched like a pagan temple nestled in the hills. The ramparts decorated with elaborate Italian graffiti looked more decorative than defensive.

Edwin pointed out to me a few landmarks: the cathedral tower, the castle wall, an old, ruined castle to the south. "She is a beauty."

"Better looking than your horse," I said mildly.

"She is at least docile, aren't you Sweetpea?" he said, patting the rump of his mount. Her ears pricked up and she closed her eyes.

My horse was chomping the grass of course. I should name him. At least I should call him something other than Stop Villain Stop. I slid off his back and looked in my pockets for an apple. The horse nuzzled my face. I offered him the apple and he took it in one gulp, almost snatching off my fingers. Edwin laughed until his hat fell off.

The horse made a try for my feather. I ducked neatly around him and pulled myself into the saddle, straining for dignity.

"Do you remember what you are to say?" Edwin asked.

"I am a distant relative of Magister Kelley, who has come at the request of his family in London to see to his affairs while he is in custody."

"*And* you were at sea, or you would have come when he was first arrested."

"And that was?"

"Over a year ago?" Edwin looked unsure.

The horse tried to drag me backwards. I think he saw a tasty rowan tree. He whinnied grievously when I forced him back on the road. "Tantalus. That's your name. Poor sod. Hell is where you are."

London's gates were business-like affairs. Attempts to pretty them up merely emphasized their purpose. But the gates of Prague were towers of lace spun of iron and stone, trimmed with gilt and polished metal. The road thrown before it was tended like a gentleman's lace collar, graced by no mud, droppings, night soil or obvious beggars. Maybe all travellers took their shoes off so as not to track mud on the streets.

Once we reached the gates, Tantalus threw a theatrical fit. He pranced ahead of Edwin's mare, bounced me on his back and broke into a canter, scattering guards, chickens and other travellers. A plump boy raced up to us, followed by a round-bodied, wobbling guard, in a neat uniform sporting an impressive badge of office. The boy caught my reins in his heavy, gloved hand. Tantalus stopped as if he'd been struck by Cupid's arrow. He turned adoring, obedient eyes on the boy, who patted his nose.

"Good day, sir," the captain said in German. A taller, skinny boy hauled a large, leather writing desk over to us and held it up before him. The captain dipped a pen in a pot of ink and nodded, one hand still on Tantalus' reins. "State your name and business, please."

"Christopher Talbot, gentleman," I said.

The captain nodded. "You'd be the young Weston girl's godfather sent to fetch her home."

I opened my mouth and closed it again. Thankfully, Edwin quickly said, "He is."

He wrote down my name without looking up. "And you'll be staying...?"

"With the family in Mála Strana at Doctor Hájek's home," Edwin said.

Tantalus snatched the plump assistant's cap in his teeth. The captain caught it and slapped back it on the boy's head. "The family is at the Cattle Market house."

"I beg your pardon," Edwin asked.

"Take the road to the left to New Town. Cross the river and skirt around until you smell the cows. You'll find the house on the far side, in the northwest corner. The family is well-liked, and if you don't mind my saying we'd be pleased to see that the young lady is cared for, what with...you know."

"Thank you," I said, because it seemed the thing to say. I ducked my nose into my lace handkerchief.

The guard captain wrote out our passport into the city and signed it with a flourish. "Welcome to Prague, Master Talbot. I am Captain Kolář."

The road to the left led to a narrow warren, with streets so close together a woman could hand a cup of milk out her window to a friend across the road and not spill a drop. I could see the spires of the church over the walls of the Old Town as we crossed the river.

"Where did he hear you were Mistress Weston's godfather?" asked Edwin, fretfully.

"You wanted us preceded by rumours."

"General rumours, not alarmingly specific rumours."

"At least we know where Kelley's family is. What are we going to do now?"

"Meet your godchild, I suppose," he said.

"Who is she?"

"Magister Kelley's ward. His wife's daughter from a previous marriage."

"Has she a Christian name?"

"Katherine, Mary, something like that."

Some godfather I would be. Oh well, it could not be helped.

I looked up the hill at the walled castle above. The brief miracle of afternoon light was already dying and the torches from the hilltop sparkled like stars. As cesspits of intrigue went, this one couldn't be more beautiful.

The New Town was a suburb, not unlike Shoreditch, though unlike Shoreditch, the city's outer wall had expanded to encompass it. There was a great deal of buying and selling and trading going on. The streets were surprisingly clean for a city this size, wide, and well built, obviously new. Still, I was glad of my scented handkerchief as we passed a midden. Tantalus dragged me toward it, because he thought he smelled something good to eat. Half of Europe had come to town that day. It was so crowded that the horses moved at the pace of the slowest farmer.

The light was dying by the time we reached the cattle market, although there seemed no slackening in commercial activity. This neighbourhood was much quieter, because cows will not tolerate a stampede of humans and did not care for noise. Barter was carried out with hand gestures. The animals chewed grass as peacefully as if they were in the countryside.

Several Italianate villas stood on the far side of the cattle market, but I instantly knew the one we sought. It was overgrown. Even the trees seemed to shrink around it. The vines that crawled along its walls were mostly dead. Most significantly to a mage, there was a small tower behind the house. It wasn't much, just a belfry, really. But a proper alchemist does not require more than a place to kneel, place his book and pray. The real work takes place underground.

The horses were not deterred by the aura of melancholy. The neglected verge made decent eating. I pulled Tantalus back to the fence and found a place to tie him. He nuzzled my hair miserably, as if to say: must you abandon us in the dark?

"Never fear," I whispered to the horse. "I shan't leave you here to starve."

"He doesn't understand English," said Edwin, testily.

"He understands." I gave Tantalus a last, reassuring pat. "Shouldn't you knock for me?"

Edwin pulled his cloak around his shoulders and rapped on the door. There was no answer. He rapped harder. Nothing happened. I looked upward at the tower. There were no lights within.

"Perhaps they are not at home," I said.

Then I heard a low, rumbling gong.

Edwin held a long sash. "You pull this and..." He gave it a hard tug and the gong rang again. This time the cows on the market must have heard because they answered with a few annoyed bovine moans.

The door opened and a shabby wench stuck her head out. She asked Edwin something in Czech. Edwin answered. The girl shook her head and closed the door again.

"What did she say?"

He shrugged. "She said the Master is not at home. I asked

about young Mistress Weston and she left."

I struck a pose, tossing my short cloak over my shoulder and holding my lace handkerchief over my face. "Pull again."

Edwin gave the rope another tug. This time we heard a flurry of steps. The door opened again. A tall, middle-aged woman appeared. She was a better class of servant, maybe a cook or housekeeper, wearing a neat white cap and apron. She had sharp blue eyes that looked at us like we were mice in her pristine kitchen.

"Madame, I wish to see the lady of the house," I said in my accented German.

"I am the lady of the house," replied the woman in English, wiping her hands on the apron.

I bowed. "Madam, would you be Magister Kelley's ward?"

"I am Magister Kelley's *wife*," she said, glaring. "What could you possibly want with Elizabeth?"

Good question. I bowed again to borrow a bit of time. "We represent...I mean...that is to say—"

"Captain Kolář's sister is a seamstress at court, and she told our costermonger who informed the neighbourhood butcher who told me you were her godfather. I decided not to disabuse her. Now tell me who you really are."

Anne told me that there are times when a prudent man kneels in the dirt. She used to box her men's ears, so I'd never paid heed to her advice before now. "Madame Kelley. Did your husband ever mention certain of his scholarly acquaintances in London?"

Mistress Kelley pulled her skirts away as if I were horse droppings. I thought she might box my ears like Anne. After some time under her gaze, I rather wanted her to. And then, to my great surprise, she said: "Wipe your feet. They are filthy."

Chapter 9

She led us into a tiny sitting room that reeked with respectability. It contained two dark wood, Italian-carved chairs, a chest littered with books, and a little basket with wool and a spindle. The fireplace contained no fire. A single candle perched on a delicate table. It scarcely shone enough light to reflect like faint prisms in the rippled panes of the dusty glass windows.

The lady gestured that we should sit. She picked up the basket and whisked off into the dark hallway beyond. Edwin's lanky frame fit awkwardly in the ladylike chair. He crossed his feet at the ankle, trying to minimize the clumps of mud that fell off his boots. The carvings dug into my backsides. I edged myself forward to rest as little weight as possible on the seat.

Edwin shivered. "How can they manage with no fire? It's cold for November."

Perhaps Edwin did not know a life where firewood was scarce. That detail revealed more than he knew. I picked up one of the books that lay discarded on the chest, and almost dropped it in shock. It was a twin of the small leather volume I found in the priest's house. Ovid's *Metamorphoses*.

"What is it?"

"Someone here reads Latin," I said, lightly.

"'Tis a scholar's house."

"Do you think a scholar works in this room?"

A short, pale, young man came through the door and gave us a gangly bow. He blinked in what passed for light in this room. This, apparently, was the man of the house, such as he was. "My good...lords?" he said, uncertain of our station.

I stood and bowed slowly. "No lords, young sir. Just a scholar like yourself."

He blushed. "John Francis Weston, at your service."

I nearly blurted my real name. I forced my tongue down against my palate. There was something prideful in the set of his shoulders that demanded truth from me.

"My name is Captain Christopher Talbot," I said. "We are come from England to see your father, young sir."

"Stepfather," he said, his lips thinning. "I am afraid that is impossible at present."

"I know he is in prison," I said, as gently as I could.

My hand reached out for him, and only then I noticed I was still holding the Ovid. His eyes flicked from me to the book, to Edwin's awkward-fitting doublet as if he were committing every detail to memory to retell later, which indeed might be his intention. I've known intelligencers younger than he.

He cleared his throat a couple of times. His voice was high in the silence. "The fire is warm."

It was the password for the Merchants of Light. I glanced at Edwin. I could either give the response in front of him or not at all.

"Go on," said the boy.

"The fire is old," I said.

Edwin did not move, although I could feel him go tense.

"The torch still burns," he said.

"The torch turning downward."

The last two lines were a secret within a secret, which should not be spoken in front of any servant, much less Edwin. I held myself rigid, willing the boy to accept what I'd already given him. The boy hesitated a moment. Then he nodded. "May I ask if you can also show some token, Captain Talbot?"

I reached into a small pocket in my doublet and felt carefully around the stitching. I drew Master Harriot's crystal out and held it up in the candlelight. I ignored Edwin, who looked surprised. Young Weston's eyes widened as I lay it into his thin hand. It was not a scholar's hand at all. There were ink stains, calluses and chilblains right enough, but he had rough patches in his palm and a burn on one finger indicated he'd been engaged in less than gentlemanly work.

Weston swallowed hard as he looked at the token. He sighed a little, perhaps hoping I'd think he was used to such things. "What sort of stone is it?" His voice went up on the last few words.

"Quartz crystal," I said. "From the New World. Though the gift of Sight is in the user, not the substance—"

"I know that," he said, sharply. "The New World, you say?"

"'T'was a gift from the Algonquin chief Lord Manteo, fashioned for its particular use in the house of Thomas Harriot."

"Harriot is very great heretic, if not a witch."

The boy was a Catholic exile, and no doubt heard all manner of ignorant nonsense spread about in the local English community. "An injustice, sir. Master Harriot is an honoured mathematician, and friend to your father's one-time companion, Dr. Dee."

"Stepfather." He scowled as he gave me back the crystal. "With the token and passwords you shared, our house is required to give you shelter, poor shelter though it be."

"I am at your service, sir." I gave him my most elegant bow, but it did nothing to soften the flint in his eyes.

"Well," he said, his voice cracking, slightly. "Please make yourself comfortable." The young master vanished into the hall, nodding with the barest minimum of courtesy.

Edwin coughed. I glanced up and he gestured at the window. I stood and put my hand between the candle and the window glass to block the reflection. Outside, in the dimming afternoon light were a band of Travellers, setting up on the slight rise between the house and the cattle yard.

"Step away before they see you."

"It cannot be the same Travellers," I whispered.

"It is."

I quickly pocketed the stone. I squinted through the rippling glass but just then the door opened, and the wench reappeared. Her long red hair fell into her face, and she carried a bundle of twigs about the size of my chest. I nearly went to help her but remembered in time that Captain Talbot would be accustomed to being waited upon. Edwin got up with poor grace and took the bundle of kindling. She dashed from the room without a word.

"We'll receive poor hospitality here," he muttered, placing the sticks of wood in the fireplace.

"They have little reason to love us."

"True," he said, glancing around for the tinderbox.

He lit a spark and set a bit of wood afire. I glanced up and saw him looking at me with a face so sad couldn't help myself.

"What ails you?"

"Oh Kit," he whispered, mournfully.

"What?"

We heard the scrape of heavy wood against stone. The door opened and young Master Weston reappeared. He dragged a small table into the room. Edwin went to help him. I still held young Master Weston's copy of *Metamorphoses,* so I opened it and pretended to read while they worked. The words were hard to make out in the fading light, but I had the Latin verse by heart:

My mind leads me to speak now of forms changed
Into new bodies; O gods above, inspire
This undertaking (which you've changed as well)
And guide my poem in its epic sweep
From the world's beginning to the present day.

The drudge returned, carrying candles, a cloth, and dishes. The dishes were stamped brass, the candle was new, and the tablecloth was a rich, noble red with gold thread woven in. Edwin moved the delicate, Italianate chairs into place. The boy lit the new taper and seated himself at the head of the table.

"My mother will not be dining with us," said Weston. "She bade me give you her regrets."

"Please convey to her my compliments," I said. "And to your sister Elizabeth?"

"She is not here," Weston said, elegantly. "Your man may share our meal. We are not so grand here, without the women."

Edwin hesitated, waiting on my word, a fine bit of theatre on his part since he was tired and starving. "Join us, Edwin," I said.

"Thank you, sir," he said, with a stronger northern accent than usual.

The wench appeared with three fine goblets and a large jug that contained a rich, pale beer. Our host took the jug and did the honours. His fingers had streaks of black ink that looked like spiders in the firelight and his translucent skin was turning pink as if unaccustomed to the heat of candles.

"First we drink as all Englishmen do, even in foreign lands," he said, with an awkward formality. "To our good and gracious Queen."

"To the Queen," I said, lifting my cup.

"The Queen," Edwin echoed.

The bitter drink tickled the edge of my tongue, and it filled my stomach with the weight of bread. Edwin drank it deeply, his Adam's apple bobbing with appreciation. Young Weston sipped his, daintily. He looked again from Edwin, to me, to the book I'd left on the chest.

"We heard you were a pirate, Captain Talbot," said Weston.

"Just a merchant seaman in Her Majesty's service."

"Did you serve her Majesty in the war?"

"I served during the Armada Crisis, yes."

"So, you're a pirate?" asked Weston.

I bowed my head. "Privateer."

"Do you believe the storm that destroyed the Armada was sent by God?"

I tried to keep my hands from shaking. It was not possible that Weston could know what his question meant to me. "I would not presume to guess the mind of God, Master Weston."

"Yes," said young Weston. "That is the accepted answer."

The door creaked open as the drudge returned, dragging a monstrous tureen filled with tripe stew. The servant girl poured soup into our plates and then left the tureen on the table, a bit of the stew splashing onto the cloth. Weston's lips pursed. He seemed to physically restrain himself from mopping up the spill with a corner of his sleeve.

I picked up the fork, which was as fine silver as I've seen in many a nobleman's house. The stew was barely salted and contained little meat, but it was hearty, full of roots and mushrooms as a big as my hand. I thought of Father Tomáš with his mushroom barley meal and wooden plates. This was poorer fare, but it was warm, and I ate it gratefully. Weston sat with his hands folded. He did not taste the stew on his golden plate. I wondered if he would eat at all or put it aside to serve again tomorrow.

Edwin stared at the boy for a long time, and then abruptly asked, "Shall we drink to the emperor, too, Master Weston?"

Weston's eyes widened. "We are loyal Englishmen here."

"Magister Kelley is a vassal of Rudolf II."

"He was knighted by the emperor," said the boy, uncertain where this was going.

"Edwin," I said, because I knew.

"How is it you remain a loyal English subject, though you are Catholic and an exile?"

"I am no follower of Master Hesketh, sir, nor is anyone in this house," said Weston, his voice thick with disdain. Or fear. Edwin nodded. Clearly the name Hesketh meant something to him.

"Surely," Edwin said, in a tone no servant would use, "It is scarcely possible for an exiled Catholic to remain loyal to the Queen."

"Edwin," I said, sharply. "Perhaps our host would enjoy one of the comforts of home. Some good, English tobacco?"

"Thank you for the kindness, but I do not smoke, good sir," said Weston, relieved.

"'Tis past time you started," I said. "*Edwin.*"

Edwin opened his mouth, and I kicked him under the table. He could not disobey me without abandoning his role entirely. He went to my pack and retrieved my pipe and the small, leather packet of tobacco.

Weston rose to his feet. "I will see what is keeping the bread. Excuse me." He stalked out.

"What has possessed you?" I asked Edwin.

"I cannot say I expected better of Edward Kelley's kin."

"You called the boy a traitor at his own board. Is this some clever stratagem to get us thrown out of the house?"

"That boy is no boy," he hissed.

Young Weston stalked back into the room and fixed Edwin with an imperious eye. "Captain Talbot, perhaps your *servant* can see to your horses. You'll want to secure them for the night."

I looked at Edwin, who looked at young Weston like a particularly strange object fished from the sea. "Edwin, go."

"Yes, sir," he said and fled as if imps were nipping at his heels. Young Weston closed the door behind Edwin.

"I must apologize for my man."

The boy smiled. "We English are an ungovernable people. In a land where queens rule, it is no surprise our servants get above their station. Please sit, Captain Talbot. There is something I must show you."

He took a ring from his left hand and passed it to me. It had a wax seal with an all too familiar symbol: the old pagan funerary sign, a torch turned down, the light that is hidden. The sign of the Merchants of Light. I used to have one like it.

"Do you know what it is, young Master Weston?"

"I know that we are required to aid any man who gives us the password or shows us a ring like this."

"But do you know what it means?"

"It also means I can ask you for aid, does it not?"

Perhaps it was the lift of the hand, or something in the smile, but I saw what Edwin saw. "Are you Elizabeth Weston?"

Young Weston hesitated as if she might deny it. Then she took a long breath and gave me a deep curtsey.

"I beg your pardon, Captain Talbot. And the pardon of your man. Though I suspect he is better born than you are. He showed suspicious skill with a fork."

I grinned. "Sloppy of him. Do you really have a brother?"

"He is away at school." She poured me a bit more wine. "You are not a privateer, either. Your hands are too soft, and your gait is all wrong. A sea captain walks as if the ground beneath him does not roll properly, and your fingers should have hemp splinters and powder burns."

"Do you meet many sea captains in this landlocked country?"

"Everyone comes to Prague. May I ask your real name, sir?"

I should have made up a name, but it was a relief to speak my own. "Christopher Marlowe, at your service."

Elizabeth Weston's eyes went round. "The theatre poet? I heard you were dead."

"I should hope you did."

She gave a most feminine laugh and a coquettish look that made me wonder why I'd ever thought she was a boy. "I am honoured to make your acquaintance. Though you had best remain dead, for I hear you are not respectable company."

"I did not imagine my reputation reached Prague?"

"Does that please you?" She smiled.

"As it would any dead man of letters. Are these your brother's books?"

I suppose embarrassment altered the timbre of my voice, because she flounced into her seat, misunderstanding the cause. "I am not the only woman scholar in Christendom, sir. My stepfather taught me."

"Magister Kelley taught you?" I asked. The Edward Kelley I remembered would not have done that. But what does one intelligencer know of any other intelligencer's true character?

Her cheek twitched. "He believed that women could learn, and we ought to learn. And I am no less modest, womanly, or worthy of respect for it."

"I said no such thing."

"You thought it. Every man does."

"I apologize for my sex. May I ask which languages you read?" I inquired, smiling at her prickly pride.

"Latin, Greek, English, obviously. French, German, Italian, and Czech. Spanish...it is like to Italian and there are many Spaniards at this court...Polish, and Slovak. I understand a little Russian as well. I wish to learn Arabic. I have some interest in Urdu."

I blushed hard because I had had the same ambition once. But even at Cambridge, no one at hand knew Arabic, much less Urdu. I had to content myself reading the Atlas and dreaming of faraway places. "Why, Arabic, pray tell?"

"The Ottoman Empire possesses many useful texts, which are not yet translated into Latin, particularly in mathematics and medicine. Also, I have heard that Arabic poetry is excellent."

"And Urdu?"

She glanced down. In another girl I'd think this was a maidenly blush, but she was clearly considering something deeper. "I have a friend who speaks Urdu. He has taught me a few words."

"You studied mathematics and medicine?"

"And theology."

"The magical arts as well?"

She folded her hands primly in front of her. "I could hardly escape it in this house."

"You are Gifted?"

Elizabeth made a face, but she didn't answer.

"It's all right if you are," I said. "I am too."

"You see into the Spirit World too." She didn't look surprised, just resigned, as if she'd known more than her share of magicians and none of us had been very appealing. If Kelley and Dee had been her chief examples, I could hardly blame her.

"Whether I want to or not," I said, as kindly as I could. "It's not a choice."

"No," she said, as if it was painful. "My friend, the one who speaks Urdu, said that our Gifts are not evil. Spirits are good and bad as men are good and bad. The fact we can see them is just a fact."

"Your friend may be right."

"But you don't agree?"

"What makes you say that?" I made myself smile.

"*Doctor Faustus*," she said. "Faustus wants knowledge and goes to the Spirit world to get it. And finds himself damned."

Elizabeth looked so sad. I wondered how young she was. She was nothing like Anne in appearance, being small boned and serious where Anne was robust and gleefully profane. And yet, she stirred in me a feeling quite like my affection for Anne. She, like Anne, was out of place in the world.

"No," I said. "That's not what the play is about."

"It isn't?"

"You are aware that even in the debased world of the stage I must disguise my stories, bury truths under layers of subtext. So, if I am...angry with those who provided my education, well it was a bit like a pact with the Devil."

Elizabeth looked at me with a steady, quiet look. "Patronage," she said. "You were poor, and powerful men gave you money."

She sounded like Will Shakespeare. "They sent me to university."

"Like my brother," she said. "And also, my stepfather. Is it true that you seek Doctor Dee?"

"Quite true."

"Might I ask why?"

"Queen's business."

Elizabeth's lip trembled slightly.

"I thought you were loyal to the Queen."

"We had no part in the Hesketh affair, but we are Catholics, and your man is not wrong that—"

"The Hesketh affair?"

She wrinkled her nose. "You really have no idea?"

"The dead hear little gossip, good Mistress."

"John Hesketh, a member of the English community here, he and several others travelled to England to promote Lord Strange as a Catholic candidate to the English throne."

Lord Strange. That name was well known to me. "Nothing came of it?"

Elizabeth pulled awkwardly at her sleeve. "He was betrayed."

"By Matthew Roydon?"

"No, by Lord Strange himself," she said. "You know Master Roydon?"

"He once carried a ring like this one." I gave it back to her.

Elizabeth looked at me thoughtfully. "Why did you not show me yours?"

Matthew and I both threw ours in the sea on the first night we met after the Armada spell. I didn't care to tell her that. "You accepted the crystal as token."

"How do I know you did not steal it?"

"You don't," I said. "But you know my right name. That gives you power over me, Mistress Weston, in ways you could not suspect."

She frowned. We spent a few choice minutes in uncomfortable silence. I ate. She did not. The stew was getting cold. The bread was just a little stale. I slipped some in my pocket for Edwin.

"Has the crown given you any instructions regarding my stepfather?" Elizabeth asked.

"I am not here to aid him."

"Are you forbidden to?"

"No."

"Can I command you to help him as a member of the Merchants then?"

"Magister Kelley is no Merchant."

"How do you know that?"

"Edward Kelley is a charlatan. A liar. I'm sorry," I added, quickly, because she looked quite miserable. "Your stepfather was an agent of the crown spying on Doctor Dee. All his communications with the spirit worlds were fake."

"The spirits told me that."

That was interesting. I wondered which spirits she communed with. "Dee gave you the password and the ring, didn't he?"

"No," she said, reluctantly. I wondered if she'd stolen the ring, overheard the password. Dee was never the most careful creature on Earth. She frowned again, playing with her napkin.

"If you help my stepfather, I will swear up and down the land that you are my long-lost godfather, come from England."

"Beg pardon?"

"As my godfather, a member of the family, I can introduce you to learned men here, men who might help you find Doctor Dee. You can stay here for as long as it takes to complete your business."

I put my fork down. "I cannot get Kelley released from prison."

For a second, only a second, she was child. Then her shoulders squared, and eyes turned to iron. "I only wish to see him."

I reached over and scraped Edwin's plate into hers.

"All right," I said. "I will help. But only if you eat that entire plate of food."

Elizabeth lifted her elegant spoon and nodded gravely. Then she ate the stew and said not another word until every morsel was gone.

Chapter 10

I found Tantalus and Sweetpea tied up in a tiny stable in the courtyard, munching on a very small amount of mealy oats. Tantalus raised his nose a bit but went back to his dinner. *I must provision this household, not just for Elizabeth's sake, but for our own.* Edwin came in, looking a good deal calmer.

"I brought your supper." I threw the bread at him, and he caught it. He looked at it as if it were a snake, then came to his senses. He sat down on a barrel and broke off a piece.

"What is wrong with you?"

"What is wrong with you?" he spat. "This is a house full of witches. Could you not feel the evil there?"

House full of witches? Ugly words coming from an ugly face. "I felt the kindness of women who went without supper to give their meal to strangers."

"You so steeped in sin that you are insensible to it. Wizards. Heretics. Girls dressed as boys. You play with forces you do not understand and cannot control. Spirits and alchemy. Rituals to alter fate. Questioning the nature of Creation itself."

I went cold. He had the details wrong, but he was essentially right. Anne had said the same. Had he noticed the altered stars? But he couldn't know about the spell. He was prattling something he'd heard at Balliol perhaps. Giordano Bruno had spoken there. It made a stir among the pious.

"Royden must have told you I was sent to find Doctor Dee because he would do as I asked," I said. "Had you no idea what that meant? You knew the little magics I practiced on the road."

"I saw you stare into the glass..." he said, and then he fell silent. His thick pale lashes trembled. He held his arms across his chest, and his lips were blue. I went to put my arm around him, but he pulled away.

"They sent Dee here with someone to watch him and he's slipped away," I said. "You met him at Rudolf's court. Heard rumours that you did not understand. Brought them back to Master Royden, who did understand, and then they gave you to me."

Edwin looked down at the straw at his feet. He didn't even move when Tantalus nipped at his head. "I did meet Dee at Brandýs nad Labem. He didn't seem evil. He said he'd been given a revelation that the Earth was not at the centre of the Cosmos. That reality itself could be ripped from its moorings and he could explain how but he didn't have the math." He looked a bit sheepish. "He drank an awful lot with Doctor Hájek and Lord Rožmberk. They talked about alchemy and a new star in the sky. The Church teaches that the firmament was unalterable."

"You told Matthew this? Why?"

Edwin blinked, surprised by the question. "It was my job. And Dee wasn't trying to hide. They were talking openly in pubs. If this were Spain or Italy the Inquisition would have them already, but Rudolf is negligent in such matters."

Dee, like me, like Matthew, knew that something had gone wrong. But instead of sulking or conforming, he'd gone to find people who might be able to help: other scholars. Here, with alcohol and the illusion of freedom Dee had endangered us all. He probably didn't even know it. "You did right." I patted Edwin on the shoulder.

His rabbit face melted into softness. "You fear wizardry too. I know you do."

"I swear 'tis not wizardry I fear." I held out the stone in my palm. He stared at it as if it were a snake. "It is just a stone. A rose quartz from America. It has no supernatural powers. It is not even of exceptional value."

I placed it into his hand. He swallowed but he did not drop it.

"It...is it a scrying stone?" Edwin asked.

"Yes."

"They fashioned it for you?"

"It was not fashioned for me."

"Oh, Kit," he said, woefully. "Can you not see that you are dicing with your very soul?"

"My *soul?*" I laughed. "Both our souls are in peril enough without occult activity."

"What do you think we fight for in this war of religions, if not men's souls?"

"We fight over the power of popes and kings."

Edwin looked grim. "I should never have...with you..."

"Do you believe that man is forbidden to eat of the Tree of Knowledge?" I asked. "Is a vindictive goatherd God waiting to smite the curious and fling us into the Lake of Fire? After all we've done in his name? Murder and mutilation and betrayal—"

"Stop," he said, looking away. "You're being cruel."

"I am cruel, Edwin," I kissed him. His eyes closed, and he was growing hard. I caressed his ass, and he trembled. "Come to bed, sweet," I whispered.

He slipped out of my arms. "Not in this place."

I sighed. It was better so. We were in a stranger's home. It served us to be cautious. I unrolled my bedding in the straw and pulled Elizabeth's copy of *Metamorphosis* out of my pocket. It looked exactly like Father Tomáš' volume. It must have been printed off the same press.

Edwin settled down near me. "What do you have there?"

"Something to read."

Edwin took it out of my hands and opened to a random page. He began reading aloud in his elegant and fluent Latin:

King Pentheus (who mocked the gods) despised him,
Deriding his prophetic speech, and cruelly
Throwing in his face the sudden blindness
Which he had been afflicted with by Juno.
But the old man shook his white head in warning:
"Better, far better, had it been for you
if you too were blind: you would then be spared
the sight of Bacchus' rites," replied the seer.

I rolled over on my side and shut my eyes to listen. The other book, Father Tomáš' book, dug into my chest hidden in the folds of the bedroll. As I fell asleep, I felt Edwin's arms go round me. I heard music outside the window.

I dreamed about rain. It was really just a dream. Or rather a memory, one I well recognized.

I crawled into the straw under the eaves. I wanted to hide my torn clothes and bruises. I did not care to add another thrashing to the first one because my shirt needed mending. My ribs ached. They were bruised, but they would recover. My soul, my shirking, hate filled, misery of a soul...I had less hope for that. The golden-haired apprentice and his three mates who thrashed me, they knew. They could see the way he stirred me. He was having none of it. Even if he wanted me too. Especially since he wanted me too.

I heard a scurrying mouse in the straw beside me. It was louder than the rattle of the rain on the thatched roof. A hand grabbed my wrist and I leapt out of my skin.

"Knew it!" said Anne, who yanked me up out of the straw. "Get up, let me see you."

She sat down beside me and dabbed at the corner of my eye. My head hurt and I could barely see, but I could not fail to notice that her cap was missing, and her sleeve was torn, and she had a cut lip. Her hair looked like it had been pulled out in chunks.

"What did you do?" I asked.

"Thrashed him."

"How?"

She grinned and showed me her apron. The pocket was sewed up with something heavy inside. There were streaks of blood on the cloth. I buried my head in her skirts. She stroked my hair. Even then, she smelled of drink.

"Come down," she said. "There's apples and porridge, and I'll fix your shirt, there's a sweet boy."

"I'm going to hell."

"Then I'll have good company," she said. "Come."

I crawled down the ladder into the main room and Anne came down with me. The room smelled of wood smoke and food cooking. Anne poured some whiskey into a cloth and dabbed it on my eye. I tried to take it like a man, but I squeaked. I could not help it. She laughed, not unkindly.

"Messed up his pretty face for you good and proper."

I sniffed. "Well, that's lovely. Defended by my little sister. They'll really fear me now."

"Don't guess he'll be bragging about it."

"What was in your apron pocket?"

"Rocks," she said.

"I bloody love you," I said.

There was a knock at the door. Anne handed me the cloth and said, "Be still."

I suddenly remembered that this was a dream. I stood, the ache in my ribs growing more pronounced. "Anne," I said. "Leave it."

But she opened the door, and Roydon stepped inside. Before I could cross the room, he took out a long knife and plunged it into Anne's heart.

My eyes opened to bright daylight. I sat up, heart pounding.

I had to find Dee. I had to protect Anne. Edwin had said that Dee had been talking with Doctor Hájek and Lord Rožmberk. Rožmberk might be out of reach, but I knew Hájek was in the city. Jahoda told me so. Elizabeth had promised me introductions. All I had to do was ask her.

I sat up. It was too early to ask her. She was no doubt fast asleep. I lay down, my heart beating in my chest. Edwin lay on his back, snoring, oblivious. I could not keep still. The stable was raw and cold, and if I could not search for Hájek, I could find something warm to eat. I pulled on my boots, took up my pack, and slipped out into the city.

The cattle market did not merely sell cattle. There were bootmakers and candle makers, costermongers, bakers, butchers, and a dizzying variety of brewers. Men and women passed me by without a second glance. It seemed like the entire world was filled of ordinary souls, untainted and not like me. I exchanged a few coins for a hot meat pie, some apples, and a small beer. I carried my bounty to the riverbank and found a remote spot where I could chew over both my breakfast and my surroundings.

The light off the water hurt my eyes. The castle perched atop the hill across the river glowing golden in the light. Swans floated up the river to me to beg a bit of crust from my hand. Dogs barked in the distance. Cattle stamped and moaned. Music floated up the river from the Old Town churches. It was quiet here. Thick red and gold leaves fell all about me.

I heard a voice chanting.

I looked downstream.

The Man-Who-Was-Not-A-Gypsy knelt by a bend of the river. He was not far, but he was enough obscured that I'm sure he believed himself hidden. He faced South and East, away from me. He pressed his face to the ground. He knelt up, his hands folded with profound reverence, and I heard him speak again.

I had never seen a Mohammadan pray before, but I had read descriptions. Jahoda said that some of the Romany were Mohammadans driven north from the Balkans by the Turks. In any case, it seemed unlikely that this man was a papal spy.

He finished his prayers, rolled up a small, threadbare blue rug and secreted it in his pack. There was something in his bearing that unnerved me. He held himself like a man who knew violence, and had little love for it, but would not shrink from it again. And there was still something oddly familiar about him...

I crept away, a bit of unchewed apple still in my mouth.

Chapter 11

The Romany band had a stall in the market. None looked like they'd indulged in morning prayers. They leaned on a table, drinking beer from a jug. Two men played the flute. A ragged little girl crouched nearby and held out a hat, which already contained few bits of silver.

"Rather wild music, is it not, sir?"

I spun around. Young Mistress Weston was dressed as a girl this time. She was quite elegant in a sea green velvet dress with a small lace ruff and embroidered gloves. The ladylike effect was ruined because her basket was almost as large as she was.

I gave her a good, proper bow. "Good morning to you, Mistress Weston. You are looking very grand for the market."

"I went to Mass at dawn," she said, primly. "Mother and I attend every morning. You are welcome to join us."

"Of course." I'd been on the road so long, I'd forgotten that civilized folk and church went together. "I wouldn't want to cause your household trouble."

The girl smiled without pleasure. "Catholic observance is not compulsory. There is a Protestant church nearby if you prefer. Most folk go to whichever is nearest or has the priest with the best voice. Some attend both services. But since we are family, we should attend together."

"Ahh," I said. "Yes."

"Your man was a-feared to find you missing when he awoke, sir," she said. "I am pleased that Anežka and I found you." The drudge I'd seen yesterday stood transformed into a respectable gentlewoman. Anežka was neatly dressed in dark brown wool, little auburn curls escaping her snowy cap.

I jingled my purse. "We are well met, since I intend to buy

provisions. You can advise me."

Mistress Weston blushed, and her eyes flashed with something like bitterness. But common sense and practicality won over pride. "Thank you, Master Mar-" She frowned.

"Captain Talbot," I said, quickly.

Her discomfort melted suddenly like sugar into a tincture of amusement. "That's a bit formal, dear godfather. I shall call you my dear Uncle Christopher."

"That makes me sound old."

"And you should call me Elizabeth," she said. "*Dear* Uncle Christopher."

Elizabeth took my arm. Anežka frowned rather barefacedly at us, but she took her mistress' basket and silently led us into the winding paths of the marketplace. The servants here must do very well for themselves, if they regard their masters so boldly. The girl did not seem to mind, but I could scarce imagine Mistress Kelley being so tolerant.

We walked in companionable silence. The scent of meat, cow blood, undercut all the other scents, including goat and fish. There was a huge tub of river carp, still alive, gaping at me. Elizabeth gently pulled me aside while Anežka examined the fish.

"I sent a message on your behalf this morning."

"To Doctor Hájek?" I asked hopefully.

"Of course not. He would not respond to a summons from me. He's too important. You will need introductions at court. A friend will provide them."

"Someone trustworthy?"

"To me he is." She put her hand on my sleeve. "Do not forget your promise. I may not be as benign as I seem."

I raised an eyebrow. I was beginning to like her. "Threats?"

She released me. "A reminder of our relative positions in this city. You are a stranger. I have powerful friends."

"Noted," I said. "What will we have with that fish, hey?"

"You can find almost anything here," she said. "My stepfather would find books and elements for his conjurations sometimes: herbs, salt, bits of quartz. There are even healing potions and fortune tellers, and animals from Africa and the East."

"Do any of the healing potions work in a good sauce?"

I saw her dimple despite herself. "Probably not."

"What shall we buy? Perhaps a pork joint? Some apples and cheese?"

"Shall we have dates? The Gypsies have them."

"Arabian dates?"

"From Dalmatia," she said. "I have no idea how they get them here with the fighting and all. You will like them. They are not expensive, and very sweet."

"By all means," I said. "Be festive."

We bought barley, fresh milk, onions, carrots, eggs, and some old-looking pale green peppers. Elizabeth steered me toward an old woman selling mushrooms. "You will want some of those."

"The mushrooms in this country are wonderful."

"You've tasted them?"

"Oh yes," I said, remembering the stew Father Tomáš fed us. My hand strayed to the book that still pressed against my skin, hidden in my doublet. Elizabeth did not notice. Her hands reached into the large stacks of silk-eared mushrooms, with a virgin's thoughtless sensuousness.

"Czechs are champion mushroom seekers," she said. "And brewers. The beer is very good."

"I had a bit with breakfast. It was all right."

"Tush," she said. "I'll send you to my stepfather's favourite hall in the Old Town. The drink there is rich as cream and twice as silky."

"You have been there no doubt in your other clothes."

She blushed. "My brother took me."

"I wonder why you and your mother do not join him."

"John is a student. He can barely keep himself. And mother won't leave. Pay the woman."

I turned and paid the mushroom seller, neatly cuffing the pickpocket who crouched by my thigh. His knife, like his face, was dark with filth, but no less sharp for it. I jumped out of the way, kicking him. He fell sprawling, blood spurting from his nose. The boy rolled deftly, ran past the old woman, and disappeared into the crowd.

"That was ungentlemanly," said Elizabeth. She handed the basket to Anežka as we strolled toward the apple sellers.

"He had a knife."

"He was a child. Anežka could have caught him."

"Is it the ordinary thing in Prague for a maiden to venture into such a place?"

"Even when we had means, Mother did all her own shopping. And you shouldn't wear your purse like that." She took mine out of my hand and secreted it somewhere in her dress. She followed Anežka into the crowd, glancing back at me with a superior smile. "Don't worry, godfather. You'll get it back."

I followed her deeper into the market. The booths wound tight like a labyrinth, and in the centre was a large stone with a cross on top. The place of public punishment was conveniently situated, so even cutpurses needn't stray far from their work to watch the show. The smell of blood was strong here, and not all of it was animal. There were stocks, a whipping post, and a hangman's platform.

I shuddered. Elizabeth stopped and put her neat, embroidered gloved hand on my arm. "We're almost finished."

"You have my purse," I said, dully. The blood smelled like metal. I could nearly taste it.

"Godfather?" Elizabeth shook me slightly. "I would like to buy one more thing, if you would pay for it."

"Of course."

She took me to a booth that sold potions. A profoundly ugly man sat behind it, wearing a twisted iron knot on a leather thong around his neck. He nodded wordlessly and reached under his counter for a small stone wrapped in velvet. Elizabeth removed a coin from my purse and gave it to him. Then she walked quickly toward home.

"I thought you said they were all charlatans."

"They are."

"What did you buy?"

"Sulphur."

I touched my finger to it and to my tongue. It was sulphur. She took it out of my hand and walked on, her neat boots making a pronounced thump on the paving stones.

"What is it for?" I asked, hastening to keep pace with her.

"Sulphur purifies air," she said. "Wind might have plague in it, this time of year."

"What are you planning to exorcise?"

Elizabeth stopped; the blue-wrapped sulphur gripped in her hand. She was breathing heavily, her face blushing dark crimson.

"Elizabeth?"

Her eyes shifted, blue like sapphires or some other poetic rot, but with intelligence no poet ever praised in a maiden. No, that is not true. The poets wrote lines about eyes like hers in our Queen, long ago when she was this girl's age, and, who knows, perhaps in truth still a virgin.

"If my *particular* skills can be of any service to you," I whispered, "call upon them, please, Miss Weston."

Anežka coughed. I looked up. A group of Romany musicians were setting up two paces from us, and Edwin's nemesis—the

Mohammedan—looked directly at us. He looked as if he knew what we were saying, and it interested him. Little chance he understood English, though. It wasn't a common language in these parts.

In the briefest of glances an entire parliamentary debate exchanged between Anežka and Elizabeth. Anežka's eyebrows barely lifted. She turned and walked demurely toward the house. Elizabeth gathered her skirts with both hands and followed.

The Mohammedan and I were left staring at one another. For a fraction of a second, I wanted to return the little flourish he'd given me in the woods. I didn't give in to the impulse. I walked past him through the mud, after Elizabeth and towards our dinner.

Elizabeth led me around the house to the kitchen garden gate. It was an elaborate, wrought iron monstrosity, with a pattern of leaves and birds that revealed as much as it obscured. On closer inspection I saw naked women twined among the metal foliage, and possibly an erect satyr. The remarkable Weston maiden took no notice.

The garden was little more than a patch. There were the remnants of tomato vines and a few winter herbs and greens. But for the most part, the garden was ploughed over. A small pear tree stood in the west corner, by the tower wall, draping long fronds of red leaves. The autumn morning light made them look like flame, but their shade made the little walled garden even darker.

Anežka stood on the kitchen stoop, the basket heavy in both hands, holding the heavy door open with her foot. Elizabeth gave me my purse. It was not much lighter than when she'd taken it.

The kitchen was the only part of the house in regular use. A good fire burned on the hearth; every spoon and cauldron gleamed. The wooden table was big enough to accommodate all our bundles, and a massive stack of books, papers, and ink besides. A heap of bedding lay folded in a corner, too large a pile for one servant. Elizabeth and her mother must sleep here to save fuel.

But the most spectacular piece in the room was an armillary sphere, a navigator's tool for mapping the heavens. It stood about five feet high, big, round, and copper, a tiny ball in the centre representing the earth wrapped in concentric circles showing the constellations and positions of the planets. I felt pulled toward it. It was the only item in the room with dust, which made the engravings of zodiac signs and planets seem prominent and gritty. No one had done calculations with this in quite a while.

Madame Kelley sat by the hearth, snapping the tops off of peas and dropping them into a bowl. She looked indignant. "What is he down here for?"

"He came to help with the bundles," said Elizabeth brightly, although I wasn't carrying any. Anežka dropped the heavy basket on the table with an exasperated sigh. Edwin thumped down the staircase. He began unpacking the basket, which earned him a far kinder expression.

"Why is this in the kitchen?" I asked.

"Doctor Dee had us put it here," said Mistress Kelley. "He said it didn't work anymore."

I touched the circles. They swung around well enough. "Works fine."

"He said it wasn't right anymore." Elizabeth corrected and then stopped and turned to me, looking panicked.

"Wasn't right?" I glanced toward Edwin, remembering what he'd said about Dee. The Cosmos was wrong. The master navigator had abandoned his navigation tools. I touched the dust between my fingers.

"Some mathematicians think the earth isn't the centre of the universe." Elizabeth frowned. "Something about circles within circles. The maths doesn't work."

"Of course, the Earth is the centre of the universe. 'Tis in

Scripture," said Edwin, without looking up from his work.

"Is it?" asked Elizabeth, glancing from Edwin to me.

"You read Latin; you tell me."

"I don't remember a description like this." She pointed to the sphere.

"Good girl, because it's not in Scripture at all." I looked pointedly over to Edwin. "It's Ptolemy's model. The Church approves it and regards the others as heresy, but it isn't Biblical. And lots of people have noted problems with the maths."

Edwin looked tense, but it was Mrs. Kelley who snorted. "Silly fools. Everyone knows the sun goes up in the east and lands in the west and the movement of the stars in the firmament goes exactly the same. Who needs maths to tell them otherwise?"

So, Dee's explorations of the night sky had gone beyond the *stellae novae* problem. I wondered what else had changed, what secrets mathematics would reveal. But I didn't know that discipline the way Dee did.

Elizabeth hustled me towards the narrow stairwell on the far side. "Go up to my stepfather's library. Anežka will bring you some refreshment."

Magister Kelley's library must contain some books that pertained to magic, perhaps to the Armada spell itself. I trembled a little as I climbed the winding stairs up into the cold, dim house. I expected a cavernous room like the one in the astral world. But the chamber was small and crowded, lit only by sunlight refracted through diamond-paned windows.

My hopes of exploring the library on my own were dashed. A young man stood by an open window, holding Elizabeth's copy of *Metamorphoses* up to the daylight. He was blonde and thin, dressed in fine furs, linen, and no small amount of gold. He had a perfectly groomed moustache, no beard and eyes the colour of periwinkles.

He looked up startled. "Captain Talbot," he said, a bit too loudly, and bowed.

I heard Elizabeth's voice on the steps behind me. "Baldhoven! Mother told me you were here!"

The boy tucked the volume he held under his arm and sprang forward to kiss Elizabeth's gloved hands. "Westonia!" he exclaimed, adoration plain on his face. "Your servant, as always."

"What a great pleasure," she said, unconvincingly. "I was afraid you had gone home to Silesia."

"I am staying for Christmas Court," he said. "Oh, my dear Westonia! When the message came, I had to come see you. Your entire household, of course. I heard you have guests from your Fatherland."

He said this last bit without glancing up from his dear Westonia's face. She stepped backward and took her hands from his.

"Lord Georgious Martinius von Baldhoven," she said, with airy propriety. "May I introduce my godfather, Captain Christopher Talbot."

The young lord gave an elegant bow. "It is a great pleasure to meet you. I was conversing with your man Edwin. Not many valets command such an impressive knowledge of mathematics."

"Captain Talbot's man is an expert in navigation," said Elizabeth, lying so quickly I blinked. She trusted this strapling only so far. That was interesting.

"Of course!" said Baldhoven, beaming. "How fortunate for a sea captain! Oh, and surely you are acquainted with Doctor Dee, since he all but invented modern navigation."

"Very fortunate." The Ptolemaic model of the universe in scripture indeed. I kicked myself silently. Luckily, the lordling had no eyes for anyone but Elizabeth.

"Baldhoven," Elizabeth said. "Why don't you take Godfather

into town?"

"Absolutely," he said. "We will talk about navigation! And mathematics! And alchemy! You must meet Doctor Hájek, the court physician. Elizabeth said you wished to be introduced. He's done marvels you cannot even imagine! Oh, wait, you do read German? Your man did not say—"

"I would very much like to meet Doctor Hájek," I said quickly. "Do you think he would join us?"

"Today?" Baldhoven blushed. He was so pale that it turned him quite rose-coloured. "Well...he is...that is to say."

"He's at Court?" Elizabeth asked.

Baldhoven moved his cerulean eyes back and forth. "He has business there."

"Is the emperor sick?" I asked, as Edwin came in the room. He went about straightening the papers and books as if he had no other purpose.

Baldhoven looked as if his collar had tightened. "It's not a thing we speak about."

"Excuse us, Godfather," said Elizabeth. She grabbed the Silesian lordling by the arm and dragged him out onto the landing. So, she only trusted me so far. Also, interesting.

I went over to help Edwin straighten out the papers. "Mathematics. Code breaking. Now that's the Dark Arts in truth."

Edwin, bless his sorry heart, looked vexed. He handed me the copy of *Metamorphosis* young Baldhoven put down to grasp Elizabeth's hands. "Take a look."

"I saw it before."

"This is Lord Baldhoven's. Same printing. It's identical to Elizabeth's." Edwin handed me a bit of paper. "Hold the page up to the light."

I held the page up against the windowpane, and saw numbers written crossways to the printed text. It was done in vinegar, lemon juice, or some other marking ink, invisible in ordinary light, but clear when the sun shone through it. It looked like the same numbers on the page that lay hidden in my pack, the cipher Edwin showed me on the road.

"It's a book cipher," Edwin whispered. "Men who study the natural arts throughout Catholic Europe use it to communicate with one another. Each man has a copy of the same volume, and the numbers point to a page and a letter."

"Father Tomáš, Lord Baldhoven, Elizabeth? No surely, Master Kelley or Master Dee not Elizabeth herself. What do they correspond about?"

"I don't know. Mathematics and observation. Celestial navigation. Somewhat about the nature of the heaven, the true age of the Earth, so on."

I smiled. I once faced a Star Chamber inquiry over a few unguarded comments about the age of the Earth. Well, also about the Divinity of Christ, and some speculation on the amorous habits of several Biblical figures. "Where did Baldhoven get it?"

"I asked. He said it was rightfully his and that was all I need to know. I am a servant after all." His voice was a little tight on that last bit. Like his question about the fire, he gave away more than he realized. Edwin wasn't usually treated like a servant. He glanced up at me under his eyelashes, but what might have happened next didn't because the children came back into the room.

"Baldhoven agrees to take you to Court," declared Elizabeth.

Baldhoven bowed at me and clicked his heels. "I would be honoured."

"The honour is mine," I said. "When are we going?"

"Now, if you find it convenient," said the lord, who's aristocratic tone indicated that he indeed found now convenient. "I assume you have clothes."

"A few minutes, if you please," I said, and bowed. I could have curtseyed or danced the Tarantella for all the boy noticed. He again had hold of Elizabeth's hand, and she did not seem offended by the intimacy. Edwin opened the door behind me. I bowed again, went out the door and down the narrow twisting stairs.

"You will need a shave," said Edwin, as we clattered down to the first-floor landing.

I patted my beard. "It's right for a ship's captain, don't you think?"

"Even a pirate tidies up for court," Edwin said.

"There's no time for a shave."

"I set it up in the stable."

"When did you do that?"

"You were gone a long time."

"And I thought you spent that time codebreaking with Little Lord So-And-So."

"It was obvious Young Miss Weston intended him to take you to Court. I anticipated your needs." Edwin smiled and patted my admittedly dirt-streaked doublet. "Like a good valet."

He had set up a little dressing stand in the stable. My cloak hung from a peg, and next to it was a green velvet doublet, with slashed sleeves showing embroidered silk and white lace. In front of that stood a small table and chair. "You look like a cat died on your face."

I let him help me off with my shirt. I shivered. The stable was cold, and the light through the window was dim. The water was warm enough though. He patted my chest down with a damp cloth. It felt good to be clean, and to be dressed in a fresh shirt.

I pointed to the green velvet doublet. "Where did this come from?"

"God alone knows. Anežka brought it," said Edwin.

I had seen plenty of cast-off finery in my theatre days. I knew the signs of carefully hidden wear. The velvet had been turned and carefully re-sewn. It was not cut to my frame, although I could make it serve. Then I remembered. Elizabeth had a brother. This garment was evidence of better days.

"Ready?" Edwin said, waving his knife and grinning.

I sat down in the chair and let him turn down my collar. I tilted my head back and felt the cold blade touch my skin.

Edwin hesitated.

I will never know what went through his mind at that moment. Had he thought to kill me? He perhaps had killed many men like this before, including men he'd taken as lovers. Perhaps he only pretended he'd never known a man before. The church bell rang the hour. Edwin smiled a heavenly smile. "You are lovely, you know."

Somehow, I smiled back. The knife scraped. It pricked against my skin as the hair came away. I breathed again.

"Don't take too much," I said, trying to keep my voice from wavering.

"I can trim a beard all right."

It was true. He could. When he held a hand mirror up for me, I saw a man I would not be ashamed to take to court.

"We must provision the family through the winter," I said. "I've bought food and fuel to last a few weeks, but it is not enough to provision the household for the entire winter. Can we appeal for more money?"

Edwin seemed confused. "Appeal to whom?"

"Who usually funds you on the Queen's business?"

He hesitated, strangely awkward. Then he shrugged. "It's not often I have to provision an entire household."

"Send to the embassy here," I said. "They'll release whatever funds we need. I did it often enough on the Queen's business in Flanders. You can go this afternoon, while I'm gone."

Edwin blinked. Something hard took place behind his pale

girlish lashes. "I'm not going to Court with you?"

"Are there two suits here?"

"I am not your servant," he said, wiping the blade on a towel. "Indeed, you still are still my charge. You shouldn't have wandered off. Strictly speaking."

I sighed. "Do you think the Merchants will speak freely to me with you there? Besides you've been to Rudolf's Court before. Someone is bound to recognize you."

"No one really looks at servants," he said, but I could tell from his expression that I was right. Someone there was likely to recognize him. Well, that was interesting.

Abruptly, he leaned over and kissed me, a sweet, enervating kiss. His mouth held just the vaguest taste of mint and honey, and his tongue caressed mine. I pressed my head into his chest. His hand still held the mirror.

"Do not betray my trust," he whispered. "You are not the only one who faces consequences if your mission fails."

I blinked. Did Royden have something over Edwin too? Why did Royden doubt his good behaviour? Or was it something closer to the bone. I stroked his temple, his brow furled beneath my fingers.

"Do not fear to lose me, Sweet," I whispered. My voice was hoarse. I held his trembling body. I wanted something more than just to have him. I wanted *him*, no subterfuge, no fear. He stepped back. He still held the mirror in his hand. He passed it from palm to palm as if he wasn't sure what else to do, his eyes fixed on the floor.

"Speak with Mistress Kelley," I said. "She'll know what is most needed."

Edwin stepped back, suddenly shy. He placed the knife and towel into the bowl. He did not look at me as he took the shaving equipment and left.

Elizabeth's brother had been somewhat larger around the middle, but the sleeves were a perfect match. I was presentable, even for court, but the entire ensemble was too Germanized for my taste. The dark colour quite overpowered my skin. Kit Marlowe in his prime preferred light colours and Italian embroidery. Then again, I was not playing Kit Marlowe. I found the hat I wore into town, wished again the feather was larger, and clapped it on my head.

Chapter 12

Elizabeth and Baldhoven frowned when I presented myself. I suppose I was not sufficiently grand after all. "I'll have Edwin bring around my horse."

"You should walk," said Elizabeth, quickly. I guessed Tantalus was not suitable for court either. She and Baldhoven exchanged an epic poem worth of glances. Whoever this young lordling was, he and Elizabeth were more than casual acquaintances.

"Yes," said Baldhoven. "Much to see. You are new to the city."

Baldhoven led me along a narrow mud path along the river that gave way to stone as we entered the Old Town. As we walked through the twisting streets, it crossed my mind that this might be dangerous. I could not have found my way back, and there were areas where the two of us could barely walk abreast. But Baldhoven moved with a lazy confidence. He obviously knew the neighbourhood well.

The Old Town was utterly clean by the standards of any city in Christendom. The neat houses had a well-scrubbed, prosperous look, with tidy shops and residences that suggested fat children and a good deal of soap. I wondered where they disposed of the waste in this part of the city. There did not seem to be a place for it in the street.

"You are a sea captain, are you not?" Baldhoven asked.

"I was in Sir Walter Ralegh's service," I said, which was true.

"I understand that Ralegh is exploring the American continent," Baldhoven said with some energy. "You must tell me about America."

"I never sailed to America."

"Oh." His face fell.

"But I was well acquainted with Master Harriot who mapped

the American coast."

"Oh yes. Thomas Harriot. His book *Algonquin!*"

"Have you read it?"

"I have," The boy blushed. "Magister Kelley had it in his library. I would love to see America someday: a wild new land, full of brave people, huge forests, ancient mountains, monstrous creatures, marvels of every kind."

"So would I," I said, in all sincerity, and then remembered the vision Madimi showed me of Cahokia, the mounds, the dying people.

"The Orloj is this way," he said. "You'll find it a modest marvel of our own."

It was.

The astronomical clock stood four times the height of a man. It resembled an astrolabe placed on a clock dial, an astonishing mess of arches, wheels, and gears covered in occult markings, with carved figures and arcane signs painted in gold. Such images found in a Spanish home would mean the death of the owner and his entire family, yet it hung on a square tower that Baldhoven told me was the city hall.

"The city of Prague has been run by the burghers from time out of mind. Theoretically they are in vassalage to the Holy Roman Emperor, but they follow no law but their own, based on old Roman tradition and whatever whim takes them. And what a whim this was!"

"Does it work?" I whispered. The mad impossibility of it took my breath away. So many in Europe spoke of astrology and mathematics only in whispers.

"I have not studied astrology. If Eli— if Mistress Weston were here, she could give you a better account."

People hurried by without giving the clock a glance. There were tall Russians in heavy white furs, black-haired Hungarians in red wool, Czech girls in embroidered waists and coloured skirts, and a small cluster of shivering, dark-skinned men who appeared, incredibly, to be African Moors. A group of bearded men in black wearing thick, fur-trimmed hats stood arguing a few feet away from us. At first, I took them for priests, but then I heard snatches of Hebrew. They were screaming about Talmud in the city square in the full light of day, a sight not seen in England for many years.

I turned to Baldhoven. "Jews?"

He shrugged. "There's a big Jewish ghetto here."

How could a youth from such a country as this grasp England's generations of burnings and secrecy, bitterness and intrigue, where an unguarded statement could kill a man. "I am never leaving this city."

Baldhoven glowed. "And you haven't tried the beer yet!"

He escorted me past the cathedral, into another maze of twisting, snaking streets, each one darker than the last, until we turned into a courtyard, went around a corner and found ourselves at the end of the street. The wall in front of me was covered over in a detailed drawing. It was rendered in thin brush strokes with very slight blurring like a woodcut, a figure with trees and vines and a naked woman holding both of her breasts that was twice the height of a man.

"This way," said Baldhoven, he grabbed my arm and dragged me to the left.

London Bridge was larger, and more choked with pedestrians, nay not just travellers but entire cottages, pie shops, even a forge. The Moldau river was smaller than the Thames but the bridge that crossed it was grand. It was neat too, startlingly clean for a thoroughfare filled with horses and people, stalls and merchandise, statues of saints and soldiers in armour. On the other side climbed a hill covered in dun-coloured cottages with red tile roofs. At the top of the hill was the castle wall, the jutting bronze tower of the cathedral inside it. I reflexively touched the brim of my hat.

"Quite a sight?" said the young lord.

"I've seen castles before." The walls looked forbidding from here. I could tell there were drawings on them, although I could not see any details.

It took us the better part of an hour to climb the hill to the castle. It wasn't far, but the path was crowded. The picturesque cottages on the other side of the river were dingy up close, filled with merchants with things to sell, who were angry to see well-dressed men disinclined to be customers. The neatness and order on the bridge gave way to chaos. The higher we climbed, the more beggars we saw.

We reached the top slightly out of breath, just as the bells of the monastery above us struck noon. I looked back and saw red roofs cast like poppies across a golden field. From here the narrow streets full of people looked like bees in a hive, dressed in brilliant colours, moving from comb to comb. The bridge was the size of a child's toy. This was nothing compared to the brilliant drawings on the outer wall of the palace, delicately rendered fauns and flowers, nymphs and sages. There were banners in the square beyond the gate, merchants' tables, soldiers in plate mail, and everything smelled of horses and cinnamon and cooking fish. Baldhoven tugged at my sleeve. I was gaping. He gave me a superior grin and walked ahead of me into the gate.

When we entered the Castle courtyard, I was surprised to see Karel Jahoda and his company of players performing before the jagged, mountainous towers of St. Vitas Cathedral. His mistress, the lady acrobat, posed before the doorway under the glaring eyes of the gargoyles, spinning a hoop in a wild pattern around her hips and arm, like a Bacchante.

Baldhoven strode past the troupe, scarcely seeing them as he pulled me across the courtyard. A woman stood on the cathedral steps in a fur trimmed red hood and cloak. She made a striking figure against the dark wall, the grim, grey sky above her scarlet head. The plainness or beauty of her face was hidden by her hood. "Well met, Lord Baldhoven."

Baldhoven took her thin, outstretched hand. "My lady, might I present Sir Christopher Talbot, a knight of England and godfather to our friend, the inimitable Elizabeth Weston. Captain Talbot, this is Lady Polyexna z Rožmberk, widow of one of the greatest lords ever to rule in the Czech lands."

So Baldhoven saw fit to elevate me to knighthood. Perhaps he simply assumed it was true. I supposed that was convenient. I bowed to the lady as a man of rank might. The hood fell from her face. She was not young, but not plain at all by any means. Her greying hair still had plenty of red, and her eyes looked like two shiny river stones in the gloom.

"Welcome to Prague Castle, sir," she said in Latin. "I have heard many good reports about you. I understand that you speak no Czech."

"Yes, Madame. That is true," I said.

"I am well acquainted with young Mistress Weston, who has impressed my family with her many talents. I am honoured to be of any assistance." She gave Baldhoven a nod. "Martinus, if you will."

Baldhoven took her arm, and we walked across the courtyard into the cavernous palace door. The hall was lit with hundreds of torches, bathing the arched ceilings and sloping floor in light. People of all classes milled around inside: priests, ladies, servants, apprentices, and even knights in armour. I stared at them despite myself. In the north and west of Europe one seldom saw men tricked out in proper armour when not headed into battle. Bohemian knights were comfortably fierce, striding around in mail like it weighed nothing. There were Spanish and Italian knights too, and a few in large moustaches and livery I could not recognize. I asked Baldhoven, who said they were from Budapest far to the south.

"Doctor Hájek must be here," said Baldhoven, looking around. "He meant to petition for payment of his bill."

"It is a bad day," she said significantly.

He nodded in the candlelit gloom. "A bad day."

"Bad day?" I asked.

The lady and the young lord exchanged a glance. "Wait here, Martinus," said Lady Polyexna. She walked off into the crowd. They made room for her respectfully, as if she were bedecked in rubies and diamonds.

"So, she is the current Lord Rožmberk's mother. Is he here too?"

Baldhoven laughed, a bit too officiously, as if he were trying to sound older. "Gracious no. She is here for Christmas Court. The company he keeps at Krumlov is not to her tastes."

"Will Doctor Hájek know where Kelley is?" I asked.

"I know where he is," said Baldhoven. "He's not in the dungeon or anything like that. He's lives under parole in a tower in Malá Strana, just outside the walls. But of course, he's at the emperor's whim. He spends most of his time in the alchemical laboratory in the White Tower."

Kelley was free. Kelley could have walked home, could have sent a message to his family at least, but he didn't. Elizabeth didn't know, or she would have come to see him herself. What fear, shame, or intrigue kept him from his kin I could only imagine. None of them improved Edward Talbot as was in my eyes. I did not ask Baldhoven. Whatever version of the story he had heard was unlikely to be true. "There's a laboratory in the castle?"

Baldhoven brightened. "Everyone knows Rudolf is mad for

alchemists." Then his face fell just as swiftly. "Well, no wonder the emperor is suffering a bad day."

I looked up and saw a face I felt I knew. A man walked through the hall at the head of a group of monks. He was thin with dark hair and pale skin, like a Spaniard. His hands were folded into the sleeves of his rough, plain habit, and the pale, wooden rosary swung at his belt like a scimitar in the hands of a Turk. He looked at all the folk in the hall with visible contempt, as if we were rutting dogs he had stumbled upon mating in his favourite stable.

The torchlight struck his face from the side, and then I remembered where I had seen him before. He was at the head of the group of monks who we met the night Father Tomáš died. He could not know me as the ragged man who fled into the moonlight from the empty parsonage, but I began to sweat. For the first time in weeks, I remembered that I was still suspected of Father Tomáš' murder.

Baldhoven glanced up at me, catching truth the way only youth can do. "Are you acquainted with Melichor Klesl?"

"No, not at all," I said. "Who is he?"

"Rudolf's court chaplain, and leader of the Counter-Reformation in the Holy Roman Empire."

"I thought Rudolf did not prefer such people."

"He has to tolerate him. This is still the Holy Roman Empire. The Hapsburgs do not leave their Holy Roman Emperor unguarded. Melichor is a watch dog. Without him Rudolf might do something insane like hand the city over to the Prague Estates and open the door to all kinds of heretical ideas."

"Has he not already done that?"

Baldhoven looked amused. "Emperor Rudolf, dear me no. He is a pure servant of the Holy Church. He merely neglects his duty to purify the realm. Due to...illness."

But he winked. I nodded, understanding he was being ironic. Open tolerance was not safe in Europe. Most places were Catholic or Protestant as the ruler dictated, and the Vatican thought that was a great deal too much latitude as it was. So, we had to speak carefully. "What I hear is that all good Czechs are Protestants. Even the Catholics."

"Especially the Catholics." Baldhoven said in a conspiratorial tone. Then he beamed a smile and turned, speaking loudly and brightly. "Here's the good Doctor!"

Lady Polyexna returned on the arm of a tall, lean figure. Doctor Hájek's confident brown eyes were set into his smooth, broad forehead, and his hair was shot with streaks of white like angels' wings. You are beautiful, I almost said aloud. I managed an appropriate nod and even lifted my hand for the sign. He folded his hand over mine quickly, as much to hide the gesture as to soothe me.

"Captain Talbot," he said in German. "It is good to meet you."

I stood, and he took both my arms and kissed my cheek quickly, first the left, then the right, then the left one again. "Is there a private place we can speak?"

"Doctor Hájek," said Lady Polyexna. "Perhaps you and the captain could visit the lions. Martinus will look out for me, won't you?"

Dr. Hájek raised his eyebrows a little, but he nodded. "I would be happy to walk with you, Captain Talbot."

The doctor took my arm. We left the hall, passed the cathedral, and exited the northern gate by the edge of what was once a moat. It was dry as bone, although steep enough to give even an invading Turk pause. Across the bridge, on the other side of this deep crack in the earth, was an elaborate Italian pleasure garden, complete with hedges and fountains. The real defensive wall lurked beyond.

Hájek pointed out stairs in the rock, which he descended as swiftly as a much younger man. I tried not to look too undignified. A sea captain ought not be afraid of heights. "The menagerie is this way. You've been to Africa, no doubt?"

"Yes, of course," I lied. "I did not tarry there long. Troubling country."

"Hmm," he said. "Yes, that business with the slave-takers. No man of conscience would wish to linger. We have embassies from the African kingdoms at this court, and the Angolan slave trade worries them. They say the English are involved."

"I understand it to be mostly a Portuguese business," I said, not lying this time.

Hájek looked at me, shrewdly. "You should keep yourself better informed. Come see the gifts of the Kingdom of the Kongo to the Holy Roman Emperor."

The menagerie was not cold, though the high sides of the moat blocked out much of what passed for winter sunlight in this country. The cages were heavily built, and there were servants tending fires. The lions paced their cage restlessly, as if they would be happy to piss on us. There was also a dromedary, as well as several other large cats, a monkey, a strange sort of bull, and, to my astonishment, a creature half out of legend...a small elephant, looking like Hannibal had abandoned him on the way to Rome.

"She's quite tame," said Hájek. "You can feed her."

A boy came forward carrying a bundle of hops. I took a long strand, folded it a bit so I could put my hand in the cage. The elephant's nimble trunk caressed my hand, sniffing it like a house cat, wondering if I was to be trusted. It felt rough like paper and smelled like musk. Her eyes looked intelligent. She was quite sizing me up. She snatched the treat and tucked it in her mouth, chewing thoughtfully.

"Right proper elephant," I said. "You are beautiful, you are."

"She is at that," answered Hájek in English. He put his hand on my arm and said, "Quiet."

I turned, expecting to see a wild animal that had gotten loose. Instead, there was a man dressed in black scholars' robes with a golden velvet cap. He had a big, red beard and sallow skin, and his chin jutted forward as if it had been bent that way. He did not seem to see us. He wandered from cage to cage like a spirit in the dim light of the moat, touching the bars, muttering in a language I didn't know. He seemed to be talking to someone, but there was no one present. Perhaps he was speaking to the animals.

"Bad day," said Hájek, and then I understood.

"Emperor Rudolf?"

Hájek's hand on my arm grew tighter. His deep brown eyes shifted from side to side, as if he were afraid. At his gesture, the boy placed the basket of hops on the ground and vanished. Rudolf patted the tiger's cage. The tiger paced about, unconcerned. I fancied the big cat preferred his master in this mood. The emperor retreated, still muttering at the air as if the air muttered back.

I plucked out another strand of hops for the elephant. She would not oblige me straightaway. She seemed as cautious of me as I was of Hájek.

Doctor Hájek nodded. "The fire is old," he said, in Latin.

"The torch still burns," I replied. It wasn't as if this were a surprise.

"The torch turning downward." Hájek smiled, and then dropped the rest of the password, which seemed reckless but maybe in a place such as this caution was less critical. "Do you see any spirits about us?"

No. There were none anywhere. "None."

"Near the emperor?"

"No."

The doctor relaxed suddenly. "What business of the

Merchants of Light brought you to my city?"

"I am seeking Doctor Dee," I said, leaving aside that it wasn't on Merchant business. He would be less inclined to help the Order of Merlin or the English Crown. I disliked lying to him.

The emperor opened the lion's cage. I held my breath, expecting blood and mayhem, but the cat came forward, tame as you please and placed his chin in the emperor's outstretched hand. Rudolf caressed the beast, as one would pet a favourite mouser, scratched him along his ear. The animal made a guttural sound of pleasure as he tossed his mane. It padded out of its cage and followed the Holy Roman Emperor as he staggered down to the far end of the moat.

I looked at Doctor Hájek. He too had been holding his breath. Hájek released the air from his lungs in a gust that startled the elephant. She stepped back with an awful moan.

"Why do you seek Doctor Dee here?" Hájek asked, his eyes still on the emperor's retreating figure. "He was recalled to England years ago."

"He came here seeking other Merchants for a magical working of great significance."

Hájek tilted his head to one side. "No Brother would have revealed that."

"His inquiries were not quiet."

"And you wish to help Dee with this ritual?"

"I wish to stop him if I may."

"Good," Hájek said. "He spoke to me. Mad things. Rewriting the fates. Moving the stars back into their places."

I blinked. "He told you?"

"Not the method," Hájek said. "Only that he needed men with True Gifts. Those like you who have been born with one foot on the other side. There are not many of you. It cannot be an easy life."

ANGELI PRIMLANI

"There are enough of us. Martin Luther himself threw an inkstand at the Devil." I made my tone light because I disliked the pity in his eyes.

"Have you met the Devil, Brother?" His tone was soft. He was kind but also intensely curious, the way all un-Gifted Brothers were when the subject of spirits and magic was broached.

"I have met no creature from the Other Realm who could match men for cruelty," I said. "It is possible that Hell is empty, and all the devils are here."

The Doctor nodded. "You are an agent of the English Queen." It was a statement, not a question.

"Yes," I said.

"Rudolf wishes your Queen no harm. Like many of us, he seeks reconciliation between Catholic and Protestant religion. If you seek those behind those assassination attempts—"

"I am not here to spy on the Holy Roman Emperor. I swear it."

He moved his hand, and I realized he had been reaching for a weapon. I took a breath. I didn't want to have a sword fight in full view of large, excitable animals.

"It is worth your life if you were to speak of what you just saw."

"Half Europe knows Rudolf is mad."

"A little respect, please," said the scholar gravely. "No man should suffer what that man suffers. Melancholy. Dementia. His obsession with occult study does him no good at all."

"Did you agree to help Doctor Dee with the spell?"

Hájek sighed. He finally turned away from the now far-off figure of Emperor Rudolf and looked at me square. "I do not have that kind of power. I have studied the lost arts of the ancients, observations of the stars and gross matter, the spirit worlds, what can be known of them. But change the fabric of the cosmos and to weaponize it as your Order of Merlin has done...I would not do it if I could."

136

I smiled. I was quite called out. "You know about the Order of Merlin."

Hájek glanced back toward where the emperor had been but he'd disappeared into the shadows far along down the endless track of the moat. I caught his arm as he turned away. "This spell is a weapon of terrifying power. Surely you understand we can't have Doctor Dee making so free with what he knows."

He didn't look at me. "Oh, I understand quite well."

"You have to help me, Brother."

"I am not an Englishman," said Hájek. "It is not in my emperor's interest to have this weapon stay in the sole property of the English crown."

"You shared the spell with Rudolf."

Hájek looked now as if I had caught him out. "I did not."

"Because you do not trust him?"

Hájek nodded.

"Brother to Brother. Is Rudolf mad?"

"Desperation is not madness. The emperor was raised at his uncle's court, the great Phillip of Spain. As part of his studies, King Phillip asked him to defend a group of heretics who were bound for execution. Young Rudolf wrote out his defence in his excellent Latin and presented it. Phillip then forced him to watch while the men he defended were tortured to death."

Well that sounded like Phillip. "Jesus."

"So, when he's tired, or has drunk too much, or he's vexed, he hears...he says he hears...the men he tried to defend. He weeps openly. He lets the tigers out of his zoo and wanders the grounds with them. Sometimes he shuts himself up for days in his closet of curiosities, his treasure box where he keeps his most precious gifts. Is that madness? Or grief and guilt from being unable to save their lives?" Hájek took a long and exhausted breath. "In his own fashion, Rudolf II is the sanest man in all of Christendom."

And you adore him, I almost said, but I kept still. Clearly his physician was grieved and guilty too because he could not relieve his pain. I simply said again, "I am not here to spy on Rudolf, I swear."

"Also, Rudolf believes a group of Carmelite monks have conjured demons to kill him."

I raised an eyebrow. "Has he cause to think so?"

Hájek shook his head. "The Carmelites don't like him."

"I'm not asking if they would do it. Can they do it? Have they done it?"

Hájek looked uncomfortable. "I don't know. I told you I don't have that kind of Gift. But you do. What did you see with him here?"

Oh, so this was why he had brought me to the moat, knowing I was an English agent. He was that desperate to know if the demons that plagued Rudolf were real. I'd seen no spirits in the moat with Rudolf. Yet that proved nothing. It meant he was only not haunted for the moment. "Nothing."

Hájek hesitated for a long moment. "I can introduce you to some of the other men Doctor Dee approached. In exchange, you can observe the emperor for me. See if his spirits are manifest in truth or mere shades of his own terror."

"How on Earth am I to observe the emperor?"

"I will arrange you to come to Court." Hájek extended a hand. "Brother to Brother, do we have a bargain?"

My instincts proved more correct than I'd known. Hájek trusted me. I didn't know if he should, but I had no quarrel with Rudolf. I clasped his hand. "We have a bargain."

Hájek smiled, the first truly genuine, unguarded expression I'd seen on his face. "Start with Magister Kelley. He worked with Dee for years. Dee certainly spoke to him about the spell, even though they quarrelled." Hájek looked embarrassed, I wondered why. "He might know where Dee went next."

"Would Magister Kelley help me?"

"I am not sure whether the grudge between them will help or hinder your errand." He made a gesture toward the stairwell. "I can take you to him now, if you like."

I sighed. I should be pleased with the offer. I'd come here expecting to have to bribe my way into a dungeon to see Kelley. But I was enjoying the menagerie quite a lot. "Let's go."

Chapter 13

We walked out the castle gates. The guards knew my companion and did not bestir themselves to challenge us. Hájek conducted me across the courtyard and out the other gates onto the Hradčany plateau. Hájek slid his hands into his deep scholar's sleeves. I wished I had something warmer than my own cloak to cover me. We continued around the castle wall and down a steep, broad staircase that led us into the Mála Strana.

"Magister Kelley is not permitted to reside within the walls," said Doctor Hájek. "He has taken rooms close by."

"That will keep his evil spirits out of the emperor's hair," I muttered.

The doctor gave me a sharp look. "You said he was not Gifted?"

"Oh, his gifts lie in storytelling. Say the name Edward Kelley and every costermonger and dairy maid has a dark tale to tell you."

Hájek looked relieved. "I heard that he afflicted a baby with donkey's ears, and the woman only cured the babe through prayer to some saint or other. Who pays heed to such offal? Here we are."

It was a plain, round, whitewashed, utilitarian-looking steeple perched on the side of the hill above a pub. The esteemed Doctor did not knock on the heavy wooden door. He stood under the window and shouted. "Hello! Come out in the emperor's name!"

Shutters flew open at the top of the tower, and a man's head stuck out, grizzled and red-cheeked and monstrously ugly, sharp eyes fierce over the stubbled end of what used to be his nose. His hair fell around his shoulders and face, silky like a spaniel's ears. In the dim light his hair obscured that his ears had been cut off so many years ago. I have heard twenty different stories about how that happened. I believe none of them.

"Aye," he shouted. "What be his Grace's pleasure now?"

The drinkers in the pub took no notice of important men of the realm, shouting and swearing outside. Such is the particular capacity of city dwellers everywhere.

"Let us up and you'll discover it," shouted the Doctor.

He looked us up and down. "Why send you two when he could send Captain Kolář?"

"The Master at Arms is a busy man, Magister. He cannot be rousted for every petty thief in the Empire."

"Petty," grumbled Edward Kelley. "Who is the whelp?"

"Captain Talbot," shouted Hájek. "Your daughter's godfather."

"I don't know him."

I made a sign that Kelley would know, a gesture known by those in Walsingham's service. Kelley looked as if he saw me for the first time. He said nothing for a very long moment. Then he disappeared. The shutters hung open, drooping like elephant ears.

I turned to Hájek. "What do we do now?"

"Wait," he said.

"What for?"

He pulled me out of the way just as a key attached to a shred of scarlet felt hit the stones at our feet. "There we go."

He picked up the key and unlocked the heavy door. It swung open upon a steep narrow spiral stairwell. Kelley's chamber door stood open at the top, giving us a trace of light. Hájek trudged up ahead of me, puffing slightly as he went. The tower stairs were high and difficult. Little wonder Kelley did not come down.

Kelley's room was little better than a cell, though I've known many players who lived with less. A bed, a chair and a low plank table comprised the only furnishings, and the table was covered with inkpots and papers, like a pile of new-raked leaves. Kelley was barefoot. His boots were by the door. I did not suppose he was expecting visitors.

He looked me over sourly. "Good afternoon, Master Marlowe. I heard ye were dead."

I bowed. "Magister Kelley. Good to see you again."

He did not return the bow. "Nice of you to take my old name: Talbot."

Kelley leaned down to scratch his leg, or so I thought. Then I saw it was gone from the knee down. His robe just barely hid that hose was fitted over a peg. It was little wonder he had not gone home. An hour's walk across the river to the cattle market would have been difficult, the more so if he was in pain. He blanched when he realized I'd seen the peg, and I quickly put my eyes elsewhere.

He sat down, heavily. "My health does not agree with the climate of this city any longer. Did her Majesty send you to spirit me away? What be yer orders?"

Orders. Right. Awkward not having any. I looked at Hájek, but he was impassive.

"Speak up. Hájek knows my business."

"All your business?"

"Just the spy business. You don't mind that do you Hájek? He just visits for the liquor."

"Not a bit," he said.

"I have no instructions regarding you whatsoever," I said. "I'm sorry."

"I'm to rot here, then. Ah." He stared out the window. "Old Sir Francis was a man of parts. He wouldna left me here. Dead, I hear. Who has our charge now?"

"Young Tom, some days. Cecil others."

"Bloody courtiers. The Armada victory made them all soft."

I suppose that was a reasonable interpretation of events. Kelley rubbed the stump of his nose. I suppose it was hard to feel at home anywhere without ears or a nose. "No matter. Let's drink, boy. Hájek, run along now. I suspect the young master wants to bend my ear without witnesses." He laughed at his own grotesque joke, and I felt obliged to go along with it. Hájek did not.

"I will return in a few hours," said Hájek.

Kelley went to the table and unearthed a bottle of something that smelled like the liquor Anežka kept, and two small cups, none too clean. He filled each one and passed it around. "How is death treatn' ye, Master Marlowe?"

"Tolerable well," I said. "I'm surprised you've heard about my demise."

"Were it not the fashion for all manner of foreign entertainment at this court, your name would be as forgotten as yer arse. What business does a dead man have in the City of Gold?"

I was seized with the fire of the very beverage that tickled my nose. It occurred to me that the Kelley family drama could be of use. I needed more time at court, more time to pry what Kelley knew from him, and this was one way to buy it. "Your ward Elizabeth petitions day and night for your return. Why is your family not allowed to visit you?"

Kelley smiled, it seemed, quite tenderly. "Despite appearances, I'm still a prisoner. I'm not allowed to receive unauthorized visitors."

"You're receiving me."

Kelley snorted. "Rudolf knows all about you, lad. No doubt he sent the good Doctor to conduct you here himself. Ask your question. You won't get another chance, so no point in being clever."

"I've been sent here to find Doctor Dee, Magister Kelley."

"Did you visit his house at Mortlake? Because last I heard, that's where he was."

"Dee has been missing from Mortlake these last two years, and I have traced him to you. Any information that you have about where he might have gone would be, to me, a gift beyond price."

"To *you?*" asked Kelley, "Or to Gloriana, our blessed Golden Britches."

"To me."

"Why?"

I wavered. To my surprise, Kelley laughed. "They're holding something over you Dead Man?"

I swallowed. "My sister."

Kelley glanced up at me. "Well, let me think on that, Dead Man. I might know something of interest about where he took himself. Assuming he did what he said he would. Might, I said. Let me think on it."

Think on it my arse. He was stalling. Kelley knew something worth hearing, and I wouldn't get it out of him. He was an experienced intelligencer and wouldn't burble to me. But I suspected I knew who could get it out of him.

"Your child is quite wild to see you. I could bring Elizabeth here."

"Did it occur to you that I might not want to see her?" said Kelley.

Given his deformity, yes it did. "Have you any message at least? She is so very concerned for your welfare."

Kelley looked melancholy. "My welfare. If it were only that at stake. I am not well guarded. If I wished, I could walk out that door right now, head for the ends of the earth and never look back. Assuming poverty and infirmity did not defeat me, I might go anywhere on earth. Hormuz. Fez. South America. The world is a large place for a free man. But I need the emperor's favour, if I am to bring my family to safety with me."

"I see."

"Pity Gloriana can't be bothered. I heard she once took personal interest in you. Made the old sots at Oxford award you your degree."

"Cambridge. And that was Lord Cecil," I said.

"As a reward for services rendered no doubt. To our lightness of conscience." He raised his cup to me.

"Amen to that lightness, which is the very spirit of the age." I clinked cups with him, and we drank together in the odd darkness of that November afternoon.

Chapter 14

Baldhoven walked me back by a quieter route, a path along the river. It spread out beside us like Aphrodite's girdle, bejewelled by the lights from boats that scattered up and down as far north as the defensive chains. As we walked by the bridge tower on the far side of the river, he pointed up. "We need not fear spirits here."

Above the arch, there was a Latin inscription. I could just make it out in the fading dusk, reflecting in the gold leaf against the dark stone.

SIGNATESIGNATEMEREMETANGISETANGIS
ROMANTIBISUBITOMOTBUSIBINTAMOR

I translated. "Reveal yourself in the form of a sign...in vain you reach for me...I am your desire...Rome, through movement of the stars...suddenly love...comes to you."

"It's an anagram, same words both forward and backwards." Baldhoven flashed his perfect smile. "Demons try to solve it, but it wearies them, so they give up and go away."

I knew what an anagram was. I'd had occasion to use one. "Do you fear demons, my lord?"

Baldhoven rubbed his white fingers together. He wore no gloves. Perhaps they were cold. "I do not have Gifts. I cannot perceive spirits."

"You know about Gifted people, my lord?"

"I know what Eliz— Miss Weston says. For most of us there is a veil. It can be penetrated. With study, discipline, and prayer an adept might glimpse light through it. But for the Gifted there is no veil. They see the Otherworld plain. Some are born so powerful they can play the strings on which the world is woven." He gave me a long look. "You are Gifted, are you not?"

I looked across the river at the castle, perched on the hill above us. It blazed with torchlight in the growing darkness. It almost took the place of the waning moon, lighting the trail beneath our feet. "Yes."

"Do you intend to marry Miss Weston sir?" He looked down at his fingernails, trying to indicate my answer was of little interest.

"Marry her?" I said, startled.

"When you take her back to England. That is why you are here, is it not?"

Where did that rumour come from? It had not come from me or Edwin. That was the problem with rumours, they tended to grow, fork and break out in some uncomfortable direction. "She's a Catholic," I began as if that were the biggest obstacle to nuptials imaginable.

"Of course, you are a Protestant," said Baldhoven. "But if you could find a way to reconcile your faiths, she must leave this place. Rudolf is not cruel, but he can be whimsical, and if Magister Kelley cannot please him..."

"I shudder to think of you toying with her since she is so vulnerable." I was being cruel to distract him. It worked. He puffed up with outrage. I added a quick, "my lord" before he exploded.

"I would never!"

"You do not want her as a mistress?"

"You mean...with one such as her? It is not a matter of rank it's a matter of soul. Do you think I would presume?"

"You have not?" I was surprised to realize I cared. There was some intimacy between them, but the idea of that girl being used by a thoughtless lord bothered me more than I thought possible.

"I suppose it is not unreasonable that you ask. She would not have me, Captain. Her heart is fixed upon other things." Baldhoven looked so mournful, I almost regretted teasing him.

Almost.

"Well, she's a sensible girl, my lord." I made my voice a good deal quieter.

"A tribute to her sex in every way."

"So, you worship at the temple of her intellect?"

Baldhoven flinched. "That is not quite all of it."

"Then explain all of it, if you would my lord?"

He turned several assorted colours. He smelled like lords usually smelled, pomade and horses, cosmetics and ink. He was probably not as young as I'd first thought him, an illusion of his delicate features. What was this young lordling doing with Elizabeth?

"When we were young, we studied mathematics together," he said. "We discovered a cipher in her stepfather's books. So, for pleasure, we intercepted whatever messages that came to Magister Kelley."

"You are *playing* at spycraft?" I could not keep the horror from my voice.

The young lordling twisted his hands. "It started that way," He trailed off, looking around at the crowd drinking obliviously around us. "The emperor and your queen, their interests do not always lie side by side...and so Magister Kelley would send her reports. And reports would come to the house for him."

"You and that child stumbled upon some matter of a genuinely sensitive nature."

Baldhoven looked miserable. "You won't believe me."

"I'll believe most things, my lord."

"Dr. Hájek says the emperor may be being driven mad using substances that when ingested make him disoriented. Magister Kelley believed his brother Matthias is behind it, but he would not act without the blessing of Philip of Spain. So, we – Mistress Weston and I – investigated."

"Ah...." The English language deserted me like a cheap whore.

"We thought Melichor Klesl was behind it, but he seems to be answering to someone named Columbanus. We haven't yet worked out if Columbanus answers to Philip or the Pope or someone else entirely—"

"You investigated the bloody Inquisition?"

"Captain Talbot, please don't be angry," Baldhoven said.

"Angry?" And then I realized I was.

"Don't you understand, Captain?" Baldhoven said, grabbing my sleeve, his hand sweating with earnestness. "The Inquisition wants Rudolf to suppress all the Czech Protestants. But half the country is Protestant. They were Protestant a hundred years before Martin Luther. Rudolf's father tolerated Protestants. He would have to kill a lot of people to enforce conformity."

I thought I felt blood rising again out of the corners of my eyes. For once, in this lad, I wished I could simply see a friend. But the stupidity of men of rank can cause as much damage as malice. "Mistress Weston is a child. What do you think will happen to a maiden who gets between Phillip of Spain and his rightful business?"

Baldhoven's pale face looked like the sweet tinge on a white rose. Dear God. He really was in love with her. "I know. You are right, sir. But then Magister Kelley was arrested, and Dee came here and talked a lot of rubbish and then he left and—"

"You talked to Dee while he was here?"

He blinked. "Of course."

"Did he talk to you about..." but what on Earth could I ask? Would he have discussed the effects of the Armada spell with—

"About the *stellae novae* and the new theories of Cosmology? Certainly." The boy clearly thought there was no reason Dee shouldn't have. Well, this was Prague. Baldhoven looked at me with pity. "I know things are different in your country. The new theories about the sun being the centre of the universe..."

"The what?" I felt as if I were in an hourglass, and someone had turned it upside down. "What?"

"Please tell me you intend to marry her and take her to safety," said Baldhoven. "I know she is your godchild, but after all that is not a blood relation and—"

"Why don't you marry her? She is not of your rank I suppose."

"Rank isn't an unmovable object. Magister Kelley was given arms by Emperor Rudolf but with him out of favour...well you have seen the state of the family. What was your purpose in coming here if not to see her safe?" Baldhoven asked. "What are you doing here, Captain Talbot?"

He looked suspicious, protective, and so desperately in love. I stood before that gaze shivering. I had to give him some kind of answer. It didn't have to be truthful, it just needed to calm him like a fractious horse. "I will. I am. Of course, I have not yet spoken with her mother."

Baldhoven looked both sad and relieved. "Good. That's good. Shall we continue?"

"Yes, my lord," I said quickly.

The Cattle Market was quiet when we reached it. I could detect the faint scent of human blood over more wholesome smells like carp heads, cows, and cooking fires. Coming from this direction, the Kelley house looked forbidding behind its tall garden walls. Baldhoven hesitated at the doorstep. I hoped he didn't wish to be invited to dinner. We'd bought nothing appropriate for someone of his rank.

"Do not worry, I shan't stay," he said. "I would just speak to Westonia."

Their conference was brief. They stood in the front garden for less than a quarter hour. She handed him a bit of parchment, which he secreted into his pocket. He handed her something. He bowed and went off into the dark city, leaving her perched at the edge of the courtyard, as if she were trapped like a cat in a window.

Elizabeth looked angry when she saw me waiting. I saw her slip a paper into her pocket. Her chin jutted as she stalked back up the walk. "You're not really my godfather, so you can stop playing my chaperone."

I ignored her bad temper. "I met Magister Kelley."

Her annoyance melted away. She put a hand on my sleeve. "Is he all right? Did they hurt him?"

I wondered what to tell her. She was still a girl. I knew what a racked man looked like, but I could not speak those words to her. "I will arrange for you to see him."

I spoke lightly. She frowned. She knew I had not said all but decided to leave it. "God be praised," she said and pushed past me into the house. I fancied I saw a tear drop on her sleeve.

Chapter 15

I discovered my belongings had been moved in my absence. I was now installed in Elizabeth's brother's room. It was narrow, with only a bed, small table and a towering stack of books. The linen was clean, but the straw tick smelled old. The chamber being too small for him, Edwin had a pallet made up on the landing next to the chamber. It would be quite hard to get past him without his knowing it. No more wandering the markets alone I suppose.

We ate a simple supper in the front room. This time Mistress Kelley joined Elizabeth and myself, while Edwin and Anežka waited on us. The food was roasted carp, roots, and potatoes heavy with cream. We didn't speak much. Elizabeth's eyes were fixed on the edge of her plate, as if she were burdened with thoughts, and Mistress Kelley had not yet warmed to my presence beyond the minimum of politeness.

Maybe it was the look on Elizabeth's face at dinner, but I could not sleep. I lay for hours with my eyes fixed on the ceiling beams, the fire making ever slighter patterns of russet on them until it burned low into the coals. Music played in the Cattle Market outside my window. The Romany again. I wondered if my Mohammedan friend would be with them.

After the church bells struck midnight, I got up. I thought I could find some strong drink in the pantry. I opened the door carefully, intending to sneak past Edwin on the landing while he slept, but his corner was silent. I edged a toe onto his pallet and heard nothing. He wasn't there. I hesitated, nervous. It was likely he'd gone out to the barn for a piss. I heard the door open below me, and a shaft of light shot through the darkness like an arrow.

"Edwin?"

The light vanished. Wherever he'd gone, his absence was my

opportunity. I crept down the stairs into the cold stone kitchen.

Elizabeth sat alone at the giant trestle table in her nightdress, writing by the light of a single candle. She held her head up with her hand and chewed her lip with concentration. She was so deep within her own world that she did not notice me. I hovered a long time before she looked up.

"Where is everyone?"

"Mother is upstairs," Elizabeth said, with a smile. "We have enough fuel that she can sleep in her own room again, thanks to you. Anežka is with her." She yawned, rubbing the back of her neck. "Did you need something?"

"My throat is sore."

"It's the smoke. So many fires with winter coming in." She nodded. "You'll want a drink."

She found the bottle, poured a healthy amount into an earthen cup, and placed it before me. She picked up a shawl from the hearth and put it around her shoulders. I forced myself to ignore the pages on the table, though their mere presence tempted me.

"So..." I said. "Father Columbanus then?"

She made a face but didn't seem troubled. "I knew Baldhoven would tell you that."

"Are you a complete fool?"

"No," she said. "But apparently I'm to be your wife."

"Baldhoven told you."

She rubbed her neck, looking tired. "He's very pleased."

"I didn't invent the rumour."

"Mother did."

"Really?"

"She had to explain you."

"Do you mind?"

"Marrying you? It is not my biggest problem."

"What is your biggest problem?" I asked.

Elizabeth looked miserable and glanced sidelong at the pages. I was interrupting her communion with her muse. I was about to retire when she said, "I've been invited to Christmas court."

"Good news comes quick."

Her eyes narrowed. "You knew?"

"I may have put the idea into Doctor Hájek's head."

"Why would you do that?"

"To help you contrive a meeting with your august parent, of course," I lied. "I thought you'd be pleased."

She glared as if I were the stupidest man alive. "Living at court through Twelfth Night will be fiendishly expensive. Lady Polyexna has offered to loan me clothes, but I need cosmetics, decent shoes, feathers, gifts, all sorts of things."

"So, you need money?" I folded my arms across my chest. I explained that Edwin and I planned to provision the house through the winter.

She took my hand and smiled as prettily as any courtier. "I have no words adequate to your kindness."

"Burns you like fire to take charity."

Elizabeth dropped my hand. "Yes."

"Well settle your pride. This is compensation from the English crown, and well earned."

"Thank you," she said. "But let's not tell mother that I'd rather keep a fire in her bedroom all winter than buy her a silk dress for court. Even with your help we cannot all afford to go. I cannot attend court without a lady's maid, so Anežka must go with us. Would you mind if Edwin stayed with Mother? He can walk up when we need him."

That would not please Edwin, but it would keep him out of my way. "It is acceptable."

She poured me a bit more brandy. The liquor smelled so strong I could taste it before it touched my lips. I nodded to her over it and drank it down.

"Master Marlowe," she said. "Do you remember that you offered to lend me your particular talents?"

I reached out my hand across the table. She did not take it. "I do."

"You are a real adept? Not just a scholar with clever words and a little Latin."

I shrugged. "Yes."

"The crystal you showed me," she said. "You use it to speak with spirits? I know that's what those crystals are for. Doctor Dee had a black one for such uses."

Many people used crystals for that purpose, but I did not need them.

"Am I wrong?"

"No."

"Do you have it?"

"Yes," I said, patting my pocket.

She squared her shoulders and jutted out her chin. "I need help managing a spirit."

I blinked. "I beg your pardon?"

"I need you to ask her to leave Mother alone."

She might have been talking about mice. I looked around. I did not see any spirits.

"Oh, stop peeping at shadows. She doesn't laze about the kitchen!"

"Where does she laze about?"

She blushed and looked at her hands. I knew what I had to ask, but I did not really want to know the answer. "Did you and Baldhoven conjure this spirit?"

She gave me a droll look. "Baldhoven couldn't. Anežka helped me." She placed her hands flat on the table, spreading her fingers as if she was exploring as much of the wood as she could reach.

She still did not look at me.

"Is Anežka is a witch?"

"No more than you or I," Elizabeth shot back.

"But Gifted enough to conjure a spirit?"

"She's not Gifted. She studied with Doctor Hájek. She was the emperor's mistress before that. Maybe 15 years ago now?"

"No, she is not so old."

"She's past forty. She was my nurse."

"Who conjured the spirit?"

"Doctor Dee. Anežka and I tried but we cannot exorcise her."

I groaned. "Doctor Dee owns the house then. If Doctor Dee gave it permission to be here, you can't banish it, and neither can I."

Elizabeth just looked me over like a fish she thought she might purchase. "I'll get the key to the laboratory." She pulled her shawl together and slipped away.

I poured what was left in the flask into my cup and downed it. It was foolish to truck with spirits while drunk, but it was too late now. Elizabeth returned with a candle and a small iron ring of keys, one of which unlocked the door to the kitchen garden.

She showed me the toe of her shoe. "Will you fare all right without boots?"

"I'll manage." My feet had stumbled through colder places.

I followed her lit candle into the dark garden. There was no wind, which was a blessing for the flame. "The door is under the pear tree."

I looked under the only tree in the garden, which I supposed bore fruit in better seasons. There, hidden from the street, was a small wooden door. Elizabeth turned a key in the lock and pushed it hard. I reached over her head to help her. It gave way easily, even though dust and traces of cobweb fell into our faces.

Elizabeth coughed so I gave her my handkerchief. She put it

in front of her face with a grateful expression. I put my hand on the top of the doorjamb, which was level with my eyes. I ducked my head over the threshold and felt around until I found an unlit torch. "Care to get me a light?"

She took the torch from my hand. "Don't go in without me."

I had seen alchemist's laboratories before. All the more reason not to go down there without light. Elizabeth went back into the kitchen and returned, bearing the lit torch.

The stairway was much colder than the garden, exuding a clammy air that made me think of plague. I could smell sulphur. Elizabeth must have burned it recently to get the spirit to leave. That works sometimes, but not if the spirit is properly dug in. She led me down a steep, spiral staircase. Her hand traced the wall as she went. At the bottom of the stairwell, we came to a door. She turned and stopped me with her hand. Her fingertips were black from the grime on the wall. She nodded and let me into the sanctum.

Magister Kelley's laboratory resembled others I'd seen. A bellows the size of a horse dominated the room. Its hollow tip pointed toward a tiny fireplace recessed in the wall. The bellows would blow air onto a fire, make it hotter, the fire of transformation.

Glass and ceramic vessels covered every inch of horizontal space, moulded in the sacred shapes common to alchemical practice: the twisted swan, the boar, the snake, the spitfire. Some were small and broken. Some were whole, monstrously big, and thick with dust. The walls of the round, cave-like chamber bore markings, where Kelley had run out of paper and painted his thoughts on the wall. I noticed the signs for antimony, and for chalk. There were traces of mathematical formulas.

A fresh pentacle was chalked on the floor. Traces of candle wax covered the edges. That was sloppy. For delicate workings one must keep the pentacle as clean and unbroken as possible. There were no spirits.

Elizabeth clung to the doorway, shivering. "What do you see?"

"Nothing."

"Look again." She pointed to the fireplace.

At first, I thought I saw Elizabeth reflected in a mirror, but the figure was too thin, and her clothes were wrong. Then I recognized her.

"*Marlen!*" said Madimi. "*You've arrived!*"

Chapter 16

I held my stone up. I looked into it, because I thought it would comfort Elizabeth if I seemed to follow the rules she knew. It was cold and heavy in my hand. The torchlight reflected off its silky surface, showing delicate flaws that sparkled when they caught the light. They looked like falling leaves, or golden snow. I stepped around the bellows to get closer, torch in one hand, crystal in the other.

"What manner of spirit are you?" I asked, grandly. "Are you good or evil?"

Madimi crossed her arms. *"Marlen, we've met before. Many times. I am an angel."*

Madimi did not look like an angel. She resembled the beggar children who lived in the river mud beneath London Bridge. But spirits can take whatever shape they desire. It spoke well of her that she did not trail conspicuous clouds of glory. She could be a demon hiding beneath a piteous shape. That's what Puritans always moaned about, demons seeming helpless, luring you in. Spirits bear a strong kinship with government men that way.

"You don't need that crystal," said Madimi.

"Spirit!" I intoned, in my most impressive manner. "Leave this woman in peace!"

"But she asked me to bring you here," said Madimi.

I whirled on Elizabeth. "You asked her to bring me here?"

Elizabeth turned pale. "Not you as such. I asked her to find help."

"Help with what?"

"With this," said Madimi. She touched my forehead, and the world went sideways.

They erected a gibbet by the Old Town Hall, near the Astronomical Clock, which still hung off to one side, functioning like the whirling eyes of fate.

A crowd stood in the Old Town Square, in silent, brown-clad rows. They were a mixed group of men, women, and children, but the air of merrymaking was completely absent. There were no Jews. There were no Gypsies. There were no foreigners in absurd hats or brilliant silks.

The women tucked their brown and auburn hair under homespun caps. The men had patches at their elbows. The children had sharp, patient faces, with eyes that looked like those of aged men. They faced the gibbet, silent, watching.

The drumbeat began. It throbbed in time with the pain in my chest.

"You have to witness," said Madimi, who stood, bare-armed and shivering to my right. "This is what we want to prevent."

Men in yellow and black livery marched about the square with drums. The rows of silent townsmen held themselves breathlessly still as they walked past. No one flinched, though one woman shuddered. Then I saw the prisoners.

The tallest was old, a round, bear-like Czech nobleman, not much humbled for all he was going toward his death. He strode through the crowd as if he wore chain and leather, like the warrior-kings of old. Some thirty other men followed, but few had his calm disdain. They had been beaten, tortured; the pretty ones walked as if they'd seen more than torture. Their clothes had rotted in whatever prison they'd been in, until wool, brocade, satin, and linen were all the same dirty water brown. Some looked at the sky, and others at their feet, and others looked straight ahead and saw nothing at all.

The leader mounted the gibbet and glared at the crowd. The crowd looked straight ahead and saw nothing.

"You always show me real horrors," I told her. "Night after

night, slaughter, murder, plague, and me always helpless to stop any of it. How is this different?"

"Because this is hasn't happened yet."

"All right," I said, biting the inside of my cheek to give myself pain to focus on. "Who are they hanging then?"

"That is Petr Vok z Rožmberk," said Madimi. "The day he dies will be almost 30 years from today. A war approaches and this country will never recover. One third of the population dead or in exile, and the rest live under the thumb of one repressive rule after another. Kings, Emperors, Dictators, Communists. Five hundred years of cruelty and death."

There was the jerk, as always, and the crash of his heavy body falling, the crack of his neck, and the nothing of death. One by one they hung them all, twenty-seven men at last. No one moved, but something sapped away from their shoulders.

"Can I go back now?"

"Wait," Madimi said, holding me fast.

There was one more, but not a nobleman, surely. This poor sod was a fat shopkeeper. They dragged him, still wearing his apron, worn and soaked with mud pressed against his legs. He knelt before the men in the yellow and black livery. I couldn't hear his words, but I didn't need a translation to know he was pleading for his life.

They dragged him forward and yanked his tongue through his teeth and shoved him against the wood of the gibbet. One of the guards produced a small silver hammer. With three quick strokes he drove nails through the man's tongue and left him there, screaming under the swaying bodies of the dead noblemen.

"You cannot let this happen," said Madimi.

"Me?"

"You can change it as you did for your own country."

"You want me to use the spell!" I said. "That's why Dee came here. He was seeking other magicians. He wanted to do the Armada *spell again, to prevent this."*

I dropped the torch. I stumbled backwards. The light burned harmlessly amongst the dust and the glassware and the stones. The sulphur smell grew stronger. Madimi reached out both her arms to me. *"Marlen! Please!"*

"No," was all I could say. "No."

I do not know how I reached the top of the spiral staircase, only that Elizabeth pushed me ahead, her torch burning dangerously close to my spine. We emerged into the empty garden, the dark rustling of the wind in the trees stiffening my fingers and my eyelashes with sudden cold. The sky had gone grey with moonlight and still with fog that rolled up to us from the Moldau, arriving as suddenly as if a net had been dropped upon us. I tripped over the roots of the pear tree. She pulled the door shut and turned the key firmly in the lock.

"Into the kitchen," she said, dropping the key into her pocket.

I did as I was bid. Elizabeth took the shawl from her shoulders and threw it around me, stamping her feet on the cold floor. The she poured a finger of something sweet smelling into a cup. "Drink this," she commanded.

I gulped the drink, which was heavy with a sweet spice. Elizabeth went around the table and sat down on the bench opposite mine. She looked much older, suddenly. Something put me in mind of the Queen, that old, virgin look. She poured a drink for herself. "What did you see?"

I shook my head.

"The gibbet?"

"Yes."

"Old Town Square and the man with a nail through his tongue."

"She's shown you these shades before."

Elizabeth sighed. "Yes, although she doesn't need to. I know what will happen to this city if the Inquisition puts the emperor's brother Matthias on the throne."

She poured me another drink and I downed it as well. "What is this?"

"Anežka gets it from the village. More?"

I nodded. She poured me a third drink, but I did not quaff it straight away. I held it between my fingers and looked at her through the haze that was beginning to lower itself over my vision.

"Does Matthias have real support beyond the Church? I know little about the politics here."

Elizabeth frowned. "I thought you an agent of Her Majesty's Secret Service."

"In Flanders. Or home in England."

"The Inquisition is the same everywhere. They wish to replace princes hostile to the Church with those who are loyal." She poured another cup of the liquor and sat across from me. "Matthias is loyal."

"Rudolph is Catholic."

"Rudolph is *lazy*," she said. "In the matter of persecuting heretics, a good deal too unconcerned for the Mother Church's taste."

Baldhoven had said this. So had Jahoda. There were Protestant noblemen south of here, living unmolested. The Church which butchered French Protestants not long ago, which made wars on both England and the Low Countries would have little patience for such laziness.

"You summoned me here. How?"

Elizabeth looked away and buried her nose in her drink. "Madimi did."

"It's not enough to be Gifted to command a spirit, you must know how to bind one to your will."

"I obviously can't bind Madimi to my will."

"What did you do?"

"Doctor Dee and my stepfather kept records of all their efforts to communicate with the spirit world. I used their notes and asked Madimi to find help. Madimi swore we could not interfere with your free will."

I sighed with annoyance. "When did you send for me? What was the date?"

She counted on her fingers like a child at school. "27th July."

Late July. Mere weeks before Matthew sent me to Prague. Madimi must have dropped the notion into Roydon's head.

"Why?"

Elizabeth bit her lip. "What did Baldhoven tell you?"

"Enough."

"When Columbanus came to Prague, Madimi said Columbanus was...new. Klesl was bad, but Columbanus wasn't supposed to be here, he would tip the balance in the wrong direction, make a bad future worse. We needed to balance him, or every non-Catholic—"

"You are a Catholic."

"I am a *scholar*," she said. "Everything here, the freedom to argue, to study, to believe as you wish, it all depends on Rudolf. Rudolf has kept it all in place at bay with nothing more than playacting as the Mad King. His brother Matthias would use Rudolf's throne to destroy every inch of freedom we have. Do you want to see blood running in the streets, like the slaughter of Protestants in Paris?"

I stood. "You know nothing about that."

Her cheek puckered slightly, amused. "Never mind. Can you perform an exorcism?"

I sat up so suddenly my head swam. "You still want to exorcise Madimi? I thought she was helping you."

THE MARLEN OF PRAGUE

"I cannot leave Mother alone here with her."

"Why not?"

"Because Mother thinks Madimi was the instigator of..." She turned away quickly, so I would not see her blush. My frank girl reduced to silence. Elizabeth opened her mouth, but no sound came out. The candlelight glinted in her eyes. I thought she might cry, but she didn't. "It is shameful."

"Not to me."

"You will think less of my stepfather."

"Not at all."

"You don't believe in sin, do you?"

"I don't rank myself above my fellow sinners."

There are worse tales told about Edward Kelley. Kelley acted as John Dee's medium for a long time, and acting was all it was for he had no Gifts. He pretended to see spirits to gain Dee's confidence.

"Why did he tell you?" It seemed dangerous.

"He could not bear for me to grow up believing Dee's humbug."

"Fair enough."

Dee was obsessed. He would not let Kelley quit, and Kelley couldn't say he'd been faking, so Kelley crafted a plan to get out. Dee had a young wife of whom he was most jealous. Kelly told Dee that the spirits wanted him to prove his devotion by giving his wife to Kelley and – here Elizabeth struggled to speak – Dee must take Johanna Kelley into his own bed.

"He never dreamed Doctor Dee would agree," she said. "And then one day he and Doctor Dee summoned Madimi here."

"You said Kelley was pretending."

"He was," she said. "And then one day...he wasn't."

"And Dee gave Madimi free access to the house?"

"Yes."

"And your mother shared her bed with Doctor Dee."

Elizabeth bit her lip.

"Willingly?"

"She says so."

"But she was angry."

"She hates all of you," she said. "Adepts, alchemists, spies. She hates the trouble, poverty, and disgrace. Joanna Dee liked intrigue. Liked Madimi. All three of them made Mother miserable."

"I imagine."

"And now Madimi won't leave. She just keeps on about the gibbet and the war that is to come. She upsets Mother. But she chose you, she likes you. She might go if you ask her."

Mistress Kelley's comfort mattered little to me, but Elizabeth looked exhausted. I drank the dregs of my cup. "Why not?"

"Should I come with you?"

"No, stay warm."

I felt my way down the spiral stairwell with one hand and clutched the light with the other. Cobwebs spun down from above me like a lady's veil. I wondered idly what would happen if I set them afire with my candle. Probably nothing. A bit of flame, perhaps before it hit the stone wall. I stepped down into the laboratory.

All around me stood dusty flotsam of old experiments: bladder-shaped beakers, a swan-necked glass apparatus, a large ceramic...thing. It seemed to me that was supposed to represent a boar, with multiple teats, but my memory was faulty, and I had never been one place long enough to study alchemy.

Madimi stepped into the circle of my candlelight. Her ghostly hair floated in the air before me like the cobwebs upon the stairs. I bowed. She was, after all, posing as an angel.

"You could have told me," I said.

"You will help me, Marlen?" She sounded like Elizabeth in an

eager mood.

"I am afraid not."

She frowned. *"I thought I made the need clear."*

"I have not the means."

"The Armada spell—"

"I can't use that."

"But why not, Marlen? You understand what is at stake, you more than most."

She pulled her ghostly locks with despair. I sat down on the stone floor next to her. "Because it isn't fair."

"All power can be unfair," she said.

"This is different." I struggled to make words wrap around the ideas I'd held barely formed inside my own head. "This is the fabric of reality. If we, the Gifted, can shape what is, fine tune it to our purposes, then we can force a man to turn left instead of right, to fall in love or break a vow. We can change things that mean all choices are no choice at all, and free will is meaningless. Effort, truth, all meaningless. We the Gifted can use this spell to erase the story of a life, write our own over it, and he would never even know."

"Is that cruel if we spare him pain?"

"We don't see all ends, Madimi. What if the new world I shape is worse? And even if I would use the Armada spell, a change of such consequence could never be accomplished by one wizard. We had half a dozen that day."

"There are magicians all over this city, Marlen."

"Not Gifted ones," I said. "Dee come back here because he wanted help."

"He needed more people," said Madimi.

"Hájek isn't Gifted, and Magister Kelley wasn't trustworthy?"

She nodded. They weren't the only disappointments either, I imagined. Half the magicians in Europe were con artists, the rest were scholars like Hájek, whose gifts were mostly intellectual. "So, Dee left Prague to find more of the Gifted ones?" I asked.

"*Yes.*"

"Where did he go?"

"*I showed you ages back,*" said Madimi.

"You've shown me many places..."

"*You didn't know how to look, Marlen. There's more to seeing than just staring about.*"

I thought back on all the all the places she'd shown me. The plague city, the lemurs, the human chessboard...

"*Fatehpur Sikri,*" said Madimi. "*The court of Akbar the Great.*"

"The Mughal Empire?" I asked, incredulous. "That's not possible. He couldn't have gotten that far."

But he'd been gone two years. It was possible with help, money, an introduction. He could be at Akbar's court wearing a ridiculous bishop's hat, a human chess piece running diagonally across the tiled floor. I would never find him and, if I did, how could I bring him back? I would never be able to protect Anne.

"Master Royden can hear you," I said, though I knew it was useless. "Tell him what you told me. Let him call me back."

Madimi wrinkled her nose. "*Royden hears but he doesn't listen.*"

"Like looking and seeing."

"*If he believed Doctor Dee out of his reach, you would return home?*"

"He would recall me, yes."

"*Back to prison?*"

I sighed. Yes, that was likely. Or they'd devise some other errand for a Gifted Marlen tied to their arm.

She looked mischievous, like a little devil child. "*Then I shall not do it. I need you here.*"

"To do what?"

"*Finish what Doctor Dee started. Recruit magicians, Gifted ones. Dee did not ask the right people. And you never know who will come to Christmas Court.*" She looked a bit sly. "*Someone unexpected might come to help you.*"

I did have an invitation to Christmas Court. If Dee were in India, the best I could do was prove without doubt he was not here. I needed a testimonial from a person with a body, someone Royden would trust. To get one I should do exactly what Madimi suggested, talk to magicians, but with my own purpose in mind.

"Good Spirit," I said. "I would ask you a humble favour. Might you be persuaded to leave this place for a few days?"

The spirit shook her head, her eyes flashed cold. "*Why do you ask?*"

"The young miss of the house and I are going to Christmas Court and—"

"*Oh!*" She looked happy again. "*You want me to go with you! Of course, Marlen. Your favour is no favour at all. You will need my help at Christmas Court, for great peril follows you close. Do not fear! You have been brought here by God for a good and worthy purpose!*" Madimi said, in a sing-song voice.

"Oh stop. I know you are no angel. You are a shadow that Doctor Dee and Magister Kelley willed into form, a trick of the natural arts, nothing more. You know it too."

Madimi towered over me, her hair twisting with the ever-stronger outline of her wings. "*Everything you say might be true. What I am is as God wills. But I am who I choose to be, just like you.*"

She patted me, as if I were Tantalus.

"You want me to save the City of Gold from the Inquisition? It isn't possible. The powerful and vile and bone breakers always win in this world. I shouldn't even be alive."

"Neither should Father Columbanus, and yet he lives," said Madimi.

"Who is he?"

"He was an Irish monk in the version of the world you were born in. He died during the Armada invasion. Now he is your other self. It happens that way sometimes, a Light worker spared from death must be balanced. By you, Marlen."

"A Light worker, me?"

"Yes," said Madimi awkwardly. "There are always islands like Prague, and they are always in peril. Those who dislike the Light, learning, inquiry, truth, and the chaos of creation, always seek to destroy them. You are sworn to protect such places, Marlen of the Down-turned Torch."

"When did I swear that?"

"When you joined the Merchants of Light. The oath you swore in Walter Ralegh's house, all those years ago to protect the Gifted and the free ones everywhere."

Oh hell. I had sworn exactly that. This is what came from joining too many secret societies, you mix up the specifics. "It is impossible. The Inquisition. The future. The wars of religion. Time itself breathing down upon us, and the stars already wrong. What can any of us do against that?"

"Perhaps nothing," Madimi said. "I am not really an angel. All this may be ordained by Fate. But it seems that we must try, even if we fail. It is better than doing nothing at all."

I squared my shoulders and stood up. She blinked, floating like a cobweb. I bowed because I could not think of anything better to do. "I would be honoured to have your company at Christmas court."

"I am honoured to follow you there," she said.

Chapter 17

I woke the next morning well after sunrise to an empty room, a cold hearth, and the worst hangover of my life. The amber firelight had given way to the thin light of day, and that light was painful. I was no stranger to drink, but last night's business had done its damage.

I lifted the cover and gingerly put first one leg, then the other, over the side. The wood floor was cold against my feet. The church bells rang out the hour. I could make out perhaps half a dozen different chimes, some close, some far away. I held on to the bedpost, listening. The nearby bells from across the cattle market were light and firm while bigger bells rang from across the river. I was sure at least one hefty sounding one was the cathedral in the Old Town. They were the sound of heaven, if heaven existed and had sound. I thought my head would split open from the flaming sword of the angel who guarded the gate.

My doublet was clean and newly brushed. My shoes had a bit of polish on them, and the buckles looked bright in the dim autumn sunlight. I had no mirror, and that was too bad. I supposed my vanity would survive.

I opened the door quietly. Edwin's pallet on the landing was rolled up and tucked neatly beside his bags in the corner. I slipped down the twisted stairs. I heard voices in the library. I tried to listen at the door, get a sense of the conversation before I joined it, but that was a waste of time.

"Captain Talbot!" shouted Baldhoven from his seat at the desk. He threw his velvet cap in the air and beamed when he saw me. I knew nothing I had done to merit such enthusiasm. Elizabeth nodded to me from the bookcase, where she perched on the ladder. She seemed undaunted by both liquor and spiritual exertions.

Edwin stood behind Baldhoven, clutching the paper he showed me on the road, the one full of numbers. His eyes clapped on me with look that comprised surprise, lust, and a sort of raw anxiety. I misliked the naked desire writ plain in his eyes for all to see. But no one paid mind to servants. "You are awake, sir?"

"Are you quite all right?" Baldhoven asked. "You don't look well."

"I am well," I said, though my headache weighed my limbs like plaster. I wished rather desperately for water. "Show me what you are working on."

"Westonia has very few candles so we should use as much daylight as possible." Baldhoven pulled a chair closer to the diamond paned windows and fussed over me as if I were an old man. He placed a table before me with two copies of *Metamorphosis,* and a stack of papers filled with numbers and Cabbalistic inscriptions. One of them was Father Tomáš'. Edwin had found it among our things.

"Your man Edwin here said that a group of *monks* came seeking this book and murdered the man who possessed it." Baldhoven stressed the word monks and gave me a significant look. I realized this meant he believed the men who killed Father Tomáš were Rudolf's Capuchin monks.

"Did he?" I grimaced at Edwin whose face was impassive.

"The message you brought from London is a string of numbers, which by themselves do not form a discernible pattern. But once we had two copies of *Metamorphosis* ...two identical copies from the same printing press...we thought it might be the code key."

"I suggested it," said Elizabeth.

"Yes, you did, my dear Weston, sorry," said Baldhoven. "These numbers break down into sets of nine. The first number corresponds to the page number in the book, the next number is the line, and the last number is the letter on the line. Like so: 177...page 177...012...line twelve...014...fourteenth letter."

"Which is?"

Edwin put the book before me and pointed to it. "S."

Anežka entered, holding a small bottle gingerly, as if it were warm. She poured the contents into a cup and placed it in my hands. She bobbed a perfunctory curtsy and indicated I should drink it. It smelled vile. The potion was bitter but didn't taste as bad as it smelled. My stomach grumbled with disrespect and then grew surprisingly still. I held still and hoped I wouldn't vomit. I sipped the potion, watching the little drama enacted before me. Elizabeth was absorbed in mathematics, Baldhoven was absorbed in the sunlight reflected in her hair, and Edwin was absorbed in avoiding my gaze. Anežka took the flask, bobbed again, and left, silently.

"So, you deciphered the message?" I asked.

"Yes," said Elizabeth. "No," said Baldhoven.

They glared at one another.

"Well?" I asked. "Which is it?"

Edwin cleared his throat and read the Latin: "*As a person in a vessel while moving forwards sees an immovable object moving backwards, in the same manner do the stars, however immovable seem to move daily.*"

From the feeling in my head, the stars seemed to move in earnest. "What does that mean?"

Edwin and Baldhoven shrugged in tandem. "I think it was encoded twice," Baldhoven said. "We have been working on mathematical correspondences between the letters."

"You are too obvious," said Elizabeth. "It is a riddle. Who is the person in the boat? Who, though immovable, appears to be moving backwards? That could refer to the Turks in the south, could it not? Which faction does the writer refer to? Protestant? Catholic? Is it someone from the Ottoman Empire?"

The face of the Mohammedan flashed before my eyes.

"I know that, Mistress," said Edwin with a bow. "But why would the Sultan's janissaries send messages in Latin?"

"Matthias knows Rudolf will not produce a legitimate heir," said Edwin to me.

"He cannot be certain," said Baldhoven. "The emperor has...well...that is to say..."

Elizabeth rolled her eyes. "Bastards, Baldhoven."

He turned scarlet. I could see why his love was unrequited.

"He is proven fertile, then?"

"He breeds like a horse," said our frank-tongued virgin scholar. "But he refuses to marry. He has six children by that mistress. You'd think he'd find the time to bed some princess for the good of us all."

This speech was Baldhoven's undoing. He took the pages out of Elizabeth's hands and made a great show of folding them up and putting them in order.

"Baldhoven," she said brightly. "Why don't you take Captain Talbot to a tavern? There is much to do to prepare for court, give him a meal, would you?"

He kissed her hand. "Of course, my dear Westonia."

I stood, surprised to find that I was able to stand. I didn't feel sick at all anymore, in fact I felt a great deal of hunger.

We followed the same path as yesterday but this time, as we emerged into the square, we walked right into my old friends the Romany band. They played in a nook by the cathedral, filling the square with their shrill and festive sound. It was a stark contrast to the cold and bluish blush of the overcast autumn sky, but the crowd liked them better for it. They threw coins and danced, girls pairing with girls, boys tossing their hats in the air.

"Pickpockets work this crowd in force, Captain," said Baldhoven.

I resisted the temptation to blow a kiss to my friend the Mohammedan. His hands struck like lightening upon the strings of some unfamiliar instrument, and his body moved up and down to the rhythm, his moustache vibrating in time. I could have watched him all night. Instead, I followed Baldhoven down the hill into the shadows.

We turned into a courtyard, went around a corner, down a short flight of stairs and opened a low wooden door. I found myself in an outdoor courtyard overlooking the river. The place was lit by torchlight and outdoor fires, and it was cold, but we could see the bridge from here. The city stretched up the hill like a patchwork of soft red and gold flowers, lights glowing in the gloom.

Baldhoven dragged me to a place near a fireplace set into the exterior wall. He waved to a round-faced, aproned man, who wordlessly dropped two foaming cups of beer in front of us and stalked away. I took a cautious sip, letting the bubbles tease my nose. It was rich and warm, like hearty bread. Baldhoven gulped his, leaving a dander of white foam on the edges of his neat moustache.

"Be careful, Captain Talbot," he said. "Rudolf has commissioned alchemists to brew it specially. It will make you see obscene visions."

I've tasted ale that you could stand a spoon upright in, so I didn't achieve obscene visions. Baldhoven drank deeply, and for the most part silently, but he was watching me too. "It is not like home," I found myself saying.

"London is your home?"

I nodded. It was more home than Canterbury.

"What is it like?"

"It is a port. The Romans set it up for trade, although there's nothing much of them left. We've kept at it ever since. Wood buildings, lots of thatch and mud. Plain décor, no graffiti the way you have here. It smells like the sea, just down the river from us. But you did not bring me here to talk about London, my lord."

"Elizabeth told me you have a seeing crystal. Might I look at it?"

"Here in the tavern?"

"Why not?"

Ahh, Prague. I took it from my pocket and placed it in his hand. He held it quite openly, looking at the light through it as if it were an ordinary piece of glass. "It is just a rock to me."

"To most men."

He handed the crystal back to me. "I am a mathematician. I do not truck with spirits or otherwise flirt with my own damnation."

"Do you believe we are damned merely for trying to understand too much of creation, my lord?" That seemed unlikely from a youth who'd been pawing through Magister Kelley's library this very morning. Something about the question troubled him. Baldhoven looked, for the first time, as if an honest answer might hold some danger.

"I was baptized into God's Holy Roman Church. I do not believe that the quest for knowledge is a sin. But there is...an extremity...in the character of magicians. Like the emperor. It does him no good, brooding on magic."

"Men can use magic to bend other men's minds," I said neutrally as I could.

"Yes, Elizabeth says such practices exist. But Inquisition or no, the Carmelite monks are holy men. Even if they could command demons, you don't believe they resort to such things, do you?"

"This man, Columbanus. He is different from the others?"

Baldhoven shuddered. "We have never met. He does not come to Court openly. He lives with the Carmelites in their monastery on the far side of the castle."

"So, he might be less holy."

"Someone killed your man's friend, the priest," said Baldhoven. "Klesl would never do that on his own. Father Tomáš was not a foreign courtier; he was a Czech village priest. He has friends who miss him. Even humble men can be dangerous enemies."

"I believe holy men do many things in defence of the Church, my lord."

Baldhoven drew his brows together. "Elizabeth and I are not children, sir. You need not speak to me as if I were."

It was on the tip of my tongue to say that children wouldn't be as stupid as he and Elizabeth, but Baldhoven stood and threw a coin on the table. I had given my lordship offence, but he was too well bred to do more than bow and click his heels a little too firmly. "Shall we return you to your hostess?" he asked, all his consonants precise and sharp.

"Of course, my lord," I said and followed him.

It had grown cold in the Cattle Market. The sky was darker than it should be, though we were mere weeks from Midwinter. The Romany band still camped there. They played tuneless music to an unimpressed crowd. The unaccustomed dark was a contagion that touched everyone.

I went into the stables where Tantalus greeted me with an air of martyred indifference. He nudged my cap with his nose, as if to say, who are you, sir? Have I made your acquaintance?

"There now," I said, softly, patting the poor horse.

The horse whickered. I looked up to see Edwin standing in the stable door, cap in his hand and a wistful look on his face. Tantalus turned his head away, snubbing me. I patted him anyway. Poor lonely horse. "Where were you last night?"

He jerked upright, suddenly tense. "Do I answer to you Kit Marlowe?"

"I wanted to give you my report of the Court. I was surprised you weren't anxious hear my adventures."

"You met Doctor Hájek," said Edwin. "Magister Kelley too?"

"And Lady Polyexna z Rožmberk."

"I was acquiring funds. You did want quite a lot of money. I found it prudent to make contact with our agent under cover of darkness."

That sounded plausible and also wrong, but I had no excuse to question him that didn't seem overly suspicious. "You found the book?"

"It's Father Tomáš'. I recognized it. Why did you hide it from me?"

"I didn't wish to upset you."

"Well, you have," said Edwin. "Why would you steal such a thing from a dying man?"

"I didn't steal it," I said. "He gave it to me."

"Why?"

"I didn't know. But since it turned out to be a *cipher key*, I assume he didn't want his murderers to find it."

Edwin leaned on the wall. He looked sadly off into a corner for a moment. "I was distraught that night. I can see why you didn't mention it then. But you should have done after, Kit. If only—"

Because he wasn't only my gaoler but my lover. I think he meant to say that. He kissed me instead. His eyes were deep hazel in this light. I looked deep into them but only saw greenish lights and lemon-coloured speckles. He fluttered his eyelids down. Yes, we can all lie with our eyes, sweet Edwin. But not with our bodies, and yours was warm to me.

"You should clean your teeth," he said.

"Bastard," I whispered.

He gave a soft, throaty laugh that threatened my calm. "I'll fetch you Anežka's tooth mixture. Reacquaint yourself with your horse. That animal will tolerate no man's affection but yours." He picked up a pewter water pitcher and went out the door.

Edwin pestered Anežka for a loaf, some hard cheese and a dozen apples and led me out of the gates. We climbed up a hill that overlooked the city. It was cold for a picnic, but it was private. We could see the city and the river, yet we might stage a Roman orgy amongst the trees unnoticed.

"There was a great battle here," Edwin said, as we looked across the river at the castle. "One of the first Protestant battles in all of Europe." He tossed a rock off the bluff. It fell a long way.

"This is a fine place to talk," I said, sitting down in the grass.

"It is a fine place to kill you if I wished," Edwin said, lightly.

Something in his lazy tone woke me up. There was a light in eye that I misliked. I took his hand and kissed his fingertips.

"Or you could kill me," he amended.

"I am quite at your mercy. Though, if I do not appear at Court, there will be questions about the missing Captain Talbot."

Edwin closed his eyes against the wind. He leaned down, picked up another stone and threw it as far as it would go. "You are to go to Court without me? Anežka told me."

"It's a problem for you," I said, neutrally as possible. I didn't look at him, concentrated on chewing the last of my apple.

"Not at all," Edwin said, lying in the grass. "I anticipated this eventuality."

I sat down next to him, cross legged. He picked a long stem of grass and pulled it apart. "I'm to be allowed several weeks without supervision? And you are sure I'll return, docile as a cow to my traces?"

"You will return to me," said Edwin. "I need not remind you of Anne."

"Go to hell!" I tried to rise. Edwin put his hand on my chest and gently pushed me back down.

"I will not hurt Anne," he said. "I swear to you. It will not be me. But you know what will happen if you were to use your freedom to escape your parole."

I lay back and closed my eyes. This was pro forma. He was threatening me so he could say he had threatened me. As he said, there was no need. I found it exhausting anyway. "Why are you encouraging the children?"

"Their knowledge of cryptography proved useful to me."

"To you?"

He smiled and blinked is pale lashes. "To our mission. You're doing the same, getting the Weston girl to host us, having the boy make your introductions."

"Did the boy blather to you about what they are up to?"

Edwin grimaced. "God, yes. He blathered."

I stood up and paced around, suddenly restless. I threw an apple core off the bluff. Edwin got up and stood beside me, almost as if he thought I'd throw myself after. Maybe he wasn't entirely wrong to worry about that. "What is it, friend?"

"Edwin Mooney, you cannot want our lives for them? The danger, the lies, never knowing if what you do is necessary."

"You know what we do is necessary," Edwin said. "Consider what would have happened if your friend Poley had not wormed his way into Babington's confidence and discovered the plot to enthrone Mary of Scots—"

"Poley was not my friend."

"Colleague then."

"Perhaps. But these two deserve better."

Edwin took my hand and turned it over in both of his, examining it as if he could see some mystery written in the freckles on my palm. When he spoke, his voice was measured, educated, the Northern accent greatly muted, the precise clip of a man who spoke Latin.

"I do not think it is for you and I to decide for Lord Baldhoven and Mistress Weston what risks are worthy. They choose their own path." He looked at me a long moment under his pale, thick lashes.

He was right. When had I become such an old woman anyway? I'd been scarcely older than Baldhoven that day I joined the Merchants of Light. I was a seeker after Truth; I dared challenge Heaven itself.

Unbidden the picture came in my mind, almost as if someone had painted it: me pushing my heretical papers off the table into a box, making room for the frying pan in the rooms I shared with Thomas. I sat down hard on the ground. I knew too well what it meant to be young and fearless, because I did not know what there was to fear, did not even know what fear meant.

Edwin sat down next to me. He brushed the hair from my face, the better to see my countenance. "Sweet, what troubles you?"

As if I would speak to him of Thomas. I kissed his rabbity face, tasting the silken sweetness of his sweat, the rose petals of his lips. I don't think I fooled him, but I did distract him. I wished I could distract myself from the unwanted view of Thomas' face, frowning with disapproval over my papers, shuddering in the candlelight as if reading the words of the Algonquin chiefs put him in danger of hellfire. The mind is cruel. Thomas was in the grave, and I had helped him there, and then I had helped wipe his fame from the Earth. Lost and prudish and beautiful...I clutched Edwin's rounder bottom to me, pulled his heavier frame down over my body. He had no love for me. He meant to dull my senses perhaps. Well, let my senses be dulled a while.

Chapter 18

Edwin needed to run errands to equip me for Court, so we walked slowly back to the house. We were not touching. Of course, we never did touch in public. But there was a dispirited nature of this. We scarcely even looked at each other. The late fall afternoon light did not last long. Shopkeepers were already lighting torches once we reached the warren that was Old Town. The streets narrowed, the sky above us getting smaller, so that the candles in various windows gave more light than the setting sun.

"I leave you here," Edwin said. "I'll cross the river to the Embassy. Arrange for funds. Heading home?"

"Probably."

He looked for a moment as if he would kiss me. I ducked my head. Somehow, I didn't want him to. Shagging Edwin didn't soothe the bite of missing Thomas. You can't force one man into the space another man left, it doesn't work that way. Not Edwin's fault really. He walked off. I supposed he knew where the Moldau was.

I could follow him, maybe use the river to navigate back to the Cattle Market. I stood alone, lost in the maze. I guessed I could find my way by following the sound of the Gypsy band, but I wasn't sure if that would take me into Old Town Square instead. I went around the corner and found myself breathless, against a wall, with a thick, heavy arm around my neck and a knife at my throat.

I did not wait to figure out which of the many people trying to kill me this might be. I elbowed him in the stomach hard and fast. Before he had time to cut me, I slipped downwards, using his weight to yank him off balance and pull him down with me. He crashed to the cobblestones, winded and probably no small amount surprised. We went down in each other's arms like lovers.

I yanked out of his grasp and sprung to my feet. I whirled around to give him a sharp kick in the head, only to find myself on my back again. He kicked my leg out from under me and was up, faster than I thought so large a man could get up. I rolled away as his foot came down, only to smash against a wall. Then I was yanked up by my collar and pushed against that wall. A punch in the gut brought tears to my eyes.

I squinted through the tears and the ghostly half-light and tried to see who my attacker was, but the knife brandished before my eyes obstructed my vision. I was shoved hard into the wall and saw stars. Then, suddenly I was free and fell choking into the gutter along the shop wall.

The Man-Who-Was-Not-A-Gypsy hovered over me, dressed as a monk. He wore a hood and a severe Dominican habit, complete with a crucifix tied to his sash. The modest robe barely obscured his powerful frame. "*Dobrý večer*," he said. I think he meant "Good afternoon." But it could have meant "I'll gut you like a fish," for all I knew.

"*As-salamu alaykum*," I said.

He was good. He registered surprise, but it only showed in a slight narrowing of his nostrils.

"I did not know you spoke Arabic," he said, in fluent English, his accent giving his words a seductive flavour. It was my turn to control my face.

"I am not nearly the master of Arabic that you are of English, sir."

He shook his head and smiled, quite beautifully. "You would never have made such a heroic figure of the butcher Timur the Lame if you could read what his victims said of him."

I was so enchanted by the sound of my native tongue spoken so sweetly that, at first, I did not take in what he said. He'd seen

Tamburlaine, one of the *Tamburlaine* plays anyway. And he knew I wrote it.

Then he extended a hand, and I took it. He pulled me to my feet with an easy gesture that spoke to how strong his arm was.

"I apologize," he said. "I didn't see you close before."

"And that makes a difference?"

"I recognize you now," he said. "I always remember exactly, a name, a face, a word. My particular gift from..."

"Allah."

"God," he said, in English.

"That was what remained of my Arabic," I said, smiling wryly. "So did you like the play?"

"You made the butcher Timur your hero." It was a condemning judgment. "I was not certain you needed to burn the Koran."

"If I could have burned a Bible on stage without being arrested you can be sure I'd have done it." I knew what possessed me to utter that blunt comment: Kit the Brat Prince of the Bankside. Stupid Kit who got his friends killed. I wanted to stuff the dangerous words back into my throat.

He seemed amused. "You neither love your Christ, nor fear him?"

"I do not know what any God needs with men like us."

"Timur was not a Scythian but a Mongol. And your geography is execrable. You consulted Ortellius' map of Africa?"

I had to stop up a smart remark. A Cambridge man is regarded as learned by English standards, but wherever this man hailed from I might as well have studied grunts from a pig farm. "What is wrong with Ortellius?"

"Nothing if you want to hang him on a wall. Everything if you would travel to Africa. *The fire still burns.*"

I blinked at him. "The fire is old."

"The torch still burns."

"The torch burning downward."

"That which keeps me alight, extinguishes me."

"That which nourishes me, destroys me."

"*Ahcchaa!*" He looked approving. "You thought we were all Europeans, didn't you?"

I hadn't. The Merchants were everywhere, carrying about bits of local knowledge in satchels, sneaking them across borders into the hands of scholars. Catholics, Protestants, Jews could all be Merchants. Perhaps even Chief Manteo of the Algonquin was a Merchant. Harriot had trusted him like a Brother.

"Come," he said, and as if he knew where I had wanted to go, he led me through the threading streets to Old Town Square and the Orloj.

"How did you know who I was?"

He did not deign to reply. He pretended to study the clock, as if he had never laid eyes upon it before. "Death and the Turk."

"Beg pardon."

He pointed. "The figures. The man, the woman, Death and the Turk."

"Murad's army marches through the plains of Transylvania at this moment. Your people laid siege to Vienna itself. Little wonder they see you as inevitable as Death."

He sighed. "There are those who want us to be afraid of each other. You are a man who escaped Death, Master Marlowe. So, what is inevitable?"

The crowd milled around us, ignoring us both. We could not have been speaking in more perfect privacy if we had been sequestered on a deserted island. So, I said, quietly, "Will you tell me your name, Brother?"

He smiled, a bit sadly. "Of course not."

"The Man-Who-is-Not-a-Gypsy is a bit cumbersome."

He considered a moment. "You may call me Nick."

"I don't suppose that's short for Nicholas?"

He smiled, thinly, and there was a strange glint in his eye. "Nick is for Nikhil."

"That doesn't sound Mohammedan."

"My father is a Muslim; my mother is not."

"How is it possible that you are familiar with my *Tamburlaine*?"

"I was in London years ago with the entourage of an envoy from the Ottoman Sultan. Your Queen gifted him with quite a fine clock."

I remembered when Murad III's delegation came to visit Queen Elizabeth. I did not guess any of the delegates attended the theatre. "You work for Murad III?"

"No, I only travelled with his embassy. I visited London for my own purpose. Master Shakespeare speaks highly of you."

"You know Will?"

"I know a lot of people," he said. "My job is not to win wars, only to lift minds. Thomas Harriot, Doctor Dee, Tomáš Hájek, various others—we're all Merchants, sir. You can trust them."

"I don't," I said. "Lying, thieving, corrupt bastards all of them."

He looked enigmatic. "You are none of those things."

"I am all of those things."

"No," Nick said. "I think a lot of people have lined up to tell you who you are, Master Marlowe. Spy, sodomite – yes, I heard that too – heretic. But what is heresy? Do you think God requires all these monsters to protect Him? God in all His Glory needs such men? God is more of a mystery than that."

When Nick spoke like that, there was a lilt to his speech that I had not heard before. Or maybe I had. It was the sound of a true believer, but in him the sound was different, less sharp, more exciting. Behind the curtain of his words lay a spectacular vista,

THE MARLEN OF PRAGUE

like the vast cosmos that Giordano Bruno described, where the Earth we stood upon was just a dewdrop in an endless field of grass...Giordano Bruno, now rotting in prison, accused of heresy. "Your God, maybe."

"There is only one God," said Nick. "All the many scriptures are facets of his wisdom that have been given to His Creations, you and me. At the court of Akbar the Great these things are discussed openly."

Akbar the Great. Akbar of Delhi. A lot of pieces fell into place. This man somehow took Dee to Fatehpur Sikri, past armies and mountains and deserts and into that warm, lovely palace where he donned silk and played chess as a human piece. Nick for Nikhil, the Merchant of Light. I shrugged casually and asked, "Openly?"

"Akbar has great meetings of holy men, all kinds, sadhus, imams, Christian priests...everyone. They sit in his great palace of Fatehpur Sikri and exchange notes on what is known of the mind of the Great One. That is how the Merchants, and our mission, were born. Reborn, I should say. There are records going back to Alexander—"

"Akbar's mission," I said.

"Rudolf, like Akbar, wants to effect a great reconciliation between faiths. Protestant Queen Elizabeth desires toleration, but if she balances on a wire, Rudolf walks a sword's edge. He is Holy Roman Emperor. He cannot defy the authority of the Catholic Church; his family will not stand for such a thing."

"Then how are we different?"

Nick looked exasperated. "We're not different, Master Marlowe, that is entirely the point. We are not interested in authority, only in truth. Perhaps that truth is religious, perhaps it is in the natural world, perhaps it lies where the two meet—it doesn't matter. What matters is truth. You know that; I know that. More importantly, Rudolf II knows it. That's why the Merchants must protect him."

I grimaced. "Akbar the Great involves himself in the affairs of European states for our own good. Not just to weaken us."

"You are weakening yourselves. How many Christians die in wars and prisons over tiny slivers of doctrinal difference? If Akbar cared about conquering you, all he need do is sit back and watch."

He was right about that. Catholic and Protestant, we were mostly devoted to destroying one another. Still, it smarted to be pitied by this beautiful, dark man.

"So," I said. "Say it's true, and Akbar created the Merchants for the good of mankind."

"Revived it. And his minister Birbal was the one who—"

"You took John Dee to Delhi?"

"Yes."

"Could you take me there?"

"I could, of course. But you want to know if I would. I will not."

"I don't wish Dee harm. I am a Brother, same as you."

"Perhaps but you are also agent of the English Crown. Queen Elizabeth flirts with toleration the way she flirts with potential suitors. But still your people live under strict control. You are allowed brilliant poetry, but every line must be cleared by a body of censors."

"Just a man named Tilney, who takes bribes."

Nick waved that away. "After your death, none of your friends spoke up for you. They wanted to. Funerals were imagined, oratories, memorials, tributes that would make you blush, sir. But not a man among them needed to be told to keep quiet. They told themselves. That is the real damage. The thoughts you will not allow yourselves to have. Your companion knows something of that."

"You are not fond of poor Edwin."

"Beg pardon?"

"My companion. He said you tried to kill him."

"The Jesuit?" he said. "I am surprised to see a Protestant agent allied with such a man. But you are both from the same country. When a man knows few who share his mother tongue, he overlooks much in a man who does."

I tried not to let my astonishment show. And failed. Failed utterly; I could see the look of pity in his eyes deepen.

Edwin was a Catholic priest?

Brother Edward. Father Tomáš had called him that.

"He serves the Inquisition," said Nick, kindly. "He doesn't like that I'm bringing Mughal and Arab science into Europe, establishing networks across religious lines."

Edwin was a double agent. I should not believe Nick, who was Edwin's sworn enemy. But I did. Oh, bless my weakened heart I did. I felt very much like a man who wakes from a dream cuddled up to a snake.

"You did not know?" asked Nick.

I flinched at Nick's sorrowful face. He placed his hand on my shoulder. The pressure of his fingers were all that held me to the earth. The clock before me blurred. Tears fell down my fool's cheeks. If he were any other man, he might have embraced me. I stepped quickly out of his reach.

"I like your poetry. It is ignorant, but extraordinary."

"Oh," I said, flushing from this unexpected praise. "Thank you."

"I shall pray for you, Master Marlowe," said Nick.

"That's kind," I said. I looked up at the Orloj, which hovered over me, lazily shrouded with fog. Nick walked away into the crowd, leaving me to curse my own stupidity. For I did not know I loved Edwin Mooney until that very moment.

I walked back to the house, keeping a measured pace so that my anxiety did not show. A throng of folk in the Cattle Market were watching the emperor's peace administered on the back of some poor sod who hung on the iron cross in the middle of the square. The crowd forced me to pause. I made myself watch the man squirming under the lash. I tried to seem as if the gruesome spectacle meant no more to me than an afternoon's diversion. I realized why the city was so clean. His blood ran downward forming a thin red river and disappeared into a sewer. All the blood flows underground. What a metaphor.

I had been so worried about what might have changed about the world, that I'd grown careless of the dangers in the world I lived in. So, think, Kit, stupid prat! You have an intellect and a will. Forget guilt about changed stars and altered fates. You sleepwalked right into this bungle.

Edwin said he'd studied at Balliol. I simply assumed that he was *spying* on Catholics, not that he was a Catholic. He'd lived in Prague before, but there were many English Catholics here, including Elizabeth Weston. Most were as harmless as she was. Roydon found him trustworthy, but the right kind of man could fool even Royden.

Will liked him, but Will liked everyone.

I assumed no believer could come to my arms so willingly. Certainly, no Jesuit. The few Jesuit missionaries I'd encountered were serious, committed men. They did not crack under torture. They would not endanger their mission with bed sport.

Unless perhaps the bed sport was the mission. I'd thought I'd seduced Edwin, but he'd seduced me. Well, that was embarrassing. But setting my pride to one side, why would he do that? What did the Inquisition want with me?

What had he achieved? Edwin now knew dangerous amounts

about the Merchants. He knew the password. He had the code key. He'd successfully infiltrated Kelley's household. I stopped walking as it struck me. Elizabeth was in danger.

No. No. Elizabeth was safe as long as she was useful. But what was he using her for? Shelter, introductions at court, distraction for me? No, Edwin needed to decipher that message he carried, the one he'd encouraged Baldhoven to help him with.

Did Edwin understand the importance of the Armada spell? He had heard Dee talk about it, clearly everyone had. Philip of Spain concluded that the defeat of the Armada was God's will. Knowledge of the Armada spell would prove to the Catholic kings that that Elizabeth Tudor was a witch. If any other prince learned the nature of the spell itself and adapted it to their own use...that did not bear thinking about.

Standing there, staring at the river of blood in the street, I thought I should do away with myself. I was meant to be dead. I should finish the job.

No. No. I didn't need to die. I could simply disappear. Edwin would not be home for hours yet. I could pack up and be out of the city before suppertime. I could give up the role of gentleman. I could find some small village and go back to making shoes as my father had done. I could head toward Vienna, perhaps to the frontier. I could join Rudolf's army, patch their boots and saddles.

Except, I still needed Edwin's good report to keep Anne safe. I drag a train of dead friends behind me. I could not add Anne to it.

I dared not run away.

Worse still, I did not want to.

A hand tugged my sleeve. I looked down and saw Anežka, smiling up at me. She tucked something inside her sleeve. Then she touched my arm and pointed in the direction of the house. The prisoner's jaw was hanging in a peculiar slack fashion. They must have broken it. I was happy to leave. Anežka pulled me out of the crowd and into a place behind the spice seller's booth. She said something in Czech, stopped, shook her head as if she had just realized I would not understand her.

"Yes, what is it?"

She pointed to several bundles and a large goose and gestured that I should help her. I giggled with relief. She only wanted help with parcels. I forced myself to smile and picked up the goose.

I hauled the bird through the kitchen gate. I got it into the kitchen, but then collapsed on the bench, shivering. Anežka clicked her tongue, grabbed a bottle of something bitter from a shelf and forced me to drink it. It made me feel a little warmer.

I could not bring myself to mount the stairs. Instead, I went out the door and into the stable. I embraced Tantalus' neck. He grumbled and nipped at my collar. It was an enormous relief to lean there and smell him, sweet and warm and uncomplicated. I could trust Tantalus, poor stupid animal.

"I thought you were having supper with Baldhoven?" said Elizabeth. She wore an enormous dark apron and held a bucket of oatmeal in her bare hands, which looked red and chapped with chilblains. I realized she wore gloves in the house all the time now. The rooms were kept so cold. It was only early December.

"That was hours ago," I said. "Do you want my gloves?"

She hesitated. Then she nodded. I stripped mine off, took the bucket and poured the oats into Tantalus' trough. The gluttonous animal stuffed his nose into the bucket and almost shoved it out of my hands. I dumped his share quickly before the dumb beast could figure out why it wasn't before his nostrils. I put the remainder before Edwin's horse Sweetpea. Elizabeth patted Tantalus. Her tiny hands did not fill my gloves, and the loose leather fingers slapped gently against his flank.

"I did not know you were tending to our horses."

"I don't mind." She patted Sweetpea, so he wouldn't be sulky at the extra attention she'd given Tantalus. "It gets me out from under Mother and Anežka's nose. Anežka is arguing with your man about supper."

I felt really slow and stupid. I could not have run away today anyway.

"Edwin is back?" I asked, patting Sweetpea in turn.

Elizabeth nodded. "He came in a few minutes ago. Why?"

"I sent him on an errand. I did not think he would return so soon."

"Just as well," said Elizabeth. "It is dark so early."

I glanced out the stable door. It was always dark here, it seemed. Elizabeth patted me, like I was one of the horses. "Are you all right? You look quite pale."

I forced myself to smile. "Of course."

"Christian charity compels me to send you to bed."

I kissed the empty fingertips of her gloved hands, then dragged myself upstairs. I did not have the strength to start a fire or remove my boots, so I lay my head on the straw tick, hung my muddy feet off the bed, and pulled the covers over my head.

"That is no way to get warm," said Edwin. He must have carried coals up from the kitchen because I heard the grate rattle and the rustle of the wood catching fire. He put the brazier down with a thump.

"Do you want help with your boots?"

I dropped my legs completely off the side of the bed and closed my eyes. I was afraid if I opened them, they would tell him everything. Edwin removed my boots. He would have unlaced my doublet, but I put my hand on his to stop him. My hand was ice cold. I should have kept my gloves. I opened my eyes just a little. He did not look a bit suspicious, only lustful.

"Leave off," I croaked. "If we are not to get out of hand, I'd best undress myself."

Edwin left, his heavy boots thumping on the steps, a sound that put me in mind of armed guards, closed cells, and the smell of hot iron on flesh. Fumbling with the laces and points like a drunk man, I stripped to my linen shift and got into bed.

Music played in the Cattle Market outside my window. The Gypsies again, howling out a strange tune in their own Asiatic language. I wondered if my Mohammedan friend would be with them. It gave me strange comfort that he liked my poetry.

Chapter 19

I woke the next morning to Edwin sweeping into my room carrying a new doublet over his arm. "Lord Baldhoven was good enough to lend this."

The doublet was blue velvet, so deep to be almost violet, though not so much that I'd be putting on the purple of my betters. It was trimmed in silver lace of fine and intricate make, and would set my figure off to perfection, I'm sure.

"Do you need help with the points and laces?" asked Edwin.

In another mood, I might enjoy Edwin tying me into this lovely suit, but my head ached. I did not remember my dreams, but I knew Thomas Kyd was in them. "Been dressing myself for years."

I let Edwin kiss me, and the taste of that kiss was lust, treachery, heartbreak, and mint all at once. He smiled, blinked his pale lashes, and left me to dress myself.

Elizabeth was in the kitchen taking breakfast standing up, while Anežka laced her into a blue frock with a pale lace collar that set off the colour of her eyes. She ate a bit of toasted bread, leaning so the crumbs would fall on the table, not on her skirt. Her hair fell in elegant curls on her shoulders. Her only ornaments were a ribbon in her hair and the ivory rosary at her belt.

"Good morning, goddaughter," I said, with my best bow.

"G'morning," she mumbled at me.

"Where are your manners?"

My lady chewed. My lady swallowed. My lady glared. "Break your fast."

She inclined her head toward the table. I buttered the hunk of dark bread, which was heavy and dark like my clothing. It had more flavour than my clothing, though it could not quite take the taste of Edwin away.

Anežka finished her ministrations. Elizabeth dropped into the chair opposite me. "You are silent this morning."

"You're in a temper."

"My head hurts," she said. "Hurry up."

It was still dark. "It is only a short ride across town."

"We're expected before noon," she said. "We're to dine with Lady Polyexna and then dress for the feast this evening."

"About that," I plucked my sleeve. "Thank you."

Elizabeth leaned over and kissed me on the cheek. "I must say good-bye to Mother. Her head hurts too, and she will not get up. Come, Godfather. Don't look so dour. This is supposed to be a pleasure trip."

She flounced out the door before I could say something bitter. I went upstairs. Edwin had packed my few belongings. On inspection I noticed he'd included both copies of *Metamorphoses* and all Baldhoven's notes and ciphers.

I went out into the damp and foggy courtyard. Edwin had saddled Tantalus for me and Sweetpea for Elizabeth. Anežka appeared, dressed in wooden clogs and a dark wool skirt. She threw a heavy shawl unceremoniously around her young mistress.

Tantalus was in his usual ill temper and tried to snap the hat off Elizabeth's head. Elizabeth moved deftly out of the way. She patted Sweetpea's nose while Edwin tightened the straps. She looked every bit a lady as if the dress were new, the gloves and hat were in fashion, and the horse had not been borrowed from a servant. Anežka said a few words in Czech. Her brown eyes danced admiringly. I fancied she'd made the same observation.

Madimi waited by the door, dressed in a ghostly copy of Elizabeth's costume. I nodded to her discreetly. She waved.

Activity in the Cattle Market had stopped, so that all the nearby merchants could gossip about us. I pulled hard to get

Tantalus' attention. He had found a bit of juniper and did not wish to leave it. We rode through Old Town, where most people carried on oblivious to us. Two women looked annoyed by the way we took up the entire street. Processions like ours were unremarkable in Old Town. We were shabby and unassuming, parvenues. Condescension didn't bother me, but I could tell by the square set of Elizabeth's shoulders that she disliked it. Of course, she'd remember the regard the family once held. Her young eyes saw judgement in every face.

I wasn't used to the closeness of the winding streets, the way the buildings loomed overhead on both sides, so high and so very, very close, like Paris only more forbidding. How did anyone duck waste thrown out of windows on such a tiny road? Tantalus, depressed into submission, plodded forward toward what must have seemed a distant light of hope. It wasn't going to be the parklike expanse of his horsy dreams, but since he was behaving himself, I was glad he didn't know that.

The Charles Bridge's massive guard tower was manned but no one seemed interested in stopping us or asking what we were up to. They waved us on without even seeming to notice us. Tantalus quivered beneath me as the sound of his hoofs changed quality. He suddenly realized there was water somewhere underneath and balked. People behind me grumbled while I got him under control, but they were good natured about it. Who hadn't been cursed with a badly trained horse? Foot traffic flowed around us like water around a stone in the river. Elizabeth waited stoically, her gloved hands folded, while I assured Tantalus he was perfectly safe.

The castle on the hill above us had torches already lit in this gloom. The bridge was crowded with hawkers, walkers and people praying and shitting and playing dice. It was like the contrast between Heaven and Earth. The light above us, the treacle of humanity, the muddy river below. How the Great excel at theatrical displays of power. I suddenly found it sinister.

We moved more slowly through the crowd than I had on foot. The sun peeked momentarily from behind a cloud turning the river from dun brown to silken blue, but it vanished again. We reached the other side, with the mill pond and its angry swans, tiny houses hugging the water's edge. Did they disappear with the spring rains? I supposed the city burghers had a way to manage that. Then we were through the far guard tower and the buildings rose on both sides, higher than before. Mala Strana, the little village below the castle, was, if anything, more crowded, roads were thinner, more people were trying to share them. We were even less significant here. Other processions preceded us from elegant houses and foreign embassies, and we had to stop three times going up the hill. The castle became more sinister from this angle too. We never quite lost sight of it, but from this angle you could see it was a fortress, with men on the wall, arrow slits manned. It was decorated in swirls of black and white Italian graffiti that made it even more beautiful and menacing, like an angel and not the comforting kind.

I expected Tantalus to balk at the bottom of the hill the way he had on the bridge, but he clopped up the stairs, remarkably docile. He seemed to know his way up. He might well have been here before. He had been of Jahoda's horses and Jahoda no doubt brought him to the palace. Sure enough, once inside the gates, Tantalus headed straight for the stables nearby. He nudged Sweetpea out of the way, trying to get to the feed box. Elizabeth stayed on but looked daggers at me.

I helped Elizabeth off her horse. "Why don't you find our hosts while I see to the horses."

She shook her head and smiled, indicating the half dozen well-dressed grooms already taking Sweetpea's reins and gathering up our belongings. "We are staying in Lady Polyexna z Rožmberk's rooms," she said to the servants, imperious as the Queen herself. She extended her gloved hand to me. I gave her my arm. I kept forgetting that we were supposed to be high and mighty.

Soon we were seated before a fire in a neat guest chamber, with warm bricks at our feet, while anonymous figures attended to our belongings. I made sure to keep my satchel close by me, so that no clever hands would disturb my papers. This didn't inspire curiosity in the servants. I supposed they'd seen secret, Cabbalistic papers before.

In swept Lady Rožmberk, a few dozen servants, and a large stocky man dressed head to foot in rich furs. With a shock I recognized him as the gaunt figure on the scaffold in Madimi's vision. Lord Petr Vok z Rožmberk was not a large man, but he took up a great deal of space, simply because his movements and manner seemed to radiate around him like the rays of the sun in ancient paintings. He was rosy-cheeked and well-fed now. His thick hair and beard grew like a shaggy wolf pelt against the sweet rabbit and ermine he wore.

He and Elizabeth were obviously acquainted. She was instantly on her feet, curtseying in a formal greeting. They spoke in rapid Czech while he kissed her hand. Lady Rožmberk said something of an introductory nature, gesturing broadly at me. I stood and bowed low. The lord gave me a nod. He barked at a servant who stepped forward to remove his cloak. Another servant appeared carrying a large Italian-carved chair.

Elizabeth said, "He asks you to drink with him."

"Tell him I am honoured," I said.

She did, and I bowed again. The lord acknowledged me with a smirk. Then beautiful glasses were placed before us filled with a clear liquid that smelled like herbs, and we all sat down.

My three companions spoke entirely in Czech, and I was ignored like a child. Petr Vok asked Elizabeth questions. She answered quietly, formally, and very precisely. If I'd not heard her chatter with Anežka, I'd have thought her awkward in Czech, but it seemed maidenly deference came hard to her.

The conversation continued for some time. Lady Polyexna seemed vexed about something that the lord, her son, clearly thought he had well in hand. She told him he was a fool; that bit required no translation. Elizabeth sipped her drink daintily as if nothing at all was happening.

After about an hour, I became drowsy. I kept awake by biting the inside of my cheek. Lady Rožmberk suddenly addressed me in German. "My lord wishes to confirm that you spoke with Magister Kelley."

"Aye, Madam," I said, rousing myself. Elizabeth's eyebrows rose.

"Is he in good health?"

"The time in prison has done Magister Kelley no favours, Madame, but he is well."

She translated for Petr Vok. He seemed satisfied. He dabbed the corners of his mouth with a massive silk handkerchief and stood. We all stood with him. This time he looked closely at me, like a horse he had just noticed in the market.

"It is an unexpected honour to be your host," he said to me in Latin. Then he laughed. "Most unexpected."

Lady Rožmberk said, "Please, sit, children. I will return." She followed him out. Elizabeth and I stood there, stupidly.

"Tell me what Rožmberk said?"

She licked her lips. "He said he is about to honour you as few are honoured and wished he could do so openly."

That sounded ominous. I poured myself some wine from the lord's bottle. It was a great improvement over the vintage we drank at Kelley's house. At least my cage was nicely gilded. "And the rest?"

"State affairs not meant for your ears."

"The lord does not trust me."

She snorted. "You are a foreign spy."

"You do not like him."

"I do like him," she said. "But he has something planned and Lady Rožmberk does not like it. She accused him of provoking Emperor Rudolf, and he said, what is the point of living if not to pull that old goat's beard?"

"They are rivals?"

"The Rožmberk family is Protestant."

"I thought in this land, the lion lies down with the lamb."

"Not this lion and not this lamb," she scoffed.

I poured her a glass of the good wine. She rolled the goblet between her hands, nervously. "What else?"

"I...I'm to be presented."

"To?" I asked, stupidly.

"The emperor. Lord Petr Vok arranged it."

"Well...that's mighty fine, isn't it?" I asked, though clearly it was not.

"You are to escort me."

That took longer to penetrate, perhaps because the cold seeped into my brain from the tips of my toes in that uncarpeted room. "I can't."

"You are my godfather, and therefore my chaperone. You must do it."

The last thing a man pretending to be dead ought to do was present himself to the Holy Roman Emperor. Royden would have a cat. "Baldhoven can do it."

"Baldhoven can do what?" said Baldhoven, who came in, brushing leaves from his cloak. He carried a large valise.

Elizabeth grimaced. "Godfather has only just heard."

"There is nothing to fear." I'm sure he thought that true. After all, there would be nothing to fear, were I Baldhoven. "He's not really mad, remember."

He opened the bag he carried and pulled out yet another doublet, this one soft green, chased in silver. He held it up to me and looked at Elizabeth. "What do you think, Westonia?" Elizabeth took hold of his arm and dragged him down to sit across from her. "Baldhoven. You and Lady Polyexna have been plotting!"

Baldhoven turned rose coloured as he braced for his scolding. I was tempted to stay and watch, but I slipped into the next room. I found a richly appointed bed with heavy curtains and silky covers. I opened the window shutters, put my head over the sill and found myself looking down at Doctor Hájek, dressed gloriously in silver and black. I pulled the shutters closed before he could see me. There was another door, which probably led to a privy, a useful hiding place. It was a privy, though it did not smell at all. Someone had dusted it with quicklime recently. No expense had been spared for the comfort of Lady Polyexna's guests. A little vomit did no harm at all. It still smelled fresh.

I stumbled out and found Edwin. He held a dark red doublet and hose in his hands.

"What are you doing here?"

"You need a valet, of course," he said. "Anežka bade me come. You are to be presented."

"How did she know when I only just heard?"

"Women have their mysteries."

My hand shook. "What if I am recognized?"

Edwin grinned, brightly. "Wait here," he said, and left the room.

I pressed my head against the door. Voices rose and fell, and then doors opened, and heavy footsteps tramped off. Then silence. Just as I reached for my cloak, ready to consider the long drop out the window, the door opened, and Karel Jahoda entered the room carrying a large box.

"Well met," Jahoda said. He came forward to greet me, kissing me once on each cheek, and a third time for good measure.

"What brings you to Christmas Court?"

"Money. We're to give a performance at Christmas Eve, one I think you'll like."

Jahoda opened the box to reveal a clever set of mirrors, combs, paint and paste jewellery. Working together Edwin and Jahoda rigged me up proper, combing silver into my beard and just above my ears. Edwin tied my collar and gave me the mirror. I looked remarkably unlike myself. I could be my father had he been able to keep two pennies together in this life.

When Jahoda stepped out, Edwin touched my earlobe with his lips, his tongue just grazing my ear. I pulled away. I needed no stiffness in my nether parts, even hidden beneath the heavy, brocaded codpiece.

He fluttered his eyelashes down, and for a moment he looked at his hands. I could not imagine these hands caressing a prayer book. Then Jahoda returned, grinning over the snowy plume of an improbable black hat. "The ladies are asking for you."

"We who are about to die, salute you," I said in Latin.

I found Elizabeth seated before a small table in a nearby bedchamber. She wore a splendid gown of yellow silk, with feathers in the collar and seed pearls sewn into the snowy white ruff. Anežka hovered, wielding a large puff full of white powder and a peacock fan. The maid was splendid herself, in a dark brown costume that brought out the gold in her eyes and made her hair almost ginger. For the first time I could see the girl who'd ended up in the emperor's bed. Elizabeth reached out her hand. She wore a white glove embroidered in gold.

"You are a picture." I kissed her hand.

She wrinkled her nose and sneezed. Anežka picked up a small pot of red paint and began mixing it with her finger. "I look like a baby chick."

Anežka said something rude in Czech and waved me out of the way. Elizabeth placed her hands in her lap, closed her mouth to let her apply the colour. The stuff on her lips gave her face an even more childlike purse. Then Anežka handed her the peacock fan and retired, scowling with irritation, taking paints and puffs and accoutrements with her.

"Your nurse does not like me," I lamented.

"She dislikes Court," Elizabeth said. Her voice was strained because she was trying to hold her face very still, the better not to disturb the paint.

"Does she miss the emperor's favour?"

"To tell the truth I think she does." She tried not to sneeze again and managed to hold it in this time, but not without pressing her hand to the front of her bodice and getting powder on the silk. I did my best to brush it off so it would not stain.

"Imperial favour would solve many problems."

"A maiden does not put herself forward at the court of Rudolf II without peril to her virtue."

Oh. I supposed that was true. It was not so at the English court, but we've been led by females for nigh upon a hundred years. I remembered stories from Old King Henry's time though.

"I look ridiculous." She pulled at her yellow gown.

"So perhaps the emperor will not demand your favours."

"Yes. I'd drop eggs into his pillows."

I offered her my hand. She took it, groaning. We made our way down the steep twisted steps under the golden light of torches and joined our party in the hall. Lady Polyexna, in keeping with the bird theme, was got up like a peacock in green, blue, and gold, with a collar of silver feathers. Baldhoven's rank allowed him cloth of silver, which set off his blue eyes to perfection. Petr Vok wore a cloak of scarlet, trimmed with gold, ermine, and some other fur I could not identify.

Only then I saw Magister Kelley behind them, huddling in the shadows, earless, noseless, and legless, hovering by the wall in a black robe. Elizabeth made a sound like a strangling bird when she saw him. He shook his head. Her hand gripped mine, but she stayed by my side. She craned her neck to keep her eyes on him, while Petr Vok led us across the cold courtyard to Vladislav Hall, like a group of silver-feathered geese.

The hall was so bright when we entered, I had to look at the polished wooden floor. Dozens of candles reflected like stars in hundreds of tiny panes of glass in the large, arched windows that filled an entire wall. I was so blinded, I did not see the faces of the dozens of courtiers we passed through. I heard the musicians...a boy singing in Italian, a lute player, something with bells...and inhaled the rich smell of old wood and beeswax.

"Sir Christopher Talbot and his ward, Elizabeth Weston," someone said over the buzzing in my ears.

"Good God, when did you become my ward?" I asked, folding my hand over Elizabeth's tiny one.

"With your shield or on it, sir," she whispered.

I raised our clasped hands, and we strode forward. I could hear nothing but the soft thud of our feet on the wooden floor. The door to the throne room stood flung open at the end of the hall. We had to walk through our assembled betters to get there.

When my eyes adjusted to the light, I was deeply thankful for our borrowed finery. I had thought Elizabeth's costume very fine, but her yellow silk creation paled before the woman in the rose-coloured gown with the demi-mask of roses and ferns, or the man dressed in faun-coloured satin, bits of silver threaded in his coppery hair. Baldhoven's dark green doublet might as well be fustian. I looked dour as a Lutheran.

We were stopped at the door, announced again in Czech, and the throne room door opened. I bowed to Rudolf II, Holy Roman Emperor, but all I could see were the tops of my shoes and the hem of Elizabeth's gown. We posed for what seemed like eternity while Lord Peter Vok and the Lady Polyexna exchanged many words with him. Then Elizabeth pinched me, and I raised my eyes to his Grace.

Rudolf II looked like an apple doll, the kind my sisters would make in autumn. He was round of face and had shiny roses in his cheeks that were helped by paint. He was well-fed but the great ermine robes dwarfed him, until he looked shrunken. He had a crooked nose, a slightly extended jaw, and full red lips, but his eyes were sharp. They gleamed at me with light reflected from all those candles.

"We are pleased to make thy acquaintance, Sir Talbot," said the emperor to me in German. "It is our custom to conduct our business in the language of our people, but we have heard that the Czech tongue is unknown to thee. Thou might address us in the German tongue."

"It is a tremendous honour, your Grace," I said.

"We have heard from those who love us that thou art a ship's captain, in service to Walter Ralegh, the English explorer of America. Is that not so?"

"Yes, your Grace."

"Thy ships dealt a blow to my good Uncle, Philip of Spain," said the emperor. "He believes God's angels lent their breath to speed thy navy."

"I saw no angels that day, but I am not so near them in rank as King Philip."

Silence rang in the hall. Someone sucked in his breath. Elizabeth made a move as if to pinch me, but she did not dare.

Then Rudolf laughed. A shiver of titters filled the hall. Some were genuinely amused, others relieved. Courtiers were courtiers everywhere.

"Well said," he said. "Please introduce thy companion?"

I could breathe again. Elizabeth curtseyed as I led her before him.

"Your Grace," I said, "May I present Elizabeth Jane Weston, known as Westonia, poetess of my own country."

"We heard of this. A girl, versifying in our court. Pray give us a song, sweet English songbird."

Elizabeth flushed. She opened her mouth to speak, but no words came. In the corner of my eye, I saw Lady Polyexna, looking vexed.

"How silent is thy songbird."

"She considers, your Grace, how best to address you. Would you like a poem in the language of scholars? Or would you prefer a song in your native German?"

She glanced at me, panicked. It struck me I had no idea if she wrote in German. I prayed she could extemporize. She made a very deep curtsey and said something poetical in Czech that made the emperor's pink cheeks turn a shade rosier.

"The language of scholars is known to all assembled," said the emperor. "Give us a lyric in the Roman tongue."

Her hand tightened imperceptibly on mine, and then she let go. She stepped forward, dropped deep into a curtsey, and then stood. Her voice trembled not a bit over the Latin verse, although I thought it was a bit weak at first.

I pray you to be my Abidas, unconquered Caesar,
Be great Alexander to me, and you will be Caesar,
The former in choosing to preserve a hundred prophets
In his feast, won praise deserving of his worth.

The latter, when a poor daughter sought a modest dowry,
Settled many talents on the suppliant.
When Augustus Caesar generously rewarded the Muses,
This augmentation entitled him to be called august.
Thus, Caesar Rudolf, if you kindly offer support
To my muses, you do deeds worthy of Caesar.
May your provident mercy care for me, lest I perish,
And may your ample Grace shelter an innocent woman.
Let my prayers be heard by you, and the requests of a
suppliant
Which a wretched maiden offers with pious groan.
Thus there will be a happy victory against reprobate Turks
Thus you will be August, thus you will be blessed.

She dropped into a curtsey so quick that her feathers ruffled as she went down. No one spoke. I bowed too because I did not think it prudent to stand and stare. I had expected her to grovel, but this was majestic grovelling.

"Well done," the emperor said, into the general hush. "A girl who forms lyrics as God creates the snowfall is a curiosity indeed. We are fond of curiosities. Our menagerie is full of beasts from all the lands of the world. We would gladly keep thee amongst them. Thou hast such an appealing shape."

Elizabeth dropped so low I thought she'd never get up again. It could not hurt that the curve of her breast in the feathered ruff looked like an egg in a nest. She rose, trembling and pale beneath the emperor's gaze.

"Thank you, your Grace," said Lady Polyexna. "On behalf of her family, and my own."

The emperor turned his glassy eyes to her. "Yes, we had heard she is the guest of thy household, Lady Rožmberk," he said, coldly.

Lady Polyexna curtseyed, though not nearly so deeply as

Elizabeth had. She said something in Czech that sounded exceptionally courteous. He answered her in few, icy, swift words. Petr Vok stepped forward and added something that made the emperor frown. Elizabeth looked miserably at the floor. I pressed her fingers with my own, but she did not respond.

Then the emperor turned to me and said, "Thou art welcome in my court, Captain Talbot. Go. We will speak again anon."

I bowed low and, with Elizabeth's hand firmly in mine, we backed out of the throne room together. The door closed before our faces, with our hostess and her noble son still inside. We stood, panting.

"We survived," said Elizabeth in English, her voice weak.

"He did not seem so bad."

"He didn't want to cage you in his menagerie."

"Better there than in his bed."

"I doubt he hesitates to take pleasure with the animals."

"What shocking notions, my dear Westonia!" I kissed her gloved fingertips.

"As if you wouldn't," said someone behind me. I turned and collided with William Shakespeare.

Had Elizabeth not held my hand, I'd have collapsed to the floor with shock. Will looked nothing like the mud-stained, bear-smelling occupant of the Bankside I knew. He was dressed in scarlet and white, his dark hair soft and clean. In equal parts, I wanted to murder him and run my fingers through his hair.

"Good *Sir* Talbot," said Will. "I am Matthew Roydon, servant to Peter Leisuer, her Majesty's ambassador to the court of Rudolf II. At your service, sir."

"Your service, sir," I said. "This is Miss Weston...um...my..."

"Godchild," supplied Elizabeth. She curtseyed and he kissed her hand.

"You are a vision, Mistress Weston. The ambassador was most

impressed with your presentation. He wishes to make your acquaintance. And yours." He nodded at me.

"It is good to meet another Englishman."

"If you are with the embassy, I should think you meet many."

"But few as august as you...a knight of the realm..."

"Godfather—?" Elizabeth tugged on my sleeve. Her eyes were fixed upon a spot several feet away. I dared not take my eyes from Will to see what she was looking at.

"Quite right. Sorry." I said to Will. "Family affairs. *Master Royden.*"

"Be seeing you, *Sir Christopher*," he said.

"I have no doubt."

Elizabeth dragged me away toward the back of the hall so hard that my arm ached. "What's possessed you, woman? Didn't you want the ambassador's help?"

"Master Leisuer? He's no use. Oh, dear God, where is he?"

Edward Kelley had gotten into the Vladislav Hall somehow. The guards did not appear to notice him, or else believed stopping him beneath their dignity. Kelley looked like a pirate in the torchlight, passing beneath the glorious Italianate sculptures like a gnomish Orpheus stalking past Cerberus. He strode forward on his peg, expertly. Elizabeth started.

Kelley put his arms around her and pulled her close. "You must forgive me, Elizabeth."

"I will not," she said, from the folds of his dark gown. "How could you!"

I looked up and saw Hájek hovering on the threshold. I stepped back. If he wished to tear Elizabeth out of Kelley's arms, he would do it without my aid.

"I miss you," she said. They were both speaking English now.

"And I you, my Rabbit." His gnarled hands stroked her shoulders.

She stepped back, her eyes red and the canary feathers a bit worse for the crushing. "Do not call me that. I am a woman grown."

"You will always be my Rabbit." Kelley tried to smile. On his deformed face it looked monstrous. I do not think Elizabeth cared.

"When will they let you come back to us?"

"Easter, surely," he said, lightly.

Hájek trod forward, heavy with reluctance. He was a decent man, Hájek. I almost pitied him. "Magister Kelley, you should not be here."

Kelley ignored Hájek. He was occupied with pressing the feathers in her ruff back into place.

"Elizabeth," I said. "Come with me."

Elizabeth looked as if I'd spoken in Angolan.

Hájek bowed. "I will take the utmost care of your guardian and return him to your family in due course."

"Thank you, Doctor Hájek," she said in German. Her voice was steady. She curtseyed to him. She then curtseyed to Kelley, but she did not trust her voice to tell him good-bye. He did her a creditable bow considering the peg leg.

I took Elizabeth's arm. She shook me off. She turned and walked back into the hall, leaving us hanging there, three flesh gargoyles under the ones made of stone.

"Go after her," Hájek said to me, taking Kelley's arm.

I found Elizabeth by the windows, pressed against the glass, one hand on her side. The frost made bright diamond shapes in response to her heated breath. I touched her back. "You are very talented," I said in English.

She did not speak. Her ears went slightly redder.

"Your parents must be pleased with how accomplished you've become."

"You are not really my godfather, sir. You forget yourself."

I saw Baldhoven looking at us. I shook my head, hoping he had the wit to leave us be. I leaned against the window myself, enjoying the cold against my back. The room had grown very warm with the crowd. Elizabeth gripped the cloth of her gown with both hands like a sailor pulling on a line.

"You called him Father," I said.

"I hardly remember my real father," she said. "He...he is the reason I am anything at all, and to see what...Everyone at court...they're all jealous vultures."

I took her hand, and she squeezed mine terribly hard.

"I know, dear. Folk are vile."

"He must be hungry and in pain and so humiliated." Tears stood in her eyes and threatened to streak through the powder on her face.

"Be still," I said. "They're coming."

She lifted her head and willed it into calm as I turned to greet Lady Polyexna and Baldhoven.

"My dear girl, you are to be congratulated. The emperor is quite taken with you," said Lady Polyexna, her eyes sparkling like the jewels in her gown.

"Tis hot as the Pit in this hall," said Baldhoven, pulling at his silver collar for a bit of emphasis. He kissed both of Elizabeth's cheeks. She did not flinch from him, though she looked as exasperated as ever.

"Enough of that," said Lady Polyexna, "Now, let's to the feast."

I extended my arm. Elizabeth rose and put her hand on my arm. I conducted her to the banquet hall, ignoring Baldhoven's anxious clucks as he hovered behind us.

The heavy doors at the end of the dark torch-lit hall gave way to a much brighter room filled with long tables and light. Huge deer heads hung on the walls, and rich tapestries woven with exotic birds and motifs as well. On the high table was the largest roast boar I had ever seen, splendid with apples and nuts and pears. Its skin gleamed in the light of a thousand giant candles. The tables were covered in silver and gold and great bunches of greens for the season. There was a musicians' gallery here too with its own group of players. They were already hard at work making merry sound to bring us in to dinner, and they played loud enough so that we could barely hear the laughter and gossip around us.

Doctor Hájek appeared at my side like one of the demons in *Doctor Faustus*. I glanced in the other direction just to see if an angel would light on that side. "Captain Talbot, a word if you will."

I bowed, and Hájek bowed, and once more we had a right, proper round of bows. Only once we were almost inside the tapestry did he stop. "Please, come to the White Tower with me, Brother," he said in a low voice.

I glanced back at Elizabeth, but she was holding Baldhoven's arm, and he beamed down at her like a man blessed. She would be all right with him. I nodded and allowed him to lead me away.

Chapter 20

We descended a long spiral staircase. The air smelled foul. Someone had been working with sulphur and phosphorous... probably saltpetre as well. There must be an alchemical lab at the base of the tower. Hájek stopped short, put his torch in the wall and extinguished it.

"We go no further with fire. Understand?"

"Absolutely, yes," I said.

"Follow me close."

He did not slow down in the darkness. After several dozen turns of the spiral, I saw the slightest glow of red, a liminal aura around Hájek's back. A fire already burned down here.

"God and damnation!"

There was a crash. The light flared to almost daylight and went out altogether. I stopped. I think Hájek also paused, but I could not see him.

"Mišak? Are you all right?" he asked in...Russian? It wasn't Czech, though it was near to it.

I heard more crashing, and then a howl of pain. Then silence.

"Mišak?" Hájek called down the stairs.

A man's voice yelled in Latin. "Yes, I'm here, Hájek. It's all right. Just an experiment gone..." more crashing "...a little wrong."

Hájek ran down the stairs. I followed him as quickly as I could. I closed my eyes. It was easier that way. I felt less like I might fall. Finally, I felt the stone doorframe with my hand. A tinder sparked. I opened my eyes.

I stood on the threshold of an alchemical laboratory that dwarfed Magister Kelley's by the length of a cathedral. We must be several hundred feet below the castle. It had arched ceilings and books that seemed to go on into the sky.

I had a flash of vertigo. For an instant I thought I was in

Madimi's Library between the worlds. But there were no spirits here, just a ragged, dense whip of a man. He was all muscle and skin. He leaned upon an immense bellows, holding a rag to his bleeding foot. Bits of glass and crockery were everywhere.

Hájek picked his way through the carnage, holding a lit candle covered by a glass shield. "Let me see it."

"It's nothing, Doctor Hájek." He turned to me. "You. Tell him tis nothing."

"You're bleeding," I said.

"Thank you," said Hájek. "Now sit down!"

He pointed at a stool and the reluctant Mišak limped carefully to it. Hájek waved me over. I took the candle and stood over them as Hájek knelt in the wreckage and badgered his patient into giving him access to the cut.

"I broke the swan," said the young alchemist.

"Never mind that," said Hájek.

"I am so close. The elixir of life."

"Yes, yes, the elixir of life."

"Oh, you will see," said Mišak. "They'll all see, will they not?"

This last was at me. Up close, his eyes seemed a bit peculiar. Was he Gifted? He didn't seem to be, but I couldn't always sense it right away. I'd known Will Shakespeare for years before I caught whiff of it.

"You work with quicksilver too much. This will have to be stitched."

"Quicksilver? No..." he said. "Not that much."

"It helps the syphilis," I said.

"It does no such thing," said the doctor, prying open one of the man's eyes. "It simply makes people rattle about inside their heads until they do not know if they're to live or die."

Mišak grinned. "It does that. May I have the honour of your acquaintance?"

"Michael Sendivogius, meet Christopher Marlowe."

"At your service," said Mišak.

"Hájek..." I said.

"Oh, sorry," said Hájek. "He's supposed to be dead. So, hold your tongue Mišak."

Mišak, helpfully, grabbed his tongue. Then, still holding his tongue, he yelped as Hájek touched his wound.

"Captain Christian Talbot," I said. "Officially."

"Talbot it is, Brother. He is a Brother, Hájek?"

"Yes, yes. Stop squirming."

"I was so close."

"To what?" I asked.

"That's supposed to be secret, but as we're Brothers," he leaned over conspiratorially. "A little trick using saltpetre."

I knew I had smelled saltpetre. "To turn lead into what? Cannonballs?"

"Not lead," he said. "Air. The purest essence of air. You could be locked in a box, deep in a mine, and with this gas you would breathe as free as on top of a hill. It just has this regrettable tendency to..."

"Explode," said Hájek. "Where's your shoe, Mišak?"

"My shoe?" He seemed confused. "By the door, on the outside. Did not want to risk a spark, boot against stone, things happen."

Hájek looked up at me, wearily. "Would you look after him? We have to get this place cleared up. The emperor is coming down."

Mišak's eyes went a bit wide, but he could not move with his foot stirruped in Hájek's firm grip. "He'll notice the swan is gone."

Hájek surveyed the damage. There was quite a bit of damage. "He'll never notice."

"He notices everything about alchemy," Mišak said to me.

"Would that he paid such mind to the Estates! Help me up!"

"No," said Hájek. "You help nothing getting dirt and glass in that cut. I leave him in your hands Marlowe, and if he's stirred an inch, it is on your head." Then Hájek was gone, taking the steps two at a time.

"What can I do?" I asked.

"Broom. Over there in the cupboard."

The cupboard contained a broom and a dozen more candles. I swept up the remains of the "swan," an elaborate glass device with a long thin neck used for a complex distillation.

Mišak sniffed the air and assured me we could light candles. I lit every one I could find. It made the room as bright as morning. The alchemist had been working over an immense bread oven cut in the wall. It was fed by the main fireplace by use of the bellows that Mišak sat propped up on. Its iron door hung open, and the walls inside were the worse for wear.

"How many explosions have you had?" I asked.

"A few. You are an Englishman?"

"I am. You?"

"I am Silesian. Why are you dead?"

"The usual reasons."

"A lady?"

"As a matter of fact, yes."

"There is a beaker of slivovice in the cupboard."

It was unwise to drink on an empty stomach, given we were about to have an audience with the emperor. I thought ruefully of the feast I'd glimpsed. "I see a stone beaker with a wax seal, and a black beaker with no seal. We've no cups."

"Who needs cups?"

"Right. Which one?"

"The stone beaker contains quicksilver."

I brought him the black one. He took a long drink and handed it to me. I took one to match him. It made my eyes tingle. Bugger. This was a bad idea.

"I'm looking for Doctor John Dee. It is likely that he approached you about a spell."

Sendivogius nodded, vigorously. "Oh yes. Yes. He did. He needed men of Gifts though." He smiled. "I'm just an alchemist."

"It must hurt," I said.

He shook his head. "Take a look at this scar." He lifted his sleeve to show me a nasty ridge from the inside of his elbow to his wrist. "Got that when a pot of heated lead spilled on me. And on the back of my head is where I was nearly sliced apart by an exploding crucible. Oh, the swan!" He paused in his catalogue of battle wounds to mourn his lost beaker.

"I thought you lot transmuted metals."

"This is for the silver mines," said Mišak. "I distilled the pure essence of air, so that men may work underground in safety. And it works. I sealed myself up in a lead box for several hours once. I suffered no discomfort. I even fell asleep. But you cannot have light and the air at the same time, you see. Impractical for mining."

"What if you covered the light with glass."

"You either suffocate the flame, or you allow in enough air and...well...I must keep trying. To create truly pure air, I must make myself pure in spirit. That is the real secret. 'Tis not the art of stirring and mixing and setting things afire but tapping into that essence which is beyond all of us. There, that is your first lesson in the Alchemical Art."

"I suppose you alchemists make a practice of courting danger."

His voice dropped to a whisper. "Nothing to the peril the Gifted are privy to."

I suppose it was obvious he couldn't be Gifted. If he were, Hájek would have no need of me. Nothing compares to us. "What of it?"

"The stories you hear about the emperor's madness," he said. "The emperor follows alchemical recipes. He *wishes to be one of us*. But he is prone to the deepest melancholia. He will never achieve the Philosopher's Stone, no matter how much time he spends in the laboratory."

"Why not?"

Mišak leaned forward and whispered. "The emperor consorts with demons."

"There's no such thing. Spirits are notorious liars."

"Spirits wear the form our hearts wish them to take. What does it say of His Grace that he wants them to look like demons?"

"It says he has balls of solid lead," said Edward Kelley, come limping in from the corridor. "What happened to Mišak's feet?"

"The swan exploded."

"Another one?"

Hájek entered carrying a heavy bag and yet another candle. "You have the lights going. Good."

He put down the taper and began unpacking his kit onto the stone floor. Hájek took out a needle, dipped it in the flame, and threaded it in some clean, fine linen. He lifted it over his head and whispered a prayer in his own language. The only bit I could make out was a plea to St. Raphael the Healer. I gave Mišak the bottle, and he drank deeply.

Hájek turned to me and said, "Hold him."

I took hold of Mišak's foot. He only struggled a little bit. The blood had washed the wound clean, but the skin gaped round the cut like a woman's nether lips, all wrong and terrible.

Hájek made the sign of the cross over the alchemist's foot three times, one at his forehead, one at his breast, and one directly over the wound. Then he anointed it with a bit of the brandy, again making the sign of the cross. Mišak breathed in sharply. I reached out for his hand, and he gripped mine hard, until tears came to my eyes. Hájek sewed up the bits of skin as if he were darning up a sock, praying the entire time. The patient took it stoically. I expect he was used to all manner of injury. In minutes the entire procedure was done. Hájek wrapped the foot in cloth.

"You cannot stay here, drunk and singed like this." Indeed, Sendivogius' beard smoked faintly like a South Sea pirate's. "Our Mišak has views on the methods used to extract knowledge from magicians."

Sendivogius sat up and for the first time in our brief acquaintance he looked entirely aware. "He is interrogating Kelley! In this Laboratory. During Christmas Court."

It was not a question, and Hájek did not answer. Perhaps he was ashamed. Kelley shrugged. Sendivogius looked at him. I could not tell from his expression whether he liked Kelley or merely pitied him.

Sendivogius stood, balanced on one foot, wobbled a bit and then took his arm. "Will you help me up the stairs, Brother?"

Hájek knelt to pack up his implements. "Tell him I am bringing the Aztec refreshment." The doctor bowed and left us, the wounded alchemist on his arm. He was scarcely gone before Kelley asked me. "What happened to Mišak's feet?"

"The swan exploded."

"Another one?"

"He fears for you."

Kelley sighed. "He has a good heart, that one."

Mišak's stool was unbroken, and Magister Kelley claimed it; I leaned against the cold sloping walls. Being left alone with Kelley felt like being abandoned in a dungeon with a large rat. I tried to ignore him, but the human mind was not constructed for prolonged boredom. "You did well for yourself in Bohemia," I said, to fill the silence.

"Fortune comes and fortune goes. Let us speak of something

else." Kelley sounded weary. "Tell me of the Armada invasion. You must have fought. You're of an age."

"There was no invasion in the end."

"Yes. God intervened." Kelley snorted. "The greatest fleet in the world, launched by the most powerful monarch in Christendom, rotten with New World gold, sails on a tiny heretic island on a holy mission to rid us of a vindictive harlot with a mere handful of privateers before her and half her own subjects wishing her dead. All scattered to the four winds by a bit of untimely weather."

I blushed but gave the expected response. "It was a miracle."

Kelley smiled at me, ugly and half toothless. "What exactly did you do in the defence of your country? You studied with Harriot and Ralegh, did you not?"

"That is a Spittalfields pub rumour."

"I have not entered a pub in Spittalfields in many years. My information comes from an altogether more reliable source. Do you entertain the company of a certain spirit? Does she show you events far away and in other times? Have you ever been to the Library?"

Oh hell.

I gave him no answer. Never mind about Edward Talbot as was. In this version of the world, Edward Kelley was Gifted. Elizabeth had warned me. First, he was pretending, and then...he was not.

"The dice might have fallen any which way. You made them fall your way. A man blows up a ship. Another ship catches fire. A storm blows the remainder out to the North Sea, the meat is spoiled, the water is spoiled, the Irish are on hand to bash out the brains of any man who made landfall. Every single matter that could be left to chance, you made the dice come up sixes in every toss."

"God's blessing," I said. Ugh. I sounded like Roydon.

"You'd better keep Phillip of Spain thinking that. Imagine if he should know that it was Devilish Witchcraft all along. He'd raise all of Catholic Europe against you. And that is why you desperately need Ionnas Dee to shut up."

"You cannot want the Inquisition for England."

"I'm Irish, you ponce. And a Catholic. You did not merely scatter the Armada. You plucked a string, and the world was one thing. Now it is another. And now I am like you."

He wasn't Irish, not really. I wondered if he'd told the lie so often he believed it. "I am sorry," I said. I could not be more sincere. I could not imagine what it must have been for him, the walls between worlds crashing down at once.

"How do the Gifted live this nightmare," he said. "Liquor, sex, tobacco, mercury, nothing helps. Sometimes pain. That was the nice part of torture. There were moments when the body is so distracted it cannot hear anything or anyone. But then I'd recover and there they'd be, talking in my head."

"Did you ask Dee to help?"

"He thought I was Gifted all along so it was not practical to ask him." Kelley said. "Tell you what...you tell me how to work this spell, and I'll tell you how to find Dee."

I sat down on the floor. Oh, Anne, not even for you.

"You need something to bargain with," I said, slowly. "You've been trading secrets with Rudolf for your parole. You've run out of tricks, and its back into the hole for you."

He did not look at me. He rubbed his stump leg just above where his knee would have been. "I can still feel my toes. They're an insubstantial shadow."

"I cannot give you *that*."

"Christ's nightgown, man! England's been safe for years now! You know what I am up against."

"England is only safe because the spell is a secret. There is still a difference between what is rumoured and what is known."

Kelley sat back, his hands flat on his thighs. "Madimi says you style yourself Marlen," he said. "As in *the* Merlin. Come again at England's greatest need."

"She styles me that. Marlowe is my name."

Kelley hauled himself off his chair. He might have paced, had the floor not been treacherous with Mišak's broken glass.

"Merlin, Marlowe, it matters not," he said. "Dee and Harriot drew on a powerful symbol, an ancient spell laid down before the Romans, to protect the isle in her greatest need. And you and your fortuitous name, a holy innocent in their damnable cause. Do you remember both histories?"

"Do you?"

"I remember the world where the new star appeared in Cassiopeia in 1573, not in Canis Major in 1577," he said. "I remember this one, with the new star in Cassiopeia happened two years ago. It is already fading, the way it faded in the other world. But slower. Most people don't remember the change, but Madimi says the Gifted do."

I swallowed. "Yes."

"Madimi says the *stellae novae* aren't new stars at all. They are very old stars that explode when they die. Stars die all the time, which is why Dee and other men who mapped the stars found another stella nova eventually. So much for Aristotle's unchanging heavens. No, we're in Giordano Bruno's infinite universe now, vast, unending, stars winking in and out of existence all around. Has my wife forgiven me?"

"Beg pardon?" I blinked at the sudden conversational lurch.

"I suppose no. I bedded Dee's wife, you know." He added an enormous sigh, as if the sexual act had been an effort that weighed him down.

"Oh," I said. Better not to mention I already knew this story. I wanted to tell him about Elizabeth and Baldhoven's little code breaking habit. But I decided that was up to her. "Elizabeth only cares that you're alive."

It was the right thing to say. Kelley's chest puffed up. "Sensible girl, my Elizabeth. A tribute to her sex."

The door opened and in walked Hájek, carrying a tray with something rich and bitter smelling. "The emperor will be down presently."

"Praise be!" said Kelley. "Is that what I think it is?"

"The Aztec cure," said Hájek. "A delicacy from the pharmacopeia of the New World kings."

Kelley rubbed his hands. He removed the glass beaker from over a candle and put the small silver pot in its place. It smelled divine, and strangely familiar. The memory filtered in upon the fumes.

"It is a restorative, effective against the lingering effects of most poisons. The Aztec called it something that sounds obscene rendered into the Romantic tongues, so at the Spanish court they call it chocolatl. I have brought us bread to dip in it."

Hájek poured the dark liquid into a small earthenware cup and handed it to me. I had to admit it was marvellous, but just as I was rolling it across my tongue, Emperor Rudolf II emerged from the darkness of the staircase.

The emperor said, in German, "Thou art most welcome, Master Marlowe. Dr. Hájek speaks very highly of thee."

Master Marlowe. Not Captain Talbot. Did every man in Prague know I was not dead? I bowed, neatly, but not obsequiously. "The honour is mine, your Grace. Please forgive me for not introducing myself under my own name."

"We understand intrigue Master Marlowe." The emperor held a wide kidney-shaped cup, more a piece of art than a drinking vessel. The glass was milky green like China jade, perched atop a thin silver stem like a sail upon a mast. The gold base was a twist of metal ferns and flowers. Hájek filled this creation with the Aztec drink. He acknowledged Hájek's bow, ignored Kelley altogether, and settled in Mišak's chair, dusting bits of glass off the seat with his own royal fingers.

Once settled, Rudolf looked quite ordinary, round faced, with a spray of freckles across his pasty skin. I knew charity students at Trinity who looked more kingly. But he sipped exotic alchemical beverages from a gem-like chalice, as actors gulp sour ale from wooden cups. I wished I could show the Bankside actors this portrait of true power.

He smiled. "Thy true master is Walsingham."

I bowed my head again. "A good Englishman believes no man his master, but we all serve the same Mistress, Good Queen Elizabeth of England, your Grace."

Hájek smiled. I pleased Rudolf too. A thin smile graced his pale lips. "Doctor Hájek told us that thou studied the magickal arts with Doctor Dee," said the emperor.

"Doctor Hájek exaggerates my proficiency, your Grace."

"Thou knowest more than this charlatan Kelley, we wager," said Rudolf, flushing red. "Thou art an adept at least, more likely a Master. And, yes, we know thou art one of those who used the Hermetic arts to turn Fate against God's Holy Armada. False modesty doth not become thee."

Oh hell. Oh hell. Oh hell, oh hell. Did Dee talk to Rudolf too? It wasn't outlandish to think he might have. "Thank you, your Grace."

"Fear not," he said. "Whatever spells England's sorcerers wrought, though you called on Hell itself, was no more than our uncle deserved. We only crave thy help."

"But your Grace—"

"Leave us," he said abruptly to Kelley and Hájek. Hájek bowed and helped Kelley to his feet. They limped away, closing the heavy door behind them, leaving me along with the Holy Roman Emperor in a chill and dripping basement.

I suddenly saw him quite differently. Rudolf was trembling. His Adam's apple rolled up and down in his throat. Sweat broke out on his face. I could see fatigue around his eyes.

"My Uncle Phillip of Spain," he said, slowly. "We are not...fond of one another."

He was just a man, brilliant, but burdened. His person was a thin blade drawn between Phillip's orthodoxy and his own Protestant and freethinking people. It was a massive burden for his human frame.

Rudolf leaned very close to me, and his voice dropped to a whisper. "We are aware of a threat against our life. It will not come in the form of poison or a knife or any traditional assassin's tools. We have been plagued by a spiritual attack that has taken its toll on our soul. As one of England's great sorcerers, I beg you to give me a spell to fight this plague."

"You do flatter me, your Grace but I know no magic of this kind."

"There is an order of Capuchin monks who have sent demons from Hell to haunt me."

Of course, he could also be mad. "I am sorry, your Grace?"

"The spirits urge us to take our own life and...this is a very great secret...one night we came into danger of complying."

Rudolf was trembling. His Adam's apple rolled up and down in his throat. Sweat broke out on his face. I could see fatigue around his eyes. He was just a man, after all. I ached for him, as I would a sick animal. Any feeling person would. "How might I be of service, your Grace?"

His eyes burned with sudden hope, and he gripped my fingers

tightly. "Thou believest. Thou believest me. We had lost all hope of being believed."

I had seen spirits conjured before. Not for nothing did I write an entire binding spell into Act I of *Doctor Faustus*. But demons from Hell? If Hell existed, I knew nothing of it. Possibly some spirits pretended to be demons as Madimi pretended to be an angel, but I did not see any around Rudolf. There was no smell of the Otherworld, just saltpetre and sulphur and chocolatl. "Where and when do the evil spirits visit you, Your Grace?"

"Everywhere," he said. "In our private study, in the throne room, in the woods. Our hunting lodge is well protected, but we cannot be there all the time. And Hájek put a charm about our bed, else we would never sleep."

"So, your Grace needs a charm for when you cannot be in protected spaces."

"Oh no, Master Marlowe!" said the emperor. "We are done with charms. We wish to fight them."

I frowned. "Fight...the spirits? Your Grace?"

"The monks."

I hesitated. "You want me to fight monks? Your Grace?"

"Not with a sword. We cannot have the order removed from the city. They are under my Uncle Phillip's protection, and we dare not oppose him openly. Besides, distance is no object for a determined sorcerer. We must do to that band of villains what they would do to their sovereign."

"Does your Grace desire that I cast demons upon the Capuchin order?"

"Exactly!" he declared. "Drive them to suicide, and we will reward thee beyond the dreams of avarice."

I had no idea if I even could do that. It is no easy thing to have spirits do your bidding. To compel a spirit to torment a human soul until he is tempted to take his own life? If the monks included a sorcerer who could do that, he was stronger than I was.

There was a knock upon the door. "Enter!" said the emperor.

A swarthy valet entered. He bowed and said something in Czech. Rudolf nodded. The valet drew back but did not leave the room.

The emperor stood and extended his hand. "We are required. Have a good rest and consider my request. We will speak again anon."

He swept out the door and I was alone. I did not remain alone for long. Hájek had gone, but stairs being a challenge for him, Kelley waited on the landing. He stepped haltingly into the laboratory. "Are you all right, lad?"

"Quite," I said. "Are you?"

Kelley shrugged. "There's worse things at this court than being ignored. What did he say?"

I did not answer. Kelley gave me a knowing look. He poured me another cup of the Aztec drink. It was very good. It seemed to restore me.

Kelley took my arm. "We need to talk about your godchild."

"Sorry?"

"Elizabeth. Baldhoven says you intend to marry her."

"It's a cover story."

"Do it. Take her home. Her and her mother both."

"Why?"

"Did Rudolf tell you about the evil Capuchin monks?"

I winced. "Is he actually mad?"

"Would you bet your family's safety on the chance that he is not?"

I could certainly see Kelley's point of view. Broke, frightened, out of favour with a mad king, even I looked like decent prospect for a son-in-law. I couldn't set foot back in England with my mission unfinished. Still, he looked like a sick hound.

"There are difficulties," I said, slowly. "They are both Catholic and circumstances in England have—"

"No one cares about a woman's faith as long as her husband keeps her in line. Make her convert."

"She will not do it."

"Tell her I command her."

"Oh, that will work."

"Marlowe," he said, his voice rising sharply. "Please. I beg you. Please."

"All right. I will do it." I smiled. I could always smile through a lie. It is my own particular skill. "I will give tidings of your continued health to my future wife, Magister Kelley. She'll be pleased to know you were not racked tonight."

Elizabeth pounced on me as I walked in the door. She was alone, to my very great relief. I did not know how I was going to get the matter we needed to discuss around Lady Polyexna. She still wore the impossible silk dress, though the feathers looked bedraggled, and she had worn much of the paint off her face. "Did you see him?"

"Yes."

"Take me to him."

"Absolutely not." Her delicately gloved hand pinched my forearm. I plucked her hand from my arm and kissed it. I went to the sideboard and poured a cup of wine from the stone beaker there. "He sent me a message for you."

I could not meet her bright eyes. I handed her the cup. She held it in both hands and sat down before the fireplace. "Tell me."

"It is your guardian's most heartfelt wish that you should adopt the Anglican confession and marry a man in good standing in that faith."

Elizabeth looked fierce. "Never!"

"He isn't the first to suggest it," I said. "Lord Baldhoven also—"

"Oh, Baldhoven!" She sat, folding her arms and looking mighty put out. "I'm sure he thinks himself terribly clever to arrange my life without a by-your-leave..." She trailed off into silence. I thought she might cry, but she didn't. She just grew more tense and fierce.

"It isn't the worst idea," I said. Then I stood stock still with surprise. Why on Earth would I say that? Was this a compulsion? Had Kelley hexed me? No, not likely. He'd done something far worse. He convinced me. Elizabeth was in danger, from Edwin, from Rudolf, from simple starvation.

I put my hand over my eyes. "It is not the policy of the English crown to demand that you change the inclination of your soul. Only external adherence is required."

"So, I need not become a heretic. Just a hypocrite." Her hand twisted at her sleeve. For a long time, she stared at the fireplace, the cold light reflected in the diamond paned windows.

"He is right. Mother and I cannot go on as we are. There is no money, and what little we have left has been spent in foolish attempts to stay in the emperor's favour. I just have one question."

I spread my hands. "Anything."

She leaned forward. "Who is this solid Anglican my guardian wants me to marry?"

I writhed under her gaze for a few moments.

"As if I would marry you anyway."

"You could go far and do worse."

"You're a rootless beggar."

I grinned. "You mean to say bugger."

"Do not be vulgar," Elizabeth said. "I understand marriage of convenience as well as any women of my class."

"'Tisn't even your class, though, is it Miss Weston?" I said. "Your real father did no more bear arms than mine. And Kelley earned his rank and title through trickery."

"True." She had a slight twitch in her cheek. "Do you wish to marry me?"

I knew she could do worse. She was not my godchild, nor any kin of mine. But having said I would look after her, I no longer had a choice, not and know myself a man of any worth at all. "I would let you study."

"Yes, I believe you would," she said. "Do you have money to keep a wife?"

"I am still in the Crown's employ."

She was quiet for a few minutes together, long enough that I thought the conversation might be over. "Will you be allowed to write if we go home?" she asked.

"Sorry?" I said.

Elizabeth looked up at me with a truly clever face.

"Edwin told you the conditions of my parole."

"No," she said, tilting her head carefully. "You did. Just now."

I was ill prepared for her pity. I passed my hand before my eyes. I did not wish to show my feelings to a child. I could not bear it.

Elizabeth looked off into nothingness. "Can we not stay here, then?"

"I suppose if I wrote in another language, under another name, I might escape notice for a while."

"Escape whose notice?" Elizabeth asked.

Her eyes were steel in the firelight. "In faith, if you are to be my wife, I have to tell you everything."

I did not tell her everything, nor anything near to it. I said nothing of the Armada spell, nor Edwin or the Order of Merlin. But I did tell her about Anne. Anne, with her tempers. Anne who drank and swore like a man. Anne who fought my battles, who loved me when no one else did, and who was hostage to my good behaviour. Elizabeth listened and held my hand when the tears began. When I could speak no more, she put her head on my shoulder and wrapped her arms around me. We sat in darkness there for a long time. It occurred to me that as marriages of convenience went, this one might do well. But Elizabeth deserved better than me. Oh my, yes, she did.

Chapter 21

I woke alone in the darkness to Madimi sitting on the edge of the bed. *"Put on your cloak. It is cold out there,"* she whispered.

"Where am I going?"

"Over the drawbridge, past the moat."

"Lovely."

"You do not ask me who it is you are going to see."

"I know who it is."

It was past moonset, near dawn in fact. The morning star shone in the sapphire blue sky. I found Will Shakespeare on the drawbridge, overlooking the menagerie. Tobacco smoke swirled around his fair head in the torchlight. I bowed to him elegantly. "Master Royden?"

"You are alive," he said, smiling. "And you came escorted?"

Will pointed behind me. Of course, he could see Madimi as clearly as the moon. She stood in the archway and gave us both a little wave. I waved and turned my back on her. Oh, you never did know who would turn up at Christmas Court.

Will raised his arms to embrace me. I obliged him. "What are you doing here Will?"

"You've been compromised. I need to bring you back to London."

"You're working for Cecil now? Or Thomas Walsingham? I can't imagine the real Matthew Royden sent you."

"As if I would serve them," Will said, sharply. "I have information your masters do not have. The man they sent with you, Edwin Mooney, is a Catholic agent."

"I know."

Will looked like he might fall over the railing into the lion's cage. The anxiety I'd felt since Nick told me was a small price for the pleasure of Will's astonishment. I must buy the Mohammedan a drink.

"Oh God!" he pulled his hair. "You are already his lover."

"He was dying of passion, Will. What was I to do?"

"You have the worst taste in friends."

"And you know he is—"

"A Catholic agent? I'm absolutely certain," said Will. "You've known this whole time?"

I leaned on the parapet. My head was starting to hurt. "No, not for long. The information came from a source I do not trust. I did not want to kill Edwin until I was sure."

This seemed to surprise, even pain, Will Shakespeare. Stupid, Christlike Will Shakespeare. "Must you kill him?"

I put my hand on his arm. "If he's truly a double agent, I do," I said, as kindly as I could. "I need to know where your information comes from."

Will looked overburdened by the number of words he was holding back. He would not meet my eyes. "It comes from me."

"I won't commit murder over Bankside gossip. I do have some standards."

This made Will squirm. "You have to trust me."

"Are you about to tell me a fanciful tale of spirits and mysteries and witches and prophecies?"

"I was a Catholic agent in York, Kit," he said all in a rush. Only then would he look me in the eye, a face full of guilt and shame and fear and relief to be speaking a hidden truth all at once. It was an all too familiar expression but not on Will Shakespeare.

I started to laugh. I leaned on the ramparts, the cold stone feeling sharp through my doublet. Will frowned. "You were not," I said.

"I left all that years ago."

"To be an actor?"

"Yes, to be an actor," said Will. "It's more a profitable and sensible life than all that stupid rot." He broke off and put his pipe back in his mouth. "Cruelty and lies, for a few lines of scripture and an icon or two."

"You know it's more than that, Will. It's the riches in the monasteries and the power over kings and queens."

"King Henry just wanted to marry Anne Boleyn."

"A Protestant martyr," I said.

"And a witch."

"That was a Catholic slander."

"Anne Boleyn was Gifted, Kit. She was a much a witch as either of us."

It made sense. There were rumours about Queen Elizabeth, but none around the others in Old King Henry's brood. If she had Gifts, it was from the Boleyn line. They were commoners just as Will and I were, even if they were absurdly rich and powerful. Maybe all the witches tormented and killed through the years were Gifted, ignorant maybe and certainly poor, but no more dangerous than Will or me. Although come to think of it we were pretty dangerous.

"We spent the last hundred years burning people at the stake. Protestants burned Catholics, then Catholics burned Protestants right back. Families turned against families, friends against friends."

"And so, I should become an actor? Hide on the Bankside hoping that no one I ever crossed notices Kit Marlowe crawled out of his grave and is giving six shows a week at the Rose?"

"There are worse fates."

"I have prospects here."

"Elizabeth Weston?" he asked, cocking an eyebrow. "Does she know?"

"She more worldly than you, sir." I sighed. "She's not exactly new to spycraft either."

"The girl is Catholic."

"No one here cares about that."

"Edwin does. The people he works for—"

"Who?" I turned on him. "And don't just say *The Catholics.* The emperor's brother Matthias? Phillip of Spain?"

Will considered this. "Edward Bedingfeld...I don't know exactly who he works for but I'm guessing it's the Holy Inquisition in Rome."

"He's a Bedingfeld?" I'd guessed he was better born than I, but not that he was from one of the great families in the North.

"The third son. He met Edward Campion while studying at Charles University. When Campion died, he found his way to the seminary in Rome. They set him up in Oxford. I was his tutor."

Will at Oxford? Will tutor to the Bedingfeld children? He answered the question I didn't ask. "I did it to please my father. That was his idea, see, get a job working for a good Catholic family, do well and they would sponsor me to university. So I went up to York, taught Latin to young men of good Catholic family until they saw in me that...what is it, potential for greatness?" Will sighed.

"You didn't want greatness?"

Shakespeare shuddered. "Not that sort. Elizabeth is no Gorgon. Long as you didn't try to kill her, and they were all trying to kill her."

"So, you met Edwin...Edward Bedingfeld...in York?"

"Edwin came to me in London, claimed to be done with intrigue. I had no reason to doubt him. He didn't really have the voice for the stage. If he'd been a better actor maybe I could have kept him out of trouble."

Campion inspired an entire generation of English traitors. I could see Edwin – *Edward* – falling under his spell so easily. Will couldn't have swayed him from the Secret Theatre. "I give up, Will. I'm an idiot. Feed me to the lions."

Will, bless him, produced a pipe from the folds of his sleeve. He filled it and lit it for me. Oh, what blessing. Edwin and I had run out of tobacco days back. No, not Edwin. Edward. Edward Bedingfeld. I had to keep that in my mind. Working for the English Catholics? No. The Inquisition?

"Kit, Is your mission here about that spell?"

"What spell, Will?"

"Anne told me," he said promptly. "The one you and Royden performed during the Armada."

Oh, Christ on a donkey. Everyone must speak of the Armada this night, just to plague me. "You want me to tell you a closely guarded secret of the Crown?"

"You didn't tell me why I needed to hide her. She thinks it was the spell."

"She's safe in London then?"

"Anne is here."

I started. "You brought Anne to Prague?"

Will jutted out his neatly bearded chin. "Anne brought me. Did you think your sister the type of woman who wouldn't come after you? She is staying with Master Jahoda, the leader of the players..."

"You can't leave Anne with them," I said. "She's likely to get drunk and start fist fights with someone." And run into Edwin too.

"She's a better actress than you think," said Will, with an enigmatic look.

I remembered her the morning of the Armada, dressed as a boy, come to London Town to fight the Spanish. There were depths to Anne I scarcely knew.

Down in the moat, a strange beast roared. It wasn't one of the lions, the sound was too sharp. Will did not look troubled, either by me or by the sound. His stupid, Christlike veneer was gone for good. Will understood my world...all my worlds...all too well. Little wonder he escaped the attention of the Order of Merlin. As a player he would be beneath the notice of those who were looking for the Gifted. Like Anne. Men of power overlooked ordinary village women, unless they were accused of witchcraft.

I suddenly realized I was near to accomplishing what Madimi wanted, assembling a group to perform the spell. Will and Anne. Elizabeth was the third, I was the fourth. Edward Kelley, assuming he could be trusted, was the fifth. You never knew who would turn up at Court, Madimi said, but we were still at least one man short.

"Kit," Will said. "Do you think it's the Armada spell that Edwin is after?"

"No. Elizabeth Weston," I said, needing a mind that was the match of my own. "She received a coded message. He's been trying to help her translate it. He's managed to get it partly deciphered, but it seems to be double coded." Will looked up at the wall above us. A guard walked the length of the wall, carrying a torch. You could see the black sky lightening barely to dark blue. "This game you're playing with Bedingfeld...Is this the same thing you were doing with Richard Baines?"

"Shut it, Will."

"You've craved death a long while. Anne thinks it's about the spell, but I don't. This has always been about Thomas."

A red veil passed before my eyes. I left those papers in his house. I kept those notes in the first place. Thomas Kyd loved me well, better than I deserved, and I made him miserable and then I got him tortured and now he's dead. And yes, I have craved death ever since, courted it, the way I courted Edward Bedingfeld, a man who I knew would one night cut my throat while I sleep. Why didn't I kill Edwin the moment I found out who he was?

"I am weary of causing the death of friends. And

Edwin...Edward Bedingfeld...is still a friend."

"To me as well," said Will. "It's all right, Kit. You aren't alone any longer."

A soft joy slowly stole over me, smoking in the dark there. Will stood beside me. Anne was far, far away from Royden. Anne was safe. We could go away. Will and Anne did not know the maddening cast of spies and alchemists who populated my days of late. They never needed to. We could walk out of this city tomorrow. I didn't know where we would go or what we would need to get there, but with Anne safe there was nothing to stop us. To hell with Madimi and her spells. And perhaps I need not kill Edwin at all...

I smiled at Will, but he passed his hand over his eyes. He looked exhausted. I heard the whisper of a packet hitting the wooden bridge at my feet. "Meet Anne and me tomorrow. There is a large pub in the Old Town Square."

"I know the one," I described the place by the river I'd been with Baldhoven.

"Sunset," said Will. "Take heart, Kit. You'll be safe away soon."

He walked away. I opened the packet. I found a goodly amount of pipe tobacco. "Happy Christmas, Will," I said, breathing the honey sweet leaves.

Chapter 22

Sunrise pinked the sky by the time I slipped back into the castle. For a time, I stood at the top of the hill by the gate, looking out at the city, breathing the cold and the damp and the sour smell of burning coal. It looked to be a rare fine morning, despite the haze. I was too cold to stay out here indefinitely. I had to return to my rooms.

I should not have been surprised to find Edwin there. He sat in the rising sunlight on the high bed, his own long legs barely reaching the ground. His arm was wrapped around the bedpost like a sailor gripping the mast in a storm.

"What are you doing here, sweeting?"

He did not answer in words. He reached out for me and pulled me to him, one arm still around the bedpost, taking both our weight as he kissed me. He tasted faintly of wine, spiced wine. I knew this kiss was a drug for me, that its purpose was to stop me from asking any further questions. It worked. I accepted the proffered lust as the explanation for his presence. In truth, for my part, this was the only good-bye I could give him.

I disengaged from his lovely body, slightly drunk with my own lust. "You'd better make a fire," I whispered. "We want a good excuse for your presence in my chamber."

Edwin slowly let go of me, controlling himself with visible effort. I felt cold where his body left mine. I took off my boots while he knelt before the massive fireplace. He folded my finery into the press, hovering in an empty silence that begged to be filled.

"You were gone all night. Did you meet with Rudolf?" he asked.

"No," I lied.

Edwin yawned. I remembered that he had been up before me the previous morning, had no sleep and not much to eat. I should take better care of my lovers. I knelt before him. "May I take off your boots, Edwin, dear?"

He did not answer so I removed them. His hose was worn. Two of his toes poked through, both swelling with chilblains. Poor Edwin. His feet must have hurt all day.

"I should have taken the part of the servant," I said. I knelt up and began unlacing his doublet. He looked mildly surprised. I slipped my hands under his clothing. His skin was cold with sweat. He leaned down and kissed me.

"Close the shutters," he whispered.

I embraced him, Edward Bedingfeld, my lover, my jailor, the man I'd have to kill. I pulled his mouth to mine, breathing in the life I would take. He placed his hand around my throat, caressing my neck, shielding his eyes behind his long, thin lashes. Perhaps he too was thinking of the moment that he'd be forced to murder me. We both trembled, dying slowly together.

I pretended to fall asleep. It wasn't merely a matter of closing one's eyes, you have to show other signs, moving your eyes under your eyelids, making small sounds, allowing the air to leave your body slowly. Matthew and I learned this trick in Harriot's house. We took turns allowing the other one to watch us as we slept.

Remarkably it worked. Perhaps the Jesuits were less thoroughly trained. They rarely expected to be a man's bedmate. Bedingfeld slipped out of my arms and went to my baggage. I saw him pull out the copy of *Metamorphoses*, thumb through it, read a page and shake his head. He placed it carefully back in my bag, dressed quickly and slipped out the door.

After the cathedral bells rang Matins and he did not return, I got up, went to my baggage and gently removed the book. I could not tell exactly what page he'd been reading. The book was too old and soft to hold a place.

I locked the door and took a good look at the decryption he and Baldhoven had done. I set aside the crumpled pages filled with mathematical equations and turned to the translation. "*As a person in a vessel while moving forwards sees an immovable object moving backwards, in the same manner do the stars, however immovable seem to move daily.*"

Vessel referred to the Armada surely. England was the immovable object moving backwards...yes, a Catholic would say that. In the same manner do the stars...in a pattern...however immovable seem to move daily? Well, that was hardly clear, but the stars, however immovable...the stars had changed. Changed daily?

There was a rap at the door. It was Elizabeth. She bobbed a curtsey. I pulled her inside, locked the door again. I gave her the Ovid and the pages of notes. "I cannot trust Edwin any longer. Lock this up for me please?"

She gave me an arch look. "If I am to be your wife, I'd as soon see danger before it arrives."

My wife. I'd completely forgotten. I was entangled in thoughts of Edwin and Will, Anne and escape. And here was my promised bride, like a bucket of water thrown on my head. Elizabeth was not my responsibility. And yet I still wanted to protect her.

Elizabeth frowned. "I've come to tell you that you've been summoned."

"Summoned by whom?"

"The emperor. Are you going to stand there lollygagging all day? If Edwin isn't here, I'll need to help you myself."

Chapter 23

Hájek looked me over, approvingly. He took my arm and conducted me out into the hall. We walked through the north palace very quickly. My head began pounding in earnest. "Why am I summoned?"

"His Grace does not confide his whims to me." Hájek chuckled without slowing his pace a jot.

We went through the courtyard, past the cathedral, and into the emperor's private palace. Hájek knocked on the heavy wooden door. Nothing happened. He pounded a bit harder. Behind the door we heard a voice shouting in Czech. I needed no translator to understand: I'm coming. No need to pound the door.

"His Grace has quirks," said Hájek rapidly over the jangle of keys. "When Rudolf invites a man to his private rooms he wants to be treated like an equal. Yet never forget he is not your equal. He is very proud, so you have to maintain a clever balance between candour and respect."

"Candour and respect," I said.

"Call him my lord or your grace, never by his Christian name. And do not cross his valet. Phillip Langer is no mere servant, but Rudolf's favourite. He controls all access to the emperor." The word favourite had an emphasis I knew well. Langer was Rudolf's lover.

The door swung open. I recognized the sallow-faced man in servant's livery who bowed to us. "Master Langer," said Hájek, nodding.

"It is a good day, Doctor Hájek," said Langer. He looked me over as if I were a carp the good doctor had fished out of a tub for his inspection. After a moment he nodded.

"Good luck," said Hájek. He patted my shoulder and pushed me inside.

Langer shut the door, spoke a few words of Czech, and pointed at the empty hall. I took off my cap, smoothed my hair over my ears, and followed the wordless man down into darkness.

The corridor ended at another carved door, which opened on a surprisingly domestic scene. A middle-aged woman sat by the fire, winding yarn. Half a dozen children ranging in age from babyhood to youth piled upon someone on the floor, laughing riotously. The man sat up, and they fell over, laughing harder.

Emperor Rudolf II emerged from the puddle of children and patted his clothing into place. I bowed. His linen and collar were askew, he had no hat, and his doublet was pried open by fingers competing to tickle him.

"My lord, the fete," said the woman by the fire.

"Do not worry, dearest." He glanced at her fondly. "Get the children dressed. They will watch the festivities from the gallery."

She curtseyed to me, and then hustled the children out.

"We must apologize, Master Marlowe," said the emperor. "It is rare that we are able to have our children with us. We beg thy indulgence. Please sit."

I took the seat he offered me. Langer entered with a wide, kidney-shaped blown glass cup on a silver tray. It resembled the one Rudolf used in the laboratory, only scarlet and gold. The emperor raised his glass cup, the mate of mine. Langer filled it with wine. He did not leave, but hovered. I guessed Rudolf would ask the questions, but Langer would make the judgement.

"Have you considered our request, Master Marlowe?"

"Your Grace," I let the wine roll over my tongue. "What you ask requires study..."

Rudolph nodded. "You want money."

I leaned forward. He did too, hazel eyes twinkling over his ruddy complexion. The emperor enjoyed conspiracy. Camaraderie. Langer continued to hover. I lowered my voice, fixing my eyes on the gold fringe of the carpet just beneath his dark, polished wooden chair. "Your Grace, as honoured as I am by your request, what you ask might be beyond my abilities."

Rudolf shook his head. He leaned back and sipped his wine and exchanged a glance with Langer. Oh yes, they were lovers of long standing, but Langer had power over the emperor. Rudolf sought his approval, not the other way around. Langer nodded. Rudolph put his delicate, erotically curvaceous winecup on an equally delicately wrought small table. "I have something to show you, Master Marlowe."

Langer produced a small, black key from a pocket in his livery. I put my wine glass down, regretfully. I could taste the sunlight on the Italian mountains the grapes had grown on. Rudolf walked through the door indicating I should follow. I did. Langer closed the door behind me but did not accompany us. I was alone, wandering the private corridors of Prague Castle with the Holy Roman Emperor himself, God bless us all.

We met servants in the halls, but they tried to make themselves invisible, standing very still against the wall. They didn't bow or make any gesture of courtesy. Rudolph ignored them. He led me to a door, which looked exactly like every other door, and opened it with the black key. I followed him down the flight of steps beyond. It was a straight staircase, just wide enough for two men to walk abreast. Some light filtered in from slits above, and I could smell fresh air.

I expected to enter another alchemical lab, perhaps a dungeon, but instead we entered a large, cavernous room, which looked a good deal like Madimi's Library, only far less tidy. The walls were lined with shelves, and the shelves full of things.

They were most amazing things! I saw a massive bezoar, crowned in gold, the horn of some creature, perhaps an elephant, but the emperor assured me it was from a unicorn. There was a box with a top of stone inlay picturing this very castle, as if we were standing on the other side of the river. Rudolf said it was a gift from a Wise Man from the Sultanate of Delhi where all the palaces were decorated in stone inlay. Nick gave him this box. I placed it gently back on the shelf.

The walls held many pictures of naked women, and one of Rudolf's face, made up of ripe vegetables, a great pear for a nose, two apples for cheeks. A clock, more elaborate than any I'd ever seen told me it was almost noon.

"Welcome to my Kunstkammer," said the Holy Roman Emperor. "I come here when I need beauty to take dark thoughts away."

He asked me to remove a box from a shelf that was slightly too high for him, while he sat down in an ornate chair. I placed the box on the table at his side and opened it. The object inside was round and wrapped in pure black silk. My stomach clenched because I recognized it. Rudolf removed John Dee's obsidian scrying stone from the box.

Dee's stone was a good deal larger and heavier than mine. It was volcanic glass, dark as a starless sky, well-polished, and about the size of a fist. Rudolph steadied his right hand with his left as he held it aloft, allowing the candlelight to reflect in its shiny dark heart as he whispered the Lord's Prayer in Latin. I wondered if I was supposed to cross myself. Then Rudolf went on in Latin and I realized he was speaking words of conjuration.

I was about to tell him it wouldn't be necessary, but Madimi put her hand on my arm and a finger to her lips. *"He loves this part."*

"I summon thee, Angel Madimi!" declared Rudolf.

And as spirits sometimes will when properly amused, Madimi revealed herself to the unGifted Rudolf. She stepped into the candlelight. *"Your Grace, I am here."*

Madimi didn't look like a waif, as she appeared to me. Her hair fell back in long, auburn tresses. She had gossamer wings and wore a gown the colour of the sky at dawn. The Holy Roman Emperor took the knee to her, the candlelight reflecting in his thinning hair. I knelt too. If his Grace was making his obeisance, Captain Talbot better not stay standing. Not that Rudolf looked my way at all. His eyes were fixed on the point where her dress touched the floor.

Take the crystal, Madimi said to me, silently.

Rudolf still held the crystal, and he was about to drop it. I lifted it with both hands. God's tooth it was heavy. I had never touched it before. I could feel Dee's essence, like a fringe. Why had he left it here? It was not a thing he'd part with willing. Then I thought about Kelley's missing ears.

"Your Heavenly Grace," Rudolf said. "Is Christopher Marlowe the man you spoke of?"

"Indeed, my dear Emperor."

"He refuses to smite my enemies."

Madimi smiled. *"He is not a man inclined to cruelty."*

I felt very inclined to cruelty at that moment, but I spoke to the emperor, not to her. "Your Grace, any spirit who would perform such offices you request would turn on us once the job is done."

"The Marlen speaks true," Madimi said with a beatific smile on her face. *"It is not meet for one so great as you, dear Emperor to meet evil with evil."*

"But I must," he said, and he still did not raise his eyes to hers. "Madame, I long for rest, deep soulful rest. But this place that I am sworn to protect. How can I leave it undefended? In the hands of my hateful brother…"

"It is not the desire of Heaven that Mathias should take your throne. Master Marlowe can think of a different way to aid you."

I shook my head, no. No. No. No. She raised an eyebrow. The emperor turned toward me. "Is it true, sir?"

"I think with the help of this..." I lifted Dee's stone in my hand. "I might be able to control the demons you want me to conjure for you, your Grace."

The emperor climbed to his feet, placed both his hands over the crystal in mine. "It is yours, Master Marlowe, and I command you to use it in my good service."

"Thank you, your Grace."

He bowed to Madimi, who folded her arms, looked cross at me, and vanished.

Chapter 24

I didn't dare leave Dee's stone in my rooms. I wrapped it in a bag and carried it to the beer hall in Old Town Square. The sun was already low behind clouds. The air all around was a greyish blue when I made my way down the hill, over the bridge, into the warm, orange-lit tavern. I did not see them at first. I was so late. It wasn't unreasonable that they might be gone. But then someone clouted me from behind and I found myself in the embrace of a tall, blonde boy.

"You're alive," Anne said in my ear. It was sweet to hear the accents of home. I turned and embraced her properly. She smelled like greasepaint, straw, mildewing finery and animals.

They were eating pork and bread dumplings and drinking tankards of beer. I had nothing in my stomach but Rudolf's Italian wine. Anne and Will pushed food on me, and I did not say no.

"Did you bring your things?" Anne asked me, her mouth full.

"My things?"

She pointed to the bag at my side. "We planned to get you away. There's a safe house." Anne glanced nervously at Will. I felt a pang, watching the two of them telegraph wordlessly to each other. Some amount of intimacy had grown up between them that I was not privy to, natural but it hurt my feelings somewhat.

"Yeah," I said. "About that. A few things happened since we spoke last."

I explained what Rudolf wanted in English, with the thickest accent I could manage. They both exchanged another intimate glance. Then Will said, "Who cares? Just leave."

"After what he told me? He'll assume I'm off to tell the Inquisition. We won't get two miles."

"But you can't help him?" asked Anne.

"I'm not truly sure there is anything to help him with. Are there Inquisition agents around? Certainly. Inquisition agents casting spells on him?" I shrugged and took a swig of my beer.

"Is that so unlikely?" said Will.

He wore the face of the former Catholic agent, not the jolly actor. I spoke carefully, not knowing what he had told Anne. "The Inquisitors I have met take a very dim view of witchcraft."

"In England, sure," he answered, promptly. "The missionaries who brave Walsingham and his tortures to bring comfort to Catholic souls are the purest of the pure. But here everything seems a bit murkier. The lines aren't so clear, so sharp, between faith and heresy, inquiry and magick."

He was right about that. Elizabeth was a Catholic. Kelley was a Catholic. I wasn't sure what Hájek was. But the Holy Roman Emperor, great personage that he was, dabbled in the Mysteries. Why should I assume I knew where the limits were here? I stared into my plate of bread dumplings. I wanted to disappear. I did so very much. But go where and do what?

Anne sat up straighter and for a moment looked as prim as Elizabeth. "Why not do his spell?"

"What spell?"

"Conjure spirits and send them after his enemies. It's only fair."

"I thought you didn't like magic."

"When a man beats you, you beat him back. Or he'll never stop." She glanced from me to Will and back, flushing slightly. Then she went back to eating. "Do what he wants, he'll feel safe and let you go. Maybe he'll even reward you, and that will give us something to live on. Unless you have another source of travelling money."

"She's right," said Will. "It doesn't have to be real."

"Spells are just theatre," said Anne. "The spells don't do the work of magick. The Gifted do that themselves." She waved her spoon in the air. "He'll be comforted. You'll be doing him a kindness."

It was a rough understanding of the Dark Arts, but Anne wasn't wrong. Someone with no Gift at all could call upon the forces of heaven and hell, mediate for days, make sacrifices, wear out their knees with prayer and nothing would happen. Plenty of alchemists knew this. They spent their lives trying to achieve what Gifted folk like the three of us could do easily.

But Anne was also wrong. There is talent and there is skill, and even the most refined wizard was better off using a machine. A spell is that machine. A fulcrum, if you will, rightly placed can move the world, if that's what you want to do.

"You wrote a spell into *Faustus*," said Will abruptly, breaking into my philosophical reverie.

"That's not a real spell." He had to know the conjuration spell in *Faustus* was fake. Will Shakespeare probably had enough Latin to debate the Pope.

"It is a real spell," said Will. "Not the Latin, the English before it. You constructed it to protect the actor playing Faustus. 'Within this circle is Jehovah's name/forward and backward anagrammatized/the breviated names of holy saints/figures of every adjunct to the heavens...'"

"You're not supposed to notice that." I sighed.

"I'm an actor," Will said. "*Of course*, I noticed you set a ward on the actor. And then declared 'Fear not Faustus...' and only *then* let him blather on in the Latin. Even that bit's got *Valeat numen triplex Jehovae!* in it. May the triple deity of Jehovah prevail...You don't even mention the demon's name until—"

"All right, stop," I said. He was right. The anagram of God's name, like the anagram on the Charles Bridge tower, was there to confuse spirits. "Yes, I built protections into the dialogue so the actor playing Faustus could not raise anything real, in case Burbage cast a man who is Gifted."

"It's good enough to keep Ned Allyen safe before a London audience, so I say it should do well enough for the Holy Roman Emperor."

"I don't have the text with me."

Anne and Will both folded their arms over their chests. They looked awkward. Then Anne raised a hand. "I do."

"You brought *Faustus* with you? Why?"

Will and Anne looked at each other. Anne looked guilty. But Will said, "What matters is, we have the text and we three actors. Call upon non-existent spirits and banish 'em."

It wasn't a bad idea, really. Rudolf wasn't stupid, but he was open to suggestion. A few words in a foreign tongue, some incense, a little cheesecloth and we could probably convince him. Hell, it might do him some good, playacting the hero's part, banishing his own demons.

"Christmas night," I said. "After the Mass, when everyone is feasting. But then we're on the road before daybreak."

Anne beamed at me. "Jahoda's troupe is performing for Christmas Eve. I have to rehearse."

"She's very good," said Will.

"Yes, I am," said Anne, helping herself to the roast pork. "And I'm going to play for the Holy Roman Emperor. That's a bit more grand than old Queen Bess I'd say."

"Play what?"

She looked haughty. The part was probably nothing much. I remembered what Jahoda's shows were like. She was probably a country damsel in some clown show, dancing and showing her legs. If she was proud of that, who was I to argue.

"It will be strange if I don't perform," she said, with her mouth full.

We'd have to evade Edwin, of course. Elizabeth...I felt a pang for my sometime fiancée. But she would recover from her absconded bridegroom, surely. Baldhoven would help her, or Hájek. I ignored the pang of doubt. "Let me arrange access into the Kunstkammer."

"I will acquire what properties you need, and she will bring them to you," said Will, looking rakish. Anne giggled.

I handed the bag containing John Dee's scrying crystal to Will. "Here is the most important one."

I found Anežka on her knees by the hearth in Lady Polyexna's sitting room, building up the evening fire. I perched on a nearby chair. I did not fancy kneeling in the cinders.

"Why do you pretend to be something you are not?" I asked in Latin. "I know you are an educated woman, as much as Elizabeth, if not more."

She described my anatomy and my relations with my mother in exquisitely fluent Latin. She only stopped when I applauded.

"How many languages do you speak?"

"Go away," she said in English.

"Were you a nun?"

She shook her head. "I was a witch. But I was young, so they did not burn me. A kind priest brought me to Doctor Hájek."

"Are you still the emperor's mistress?"

She pushed her honey-coloured hair behind her ear, and I caught a bit of a smile. She began sweeping the ashes from the hearth with a vengeance. "Would you pander me then, Captain Talbot?"

I grew hot and not from the fire. "The fire is old."

She gave me a side long look. "The torch still burns."

I'd guessed correctly. "Do you know Rudolf's favourite, Master Langer?"

She sighed and sat back on her knees. "I suppose. But you must want me let into Rudolf's private rooms for a purpose."

I sat down on the fireplace, so that we were on the same level. Anežka closed her eyes and wiped the sweat from her forehead. I suddenly saw lines in her face, the ink and writing calluses on her fingers. She had played the servant so well that I honestly had not seen all the tell-tale signs of an educated woman, a physician, a Merchant of Light, in fact.

"I need the key to the Kustkammer."

She rolled her eyes. "Oh, you don't want much."

"Can you get it?"

"From Langer?" She looked thoughtful. "Perhaps. If I know why."

"You know what the emperor suffers."

"Better than you I suppose."

"I have been asked to cure him."

She shook her head. "There is no cure I know."

"Maybe not," I said. "But I have something I'd like to try."

She looked at me with piercing eyes. "If you can do aught to help Rudolf, I will happily assist you."

Anežka cracked kindling as if they were my finger bones, but she smiled at me. Yes, she was a woman who even now could be a temptation to an emperor. I sat down in the ashes on the floor and explained to her what I needed.

Chapter 25

I went to my rooms. I hoped to organize my belongings so that they could be scooped up quickly without being obviously packed. But Edward Bedingfeld was already there, waiting. He sat on the edge of the bed, his hands on his knees, tense as a man awaiting execution.

Having no idea what to say made it easy to abandon all thought. I went to him, put my hand at the nape of his neck and lifted his lips to mine. I kissed him hard, his lips both warm and cold under mine. His arms went around me, and we were down on the bed, everything, all plans and thoughts just lost in the salt of his skin beneath my tongue. I knew that as we crawled together in a cluster of elbows and knees that I wanted simply to say good-bye, and this was the only way.

We lay together after, bedclothes wrapped cockeyed around us, his soft bottom warm and round under my palm, shuddering with the ecstasy of proper sin. Edwin rolled over and buried his head in my chest, like a small animal, a cat who wanted attention, but only in this moment, only in his time and on his terms. He licked a spot just above my heart, which made me shiver all over. "You are the devil, Kit Marlowe."

"Am I?" I wondered if Edwin was an actual priest. Not all Catholic agents were, but one could not read the sacraments on his skin the way it was said that you could see a Devil's mark on a witch. It hardly mattered. This was the last time. Christmas morning, I would be on the road, vanished from world of the Great and Near Great, leaving him alone. If he would give up spycraft and wander the world with me, would I take him? I wished I could ask.

"Do you believe in the Platonic view of the cosmos, Kit?"

I don't know what I expected him to say but it wasn't this. "Beg pardon?"

Edwin looked up, his chin digging into my chest. His eyes were soft with something akin to love. But no. He wanted something. "God is in his Heaven and the angels below him. The planets, the moon, the sun, and Earth. Man at the centre of it all."

I felt uneasy. I was starting to suspect this was about the Armada spell again. "Who cares about all that?"

"You are a Mage."

"Not a very good one. Magickal arts require great spiritual purity. Picture me on my knees in a drafty tower." I closed my eyes and stretched out my body to give him a good look. He enjoyed the view quite a bit, but he was good at his job and not distracted overmuch.

"Can we drop the pretence, Kit," Bedingfeld asked, softly. "Tell me what you know about The Mohammedan."

I had quite forgotten about Nick. He was tracing little swirls on my skin with his fingers. "I don't know anything about him other than he hates you. Do you want to tell me something? Or is this just adding spice to your bed sport?"

Bedingfeld sighed and flopped over on his back. "You think you are so wicked, Kit. Some particular sinner. The truth is you're an innocent."

"Oh?" I had been called many things before but not an innocent. "In case sweet Matthew left you any doubt, I am being compelled to betray John Dee, a friend, through threats to my sister. How innocent is that?"

"So why not help me instead?"

"With what?"

"Magicians," he said, nearly spitting the word. "The Merchants of Light and Order of Merlin. They are trying to disrupt the natural order of things. Wicked people with a demonic agenda. You are their victim."

Victim. That was a stranger word for me than innocent. I had never seen eyes so naked, as naked as his body, as naked in some ways as I suspect Edward Bedingfeld had ever been. He didn't know that the Merchants and the Order of Merlin did not share the same goals. He was fishing. What in the hell did he want?

I should have left him at this moment. But Bedingfeld understood me better than I liked. The truth was—oh dear God—I was curious, and curiosity was the one true failing of my character.

"All right," I said. "Let's talk."

We sat together at a small table, a bottle of wine between us. Edward Bedingfeld looked neat in shirt and hose. God alone knew what I looked like. I was cold without a doublet, but I felt the need to match him, to make him feel as much as possible as if he were looking in a mirror. It was an old provocateur's trick, but who knew which of us was using it on the other. I took a sip of the sweet, fortified wine, turning the wooden cup in my hand as if I sought wisdom in its depths. I placed the cup on the table, as if I were placing a chess piece on a board, and cultivated a thoughtful look, with just the slightest look of evasion.

"I was a prisoner of the Order of Merlin and I detest them." Start with a truth. Walsingham's training prevailed.

"I know." He sounded sympathetic, but he was, after all, an actor. He waited for me to fill the silence, and I paused just long enough to suggest the trick worked.

"I was born with the Gift or if you will the Curse. Some say it runs in families."

"Satan tempted you," prompted Bedingfeld.

"Spirits spoke to me of power, heresy, wealth, fame, and renown. They whispered to me of the Heretic Queen, her beauty and her immorality. And of the unnatural uses of men with men."

I couldn't resist looking directly into his eyes. I had no idea if demons whispered to him of my body and the bodies of others, but I did know he burned.

He could not meet my gaze. He crossed his legs and folded his hands over his knee. "Do you abjure your loyalty to Hell?"

"I do," I said.

"I understand," he said. "I am quite like you."

I raised an eyebrow, pretending to misunderstand. "You have Gifts?"

Again, he wouldn't quite meet my gaze. "No. But temptations, yes. Not just of the body, but for the other uses of the world. Original sin was not a desire for the flesh, but for knowledge. The knowledge of good and evil."

"Fruit from the forbidden tree," I whispered.

"You tried to leave the Secret Theatre, become a poet like Master Shakespeare bade you. But Master Royden put aside the mask of friendship and locked you in a tower."

That was an accurate view of both Will and Matthew. I placed my hands on the table between us. The best, most delicious lies were the absolute truth. "I cannot bear my position any longer."

"What would you do, if you were free to serve your own desire?"

"I do not know." Also true. I flushed with shame. I'd been a Queen's man my entire adult life. It struck me that Anne would agree with Bedingfeld's assessment of my situation. Where could I go? I could hardly go back to Cambridge and study theology. I would make a poor alchemist. The life of a common actor was no refuge...

"Kit?" Bedingfeld asked.

"Sorry." I did after all just miss my line. "If I could only find a true cause to serve—"

"I can protect your sister," he said, quickly.

I feigned surprise. "Is that possible?"

"Powerful friends would protect her, were you sworn to their service."

I was abruptly, shockingly angry. Bedingfeld offered me the same bargain Royden had. Serve my cause in exchange for your sister's life. Only knowing her safe kept me from choking the lovely Master Bedingfeld to death. I swallowed hard. I let my hands tremble. He would think it was fear or desire, not rage.

"I would do anything for Anne." It was, again, the absolute truth.

Edward Bedingfeld's pale lashes caught the light, like a golden fringe. "My mission does not interfere with Her Majesty's interests. My target is quite different."

"The Mohammedan."

"Yes."

"Why does he want to kill you?" I asked.

The look in his eyes was truly terrifying. He looked like an actual Jesuit, fanatical as the poor bastards I'd seen tormented in Walsingham's prison. "He serves a foreign prince. A corrupt man who has strayed from the purity of his faith just as the madman Emperor Rudolf has."

"Murad III?" I asked, blandly.

"Akbar of Delhi."

I tried to look shocked. "What on Earth does he want with you?"

"There is a battle for the soul of all of Christendom. Some of the Children of our Lord Jesus Christ have turned against the faith but to have an outsider...a Muslim...interfere in our affairs...we must destroy him."

He had broken out in a sweat. I wondered if I would give the game away if I didn't react to that. "How is the Sultan's man interfering with all of Christendom?"

"Kit, do you really think this move throughout Europe toward questioning and alchemy is the organic working of sin? The Merchants are not a Christian organization. They are Muslims, infidels, outsiders. They have corrupted the English, and they are corrupting the Holy Roman Emperor. They consort with devils and turn princes away from their rightful work."

"Which is?" I asked, all innocence.

I honestly thought he'd say something mealy-mouthed about fighting the Turks. He knew me as a Protestant agent, however nominally. But love made him lose his reason or maybe it was just hope that he had found a friend, a partner in more than bed sport. "Purge heresy and return Europe to the true Church." Edward Bedingfeld smiled, joyfully unmasked at last. There it was. He had confessed he was a Catholic sympathizer.

I was suddenly afraid. This had to be a trap. He gripped my hand, and I felt the sweat of his palms. I pulled his hand to my lips and kissed the salt of him. He was in danger if he misjudged me. And he had. I drained my cup. The fire of the wine gave my eyes the flint he hoped for. "What must I do?"

He withdrew his hand from mine and placed it on my bent head. Oh, dear Lord, we were going to have less sex and more praying from here on. "Swear to me by the God we both love to serve the Holy Church."

"By the God we both love?" He could not be this stupid. He knew such an oath from me meant nothing.

"You are like me," he whispered. "I've known it since I saw your *Faustus*. A man searching for forbidden knowledge, cut off from God. The demon tells him that he carries Hell inside him wherever he goes. I knew you understood me."

How right he was and how wrong. He thought I suffered over my unnatural urges or separation from God, not because Thomas was arrested, and it was my fault. Bedingfeld cradled my head in his hands. "It is all right, my dear," he murmured. "You are only a man. If you come to Him with a repentant heart, God will forgive you."

No doubt he thought he had reached me. He could not know that I had loved Thomas tenderly. Separation from God's favour was as close as he'd ever imagined to a broken heart. His embrace felt like clasping a statue. Thomas was foolish and disapproving but warm, gentle, soft. Edward Bedingfeld was a graven image. Thomas loved me. I was an instrument of Bedingfeld's damnation.

I pulled away. Let him think he had turned me. I allowed the tears to fringe my eyelashes, so that he would see them and not my eyes. "I am yours to command."

"Elizabeth Weston's Polish lover—That doggerel we translated has meaning. You will discover it for me."

I glanced up. He looked serene, smug even. "If I do this, you will give me absolution?"

"I will arrange your confession. Full reconciliation with the Church, our Mother. Full admission into the society of the faithful."

"Because this message is so dangerous?"

"It is."

"To Prince Matthias?" I asked. "King Phillip of Spain?"

"To God," he said.

"You want me to spy on Elizabeth Weston."

"She is a good Catholic. Once she is your wife you can control her." Then, with no trace of irony, he kissed me. I found myself detached, puzzled. How could a creature with this little imagination and understanding of his fellow human beings fare so successfully in the Secret Theatre? I licked my lips. "When can I meet your confessor?"

"This afternoon." His excitement was palpable. "Then you too will live forever in Our Lord's perpetual blessing."

"God be praised," I made myself say.

Edward Bedingfeld beamed and recited a prayer in Latin. Great. I think he really was a priest.

Chapter 26

After he left, I went to find Elizabeth. She was eating breakfast with Lady Polyexna. Our hostess stood. "We were pleased to hear the wonderful news. Congratulations on your upcoming marriage, Captain Talbot."

I bowed. "Thank you, my lady."

She cupped Elizabeth's chin with her hand. "Make certain you rest this afternoon. No one sleeps much on Christmas Eve."

Christmas Eve. Christmas Eve already.

Elizabeth curtseyed as the Lady left. She pushed me gently into a chair before the fire and poured me a glass of something that tickled my nose before it touched my lips. It tasted like herbs and glory. "What has happened?"

"I need you to trust me, Sister, with your true mission at this Christmas Court. It is more than simply seeing Edward Kelley, isn't it?"

Elizabeth looked into the fire. "I would rather not say."

"May I try to guess?"

She looked guarded, but she nodded.

"You and the Silesian Lordling who adores you in a pure and godly way are working with messengers from the court of Akbar the Great to help Rudolf's alchemists communicate with his. You are using the book cipher left in your house to decode messages, but you need to decipher the riddle within a code..."

"It isn't a riddle," said Elizabeth. "It's a translation of a quote from the astronomer Aryabhata who observed the movement of stars over a thousand years ago."

"I don't understand."

She took my cup from me. "*As a person in a vessel while moving forwards sees an immovable object moving backwards, in the same manner do the stars, however immovable seem to move daily.* This cup is the boat. I am sitting on the boat. You are on the shore of a great river." She put her finger on the lip of the cup and started to move the cup from one side to the other.

"I still don't understand."

"Stars only seem to move. It's the Earth that moves."

I blinked. "But Ptolemy—"

"The Church decided Ptolemy was correct a thousand years ago and no one was allowed to contradict him. Now we look at the stars for ourselves. And the Church says we must not see what we see."

I gently took cup out of her hand. This barely marriageable girl was speaking truths learned men had been put to death for. "What has this to do with you?"

"I am meeting a man who is interested in Aryabhata. This confirms that his observations have been shared by scholars in other parts of the world."

"Elizabeth. You must know you are in danger."

"Not at all," she said. "Not in Rudolf's Court. A simple meeting at Christmas Court. No one will notice."

My mouth grew dry. "The Inquisition knows about you."

She scoffed "What, you mean Klesl? He's not—"

"I mean Edwin."

"Edwin is the Inquisition?" She looked grave. "He's seen the ciphers. He knows about the book code."

"You must warn Baldhoven," I said. "And you and I should leave."

Elizabeth looked scornful. "No."

"I command it."

She pursed her lips. "Have a care, Master Marlowe. We're not married yet. This is my home. I have powerful friends here."

I opened my mouth to protest and then closed it again. She

was right. Only anonymity made the open road safer than this Court. Elizabeth had no practice blending into the common people. Nothing in her life would prepare her for that sort of disappearance.

"You work for Nikhil of Delhi?"

I must have sounded condescending instead of frightened. She lifted her chin and looked cross. "I work for the truth. Why don't you, Kit Marlowe? You're a Merchant, aren't you?"

Had things gone a different way, this woman would have made an extraordinary wife. I felt the cords of obligation surrounding me. Edwin's cords, Rudolf's, and now Elizabeth's. The open road beckoned, and I couldn't be further from taking it.

"What would you have me do?" I asked.

She smiled. "Come sit for a portrait."

The last thing a dead man ought to do, was have his portrait painted, but there were things Elizabeth could do on my arm that would be inappropriate without me. There were artists who painted portraits of gentlemen in Vladislav Hall, doing simple sketches for vain men waiting for an audience. It wasn't strange for an affianced lady and gentleman to order a portrait together.

Elizabeth and I walked arm in arm into the Hall at mid-day. The place was decorated for Christmas, but it was still a working day at Court, with men with business with the emperor standing and sitting wherever there was room.

The painter she chose had a lean and hungry look and was clearly not one of the first rank of painters. His scribbles were rough, which was a relief. A dead man doesn't need a good likeness. I asked his rates, and while he answered my questions, his eyes drifted toward Elizabeth. They clearly knew one another. He agreed to come to our rooms for a sitting, but there was something about his hands that seemed odd. They were stained with ink, not paint.

"Our contact?" I asked Elizabeth, back in our rooms. "He's no painter."

"He is in disguise."

There was a knock, and she answered the door. The young man dragged his artist's easel into the room. He tried to bow, dropped his paint box, and his hat fell off his head. "How are you, Westonia?"

Elizabeth picked up his hat. "Have you eaten?"

"I ate yesterday. Do you have the message?"

I went to the table where some apples sat in a dish and offered him one. The stranger sat down and munched on it gratefully. Elizabeth brought the pages with the words Baldhoven had deciphered and placed them in his hand. He dropped the apple on the floor as he stared at them.

"They have known this in Hindustan for how long?"

"Four hundred years after the birth of Christ."

"So long ago!" He rubbed his hand over his beard. The juice from the abandoned apple smeared on his face, but he did not care. He held the page as if it were precious.

"May I ask its significance?"

The artist-who-wasn't-an-artist glanced at Elizabeth, and she nodded. "Are you familiar with the heretical text *De revolutionibus orbium coelestium?*"

"On the Revolutions of Heavenly Spheres?" I asked. Thomas Harriot had that in his house. I'd glanced at the pages but never read it.

The stranger nodded vigorously. "You understand in this era where Giordano Bruno is jailed for his thoughts that we have to be enormously careful."

"I am not an astrologer."

He carefully placed the paper on the blue brocaded sofa fished the apple off the floor. He took a bite. "Right, so Ptolemy's view of the universe, as every educated man in Christendom knows, is that the Earth is the centre of the universe and all the planets and stars and moons and everything in the cosmos just goes around and around the earth."

"I know."

"Except it doesn't!" he nearly shouted, and then modified his voice. "It...probably doesn't. It might not. There are those of us that believe that Copernicus is right and the Sun, the symbol of the Lord God himself, is the true centre. Some Arab mathematicians have suggested this and now...the Mughal Empire! A thousand years before the Arabs, this man Arya—how you say?" He looked at Elizabeth.

"Aryabhata," said Elizabeth, pronouncing the name it in a way that reminded me of Nick.

"For one thousand years, since the death of Hypatia of Alexandria, Christendom has been trapped in a Dark Age of inquiry. We are permitted moral questions, philosophical questions, how many angels dance on pinheads, but we cannot question Church-approved texts because if they are wrong about the natural world, they might be wrong about—"

"Master Kepler, please," said Elizabeth. "You are shouting."

He calmed himself. "Forgive me. Can I trouble you for some beer?"

She went out of the room, leaving me with this very young man, chewing his apple and staring into the fire. The pages with the thrilling words from Delhi sat next to him, unremarked. They blazed in front of his eyes.

Young Master Kepler shook his head. "You are Christopher Marlowe."

I sat on the stool by the fire. Everyone must know. "I am."

We sat in silence. I wondered if I was about to hear another critique of my plays. But after he chewed the apple down to the seeds, Kepler asked something unexpected. "Do you remember the *stella nova* in Cassiopeia as Elizabeth does?"

I started. Of course, he was Gifted. That was hardly a shock since he was one of the Merchants. "You must have been a child when that happened?"

"It is one my first memories of my mother," Kepler said. "She pointed it out to me. She was always working, drying herbs, shelling peas, but she knew stars and eclipses, taught me everything there was to know about the Firey Trigon...." he trailed off, staring into nothing. "She cannot remember this now. When the star appeared in Cassiopeia again two years ago, she scarcely looked at it. As if she had been cut off from the part of her mind that cared."

I shuddered, gooseflesh pricking my arms. "You are Gifted. She is not."

Kepler sighed heavily. "People say she is a witch, but she just knows what everyone knows. She only knows it better." He looked at me sidelong. "My mother is brilliant. She remembers every sick sheep and child's winter illness. But she can't remember that. What happened to her?"

He spoke with raw grief, as if his real mother was lost to him. I had no apology adequate to the crime. It was on the tip of my tongue to say I envied him. A bond of mind and heart was beyond my experience. I thought of Edward Kelley, doors to the Otherworld flinging open as we performed the spell. "Was she Gifted before?"

"It would explain the witchcraft rumours,'" he said. "I assume most accused witches are Gifted if they're not just victims of slander. I keep my real thoughts under a bucket all the time. Our Gifts are a lonely thing." He tapped his head with his fist still clutching his apple core.

I realized suddenly we had six Gifted. Will, Anne, Elizabeth, myself, Kelley if he could be trusted, and now young Master Kepler. We could perform the Armada spell if we wanted. That felt heavy and dangerous.

When he was gone, Elizabeth dropped onto the chair next to mine. "Anežka told me that you had a plan to help Rudolf. A counter-spell to save him from madness."

"It's not really much of a counter-spell."

"Let me help you," she said. "Who knows, maybe he'll find a way to expel the Inquisition."

"I doubt that."

"What spell is it?"

"Stagecraft, mostly," I said.

"If it works, could we stay in Prague?"

"I don't know."

"Would it prevent the future that Madimi keeps showing us?"

"I don't know."

"But I can help?"

I took her hand in mine. "Of course, you can help."

I told myself as I wandered the courtyard that cold morning, strictly speaking Elizabeth was not my problem. She was nearly an adult woman. I knew intelligencers younger than she, but it was not a life I wished on anyone. Thoughts of what could happen to her without the protection of marriage troubled me. I needed to make some provision for Elizabeth.

As I strode between the cathedral and Vladislav Hall, I saw a member of the Romany band sitting on the church steps, playing a pipe. The obvious answer came to mind: Nick.

Dee could get to India because the Turks let Gypsy traders cross battle lines. How else? It was no easy journey. I scratched my head, as if the pressure would bring Ortellius' atlas in front of my eyes. I studied it closely while writing the second *Tamburlaine* play. Timur the Lame invaded Delhi, the Mughals descend from him.

Nick...Nikhil...would not take me to India, no. He did not trust me. But if Nick could take Dee to India, he could do the same for Elizabeth.

I approached the musician. He had a small, red hat at his feet, with a few coins in it. He had a moustache identical to Nick's. Indeed, he looked a good deal like Nick. I wondered if he was Roma at all, or if he too was an agent of Akbar.

"I am a friend of Nick," I said, in awkward Czech.

He left off playing his pipe long enough to say, "I know no Nick." He went back to playing, but his eyes were on me.

I leaned over and whispered, "The fire is old," in Latin.

He nodded and pointed to his hat. "Still, it burns," he said in Czech, glancing up at the passers-by.

I saw Melichor Klesl. He wasn't looking at us; what we were doing probably didn't merit his attention. I leaned over and put a coin in his hat. "Tell Nick to find the English poet," I said, in Czech. This was exhausting my linguistic ability. He shrugged but nodded.

I headed through the courtyard out the castle gates. Perhaps Klesl was watching me. Perhaps he wasn't. I wondered who else in the crowd might be watching me.

Bedingfeld waited for me outside the gates. Anne hovered by the wall nearby among the crowd, bundles on the ground next to her. I couldn't risk having Bedingfeld see me talking to her, so I walked right past. She had the wit not to speak to me. I walked with determination toward Bedingfeld.

Madimi was at my shoulder. *Mistress Anne asks where to take the bundles.*

I blinked. Of course, Anne need not speak to me when spirits could pass messages undetected. *Have Anne ask for Anežka at the servants' door.*

"Is it a long way?" I asked.

Bedingfeld smiled. "No." He took my arm and guided me through the square. It worried me that Madimi followed us.

Chapter 27

We went across the moat and turned north, through the small gate, down the hill, into the woods. There, screened from view by the woods, we found a small building, not far from the castle walls at all. It was a small wattle and daub mud thing, the kind of place you'd see in London slums. I was reminded of the tavern in Deptford. I could be gutted like a pig in that hut and my screams would not be heard.

Bedingfeld touched my shoulder. "Cathedrals are for ordinary believers. Great hearts and great faith do not require frippery." *Coming along?* I asked Madimi, who hovered by the trees.

She shuddered. *You will understand.* She looked disapproving.

I did understand. An UnGifted man would not be troubled entering that humble place. To me it was like walking through the Thames after the boatmen dumped their sewage. I felt an overwhelming desire to vomit. Ordinary Catholic Churches never felt like this. They never really felt like much of anything, except sometimes you could feel the loving care that the craftsmen placed in the stones, the life's work of hundreds of people. They never felt evil. This felt evil.

I glanced at Bedingfeld. He clearly felt nothing. No trace of Gifts there. I pulled on all the discipline of a decade in the English Secret Service and forced myself to walk through the swamp of utter malevolence in the front door.

The room inside looked ordinary; indeed, it was rather pretty. The chapel was plain and whitewashed, the altar unadorned except for a small iron crucifix. Behind that altar was a small, unassuming man in a simple monk's robe.

I wanted to accept his welcoming kiss of peace without

flinching but when I looked at him, this is what I saw: layers. This man had a skeleton. This man had a body of organs and muscles that had been stripped and laid bare to the elements. This man had a wrecked tattered garment of skin that was lain across his tormented inner self like a bandage wrapped around agony. I suppressed a wave of nausea. I returned his kiss of greeting, his skin powdery under my lips.

"Father Columbanus," said Edward. "This is the English poet and notorious atheist Christopher Marlowe."

Father Columbanus had reddish hair. Yes, yes, Kit, focus on his hair. Focus on the sprinkling of freckles across his nose and face. Focus on the perfect teeth in his smile. They were as white as Nick's, whiter even, as if they were the bleached colour of the bones underneath...don't Look, don't Look, don't Look...I made myself smile. I made myself bow. Focus on the carefully polished stones. This place was modest but immaculate, well maintained, perfect There was a drain in the middle of the floor; I wondered why. Did this place flood or did they need to wash away blood as in a slaughterhouse?

"We flood, sometimes," said Father Columbanus. Gifted? He couldn't be Gifted and stand in this terrifying place without screaming. He just saw me looking at the drain in the floor, looking ill.

I forced my face into an expression of ordinary penitence. "I am glad to meet you." My own voice sounded quite normal. I was too good at this.

"Father Columbanus was sent to us by Rome," said Bedingfeld. "He is tasked with removing the unclean reprobate Rudolf II from the throne and replacing him with Prince Matthias, a servant of the true Church."

I glanced from Edward's shining face to Father Columbanus's... distorted, terrifying... no, actually quite handsome, peaceful one. I realized I had seen him before in the moonlight, walking with Melichor Klesl to Father Tomáš's house. Had he killed Father Tomáš? Why? Did Bedingfeld know? His grief for the old Czech priest was real.

Father Columbanus frowned. "You put enormous trust in him."

"I have watched him for a long time," said Bedingfeld. "He has no love of his Protestant masters and no loyalty to Rudolf."

Father Columbanus put both his hands over mine. "Young man, be at peace. We will wash your sins away with worthy deeds."

He led me behind the altar. I expected to see human or animal sacrifice, ravens, blood, bones. Instead, there was only a smashed cup. It was made of glass, interwoven with threads of gold metal. This was one of Rudolph's prized cups. The glass was mottled scarlet and amber. I reached down but he pulled me back.

"Do not touch that," Columbanus whispered. "There lies the symbol of all the wicked Emperor's corruption, his greed, his lusts, his filthy whoredom, his *tolerance*." And you could hear in his voice that the sin of tolerance was worse than murder, rape, torture, blasphemy. I could feel the sick current around me ripple. It wasn't sorcery, not as such, not what most would reckon sorcery anyway. This man hated Rudolf and all he *tolerated*. He believed meditation on his hatred a form of prayer.

I made myself look at his flayed skeleton. He was not himself Gifted. Something had happened to him, something that had allowed someone else to use him as an Instrument. My opposite number, meant to be dead as I was meant to be dead. The tipping point who could make a bad future worse.

"I am in the emperor's confidence," I said, numbly. "I will do whatever you ask."

This horrible creature smiled at me. I didn't want to be

anointed by such a creature. In the hands of an ordinary priest, it was harmless nonsense, but in his hands, it would become something horrific. I knelt before him. He offered me his ring, and I kissed it. I imagined I smelled blood.

Bedingfeld helped me to my feet. Father Columbanus turned away from both of us, toward his altar. He lifted a beatific face to the sunlight and fell into his prayers. We were dismissed.

Bedingfeld took my arm on the path back to the castle, and I must say I needed it. "He trained in southern France, putting down heretics."

"Was he in Paris during the Massacre?" I asked.

"You shouldn't call it that," said Bedingfeld. "It's an English habit."

That was not a no. I caught a glimpse of Madimi in the trees. Perhaps in the world where I had died in the tavern at Deptford, Father Columbanus had died in the Massacre. Some Protestant fought back, got the better of him. Now he was here, and I was here. Balanced. Of course, that assumed I was a creature of Light. I laughed.

Bedingfeld looked curious. "What is funny?"

I patted my lover's arm. "You have delivered me from evil."

He relaxed. "I know that joy, my friend."

I had quite a lot to do in one Christmas Eve. I had to trust Anne and Anežka to set up the spell for me while I attended Christmas Court and Mass with Elizabeth and the Rožmberk family. Will would have to attend too, since the real Master Royden would be expected. Then revels would begin. We could slip away after an hour or two, have our private audience with Rudolf, then be on the road at dawn. I had to pack. I had to dress.

I stood at the wall, looking down over the city. Lights glowed all over town. People would process up this hill by torchlight to attend Mass in the Cathedral. If they were an attacking Turkish army, I could kill them all with a pot of boiling lead. But since they were only revellers I saw just the odd guardsman with a crossbow, looking as if he'd rather be drinking with the crowd. It was afternoon, but it got dark so very early this time of year.

Jahoda's troop had built an elaborate stage in front of St. Vitus Cathedral. Huge mirrors hung on either side of the stage. Two of the actors perched atop barrels, lighting massive candles, the biggest candles I had ever seen. They were fixed cleverly in a large lattice of holders. The mirrors reflected the light from the candles onto the stage until it was as light as mid-day. I watched them work in a kind of awe.

Anne appeared at my elbow. "I got your message. Madimi likes to talk, doesn't she?"

"Are we ready for tonight?"

"Will is working on it. Kit, there is something I must tell you."

I sighed. "What is it?"

She squared her shoulders, her eyes glinting in the torchlight. "Thomas Kyd. I'm so sorry. He is dead."

It would have been unbearable from anyone but Anne. She looked at me with such constancy that the ground stayed steady beneath me. I leaned on the wall. Oh Thomas. "When did he die?"

"Three days after Feast of the Assumption."

"He was still in prison?"

"I don't think he ever saw daylight." She leaned against me. "I never did find his play for you Kit. Will thinks it disappeared the night of the Armada—"

"You need to stop talking so about that," I hissed. "You and Will possess a secret that could rewrite the maps of Europe. It's not for gossip."

She grew silent. I thought she was offended. The darkness that clouded her face wasn't just the gathering dusk. But she put her hand on my forearm, strangely tender. I fought back tears. "You were never the same after the Ar—after that. I thought you would confide in me, but you never did."

"You were right. There is something dishonest about fighting battles with magic."

Anne shuddered. "Do you remember the old folks talking about that time Bloody Mary's men burned that old woman. She screamed for days."

"I do."

"Is Royden wrong to want to stop that?"

"What does it profit to erect Protestant pyres in the place of Catholic ones."

"Is that a danger while Elizabeth lives?"

"No. But a future Protestant ruler might. And Royden wouldn't mind that."

"So...monster."

"We're all monsters," I needed to change the subject, if only to push against the tide of despair that would take me down if I let it. "So, you're one of Jahoda's players now?"

"Don't condescend," she said.

"You don't speak Czech."

"I memorized the words by the sound. Priests do it with Latin all the time."

"You're not wrong."

"Will says I have real promise."

"And you and Will are...?" I meant to tease but she went red and clouted me on the head. "Oh ho!"

"It's not serious." She said haughtily. "He's married."

"You're married."

"I think he likes his wife a bit more than I like my husband."

I remembered something from one of my visions. "Did you have a child?"

Anne sighed. "I wasn't much of a mother even before I became a fugitive. But...yes. Two. Better off without me if you ask my opinion."

Her cheeks were going redder in the gathering gloom. I kissed them, in the manner of people here. "None of this is fair to you."

"I get to perform before the Holy Roman Emperor, that's no small beer." She clouted me again. "I'll be at the steps of the White Tower after the show."

She walked off jauntily. She seemed reconciled to exile, indeed happier for it. Leaving Jahoda's troop was a bigger blow than leaving Canterbury. I would have to talk to Will about that, and about corrupting my sister, I supposed. And about Thomas.

No, I couldn't think about Thomas right now. I had so much to do in the next few hours.

Chapter 28

The castle courtyard dazzled with torches. Pretty girls moved amongst the revellers carrying big jugs of hot red wine. The entire court was assembled, dressed in warm brocades and furs.

As we hovered in the doorway, someone blew a trumpet next to us. "Sir Christopher Talbot of England and Miss Weston!" someone shouted, first in English, and then again in German and then again in Czech. I thought my head would roll off my body, it was so loud. Elizabeth winced too.

No one glanced up, although I fancied the emperor's eyes flickered in our direction. As we moved into the crowd, I spotted Will with the English ambassador and his retinue, better dressed than me, in greens and reds and blues. He nodded to me. I returned his nod. Elizabeth glanced from me to him, but she said nothing. She pulled on my arm as if I were a stubborn horse and drew me toward our own party.

Lord Petr Vok and Lady Polyexna sat together, sharing a cup of wine in fair sight of the stage. Baldhoven was with them, dressed in ermine and blue. He crossed to meet us, the moonlight trim on his costume highlighting the colour of his hair.

"Happy Christmas," he said, in English. He gave me a cup of wine, which was hot and smelled like cloves.

Elizabeth took my arm. "What is your man doing?" she whispered.

I looked up at a small platform on the side of the stage. Edward Bedingfeld stood by the large rack of candles with Jahoda. The stage itself was as bright as mid-afternoon, but the two of them were in shadow. They seemed to be arguing.

Another trumpet sounded, and the entire courtyard parted. His Majesty the Holy Roman Emperor processed through the throng and seated himself in the royal chair. The crowed pressed

Elizabeth and me against the wall. Jahoda left Bedingfeld fuming and leaped onto the stage. He stood in the reflected light waiting.

The emperor raised his hand, and the crowd was silent.

Jahoda bowed and began speaking in Czech. Bedingfeld hovered in the shadows, glaring at him. Elizabeth tried to stand on tiptoe.

"What is happening?" I asked.

"They are going to perform a play for the emperor."

Baldhoven said something anxious in Czech over his shoulder. She answered him, shortly. He shrugged, glanced at me, and turned his attention back to Jahoda. Since I did not understand Jahoda's lengthy speech, I examined the crowd. Sendigovius was whispering with Hájek. Will stood by the English ambassador, looking smug. Lady Polyexna stared fixedly at the stage. At her side, Lord Petr Vok watched Rudolf.

I suddenly remembered Madimi's vision of Petr Vok standing on a scaffold, the noose draped around his neck. He looked at the emperor with an expression not unlike the one he'd worn looking out at the crowd.

I thought I heard Jahoda say my name. My real name. I blinked. It was hard to be sure. Proper nouns change case in Czech. Elizabeth's hand tightened on mine.

"I swear I did not know," whispered Elizabeth.

"Know what?"

"Just be still," she said. "No matter what happens. Be. Still."

Jahoda bowed again and the drumming began. The stage filled with actors dressed as demons. They began speaking the prologue. I noted the actor dressed as an alchemist in the shadow by the stage. No, not any alchemist.

Doctor Faustus.

It was Anne. She wore men's clothes, but it was definitely Anne.

THE MARLEN OF PRAGUE

"Not possible," I said.

"I'm so sorry," said Elizabeth. "Lord Rožmberk hinted but didn't say outright."

Anne said she had the text with her. Will said she was a better actor than I thought. I certainly never dreamed this. "Who translated it?"

"He did not say."

Anne playing Faustus said in Latin: "the purpose of logic is to argue well," before lapsing back into Czech.

I sensed Matthew Royden before I saw him. This happens sometimes with Gifted people, but more often with those who had done spell work together or shared a bed. The Armada spell had made this bond as solid as iron. I turned, and he was not even three feet away. He wasn't looking at me, though. He was looking at the English Ambassador's party. Will Shakespeare had not seen him yet.

"Wait for me," I whispered to Elizabeth.

"You have to stay," Elizabeth whispered. "Lord Rožmberk will be offended."

"I will come back," I said, although Lord alone knew if I would be able to. I edged away in the crowd. I didn't bother sneaking up on Sweet Matthew. He knew I was here the same way I had spotted him. I simply sidled along until I stood next to him.

"Hello Matthew," I said.

"Holy Roman Emperor," he said. "Quite a triumph for a theatre poet."

"This was not my idea."

"And your impending marriage. You've got more lives than a cat."

"So, you've come to congratulate me?"

"Of course not, Kit. I'm here to kill your sister. As promised."

I smiled. "There is no need for that, Matthew. The bargain

was I look for John Dee. I have done as you asked."

"Yes, you've been quite splendid at living up to the letter of the bargain. Although, I don't see Doctor Dee anywhere. I'm sure you'll tell me he was here and left."

"He was here," I said. "He left."

"I really can't see how your sister's performance fits in with your plan."

"There is no plan. Surely you don't think I would make a plan this stupid."

"You are absolutely the only man I know who would make a plan this stupid."

Quite suddenly, the guard captain Kolář appeared at my elbow. He pulled at my sleeve. "Captain Talbot? May I be of service?"

Matthew finally turned to face me. "I cannot do anything about this here, or about your impending nuptials with Edward Kelley's ward. But mark my words, you will not make a complete fool of me." Matthew turned his back on me and walked off into the crowd.

I glanced up at the dais. The emperor clutched the sides of his chair. His eyes bored furious holes in Lord Rožmberk. Petr Vok matched him, stare for stare. They did not seem to notice me at all. I wanted to stay. I am vain enough to risk my life to watch my own play. But Kolář placed himself in front of me. "Go. For the maiden's sake, if not for yours."

Over the guard's shoulder I could see Sweet Matthew by the English Ambassador's party. He was within a hand's reach of Will. I tried to push past Kolář, but he was a much larger man than I. He turned me around and moved me with a gentle, firm push along my back. A casual viewer would think we were strolling along together, but I was not sure my feet entirely touched the ground.

I found Elizabeth standing in the doorway. I craned my head and saw that Will was surrounded by a group of men, arguing with him. Matthew had declared him an imposter and was believed, it seemed. But there was a crowd between us, and Kolář was wasting no time.

Elizabeth took my hand. We edged behind the line of spectators, following the guardsman. No one stopped us. The crowd was watching *Doctor Faustus*, enraptured by my words even in Czech.

Kolář took us to the White Tower, but instead of going down the spiral staircase, we went up. We climbed to the second floor where we entered a long, dusty corridor that seemed to go on forever. There was a chink in the wall every few feet. A guardsman stood at each one, crossbow in hand. We were inside the castle's defensive wall.

"Wait here." Kolář bowed to us and left.

I sat down on the floor. I could not help it. I felt so light-headed. "Why is Jahoda doing my play?"

Elizabeth stood next to where I sat. "Lord Rožmberk commissioned it to pester the emperor. Your play predicts damnation as a consequence of an overabundant interest in magick."

I put my head in my hands. "There must be scores of Faust plays. Why use mine?"

"I don't know," Elizabeth said. "I didn't know, Kit."

"She could not have," said Bedingfeld. I looked up and saw him at the doorway at the top of the stairs. "You must get out of the castle, Kit. Rudolf thinks you conspired with Lord Rožmberk, and he is not well pleased."

"I am sorry," said Bedingfeld. "I am so, very, very, very sorry."

"Why are you sorry?"

"Because he translated it," said Matthew Roydon, from

behind me. "Didn't you Edwin?"

Edwin looked legitimately embarrassed. "It was winter, I had the play, we were bored and to pass the time...The rhythm's all wrong. I just went for the meaning." Somewhere under Bedingfeld's layers of subterfuge still beat the heart of an Oxford scholar, angling for a bit of praise.

Roydon drew his sword. My hand went to my belt knife, wishing for a rapier. There were perhaps three feet between us. I might get the better of him if I rushed him.

Elizabeth put herself between us. "Master Marlowe knows nothing of Czech politics. He does not even speak the language."

"Get behind me, Elizabeth," I said.

"No, I shan't." Elizabeth took a step toward Matthew, who did not move so much as an eyelash. "Master Marlowe is the guest of the Rožmberk family. He met with the emperor himself. Think twice, Master Roydon, before you threaten him."

He bowed to her. "Please stay back, Mistress Weston. This business is not your concern."

"Where is Will, Sweet Matthew?" I asked.

"Will?" asked Bedingfeld, looking confused. "Will Shakespeare?"

"Will Shakespeare is facing consequences appropriate to his fraud. I would have a care for your own troubles right now."

"Is Shakespeare *here*?" asked Edwin, looking bewildered. Oh, he knows Will told me who he was, and that means I was playing him. We were all very knowledgeable, but there were drawn swords and close quarters, and that made frank conversation inconvenient.

We began to circle in that narrow space, but Elizabeth placed her huge confection of a dress between us. It was impossible to stab anything but cloth.

"Where is Will Shakespeare?" I asked Royden again.

"Where is your sister Anne?" asked Matthew. "That was her on stage, wasn't it? The strumpet playing a man in your play—oh but you didn't know. This was some scheme that involves your play and your sister and William Shakespeare and bloody Lord Petr Vok z Rožmberk but somehow you are oblivious?"

Just then, two guardsmen put down their crossbows and picked up their swords. They'd paid us no mind when Kolář brought us here, but foreigners with naked blades, shouting got their attention. Roydon looked from them to Elizabeth to me to Edwin. Edward Bedingfeld. I must remind myself. Even if he would stab Sweet Matthew for me, he was still the enemy. A guard called out to us. Bedingfeld answered in Czech, but he put his knife away. Elizabeth spoke quickly, trying to reassure them.

I stepped close to Matthew, so that no one else would hear me beg. "Dee is not here, but I know where he is. I can still do my job. That is what matters, isn't it? That we stop Dee from talking?"

Matthew looked uncertain. What did matter to him? It had been so long since we'd spoken as friends, I really didn't know. England safe, surely. Dee's discretion. My silence. Surely all that was far more important that his anger at me for blundering into the politics of the Holy Roman Emperor.

"You can't deliver Doctor Dee. He is gone. Everyone knows this."

"I need time. Please, release Master Shakespeare."

"Time?" He frowned. "Time for what?"

I breathed in. Somewhere inside that carapace of fear and orthodoxy was a man who would understand me. I leaned in close. "Merchant business, Sweet Matthew. I beg of you. I just need one night."

"One night." Royden scowled. I thought him unmoved but then he nodded to the palace guard, sheathed his sword. "I do not have the authority to release Shakespeare. But you have your night, make profitable use of it."

He walked out.

I stood in the doorway watching him go, trembling. He was still Matthew Royden, Merchant of Light. I heard Elizabeth talking to the guardsmen behind us. She was speaking Czech, and I didn't understand a word. Edward Bedingfeld sheathed his sword and stood by my side.

"Will Shakespeare is here?" he asked, with the weight of everything he knew that meant behind it.

"The English embassy has him," I said. "I doubt he's in for an easy night."

"That is nothing," said Edwin. "I can secure his release."

"How?"

He looked significantly at Elizabeth. "Leave that to me." He turned and bolted down the stairs.

Chapter 29

The courtyard was full of revellers. I put my arm around Elizabeth, and we sauntered slowly in the direction of the castle gate, pretending that we were sneaking off for a little holiday privacy. Few paid us any mind. A huge throng of people climbed the hill carrying candles and lamps on their way to attend the Midnight Mass at St. Vitus, and we were forced to slip down the hill against them.

Elizabeth's teeth were chattering. "What do we do now?"

"This neighbourhood is not the best. Stay close to me."

I led her down the winding paths into Malá Strana. We entered the familiar courtyard, with the pub full of revellers, just beneath Kelley's tower. No light shone from his window. She had the sense to step into the shadows. I went into the crowded tavern. Kelley was there all right, all but on his face with drink. I grabbed his collar and dragged him unceremoniously out.

He slipped a bit on the wooden leg, but it did not hurt him. Much. "I ought to knock your teeth in."

"Father?"

He turned and slipped again. If I had not caught him, he would have fallen. "What did you bring her here for?"

"Hide us," I said. "Please."

Kelley was sober in an instant. He opened the door. Elizabeth went up first, I followed. Kelley held the door open so we would have light to climb by. The door shut, plunging us into total darkness. I heard the slow scrape of Kelley's peg leg on the stairs.

"How far is it?" Elizabeth asked, a little winded.

"Five turns up. When you touch wood, stop."

I followed the sound of her voice, counting turns under her breath. Kelley was not far behind us. Her breathing quickened and seemed closer in the darkness. "I found it I think."

"We need the key," I called down to Kelley.

"It isn't locked," he said.

The door groaned as I pushed it open. Moonlight seeped through the cracks in Kelley's shutters. The bare traces of light seemed bright as the light from a thousand torches as we stepped into the tiny room.

Kelley came in behind me. "Let's begin with moonlight." He opened the shutters and placed his head out the window. The angle of the wall there made the window much like a skylight. Kelley could stand near erect and place his head and shoulders out over the roof.

"What do you see?" I asked.

"Look for yourself."

Snow fell, looking golden in the torchlight from the castle and the even brighter moonlight. From this distance I could see the great tower at St. Vitus. We could hear church music clear and true even above the louder music from the taverns in Malá Strana.

The play was still going on. My *Faustus*. I always dreamed my work would be performed on the Continent, but not like this.

I turned and saw Elizabeth looking around the room, observing what Kelley had hoped moonlight would obscure: the thin bed, dirty table, rubbish in the grate, the stinking rags he used to wrap his leg in. She had the wit not to burst into tears. She did not even insist that Kelley sit down, though he was sweating with pain. He offered her his chair. She sat upon it, as regal if it were covered in cloth of gold.

"Can I offer you some hospitality?" Kelley said. "It is my custom to take meals downstairs, but there is bread, I wager, and some sort of wine. Why are you here?"

"You said he meant to honour me."

"Who?" asked Kelley.

"Lord Rožmberk. He chose the play before he learned Kit's identity." Elizabeth folded her hands in her lap. "He said it was a remarkable to dine with a dead poet, that day you met him. He thought it was a joke, really."

"Boy, you don't want to be subject to the emperor's whims." Kelley put his hand on his thigh, just above the stub of his leg. "Besides, the compliment was for me."

"Father, please," said Elizabeth.

"Well, not me personally," he said. "Dee, Hájek, Sendivogius, all of us. Rožmberk meant to shame Rudolf in front of the Italians and Spaniards, force him to stand up to the Church openly. It's not a joke, it's a political ploy."

"And they are going to kill him for it," I said sharply.

"I doubt that," Kelley said. "He's still the Holy Roman Emperor, defender of the bloody faith against the Turk and all."

"I would not take the threat to his person lightly."

"Did he ask you for help fighting Black Magic Monks?" Kelley smirked.

"Hájek said that was a secret."

Kelley snorted. He and Elizabeth exchanged a look that shut me out of their club of two completely. Of course they would think that nonsense, paranoia. They thought the Church meant courtiers like Melichor Klesl. Father Columbanus did not enter their imagination. I had not told Elizabeth. I needed to.

"So, just for sake of argument," I said. "What if the emperor did ask me for help fighting evil spirits sent by Black Magic Monks?"

A pebble hit the shutter.

I went to the window. Edward Bedingfeld, Jesuit and provocateur, stood in the narrow street, bundle under his arm, leading a horse. I was absurdly glad to see him. Then I realized the horse wasn't Sweetpea or Tantalus, and I felt a trickle of dread.

"Throw me the key," he said.

"I'll come down." I took the steps two at a time and all but slid down the last turn. Bedingfeld stepped back so I could get out the door.

"Will's freedom is secured."

"So quickly?"

"There is much about Master Shakespeare that might not be apparent."

Oh, right. Bedingfeld knew Will as a Catholic agent. There must be a Catholic sympathizer among the embassy staff. "Where is he?"

"Drinking sack with Mistress Kelley in her kitchen," said Bedingfeld. "But you, my dear, need to leave the city as quickly as can be managed. Rudolf's displeasure is likely to fall on you. I can escort you to Father Columbanus where you will be safe until we can remove you to a better place."

Remove me? Kidnap me was more like it. I spoke quietly, carefully. "I need to make arrangements. Anne, Elizabeth, even her mother. These women look to me for safety. I cannot abandon them. Give me until the morning."

Bedingfeld nodded. "Meet me at the city gates at dawn." He almost added "my dear," but did not. He slipped off into the darkness of the city. I watched after him. I would probably never see my Edwin again I thought. I hoped.

Dawn. It would be enough time.

Chapter 30

Anežka met us at the gate without even a candle to grace her. She led us through servants' corridors and other disused passages, through a side door to the stairway down to the Kunstkammer. She knew her way like a cat. We edged along stairs in near total darkness, unable to do more than follow, trusting that each footfall would meet actual steps.

Anne was already by the door, her hand holding a taper, unfazed by the pain of the wax dripping down onto her fingers. "Is Will with you?"

"Edwin has Will."

"Bedingfeld? But—" She frowned but she handed me the scroll in her hand. "It's all right, I have the text he wrote."

We entered the Kunstkammer. Anne and Anežka, true to their word, had set up for us. There was a bank of candles, a transparent curtain of cheesecloth, and a solid one that, when pulled away, reflected objects onto the curtain.

"We're not using *Faustus*?"

"Will thought Rudolf would recognize *Faustus*, given..."

I looked archly at her. "It was a fine performance."

"I should have told you?" She wrinkled her nose.

I took a breath. "Let's get inside."

"Will scribbled this down in the pub. He said to read it from the side like the actors..."

"I know, I know." I sat down near the bank of candles and looked at the text. "Yes. Do you have John Dee's scrying stone?"

Anežka handed me the round ball wrapped in cloth. She then helped Elizabeth off with her ruff while Anne unravelled some thin, translucent fabric around her body.

"Are we sure he will come?"

"Doctor Hájek will see to it," said Anežka. "They will enter through that door you just came through."

Without Will to stage the thing, I was a little at a loss. I was a writer who walked in, handed the sides to the manager and walked out. Will did every job there was to do in the theatre from courting patrons and bribing the censor, to painting props and feeding the bear. I, a man of the secret theatre, powerfully envied his years in the ordinary theatre. There was a parable in that. So, what had Will intended with this set up? "Is there a mirror behind that cloth?"

Anne went and looked. "Yes."

I guided Elizabeth to where the light would catch in the thin translucent cloth she was wrapped in. The bank of candles felt like standing in front of a bonfire. Then I stood in the centre of the room. Her reflection in the mirror shone onto the cloth. She seemed to float in front of me.

"Drop the cover, Anne." She did and Elizabeth disappeared. I looked down. Was there anything I could do to mark this spot that wouldn't be noticed? I removed my earring and placed it on the floor. It was small enough to be unnoticed, but my toe could find it in the dark. If I put my foot on the earring, and made Rudolf stand just to my right, he would be in the perfect position.

"Shouldn't Anne do this?" Elizabeth asked. "She's an actor."

"Just say what is written on the scroll."

She unrolled it. "It's in English," she said, and began to recite:

> *"Fear no more the heat o' the sun,*
> *Nor the furious winter's rages;*
> *Thou thy worldly task hast done,*
> *Home art gone, and ta'en thy wages:*
> *Golden lads and girls all must,*
> *As chimney-sweepers, come to dust.*

Fear no more the frown o' the great;
Thou art past the tyrant's stroke;
Care no more to clothe and eat;
To thee the reed is as the oak:
The scepter, learning, physic, must
All follow this, and come to dust.

Fear no more the lightning flash,
Nor the all-dreaded thunder stone;
Fear not slander, censure rash;
Thou hast finished joy and moan:
All lovers young, all lovers must
Consign to thee, and come to dust.

No exorciser harm thee!
Nor no witchcraft charm thee!
Ghost unlaid forbear thee!
Nothing ill come near thee!
Quiet consummation have;
And renownèd be thy grave!

"Will wrote *that* in the pub?"

"Oh, Will scribbles in pubs all the time. Is it all right?" Anne replied.

"It will serve," I said.

We walked further into the darkened space of the Kunstkammer. The strange curiosities adorned shelves that seemed to stretch upward into oblivion, the shadowed darkness at the top of the chamber. "Like the Library," Anne said, taking my hand.

"You've been there too?"

"Long before all this. We both didn't fit in in Canterbury, but you left, and I stayed. I found my way to the Library. Feels like this place."

I placed my hand on hers. "I am sorry for all this trouble."

She shook her head no. "What would I have done if Will Shakespeare hadn't come for me that day to tell me you were alive? You freed me, Kit. You and him."

"Free to wander and starve?"

"There's more than one way to starve. Now let me see to these chairs." Anne began briskly moving things about the room so that Rudolf would be naturally inclined to sit where our illusion would show off to full effect. Then four of us sat in together for a long time, the candles burning ever lower in their sconces.

It was cold, which made staying awake easier. Just as I was beginning to doze, I heard footfalls on stone. The door opened and Emperor Rudolf entered, simply dressed, in a black doublet and breaches. Hájek was not with him. His favourite Philip Langer stood behind him, also in black. Langer held open the door. Will entered. Then Johannes Kepler. Then, dragging his leg, came Edward Kelley.

Myself, Anne, Elizabeth, Kelley. Master Kepler. Will Shakespeare.

Six of the Gifted.

Oh hell. Oh hell. Oh hell. Oh hell.

Langer said. "I brought you his papers, your Grace."

Rudolf took the pages he gave him and brought them to where I still sat on the floor. He kindly bent down and showed them to me. "This is thine, Master Marlowe?"

He did indeed have a copy of Baldhoven's ciphers and the note that Edwin had carried across Europe. "Yes, your Grace."

Rudolf extended his hand to me, and I looked at it stupidly. "We would help thee to rise," he explained.

I cautiously gripped his hand. It was surprisingly cool. He pulled me to my feet. Anežka and Elizabeth were already on their feet. They were standing together, disoriented. Anežka was holding Elizabeth who kept looking at Kelley. Kelley leaned against the wall, sweating from the exertion. Those steps couldn't have been easy for him. The young scholar Kepler had his arm.

Rudolf reached behind him, and Langer produced a bottle and a pair of splendid glass cups which he filled with wine. I ought not have taken it. One does not accept meat or drink in faery lands. But Rudolf anxiously hovered, the two beautifully encrusted vessels dazzling in his hands.

I accepted the drink. "Thank you, your Grace."

"No, none of that," he said. "We are brothers in this place."

"The fire burns warm," I said.

"It has been warm for December. They say the snow turns to rain."

So. Not a Brother then.

"Of course, your Grace." I said, remembering Hájek's warning. Candour and respect.

"And this is thy sister," he said, turning mild eyes on Anne. "Doctor Faustus."

She bowed as a man would. "Your Grace."

"Thou didst promise to give us aid, against those who would afflict their King and Emperor."

I swallowed. "Yes, your Grace."

Rudolf beamed. "Thou hast no idea what hope thou givest us."

Elizabeth was not hidden. She was standing in the middle of the room. Madimi was nowhere. I wobbled. "Your Grace, I do not wish to offend, but I am in no condition to summon the spirits to your command. Battle with demonkind—"

"Do not worry about that now," said the emperor gravely. "We would not require such a thing of thee on Christmas night. Thou

295

wilt teach us the ritual of the Armada."

I felt a strange buzzing in my ears. Rudolf II, Holy Roman Emperor, patted me on the head like a dog. "We doubted that thou wert the adept we needed, Master Marlowe."

"Your Grace, I am not—"

"But then we saw thy marvellous play, and thy marvellous sister and we knew thee to be our salvation." He took my face in his hands and kissed each of my cheeks. "How very enterprising of thee to have thy words translated."

Oh no. No. This is what it felt like to go mad. I had no idea what to say. Rudolf would not have listened to me.

Rudolf clapped his hands. "Now, shall we begin?"

I looked numbly down at the chalk in my hand. "Begin?"

"The ritual, of course," said Rudolf.

"The ritual," I said, numbly, knowing I was about to say something incredibly unwise.

Rudolf blinked, but he smiled generously. "Is there aught thou needest?"

"Would you all see men burned alive at your whim?" I said, like a waterwheel gathering speed.

"Master Marlowe there is no need—" began Edward Kelley, seeking to save me.

"How many will die if I teach you this ritual?" I tore recklessly on. "Die starving. Die at sea. Die burning. Like the Spanish sailors who encountered the fire ships. Oh, but what is a common sailor to Great Men?"

"Shut up, Kit," said Anne.

Oh, I should shut up. Oh. I should at least stop the tears that ran unmanfully down my face. "A hundred common men. A thousand. A hundred thousand."

Rudolf placed his hand over mine. "Sir, thou knowest this realm is in danger. Thou knowest what forces would remove us and put a villain in our place."

"Men survive tyranny," I said. "They would not survive this. There are infinite probabilities. We picked the thread of time with the probabilities we wanted. And we yanked the world with us."

"It is as we thought," said Rudolf. "You chased the Armada back to Spain, not God."

"So, the Spanish ship foundered, so a man set fire to a powder keg, so the wind blew them up into the North Sea where they rounded the Irish coast and the choice between starvation and being clubbed to death if they landed. One hundred thousand men died."

"In war."

"In war ordinary men and women can run, fight, hide. How do you fight the rearrangement of reality itself? You can't! You don't even know it happened. This is the end of free will, free thought, all ordinary folks turned into puppets in the reality-shaping Theatre of the Great!" I began to laugh. They all stepped back from me as I sank to the floor. I just wished...if I could only see Edwin one last time...

"A world where control of reality itself was put in the hands of princes would be an endless nightmare."

Philip Langer said, "But in the hands of a good prince, an educated prince..." He looked at his sovereign. He thought Rudolf was such a prince.

Clearly, Rudolf thought he was. "A good prince owes it to God to make his world better for his people."

"I would entomb myself alive," I said, "if it would keep this ritual out of the hands of all princes, forever."

Rudolf turned red. "That can be arranged."

And then someone put a sack over my head.

Chapter 31

My eyes opened in utter darkness.

It is not that easy to bash your brains out against a wall. Some animal instinct for survival kicks in. Maybe it is just aversion to pain. I desisted after a few minutes and tried other ways of exploring my newfound madness. No place like prison to do that.

All prisons smell the same. I did not mind the dirt and the stink of well-used straw, and I was delighted with darkness. I had seen men suspended from chains in the wall, their arms gone pustuled from the iron rubbing against their skin. I hugged my arms to me and stared up into nothing.

Days went by in the black. Perhaps it was hours. It was hard to tell. I listened for screaming. I could not hear anything. It was so quiet I could not breathe. The sound of my breathing was too loud. I forced myself into a sitting position. I could sit up, it seemed. I could even stand although I had to bend my neck a trifle.

By touch I discovered the food they left. I was glad I could not see it, because I knew I had to eat it. Starvation killed in prison. It did not do to be finicky. I chewed the hard bread slowly, softening it with my spit.

I was in a much larger cell than I'd thought. I fumbled around for an opening but did not find one. Boredom finally came. Boredom is the final cause of madness. Your mind clears despite itself and then you have nothing to do but think. They would interrogate me sooner or later. That was the entire point of long solitary imprisonment: to make a man ready to talk. I looked forward to interrogation, if only to break the tedium.

It did not come soon.

Sometimes I would wake up and there was new bread on the floor beside me. Sometimes I found water. I began to hate the smell of my own piss. Then I forgot about the smell. I forgot everything comfortable and safe.

I tried to remember poems. I recited bits of my own into the darkness. I sometimes heard rats scrabbling. I did not mind them. I, once so particular, lay my head down for them to walk upon.

I sang every song I knew. Some were bawdy, some sentimental, but in the end, I found myself singing the old hymns. I could not remember which was the approved text, so I slipped back and forth from Latin to English and back again. I do not suppose it mattered. Music gave me moments of deep unnatural joy, even here. It made me imagine that somehow help would come.

But help did not come. Philip Langer did. I shut my eyes against the brilliant light from his candle. He was an outline, a shadow that made kind sounds. "I had some trouble getting to see you, sir. Are you well?"

I shrugged. "I am as you see."

He pressed a flask into my hand. "Drink this."

"Poison?"

"Whiskey."

I took a sip. It burned my chapped lips nicely. I laughed. In the damp, it sounded like a man choking. Not I. Some other man, far away from this filth. Langer sat on the filthy straw with me. "Your hand is warm."

"What of it?"

He placed his hand on my forehead. "Oh, this is not good."

"Yes, yes, I'm fevered. It's a prison."

"Why will you not tell the emperor what he wants to know?" asked Langer. "Do you know..."

"Yes," I said wearily. "I know about the darkness that's coming."

"You've had prognostications?" Langer bounced a little. "Visions."

"You could call them that."

"Please?" he pleaded. "How can you deny us when we would use it only for good."

A star out of place. A missing play. Twenty thousand people burning, set in motion by my own hand. That was how I could deny him.

"Let me take you out of this place," he said. "We can find your lover, Edward. He will nurse you back to health. You can have food, water, a decent bed."

I laughed until my voice cracked. Edward? The Inquisitor? "No."

"Will you not tell me?" he pleaded.

I almost did.

I really wanted to.

Thomas Kyd, stretched on the rack and hating me...was that the spell too?

Langer was gone. The light went with him. I was left in darkness. I felt so sick.

Decades later, another light appeared. Guards placed a table before me, put me into a chair. My bonds were loosened. I could rub my wrists, even scratch. I smelled terrible. The door opened, and the Holy Roman Emperor was escorted into my cell. "Good evening, Master Marlowe."

I said nothing. I was not sure this was real. He poured me a glass of wine. I could taste it. That boded well. I tried to bow but I fell off the chair. It was years before the guards lifted me back into it. The emperor did not seem troubled by this. He had brought his pet monkey. It sat on his shoulder.

"We have come to secure thy release." He reached out his hand. He was holding a milky white scrying stone. It was larger than mine, though smaller than Dee's. He gestured to the guards.

One of them lifted my hand and another placed the stone in it.

Rudolf frowned. "Tell us what thou seest."

I shook my head. It hurt so much. "What would you have me see, your Grace?"

"Foolish boy," he said. He gestured for me to continue.

I squinted at the stone, obediently. "War. Pestilence. Death. The Church will raise your brother against you. But the real horror comes after—" I could not say "after your death."

"Then why wilt thou not tell us how you destroyed the Armada?" asked Rudolf, plaintively. "We only want the means to defend our country."

"I will give you any other means," I said. "I would protect this country, its liberty, its freedom to think and study and believe, with my own life. I will teach you ways to turn back the Capuchin monks who torment you. I will myself turn lead into gold…"

"We have alchemists. We have protection charms and astrologers." Rudolf smiled, grimly. "We need a weapon."

"No, your Grace."

Rudolf II, King of Bohemia and Holy Roman Emperor blinked. We shared a complete, stunned silence. I could hear the guards breathing grow heavy. He was beginning to blur in front of me.

"Is it because we are not worthy?" Rudolf asked.

"Your Grace?"

"The Hermetic arts require a spiritual purity that no prince can indulge. This is why devils can plague us."

"Your Grace. I am no example of purity."

His jaw turned square and his eyes flinty. "Thou art a prideful man. I have heard this."

"Master Marlowe," said the Holy Roman Emperor. "So far, we have shown thee great courtesy. Thou art in our custody and thou hast not been touched. We can see to it that changes."

My heart beat harder. I am no coward, but I had a professional's knowledge. I had been in prisons before, on both sides of the iron door. I knew I could not hold out against torment.

He stood. He looked down at me as if I meant less to him than his pet monkey. I probably did.

"Thou wilt tell us what we wish to know in time."

"No, your Grace," I said. "I won't."

I lay in my own filth again and waited for the proper interrogators to come, and I wondered if I wasn't simply being an ass.

Perhaps it was wrong not to give Rudolf the spell. Why not let him set twenty thousand men afire if it would preserve the freedom of this place? I loved this city. I had no love for the Inquisition. Who was I to dictate what sins no prince should commit?

It did not matter. I could not do it.

And yet, I might. I knew how pain makes you fall in love with those who inflict it, how the power to give or take away food, respite, comfort, the power to stop pain itself makes the interrogator seem godlike in his victim's eyes, how lack of sleep and food distempers the mind. I would beg and grovel for a bit of food, an hour of rest, a moment to hold my bowels into the cavity of my skin. Many people will tell you that a man who is strong enough will never break under torture. It isn't true.

Well, let me qualify that. There are men, women too, so deeply spiritual that they can transcend pain for a very, very long time. An old hand at the Tower witnessed Anne Askew's interrogation during the time of Old King Henry. He opined that women had higher pain tolerance than men. It was God's blessing on the fairer sex to endure childbirth that kept her head clear, not faith at all. But others said that God took her pain away.

I have no idea. And in any case, I've never given birth, nor was I likely to develop a powerful faith. It is worth noting that there are legal restrictions on torture in England that they do not have in Catholic countries.

The mere threat unmans most men.

The mere threat unmanned me. It did not matter. I could not allow myself to break. There was only one way to accomplish that. The trouble was...how?

I felt my way around the cell. The walls were damp and smooth. There was no window. The door was solid. There were not even hooks in the wall to put in chains. I was not that kind of prisoner. Well, not yet.

I had no furniture. There was nothing sharp, nothing that would cut or puncture. No fixture I could hang myself from. The cell contained but straw and stone and damp, foul smelling earth.

I thought about bashing my head on the wall again, but I had tried, and it had not worked. I could rush a guard when they brought me food, but they would not kill me. They'd simply restrain me, and I'd have lost all chance.

I could stop eating, but that would take too long.

Suicide is bloody difficult. And in any case, I did not want to die.

"*It was difficult to find you,*" Madimi said. "*There are wards and charms on this prison.*"

I turned my head to better see her. "But you found me anyway. Peerless spirit."

She shook her head. "*I cannot stay.*"

"Why not? You visited me in prison before."

"*Not this prison. Rudolf knows how to hold magicians.*"

"Where am I?"

"*Vysehrad.*" The name meant nothing to me. "*The Old Premyslid castle down the river. It is abandoned, except for a handful of underground cells near the water's edge. He wants you kept secret even from those who keep his secrets. Why will you not tell him?*"

I turned my head to the clammy wall. "If you came to plead for that go away."

"*You are my friend Marlen,*" she said. "*It is not foolish to fear this spell, what even good powerful men would do with it. It comes.*"

"What comes?"

Then I saw it. It looked like a large, flapping bird, a cluster of them rather, a flock with many eyes and many wings and many, many claws. Madimi's eyes grew huge, and then she disappeared. The thing went with her, dragging its claws into her flesh and rending it like paper.

Wards and charms on this prison. That was very thorough.

"*Come to the Library if you can.*"

Trouble was if spirit guards prevented Madimi from getting in, surely, they would keep me from getting out. I could not simply slip from my skin and be in the Library.

When one is afraid it is difficult to leave your body at all. The slightest distraction, the tiniest tension, a bug, an itch, the pressure of a straw against your back, that's usually enough to bring you back. It is the soul's natural state, unless one is close to death.

But the darkness, the emptiness of the cell and long hours of enforced inactivity...it was the next best thing to a full ritual circle. If I lay perfectly still no one was likely to interrupt me. The hard packed earth of the floor would provide a natural ground. Besides, I'm very good at this.

I waited for my meal to come. I did not want to chance the

guard bringing a light in and noticing what I was up to. I cleared a bit of space by touch. I ripped a bit of my shirt and covered the food, took a tiny sip of the water, and poured a bit on my hands. I traced a circle in the dirt.

Placing myself in the centre, sitting cross-legged as Lord Manteo and Wanchese showed me the night of the Armada spell, I folded my hands and closed my eyes.

I counted my breathing. Five breaths in. Five breaths out.

It did not work.

No matter. I stilled my thudding heart. I knew where I was.

I felt my breathing grow ragged. Emotion would keep me in my body.

Deep breaths. Five breaths in. Five breaths out.

Let go of the earth.

Let go of the sky.

Let go of time.

Let go.

I was outside the cell.

The floor sloped downward into darkness, but that did not matter. I could float. I could walk through walls. I could see the cord that snaked between my spiritual body and my real one trapped in the cell. If I severed that line, my real body would die.

I could wander freely inside the castle. The cells were empty. This really was no ordinary prison. It was only for special prisoners, the most secret, or the most dangerous. I wondered which I was. Most of it was a complete ruin. The upper floors had cows living in them. I liked being up there. I could see the moon through the holes in the walls.

I tried to leave that way, but it felt like hitting a wall of flame. It threw me backward, almost all the way back to my own body. I found myself outside my cell again.

I found the interrogation room. There were some very impressive instruments, well-tended, razor sharp. Some were newly forged. Old Sir Francis would approve of an interrogator who took such good care of his tools.

I wandered downward. There was water far below, the silvery Moldau river flowing past. I could hear people shouting from boats on the river. My cell was almost parallel with the waterline, but when I tried to go through the bluff I bounced backward again.

This was silly. There was no reason whatsoever for me to adhere to geography. When Madimi took me to the Library, it was instantaneous, because it was disconnected from time and space entirely. A place between the worlds.

Well...here went nothing.

I pictured the fireplace. I willed myself with all my might. I tried to see the books rising to infinity all around me.

It did not work. But I did alert the guard.

I could see it clearly this time. It had wings going in many directions, the feet of a bird, a head made of fire and a thousand eyes. It was hell and wrath and flame and despair, and it was not going to let me pass.

I put my hand where my sword would be. Out here, the sword is just a manifestation of my will, but the non-Euclidian horror bird drained my spirit just by looking at me. Still, nobody said willing oneself to death was easy.

I drew my sword.

I whispered, "That which nourishes me, destroys me."

I rushed the monster.

I opened my eyes.

I lay panting across my hand drawn circle. My entire body was on fire. I screamed; all my limbs jerked about. I felt myself going mad with pain. I was detached. Was this death? Had it worked?

For a long moment I thought it had.

Then I threw up and knew I was still alive.

I tried again, of course. Each attempt was less successful than the one before it. On the third try I did not get out of my cell. The Harpy positioned itself outside the door. I did not have time to create a sword. I rushed at it and ended up back in my body, ringing with pain like a bell.

If Rudolf's mages had created a prison to hold an adept, then the spirit guards would know not to kill the prisoners. I spent an unpleasant hour hitting my head against the wall again, but only succeeded in bleeding. I might give myself blood poisoning but that would take even longer than starving myself.

I wasted a few hours on raw panic. That did not help.

I left my body a fourth time to see if my sword could cut the link between my astral and physical body. It did not work. The Harpy had a good laugh while I tried.

I realized that if the Harpy were conscious, perhaps I could talk to it.

I went out of body a fifth time. Hello, Harpy, I said.

I was thrown back into my body so fast my teeth rattled in my head.

I put my head down on the floor of my cell and wept. That accomplished nothing but I felt better afterwards. I fell asleep. When I woke up, I could think clearly again. I nibbled a bit of food and applied my mind to the problem afresh.

Perhaps I could reconstruct the binding spell in Act I of *Faustus* to bind the Harpy. But I needed its name for that. I didn't know it.

I wondered if I could stab my physical body with my spirit sword.

And then I knew.

I knew what I could do.

It was horrible.

I could not reveal the Armada spell.

But I could use it to take my own life.

See the actual Armada spell required a full circle, six fully Gifted mages, ritual tools and calculations to control the world we would create. Keeping the Armada from landing on England's shore required the manipulation of a complex series of probabilities. Killing one man, that was much simpler, especially when that man was already supposed to be dead.

It was morally problematic and hideously dangerous. I might partially undo the Armada spell itself. But I suspected not. The weave of reality has a natural feel to it. If a thread has been kept in a little way past its time, it's not that hard to snip it back out. I wondered if I would kill Father Columbanus along with me, restore the balance. Didn't really know. This was an experiment.

I redrew the circle. I could feel the Harpy watching me, but it did not matter. I would not leave my body this time. In fact, it was very, very important that I be rooted to the ground.

I placed both hands on the floor on each side of me.

I hated Magick.

I always knew it would kill me.

I dropped deep into the trance.

I could remember the smell of Lord Manteo's tobacco. I could feel the walls of the high room at Greenwich around me. I remembered Doctor Dee's hands on mine, guiding me over a globe. We were going to shift the Earth, he told me, in his sweet, slightly raspy voice. When we moved the globe, the world would follow us.

This was memory, no dream, no spiritual vision. I

remembered what to do.

I had not needed the globe that day.

Just the way I never really need a crystal.

I could reach my mind deep into the ground and gently...push.

There are infinite threads of reality all around us.

Choosing one is like strumming a stringed instrument. The Greeks were right. The threads of time are woven on a loom. When Fate thinks it is right, they cut the thread with heavy, metal shears and pull it out of the pattern.

I found my own thread.

I could touch it. It felt like paper in my hands, and ink, and the sweet, sweet scent of skin, and the taste of sweat on a man's body, and brilliance of candles and the roar of the crowd when the show is good.

I touched my thread, but someone else already had it in his grasp.

Will Shakespeare stood in the kitchen of Elizabeth's house with Anne. I could hear the sound of the Cattle Market outside, all drunken fights and music. They had dragged John Dee's dusty model of the earth to the centre of the kitchen. Will was smoking a pipe. I could smell the tobacco smoke wafting over his head.

Anne held a lit candle up to her face, which gave her an evil look. She traced a circle with chalk. "Is this East?"

Elizabeth was behind me. "Yes."

"Prime," said Anne. Her Latin pronunciation was off, but it did not matter. The candle flared. She moved to the south. "Secunde." The candle flared again.

I realized what they were doing. It was the Armada spell. Somehow, they had recreated it. Morally problematic. Hideously dangerous. "This is a terrible idea."

"*Nobody asked your opinion,*" *said Anne, moving West.* "*Tierce.*"

Will exhaled smoke and waved it over his body like Lord Manteo had, only as far as I knew Will never met Manteo.

"*Quarte,*" *said Anne, and the candle flared in the north. The circle was closed. Will slipped into the warded space and handed his pipe to my sister. She gave him the candle and took a good pull. She did not cough like a dame should.*

"*Are you certain this will work?*" *asked Edward Kelley. What was he doing there, out, free, in his own home? Oh, this is how they knew what to do. He had seen the spell in his visions, not all of it, but enough to make educated guesses.*

Will shrugged. "*He started his spell. We can feel it working. We have nothing to lose now if we can't take it back from him.*"

"*Do not do this,*" *I said.* "*I want to die.*"

Anne scowled. Master Kepler looked in my direction and took his place in the circle.

"*Did you think there was only one possible way of doing magick?*" *It was Nick. He grinned, and looked at Will with affection and trust, as if they'd known each other many years.*

Will put a stone in Anne's hand. "*Imagine this is the world.*"

"*This is the world,*" *she said.*

"*With the right fulcrum, we can move the world,*" *said Johannes Kepler.*

"*Stop,*" *I said.* "*Let me go, damn you.*"

Will spoke to me, although he didn't look up. "*Since when do you believe in damnation?*"

Elizabeth folded her gloved hands. "*It is not for you to decide what risks we should take.*"

Edward Kelley smiled like a pirate. "*We don't care for your rules, Dead Man.*"

"*What are you doing? What are you changing? You don't even know!" I protested.*

"We know it will save your life," said Anne.

"And when another stella nova *appears in the wrong place in the sky?"*

"We will observe it," said Kepler.

"And measure it," said Nick.

"And wonder," said Will. He grasped my thread and pulled.

Will and Anne and Elizabeth and Edward Kelley and Master Kepler and Nikhil of Delhi looked at each other and smiled. Their hands closed over John Dee's armillary sphere, big, round and copper, with the brass ball in the centre representing the Earth. They moved the stone together...

I woke up in my cell.

I was still alive.

I failed.

Or they succeeded.

Or I dreamt the whole thing.

Either way I sat alone in the dark.

Chapter 32

And then comedy piled upon tragedy, because Edward Bedingfeld came to see me. He was tonsured and dressed in robes with his face clean shaven. He wore no ornaments save the crucifix at his belt, and he held a prayer book in his hands. His slim fingers pressed upon it while I was dragged to my feet. The guards brought him a table, a chair and a light, and then bowed while he took the seat.

"Sweet Christ. Tell me you are not a bishop."

"I am not a bishop." Oh, his voice. It was still exactly the same. How strange that was. "I am in the service of the Holy Inquisition."

"You mean Father Columbanus."

"We champion the true faith. Did you think that Rudolf's infamous tolerance extends beyond the territory that surrounds the City of Gold? It's the city fathers forcing him to tolerate moral laxity in the face of heresy. In the villages, the local lords stand firm for the Mother Church."

"Not Petr Vok."

"The heretic Lord Rožmberk is not universally loved by his people."

"I imagine the Protestants love that he's Protestant."

"Heretic." He corrected me firmly, leaning back in his chair.

"So," I said, through a dry and rough tongue. "How did you get into my prison? Can't imagine Rudolf sent you."

"All gentlemen prisoners are allowed access to spiritual counsel." He made the sign of the cross over me.

"Oh, please none of that."

"I wish to bless you."

"Bless yourself, you arse."

Bedingfeld sat down and regarded me patiently. "I am not the reason you are here. Good King Rudolf holds you, not the Mother Church. He plans to break you once the Holy Days are done. This spell you know, he wants it very badly."

"So, you came here..."

"To offer you spiritual comfort." Bedingfeld smiled.

"Please credit me with a little intelligence."

The smile went away. "I need to know what the coded message means."

I almost laughed at the triviality of the question. "Are you mad?"

"That message was meant for your infernal Merchants of Light. You do know that Lucifer also styled himself a bringer of Light."

I was getting tired. "Spare me. I cannot manage riddles."

"A riddle," Bedingfeld said, with a grim smile. "So, math will not avail us. I must guess its meaning."

I shrugged. Bedingfeld bit his lip, and waited, clearly hoping I would babble to fill the emptiness. But when I spoke, it was not what he expected to hear me say. "Father Columbanus killed Father Tomáš."

Bedingfeld broke a sweat. His skin went pale under the freckles. I took his clammy hand in my filthy one. He frowned but he did not pull away. "Kit, this is beneath you."

"He did not tell you?" I licked my lips, to make them supple enough to work. "You probably do want to overthrow the Protestant Queen. You wouldn't be the first. But you're not a murderer of scholarly old priests."

"You do not know me," he said, softly. He drew his hand away, produced a handkerchief and wiped the grime from his pale, thin hand. "Is this how you tempted men at Cambridge to betray their fellows?"

"Did I take them to my bed? Yes. Sometimes."

I tried to catch his eyes. He still looked cool. "My brother was at Cambridge with you."

My ears turned hot. Blood left my heart and poured into my head. "I remember no man named Bedingfeld there."

"He did not use that name," he said. "The University would not admit a known Catholic. I begged him to come here or go to Rouen or Rome. But he wanted to stay in England. He wanted to learn. You approached him in the guise of a friend."

He had been so quiet in the beginning. I thought it professional reserve, desire, or shyness at my fame. But Edward Bedingfeld had hated me.

"They racked him," he said, wretchedly. "They knew he was no threat, but they racked him all the same. Do you know why?"

I did. "So he would tell them of any traitors he knew."

"My brother had no designs on the throne. He only loved God."

"This is no time for people who only love God."

"If you at least loved your Protestant God, I would understand you."

"You lot would plunge our country into another cataclysm of human pyres, and if your brother was caught up in that, there is no doubt I did the catching. And I am glad of it." I spat. "Glad of it."

Bedingfeld gripped my shoulder. I thought he would punch me, but instead he dropped back into his chair and put his head face down on the table. He was shaking. We sat together without moving for a long time. And then I realized my spell had worked. The vision of Will and Anne and the rest had been a dream. Here sat before me the means to take my own life.

"Revenge for your brother is not without honour," I said. "Kill me, Edwin."

Bedingfeld sat back. Sweat had broken out across his skull,

where they had taken his hair. He placed a vial in the middle of the table.

"What is that?" I asked, though my mouth had gone dry.

"Anežka sent this."

"Is it poison?"

"It is for you," said Bedingfeld, measuring out each word. "I think you must decide if the secrets you keep are worth dying for."

I could hear the water dripping on the walls far, far away. "They are."

"Greater torments await you in Hell." He nodded at the potion.

I took the bottle in my hand. "Perhaps."

His fingers closed over mine. "Or you could trust in me. Confess your sins. Be restored to your Maker. Be spared all this suffering. For I do love you, Kit Marlowe. If you die here, I will mourn for eternity." Edwin knelt before me and laid his head upon my breast. I breathed the smell of him, the faint touch of incense, wine, horses and ink.

"I do not need forgiveness."

"I do," he said. "The things I did in God's service...I see them behind my eyes at night. I can never be free of them."

I kissed the edge of his tonsure. "We are the same."

For a long while we clasped each other. And then, gripping the vial in my palm, I pulled him to his feet. I kissed him. He was warm and soft and tasted of roses. I did not want to think what I tasted of, but he did not mind. We slipped to the floor together, like angels falling in the dark. The cold was nothing to the warm of him.

"Go, my Sweet Edwin," I whispered. "You cannot know the gift you've given me."

He rose painfully to his feet, like a much older man. "I will pray for you with my last breath."

Then he was gone.

I hid the vial in my cheek so the guards would not take it, but they did not search me. The spell gave them a burning desire to lock the cell quickly and return to their card game or women or what you will.

I had the instrument of my death.

I'd won.

What a miserable victory it was. I did not want to die. Perhaps a saint could meet death at peace, trusting a loving God to embrace them in the afterlife; I had never believed in that.

I spent an hour or two considering my fate. It was mere procrastination, but when one has only a few hours left, one becomes greedy. There was no reason to rush to oblivion.

I am not a heroic man. I never wanted to sacrifice myself for a cause. Martyrs revolt me. Fanatics terrify me. I wanted to live free and die a sinner. But I always knew it would come to this. I think I knew well before Deptford. I walked this road every night I sat shouting heresy in the tavern. I wrote spells into *Faustus*, betrayal and torture into *Edward the Second*. The lost pages of *The Massacre at Paris* contained line after heroic line of the cries of burning men. Thoughts my fellow wizards spoke only in whispers, I used as poniards to goad my arguments. I could not bear silence like a government man should.

And here, from Sweet Edwin's hand, came my deliverance. My enemy and my love. It would make a good play. Pyramus and Thisbe without the lions.

I was not a good man, but I was not a bad one either. I hurt many people, but maybe I had helped some. I loved greatly and drank deeply from the wine cup of life. I did not believe that was sin.

I raised the vial to all my ghosts. "Cheers."

I drank it. I sat down in the straw and waited.

I was in the Library.

Elizabeth was splendid, dressed in the brilliant yellow silk, firelight glinting in the seed pearls in the collar. She gripped the sides of the chair. "Kit?"

"How did you get here?"

"Nikhil taught me," Elizabeth said. "He tried to reach you himself, but he said he did not know you well enough."

"But I did," said Anne, standing behind her, the fire roaring up to put her in shadow. She looked up at the books. "Goes on forever and ever, doesn't it? The repository of all human knowledge, all the books that have ever been written or ever will."

The lost plays of Euripides. The wisdom of Alexandria. The Spanish Tragedy by Thomas Kyd, a play written in a world that was lost.

"We need to tell you the plan."

"I am dying, my girl. That is the plan."

"Nikhil said you would say that."

Anne nudged me with her foot, hard. "Does this hurt?"

It hurt. My side hurt. I had been lying on it for too long. It was festering from the pressure. I could hear howling, a man in torment more specific than mine. Pain and madness produced different timbres in the voice. I screamed with him for a time, creating harmony in hell.

The floor of my cell was wet. No more than wet. Apparently, the cell was lower than the corridor because I could hear water pouring through the bars. Prisoners squealed like pigs before a burst dam.

"Madimi?" I asked aloud. "Am I drowning?"

But Madimi did not answer, for I was in the Library. Elizabeth was there with Martinius von Baldhoven. They had a map of the city on the table between them.

"That will be hard walking," Elizabeth said. "And the water—"

"He will not need to walk," said Baldhoven. "If the Moldau is flooded, there is no need to get him so far. You can put the thing here and float him right down the street."

I opened my eyes.

The water was a bit higher. I could hear rats, their thick, fat tails slithering away into holes above. I saw Madimi.

"Where is the Harpy?"

"Gone," said Madimi. *"I do not know why."*

I did. The spell had taken care of him too. Not sure why that mattered. I could die perfectly well with him here.

The water was up to my torso.

I held my head above water for a while, but I had to lean higher and higher. I felt so drowsy...

Madimi kneeled next to me, cradling my face with her hand.

"Not long now, is it?" I asked.

"Your heart is slowing. We must be very careful."

"It is better so."

Her tears dropped on my face. "Open your eyes," said Madimi. "It is time."

I smelled saltpetre.

The smell was monstrous.

I could not move. I felt nauseous and the ground I lay on kept rolling, like the bottom of a ship.

The air felt heavy and strange. I would have vomited, but I had nothing inside me, so I simply gagged.

Well, guess what, Edward Bedingfeld. You were right. Hell exists.

A hand held my head upwards.

"Drink this," said Anežka.

I felt so cold. My hands could not hold the cup, so she held it for me.

A man's voice said, in Latin. "Do not worry, Brother. This tube is filled with the elixir of life. It is sound and will see you through to safety."

"Sendivogius?"

Sendivogius rapped on the top of the wooden tube. It smelled of pitch. "You will bide under the water for a time. Do not let the light go out or you will suffocate."

The bottom lurched, as Anežka climbed out. Then a large cork plugged the hole.

I was alone in a tube, with only the light of a burning bit of saltpetre to see by. It might as well have been the sun. I lay on the side without the pressure sore and basked in the tiny light.

The tube sank into water.

I was not afraid.

I was mostly curious. The contraption moved. Was I being dragged along the bottom of the river? I was definitely underwater. I could breathe easily. I wondered what I ought to do if the light went out. I wondered how they planned to get me past the defensive chains. I longed to get a good look at it from the outside, to get Mišak to explain how he made it airtight.

I heard shouting far away. I imagined...no, perhaps I dreamed...the tube floated through flooded streets. I brushed by bundles, other boats. I heard a woman shouting in Czech: get on the roof. I did not know why I understood her.

I must have slept because I did not know when the vessel reached land. A light shone on my face. Someone held a lantern over me. A woman's hand touched my forehead. I heard voices speaking in yet another language I could not understand.

A man lifted me in his arms. He smelled faintly of sweat and cinnamon.

"Englishman," said Nick. "Do you know where you are?"

"Am I dead?"

"No." He chuckled. All the layers of sound resonated in his powerful chest, like wind through an organ. I lay my ear against him, hoping he would make that sound again. I could smell the slightly mouldy smell of damp wood burning.

I could smell meat cooking. Someone played two notes, adjusted something, and played them again. A hand rapped a tambourine, and I could hear the tremble of handheld drums.

"We are with the Gypsies," I whispered.

Chapter 33

I woke to the sound of rain hitting the wooden roof of the Romany wagon. Wagon was actually not the proper word for it. I've seen farmhouses that were less well appointed. Thick silk rugs lay on the floor, and more silk hung on the walls. I lay in a tiny but comfortable bunk covered in almond-coloured furs. My hair was damp. They had washed me. Whoever owned this bed did not want me to soil it.

I thought I might lie there forever. I might have, if nature had not driven me to relieve myself. I looked over the edge of the bed and found Elizabeth lying on the floor. Her eyes were closed. She stroked the red silk rug like she was petting a cat. It had an intricate pattern of white and gold flowers. They were not embroidered. Every fibre was a different colour. Some patient hand had placed each bit of coloured silk to make the pattern.

She opened her eyes and smiled. "Hello, husband. Do you need something?"

I told her what I needed, and she produced a chamber pot made of stamped brass. It was almost too pretty to use. When I was done and the contents tossed out the door, Elizabeth bustled about, tucking and wrapping things around me until I was likely to strangle.

"Why are you here?"

"I'm your nurse," she said, with a bit of wickedness.

"I thought Anežka would be more appropriate."

"Anežka could not come," she said. "She was needed in the city. We planned to go to Kutná Hora. Master Sendivogius has friends in the silver mines there. But the roads are washed out so we must wait."

I fell asleep. When I woke again, the rain had stopped. Elizabeth was gone. The wagon door stood open. I got up. I had no shoes or hose, so I hovered, barefoot and wearing only a shirt. It was remarkably warm for winter. I lifted my head and sniffed the air, rich with meat roasting and damp wood smoke.

I wobbled down the ladder and placed my feet upon the wet, trampled grass, sighing with pleasure. The steep hills around me were grey with leafless trees and filled with large winter birds.

The Romany had circled their covered wagons around a large fire and laid down logs to make a trestle table. This was a big group with young children with them. From time to time one of the women would absently snatch a child away from the fire, or pull an inedible item from a mouth, but they went on talking and working. Nick sat at the trestle table smoking with the Roma man I'd met in front of St. Vitus Cathedral. The Roma smiled and waved his pipe at me, but Nick looked enigmatic. I could not tell if he was angry, concerned, or pleased. Then Nick stood and walked to me, treading down damp streaks of grass.

"What a beautiful day this is," I said.

He grimaced at me as he took my arm. "Come for breakfast."

He led me to where Elizabeth sat by the fire, apart from the other women, dressed in a loose red shift and wide yellow skirt. A book lay in her lap, but she was not reading. Instead, she gazed forward, her mouth forming silent words. Praying, I thought first. Then I realized she was composing.

Two young Roma women looked at me and giggled uncontrollably. Elizabeth turned pink when she saw me. "Have you no breeches to give him?"

One of the women handed me a bit of chicken and bread. She pinched my cheek and said something rude. Elizabeth turned redder and they laughed harder.

"She thinks you are too thin." Nick said. "How will you catch a wife?"

"She did not say *wife*," Elizabeth said.

"Do you understand them?" I asked.

"I understood that."

I blew the woman a kiss, and she made a great show of scolding. I meekly turned my attention to the food. Nick stood away from us, poking the fire, his boots right in the ash, almost to the embers.

I pointed to him. "Will he not burn?"

"He is always cold, he says."

"Even in spring?" I asked.

"It is January. Just past Epiphany."

I looked at the great hills surrounding us. "Where are we?"

"South and east of the city," she said.

"Not far enough to avoid pursuit."

"I don't think we need worry about that."

"No?"

Elizabeth made a face but did not say anything.

"You do not like our hosts."

"They ask the rudest questions," my lady declared. "Am I married? Why am I not married? How many babies do I have? Do I want babies? Where did I learn to read? They call me the Abbess."

I laughed. "I am sure they mean no harm."

She smoothed her skirts. "I do not care to be mocked."

"That's why it is such fun to mock you. I did not think the Travellers suffered strangers."

"They accept us as a favour to Nikhil."

"So, they bore you away without so much as a by-your-leave?"

She started to laugh. The other women did not know what we were saying, but they laughed too. Maybe I simply looked funny. I have seldom felt so undignified in my life.

"What are you writing?" I asked to make her stop laughing. It worked.

"Writing?" she asked. "Nothing. We have no pen or paper to spare."

"You were writing up here," I said, tapping her head.

"Oh," she said. "A bit of indulgence, really."

"Speak some of it for me?"

She rose slowly to her feet and folded her hands, as she had done at court. "I was going to call it *Metamorphoses.*"

Well, no one would ever accuse Elizabeth Weston of excessive modesty. "Please."

The severity of Heaven calls out the angry winds
The massed clouds are perpetually sodden with rain
The furious Moldau is greatly swollen with storm-waters
Impetuous, it is breaking its own banks,
And in its abundance it overflows in a flood across the wide
plains
So the swift river overwhelms the dry fields.
Foaming, the headlong flood sweeps over all,
And tragically, everything is borne off by the maddened water.
Here grain, here jumbled fruit bobs on the waves,
There a man, a bed, a woman swims:
See, beams, pinewood, roofs, floating,
Strange things are whirled round in the rapid eddies.
Here grain, here jumbled fruit bobs on the waves.

I remembered soft bundles hitting the side of Sendivogius' tube. The shouting. The water that filled the floor of my cell. The prison's unearthly quiet. The guards who did not bother searching me for contraband. The roads were washed out. Anežka had to stay in the city. She was needed.

"Was there a flood?"

Elizabeth looked as if she might speak, but then inexplicably, she turned on her heel and stalked into the forest. I followed her into the trees. The ground was soft with slick. Water dripped from the empty branches. I quickly fell behind. She was young and strong, and my legs protested after the enforced stillness of prison. I pushed through a clump of brush and nearly plunged to my death down the steep rocks above the burgeoning Moldau river. Because, oh yes, there had been a flood.

The city was gone. I could see the spires of the cathedral, and the top of the powder tower with its inscription still proudly keeping demons away. The castle was protected by the hill and the walls, but the Old Town Square, the Little Town, the bridge, the chains, the bargemen...all lost, all lost.

"What have I done?"

Elizabeth took my hand. "Come back to the fire. Nick and I will explain."

Will met us as we walked out of the woods. He carried a tambourine and had damp hair, like the country lad that no doubt in his heart he was. We joined Nick's friend at the table. He introduced himself as Gregor and offered his pipe. Will placed the tambourine on the table and accepted.

"What did you do?" I asked him.

"Good morning to you too, Master Marlowe," Will said. "I'm starved."

Nick came back with a bit of roast meat and bread. "How is the boy?"

Will ate Nick's offering with gusto. "Master Kepler and Mišak are mucking about with Kelley in his tower with star charts and maths. They're all well clear of the river up there. Why is Kit so glum?"

I picked up the tambourine, folding the soiled, red ribbons around my fingers. "What's this for?"

"Your very secret spell. Oh, this is good." Will sat down next to Elizabeth who nudged him away so her dress wouldn't get wet.

"Gregor's musicians circled the house and played music, to raise up energy from the audience. Like during a play."

Gregor's musicians? Suddenly I saw the people around me with different eyes. The chattering women, the cautious-looking men. These people saved my life.

"Like doing a play?"

"We needed to raise energy to take a spell already in progress back from the magician who cast it. And we didn't have a lot of time with the water rising."

Nick shook his head. Gregor said, "It worked."

"It works six days a week and twice on Saturdays," Will pointed his bread at me. "If you didn't hold yourself aloof from your creations, you would know that."

"A play isn't magic, Will."

"Plays are the old rites of the temples of Dionysus. The public transformation of the audience through catharsis. Even Aristotle knew that."

"Oh, you read Greek too."

"*Any*way," said Will. "The more people you have, the more enthusiasm you can direct. That gave us the raw power we needed."

"To flood the city?" I was shouting. "Are you mad?"

"Kit," said Nick.

"One man's life is not worth that."

Will crossed his arms across his chest. "No, it isn't."

"You had no right—"

"I did." Anne was behind me. She was dressed from head to toe like a Romany man, with sash and vest, her thick braids bearing traces of mud. She took her place at the table. Gregor nodded to her and passed her his pipe. She took it, gave it a puff and glared at me.

"The fate of the world entire does not rest on you, Master Marlowe," said Nick. "The rain began Christmas morning. We did our spell two days ago."

Nick explained the rains began after my arrest. Everyone at court believed it would turn to snow, so Christmas feasting went on as usual. The great men on the castle hill were blissfully unaware that the great river had begun to rise. By years end, the streets of Malá Strana and Old Town were awash. Townsfolk climbed onto their roofs to escape the water, floated on planks, put all their possessions on their heads and swam in the streets. The young, old, and infirm drowned. The pious prayed to God and the rest fled.

My friends took refuge in Kelley's home, and so it happened they had four Gifted in one house two days before Epiphany, when Anne sensed me begin my suicidal spell. It took an hour to find Nick and another to find Kepler. Anežka brewed her potion while Mišak readied his submarine. Will found Edwin, gave him the mixture and told him what to say to make me take it.

The guards did not stop to make sure I was really dead. They threw my poisoned body into the yard. The rising water made my ride in Svendigovious' machine easy. I passed right over the defensive chains and through the flooded city streets.

"It could still have been you," I said. "The chain of probability can reach back into the past..."

"We know what changed," said Will, evenly.

"How can you possibly?"

Anne snorted. "Suicide is a sin, you know. Even *Catholics* know that. I had no *right*? You rip apart creation to kill yourself, but *I had no right*?" Her skin was going blotchy with red patches of fury. "You think you are alone making choices that affect only you. But all of us are here to save you. Not humanity, or Christendom, or the crowned heads of Europe, just you. You sacrificed everything to save me from Royden. Do not tell me what I am allowed to do."

Anne made a small, frustrated sound. She passed the pipe to Will, got up, and left. Gregor got up and followed her. I heard them arguing in a mix of Czech and German. Elizabeth looked disgusted at me and got up from the table. Nick followed her, leaving me alone with just Stupid, Christlike Will Shakespeare.

"She isn't happy with you," Will said, laconically. He looked around him at the gathering. "This should be in a play, people on the run finding each other in the woods, secret revels, magical strangers, girls dressed as boys..."

"Write Bohemia into a play and watch Royden come after you for sure."

Will chewed his bread thoughtfully. "Could change it to France. Or ancient Greece. Or an island in the middle of the ocean. Wizards and clowns and girls dressed as boys. Lovers lost. I'll say there's a coast in Bohemia. Claim I never even saw a map." He grinned at his own idea.

"Anne doesn't know better," I said. "But you should."

He looked annoyed. "You're really arrogant, deciding what we can and can't do, as if your Merchants of Light are the only ones who understand magic. Theatre folk have always known. Words, stories, the changing of people's hearts, just by telling a story honestly.

"We decided the story we were going to tell, Kit. To save your life, we changed a single heart."

"Whose heart did you change"

"Lovers lost," he said, drumming his fingers on the wood.

I stood up from the table and went to where my friends stood at the fringe of the woods, water dripping down onto them from the trailing leaves. They stopped arguing to give me an arch look. "Where is he?"

"Walk into the woods a few minutes," said Gregor. "He is on the other side."

"He may not be what you expect," said Elizabeth.

Nick said nothing. I hovered, looking from one face to another. I could not tell if they were pleased or sorry about what I was about to find, but they didn't look angry anymore and that was something.

"Well," Anne said, "Go on then."

I pushed through the trees until I broke through to a large clearing full of tall, damp grass. I saw a man and a horse, sitting by a solitary fire. It was Edwin and Tantalus. I walked to him. My hands itched as the tops of the stalks tickled them. I should have cared about snakes or small animals I might tread on, but I did not. Edwin kept his eyes fixed on my horse, patting him gently.

"You saved Tantalus?"

Edward Bedingfeld nodded. "He ran out of the stable before it flooded. It seems he doesn't hate me after all."

Tantalus nipped at the top of my head. Edward...Edwin...still wouldn't look at me. "You said it was poison."

"You assumed it was poison. You had to decide if your secrets were worth dying for." His face twitched.

"Why—" I didn't know how to ask. Didn't you hate me? Did you really love me? Were you just witched into it?

"Why help you? I don't know." He nodded, still with his eyes on the horse. "They tell me I have changed."

"How?"

"I think...I lost my faith."

"Just like that?"

"No," he said. "Or yes. Slowly perhaps. Then all at once. I might have killed Father Columbanus. I'm not sure."

I breathed in the scents of horse, dew, grass, forest, and him, a deep, powerful breath that filled me up with light as I did. "Why?"

Edwin looked lost. He blinked rapidly. "I was arguing with him. I remember that. He wanted to...to use the power of God to curse someone? Drown the heretic king and all his court in the rains?"

"Columbanus caused the flood?"

"The rain just came down in sheets. It was like a baptism, but its opposite, showers of unbelief." He trailed off, frowning. "But then...the clouds cleared and...you won't believe me."

"Try." I breathed in the smell of mould, woodfire and roasting meat.

Edwin nodded. He was pale under his freckled skin. "I saw the unchanging stars rearrange in the sky. It was as if a great hand plucked them out of their places, changed the constellations? And then I pushed the old monk right into the rising water. And then I was standing in the Cattle Market. It felt like I was waking up. Tantalus found me, and I took him back to Kelley's house, and Will Shakespeare asked me to save you."

I looked back toward the woods. Will had crept up to watch us from the edge of the clearing. He shrugged at me as if to say, take love when it is offered on a plate. I should have punched him in the eye. He deserved it. He was also right.

Then Edwin did look at me, and I could see something in his eyes that was clearer than before, like a cataract had faded. "I am sorry, Kit. Will says I was quite different before. I don't remember. It's like a dream about being a character in a play."

"And now you're in a different one."

"I was never that good a player. I didn't have the voice—"

He had no voice at that moment because I was kissing him. He tasted like the spice the Romany women put in the food. Small crickets seemed to chirp around us as if in approval. I supposed anyone could see us kissing here, but I didn't really care. Will Shakespeare, not so Christlike and not so stupid, he wouldn't mind.

Edwin's eyes closed tight, as if he would be struck down if he opened them. I pulled away gently, my hands gently wrapped in his thick hair. I kissed his plain, freckled face, his eyelids, brows, the tip of his nose. "Master Bedingfeld," I whispered. "Look at me, sweet. It seems I must leave."

Edwin's pupils were wide, encompassing so much darkness in his gold flecked eyes. "Yes."

"Come with me?"

He shook his head. "How do you know I won't betray you?"

"I am trusting you. Edward Bedingfeld. I cannot compel you to do right. But I have faith." It was strange to hear those words on my own lips. "I have faith in you."

He clutched me and buried his face in my doublet. I thought he might be praying. But the stood and squared his shoulders. "Then I will endeavour to be worthy. To the ends of the Earth."

"To the ends of the Earth."

The End of the Earth was where I aimed to take him, for I could not leave him in Europe. This new Edwin was sweet, docile even, but there was something unnerving about him. Something wrong. So that night, I went to Nick and asked for his help.

Nick made a fire, swore in his own language the whole time, slapping his hands against his chest. He sat down before the tiny blaze, shivering, his bare feet so close to the flames I thought his toenails would catch fire. We sat on the bluff watching Edwin alone in his clearing. None of the Romany would go near Edwin. Even Will, Elizabeth and Anne steered clear. Nick fumbled around in his pockets for a minute, mumbling again in a language I'd never heard. Then he made a small cry of pleasure and produced a small pipe and a tightly wrapped packet of tobacco. He opened it and sniffed. "Still dry. God is good."

I climbed up next to him. The smoke from his pipe combined with the warmth of his breath in the cold damp air. He offered me his pipe. It was stronger tobacco than I was used to.

I looked up where the Stella Nova was supposed to be. It was gone. So, Edwin's mind was not the only thing that had changed.

"You should have left me in prison."

"Oh, Mišak wanted to try his submarine device," said Nick.

"Did you not think it might explode?"

"I helped him test it."

I wondered how could have had time to do that. "When?"

"The day before Mikuláš."

The feast of St. Nicholas, more than a week before Christmas.

"I intended to use it myself. Gregor's people are kind, but I put them in danger every time I come here."

"Will you do what I ask?"

He considered. "Gregor's people will take you overland to Odessa, then Baldhoven's funds will get you passage across the Black Sea to—"

"The Mughal Empire?"

"That's what you wanted?" He curled and uncurled his toes.

I must have looked troubled. I had been alone in darkness so long that being surrounded by friends, filled with good food, the wind on my face felt wrong, as if the world would tilt again.

Nick placed a hand on mine. "Will you not walk in Timur the Lame's footsteps? Walk the city he sacked? Read a decent map for once in your life? Fatehpur Sikri is beautiful. The palace is on the plains near the Yamuna River. It is so warm there that the court spends much time outside. They stretch huge silk cloths over the courtyards for shade."

"Sounds like heaven," I said, shivering. "A warm, shady heaven."

"On days when the heat breaks, Akbar holds conferences of

learned men of all faiths. Hindus, Buddhists, Muslims, Christians, Zoroastrians, Jains, Jews. They drink warm drinks and dispute the nature of reality."

"And then they murder one another?"

Nick laughed. "Akbar would not tolerate it."

"You must think we are barbarians," I said, bitterly. "Hacking each other to death over tiny bits of dogma."

He pondered that for a bit.

"The Ottoman Turks have zealots too," he said. "Ignorant mullahs persuaded the Sultan to destroy the observatory at Galata, because observing the stars is bad luck and against Islam. In time, we will need to extend the Merchants there. Wherever men kill those who seek the truth."

"Perhaps that is not so unwise," I said. "Killing us, I mean."

"You do not believe this. Learning is how we will grow out of our monstrous tendencies. We learn and we meet, we teach, and we grow. That is what the Merchants of Light are for. I would take you to Fatehpur Sikri gladly. You would do well there."

"But not Edwin," I said.

Nick looked uneasy. "He tried to murder me more than once. I still remember that man."

"Even if he is gone."

"If he is gone."

I didn't really know. I might vouch for Edwin before the throne of Heaven, but that meant nothing since I didn't believe in the throne of Heaven. Now Edwin didn't believe in it either.

"I can bring your sister. It's hard to go so far alone."

I shook my head. "Anne wants to stay with Will Shakespeare."

"As his lover?"

"On his stage."

"But you must come with me, Brother," said Nick. "There is no safe place left for you here."

"And leave Edwin?"

"When the flood recedes, he can go where he will. But you?" Nick shook his head. "Where in Europe is safe for you now?"

The idea was daunting. To go so far away alone? I wrapped my arms around my knees. They were bones and rags of skin. I felt as though I were holding myself together with my hands. "I should be dead. I chose to be. I wished to be."

He touched my shoulder. "You were spared—"

"Please, do not say I was spared by the hand of God."

"You were spared by the diligence and determination of your friends. Can you not see wonder in it, Master Marlowe?"

"But Edwin... Nick, even before the spell we were much alike. More than you know."

He thought about that for a while.

"You mean that you have both done terrible things, and like many men, you did cruelty and violence for those in power. But that is where the similarity ends, I think. You give of yourself. You care when there is no profit. Your Edwin, I knew him many years. He had companions in that time, but they never stayed long. He never inspired loyalty. Even his love for you was as nothing compared to his purpose."

I sighed. His breath was warm on my neck. "But he's changed. Because you changed him. You are responsible for him now. Surely you see that."

Nick passed me the pipe, and we smoked for a while. Night was falling all around us. I could see the stars pricking the sweet dark cloth of the sky.

"He cannot stay here. He is a new man. He deserves a new chance."

"Perhaps." Nick looked up at the stars.

"He could help us."

"Or he could destroy us."

"That which nourishes me destroys me."

Nick smoked silently for a bit. "I wish I could consult with my mother," he said. "He does seem...dazed. Like a new-born lamb. It might be dangerous to leave him for any predator."

I thought about the lines from Aryabhata. We were in a boat, and the far-off stars were the shore. Oh, yes, that would pull a few ecclesiastic beards. Just like the things Chief Manteo said about the endless age of the Earth. How could creation wink into being in only the few thousand years dictated by scripture, he said. And if that were true, what else in the scriptures were wrong.

Maybe everything.

"Do you have Greek texts in the library at Fatehpur Sikri?"

"We have texts older than theirs," said Nick. "Wisdom from China, Persia, from the land of two rivers."

"Are the stars the same at Fatehpur Sikri?"

Nick frowned. "The angle is different. It is very far to the south."

"Do you remember the *stella nova* that disappeared?"

"The one in the Camel's Hump?" He pointed at the sky. "Cassiopeia, as you'd say? Which has now disappeared but was there before we freed you."

"In your collection of ancient wisdom, do you think there is reference to a spell that would change the stars like that? How to help someone changed by it."

Nick hesitated. "If such a document exists in Akbar's keeping, my mother would know."

"Your mother?"

"She is the real scholar in the family. Like Miss Weston."

"Would you take me to Akbar's court to meet her?"

Nick smiled. "And Edwin? Yes. I suppose I must."

It was a difficult journey, and it took almost a year. First the Romany smuggled us to the other side of the battle lines, which was their especial skill. They traded with both sides. Then Odessa, across the Black Sea, then overland through the Persian lands to Hormuz where we took a boat across the vast Indian ocean to the ancient city of Karachi. Then we rode camelback with a caravan through the deserts of Rajasthan. There were Romany there too, both in Karachi and in Jaipur, relatives of Nick's protectors in Europe. Then we made our way to the great city of Akbar himself. And this, Madame, is what brought me to you.

Fatehpur Sikri is a beautiful place, as Nick said it was. I am making good progress with Sanskrit and Urdu, and your husband's help in the great library has been very fruitful. He has found texts that could be useful, but they are in languages that I do not read, and it will be years before I can make any sense of the magical texts he found.

I sit in the shade, drinking tea, translating texts into Latin. Nick comes every once in a while, takes my translations away and leaves questions from the West for me to research. I've recognized John Dee's writing more than once. Good old bastard. He left before I arrived, heading even further East. I no longer even cared.

I was presented to Emperor Akbar once. He treats me like a curiosity, much as Emperor Rudolf views Elizabeth. He glanced at the pages I produced and nodded with approval, but he did not read them. I'm told he cannot read. He was a wild child in youth and never learned. I have watched the games with human chess pieces, but I cannot bring myself to join them yet.

It is a quiet life. If it lacks excitement, it also lacks fear. A decent trade, no doubt. But the food, the smells, the weather, the language, the very angle of the stars are odd to me. It is one thing to explore the world. To know you can never go home again is quite something else. If Edwin were not with me, exile would all quite unbearable.

Madame, knowing my story, will you help me with Edwin? He is quite lost, you see. And that pest of a spirit Madimi would plague him. He can't see her, but there is nothing there in the place where his faith was lost. He catches glimpses sometimes and thinks it is his God, then knows it isn't, and his heart breaks again.

We sit by the Yamuna River and look for the *Stella Nova*, which is no longer in Cassiopeia. He cries because it is gone. Maybe he understands why the stars changed, maybe he doesn't. It doesn't matter. The moonlight over the is beautiful. And we are safe. That should be enough. Madimi says it is not, but she is not wise as you are wise. For you know there was a star where there should not be a star, and now the star is gone. Again.

I am told you have knowledge that could cure all hearts. Hearing my tale, would you help Edwin?

Please?

THE END

Acknowledgements

No one ever goes on a journey like this alone. I had lots of friends, guides, editors, and well-wishers who supported this project and contributed to it spiritually. I'd like to thank first of all my editor at Guardbridge Books, David Stokes and my agent Bob Mecoy, Laura Haywood-Cory, Claire (C.S.E.) Cooney, Tina Jens and everyone associated with Gumbo Fiction Salon in Chicago, who cheered me on during the last round of rewrites. When it comes to research, I have to thank my parents Saroj and C.J. Primlani who took me to Fatehpur Sikri, Markéta Špinková and Jana Fričová, Petr Trávníček and Zuzana Travníčková for their hospitality and encouragement, including taking me to Brandýs nad Labem, Michal Pober and the Alchemy Museum in Kutna Horá, Richard and Meghan Greene for their hospitality in London, and the Brodiloví family, especially Marie Brodilová who was the reason I learned Czech at all.

I want to also thank my beta readers Mary Anne Mohanraj, Michael Maltenfort and Christina Rizen, and Scottie Ballard, who I could call up randomly and ask for a pre-King James Bible English translation of a quote and she'd give me three. I was also blessed by everyone I worked with at Accidental Shakespeare Theatre Company, especially Sherry Legare, Benjamin Dionysus, Julia Kessler, Catherine Cefalu, Gary Henderson, Chris Aruffo, John Amadeo, Mary-Kate Bullaro, Jim Campbell, Danielle Aeschbacher, Becky Heydemann, and Margaretta Sacco.

Mark Mitchell helped me in a thousand tiny ways, especially driving on a particular long trip to southern Illinois. Eric Cherry sent a clown with a pie to my door. Greg Briggs, Albert Ervin and Thomas Prus spent a lot of time discussing Christian theology with me. Raymond Johnson told me weird stories about pre-modern Prague during long afternoons in *The Prague Post* copydesk office. Truly there are many others whose talent, warmth, and overall encouragement contributed to my life, even if not this book directly. Even if your name is not on this page, you are in my heart.

About the Author

Angeli Primlani is a Chicago-based playwright, director, producer, and actor. She was a journalist for a while, including four years as culture and features writer and online editor for *The Prague Post* in the Czech Republic. Then the newspaper industry collapsed, and she crawled back to the theatre because when you have to go there it has to take you in. She was the founding Artistic Director of Accidental Shakespeare Theatre Company where she directed tons of stuff. Her journalism work has appeared on NPR and in many publications in North America and Europe. She's worked as a playwright with Rasaka Theater Company, Otherworld Theater, Clock Theater, and Pork Filled Productions. Her full length play *The Black Knight* premiered with Lifeboat Productions in spring of 2022.

Author's note:

In the 21st century the word Gypsy is increasingly considered a slur. The appropriate name for this group in the modern context is Romany or Romani or Roma. The trouble is this is relatively new and not universally understood. Different groups of Romany people prefer different names for themselves. Some groups even accept Gypsy. But my problem here is the mostly non-Romany audience, because if I use the word "Romany" or "Roma" lots of readers will actually think...sigh...that I'm talking about people from Rome or Romania. I didn't want anyone to be confused about who I was talking about.

This text strives to make a historical cultural connection with India where the Romany people have linguistic, cultural, and genetic ties. I've used Gypsy and Romany interchangeably, because I suspect, with one or two exceptions, that's what most of the characters would have done. This is a less-than-ideal solution. If it isn't certain what the accepted name was in 1595, we don't live in the 16th century, and Romany should be used in the modern context. I apologize to anyone I offend with this solution.

More historical fantasy from Guardbridge Books.

Drakemaster
by EC Ambrose

A desperate race across medieval China during the Mongol conquest to locate a clockwork doomsday device that could destroy the world with the power of the stars.

"Expertly researched with unforgettable characters and superb writing, this is one not to be missed." — Brendan DuBois

The King of Next Week
also by EC Ambrose

When a captain trades his cargo of ice to bring home a djinn bride, his life in post-Civil War coastal Maine will never be the same.

"Historical Fiction at its best" — Beth Cato

The Elephant & Macaw Banner
by Christopher Kastensmidt

Adventure in Colonial Brazil,
A pair of heroes face the monsters of Brazilian folklore.

"A fantastic romp... with epic battles, creepy creatures and wonderful set pieces." — Aliette de Bodard

All are available at our website and online retailers.

http://guardbridgebooks.co.uk

Printed in the USA
CPSIA information can be obtained
at www.ICGtesting.com
JSHW022028111023
49889JS00002B/13

9 781911 486756